REFUGE

FINDING PROVIDENCE - BOOK 2

JILL BURRELL

CHERRY CREEK PRESS

To my Husband.
You are my Rock.

CHAPTER 1

*J*ake Winters was convinced paperwork would be the death of him. It couldn't be today though because the ranch hands expected to be paid.

He hit submit on the first phase of paperwork for the government solar project and stretched. This was only the first of many phases and already he regretted his decision to install solar on his land. Not because he didn't think it would be worthwhile but because of the virtual mountain of paperwork it required.

He couldn't think of anything else to do with the large section of land that was too sandy for growing crops. This ranch was his life, and the solar project was his way of adding to the legacy he'd been left.

He pulled a checkbook from his desk.

"Ah, the dreaded paperwork!" Lottie stepped through the open office door.

Jake flinched, both welcoming and dreading the distraction. He hated being cooped up indoors, and interruptions prolonged the torture.

"Need something?" He set the completed paychecks on the corner of his desk.

Lottie Hamilton—his cook and housekeeper—was like a second mother to him. She and Zane, his ranch foreman, had both been with the ranch since before Jake was born.

"I'm headed to town. Do you need anything?" When Jake shook his head, she asked, "Do you want to look over the menu and grocery list?"

Jake tossed his pen onto his father's old mahogany desk. A desk whose rich, dark color belied its age. Of course, Blake Winters had hated paperwork as much as Jake did.

Man. It had been three years since his father died, but his absence still hit Jake hard sometimes.

He scowled. "Why would I want to do that?"

Lottie propped her hand on her hip. "To see if you want to change or add anything."

"Have I ever changed the menu?" Jake bit back a sigh. "Your cooking is amazing, and you anticipate my needs better than I do."

"Too well, I'm afraid." Despite Lottie's stern expression, the laugh lines around her eyes softened her features. She had her jet-black hair pulled back into a ponytail, an obvious sign of her no-nonsense-get-things-done mood.

"What's that supposed to mean?"

"It means, Jake Winters, you're spoiled. You're too comfortable. You need something, better yet, *someone* to shake you up a bit. I may not always be around, you know. What would you do then?"

Here we go again.

"This ranch is your home, you can't leave. And if you ever did, you'd have to go without Zane, because there's no way I'd ever let him go." Zane had held this ranch together after Jake's father's first stroke five years ago. At twenty-four, Jake hadn't been ready to assume the magnitude of responsibility thrust upon him.

Lottie rolled her eyes. "Whatever."

She enjoyed reminding Jake what a pitiful bachelor he was. And she'd grown more persistent in recent months—since his cousin, Ben, got remarried.

His usual response of, "I'm too busy for a wife," always earned him a scowl. Today, he kept his mouth shut. He learned a long time ago not to mess with Lottie when she had her hair in a ponytail.

"Well, I'm leaving. If you're lucky, I'll come back. If not... good luck." She laughed as she walked away.

Finally, some peace and quiet. Now there was no chance of interruption. Unless the phone rang. His mom knew he spent Friday afternoons doing paperwork and frequently called to chat. He'd better be careful, or he'd jinx himself.

He opened the window beside his desk, needing the fresh air like crops needed sunlight. As usual, his office had grown claustrophobic. Of course, the breeze blowing through the window wasn't exactly *fresh*. It carried the unmistakable scent of the manure they had hauled to the grazing pastures on the outer reaches of the ranch earlier in the week. The alfalfa fields that took priority were fertilized weeks ago.

A grin pulled at Jake's lips. Lottie would chew him out when she came home for *"stinking up the whole house."*

Focus.

The occasional low of cattle, clang of a metal gate, and drone of a tractor pulled at his attention. He wanted to be out there, not in here. But running a successful ranch required paying the bills and ordering supplies.

Jake's head snapped up at the screech of rubber on asphalt followed by the crunch of crumpling metal. A chill raced down his spine. He surged to his feet, heart in his throat, and bolted out the back door of the house. *Had one of his men been injured?*

A cool breeze hit him as he scanned the closest pastures where half a dozen horses grazed, followed by the stables, and what he could see of the stockyards. He saw nothing amiss. The green pastures and distant rolling hills looked as serene as always. *So where did the sound come from?*

He jogged to the paved lane beside the house, his gaze darting to the highway. Every muscle in his body tensed as he took in the black car wrapped around the steel beam encased in brick and concrete that supported the Double Diamond name and brand.

Jake fished the cell phone from his pocket as he sprinted toward the accident. He punched in 911 as he skidded to a stop at the wreckage. Wrenching open the front passenger door of the crumpled black sedan, he sucked in a sharp nitrogen-tainted breath. He scanned the interior of the car—the blown airbag, the shattered driver's side window, and the unconscious, bleeding driver.

"911. What is the address of your emergency?"

Recognizing the operator's voice, Jake turned away and swallowed hard, fighting the nausea threatening to overwhelm him. "Janice, this is Jake Winters. Send an ambulance to the Double Diamond Ranch. A car crashed into my front gate."

"I'm dispatching one now. Stay on the phone with me, Jake. I need you to tell me how many people are injured and how severely."

He glanced at the empty back seat. "Only one." He turned back to the unconscious driver sandwiched between the door and the center console. Blood flowed from a gaping wound on his head.

Jake pressed his fingers to the warm, sticky blood on the man's neck. A faint, slow pulse pushed back. A low gurgling sound confirmed the man still breathed. *He's alive.* Barely.

"He's in bad shape. Tell them to hurry, Janice!"

A low moan from the back seat drew Jake's attention. He inspected the area he'd previously thought empty. His stomach dropped at the sight of a woman crumpled on the floor.

Another low moan rose as he opened the back door.

A slender figure with a mass of auburn hair lay in a heap. Blood oozed from a gash above her left temple. She groaned and shifted.

"Easy... Don't move." He put his hand on her shoulder to calm her.

She turned her head, and the greenest eyes he'd ever seen stared at him.

"Help me. Don't let them kill me."

Jake's brow creased. *Kill her? Them?* Had she hit her head so hard she'd become delusional? "You're going to be okay. Help is on the way."

"Please, don't leave me." Her pleading eyes closed, and her face scrunched in pain as she rolled forward.

His gaze ran down the length of her arm, tucked behind her back at an awkward angle, to her bound wrists.

"What the..." Jake's lungs seized. He tightened his grip on the cell phone. "Janice, send another ambulance and get the sheriff out here! Quick!"

~

JAKE PACED the hospital waiting room, the smell of antiseptic and stale coffee causing his knotted stomach to churn. He'd been here over an hour.

The woman had awakened as the EMTs prepared to load her into the ambulance and again pleaded with Jake to stay with her. Feeling compelled to stay by her side, he'd ridden here in the ambulance. Until the nurses told him he needed to wait in the waiting room, that is.

During the ride, the EMTs had grilled him with questions he didn't have answers to. And he wanted answers. He couldn't get the image of her wrists, duct-taped so tightly together her fingers had turned blue, out of his head. The fear of further injuring her kept him from ripping the tape off.

While waiting for the ambulance to arrive, he'd scanned the surrounding area, wondering if there had been another passenger who had escaped the car. He'd spotted no one in the open landscape.

His mind reeled when he'd realized the center seat leading to the trunk was pushed forward. Had she been in the trunk prior to the accident? How had she managed to work her way into the back seat with her arms bound behind her back?

Thankfully, the ambulance made good time covering the fifteen miles from town in half the time it usually took to reach the ranch.

"Jake." The County Sheriff—and coincidentally Jake's older brother, Robert—burst through the door. "Tell me about the woman."

Though Robert was eighteen months older than him, they stood eye-to-eye.

Jake shrugged. "They haven't told me anything yet. How's the driver? Did he make it?" He'd left with the woman before they managed to extricate the man.

Robert shook his head, a sober expression on his usually cheerful face.

Deep down, Jake had known the man wouldn't survive, and a part of him was glad he hadn't. Any man who would bind a woman and stuff her in a trunk deserved what he'd gotten. The other part wished he'd survived so Jake could see him arrested. After he punched him in the face. A twinge of guilt sliced through Jake. Neither part felt very Christ-like, apparently.

"So, what are we dealing with here?" Jake asked.

"It's clearly an abduction. I found a Colt .38 on the driver, as well as several strands of her hair and a strip of duct tape, that was likely over her mouth, in the trunk. I'm not sure how she managed to work it off. But there's no ID for the woman. We don't know her name, where she's from, or why he abducted her."

A sick feeling settled in Jake's gut as he considered the possible *whys*. "She was lucid for a moment before the ambulance arrived. She said, *'Please help me. Don't let them kill me!'*" Unable to stand still, Jake paced again. He hated to see people hurting. "Do you think her escaping from the trunk into the back seat caused the accident?"

"That's my guess, but I have no idea how she managed it with her hands behind her back. I figure she either distracted the driver or intentionally caused the accident." Robert put his hands on his hips. "Judging by the skid marks, he was speeding, contributing to the loss of control and the force of the impact. According to his ID, his name was Brian Barnes. He doesn't have a record. I need more time to dig deeper on him."

A door behind Jake opened, and he whirled around to find his uncle, Dr. James Young, entering the waiting room.

Uncle James gave them each a nod. "Do either of you know the young woman's name?"

Robert shook his head. "We haven't found any ID for her. How is she?"

"She's bruised, broken, and very lucky. But she should make a full recovery." He motioned for them to follow him.

Jake's gaze went to the slender woman on the bed the moment he stepped into the hospital room. The bruises on her cheeks and around her eyes looked garish compared to her pale face and the bandage above her left eye."

"The left side of her body took the brunt of the impact." Uncle James made a sweeping motion down the length of the woman's body. "They were all clean breaks, but we sedated her so we could set her bones without causing her additional pain."

Poor woman. The neck brace, a cast on her left arm spanning from above her elbow to her fingers, and the bulge under the blanket from mid-thigh to toes, made the slender figure bulky and lopsided.

"She cheated death today, probably even twice." All three men were quiet for a tense moment before Uncle James spoke again. "The trauma caused by the abduction may take longer to heal from than the broken bones."

Both brothers' gazes snapped up to meet their uncle's.

Uncle James pointed to a lighter bruise by the woman's right eye. "She was taken by force. Most likely knocked unconscious before being bound. I hate to imagine what he intended to do with her."

Heat coursed through Jake's body, and he clenched his fists. He couldn't tolerate men abusing women and children. He recalled one of his childhood friends, Shawn, showing up to school with bruises inflicted by his stepfather. Jake had also seen Shawn's mother with a black eye and a split lip once. He told his parents about it and they went to the authorities, but Shawn's mother refused to press charges. It wasn't until almost a year later, when her husband beat her so badly she nearly died, that she finally pressed charges. Shawn's stepfather went to jail.

"The driver had a gun on him," Robert told their uncle. "And she told Jake, '*Don't let them kill me,*' before she lost consciousness."

"Them?" Uncle James' eyes widened. "If she had more than one captor, she's still in danger."

Jake's body tensed as an urgent desire to protect this woman filled him.

"I'll keep an officer posted outside her room," Robert said.

Uncle James stepped toward the door. "She's not likely to awaken for some time. We'll call you when she does."

Robert scratched his jaw, an obvious sign of his impatience. He was probably torn between waiting for her to wake up and getting back to work looking for answers.

Jake rubbed at the tense muscles in his neck—his giveaway of the anxiety pulsing in him. He saw again the fear in the woman's eyes as he recalled her plea for him to *stay with her.*

"I'll wait with her." He looked at Uncle James for approval.

Uncle James' brow furrowed. "The EMTs said she asked you to stay with her when they put her in the ambulance?" When Jake nodded, he said, "In that case, I think it's fine for you to stay."

Jake hated sitting around doing nothing even more than he hated paperwork, but he had to know if she would be okay.

He looked at Robert. "I'll call you as soon as she wakes up."

"Are you sure you want to stay? I know how busy you are at the ranch."

At Jake's nod, Robert backed toward the door. "I'll look into the driver and go over every inch of that car with a fine-tooth comb."

After the door closed, Jake turned back to the woman. *Who was she and what had happened to her?*

CHAPTER 2

*J*ake stepped out of the room long enough to call Zane. He informed him he wouldn't be home for a while and that the ranch hands' paychecks were on his desk.

He returned to her room and sat on a chair facing her bed. Despite the paleness of her skin and multiple scrapes and bruises, she was a beautiful woman. Long, wavy auburn hair framed an oval face with high cheekbones. Dark eyebrows and long dark lashes stood out amid the bruising around her eyes.

He studied the smaller bruise Uncle James pointed out. How long had she been held captive and bound like that? How long had she lived with the fear that filled her plea for protection?

His gaze continued to roam over her. Prominent collar bones peeking out of the neck of her hospital gown emphasized her slender figure. His eyes stopped on her left hand. No ring. Or had they removed it to put the cast on?

It didn't matter. It's not like he needed a woman to complicate his life. Besides, she probably had a boyfriend, if not a husband who was worried sick about her.

Unable to sit still, Jake paced the small room. His work on the ranch left him little time for a social life, let alone a serious relationship. A rancher didn't always have a lot of time to devote to a family.

His father had been a good man, but he'd always worked long hours. So his mother had focused on her three children, worked part-time, and involved herself in civic activities.

His thoughts turned to Lydia, the woman he'd fallen in love with at college. A few days on the ranch had been enough to convince her she didn't want to be a rancher's wife. His stomach soured at the memory of being forced to choose between his love for her and the ranch. He simply hadn't been able to walk away from the ranch he loved.

It wasn't that Jake didn't want to marry and have a family. He did, but on a ranch the size of the Double Diamond, a wife could feel neglected during the spring and summer months when there was so much work to do. He recalled not seeing his father for days on end during calving season—that lasted for months—when he was young. Once he was old enough to help, Jake longed to see less of his father and more of a hot shower and his bed.

In the winter, however, the ranch could feel isolated. Lonely. He'd found that out firsthand last winter. For the first time in his life, he'd been alone at the ranch. Technically, he wasn't alone; Zane and Lottie lived nearby in their own house. And even though they ate meals together, the evenings were very long and very quiet.

Jake had promised his dad before he passed away that he'd take care of the ranch and continue to build on his grandfather's legacy. But what was a legacy if there was no one to leave it to? He may be pushing thirty, but he had no plans to marry and have a family anytime soon.

Jake had been at the woman's bedside for nearly an hour when she moaned. He stepped to the bed and watched her eyes flutter open. Twin emeralds stared at him.

Her brow furrowed. "Who are you?" The words came out gravelly. "Where am I?" She tried to sit up then winced and fell back against the bed.

Jake put a hand on her shoulder. "Stay still. You were in an accident." He stepped to the door and told the nurses to get Dr. Young. Then he texted Robert.

The woman's gazed darted around the room as if searching for answers. "What happened?"

Jake froze beside her bed. Was she referring to the accident or her abduction? "Um... you were in a car wreck."

Her eyes widened. "Was I driving?"

"No."

"Was anyone else injured?"

Jake debated how to answer. *The man who abducted you died. Oh, and by the way, you were abducted.* He didn't think that would go over very well.

He heaved a sigh of relief when his uncle arrived and began checking her vitals.

Robert walked through the door as Uncle James finished his exam.

"Now, young lady, can you tell us what happened to you?" Uncle James said.

Her brow furrowed again. "I... I don't remember."

"What is your name?"

Her eyes widened, and her right hand gathered the blanket into a tight fist. "Um... I... don't know."

Uncle James exchanged a sober look with Jake and Robert. He asked a couple more simple questions: *"What year is it?"* and *"Who is the president of the United States?"*

Both times, she gave a blank stare and shook her head.

Tears gathered in her emerald eyes.

Jake's gut clenched. *Poor woman.*

"You've been in a serious car accident," Uncle James said. "Apparently, the trauma and concussion have caused some memory loss."

"Memory loss? Like amnesia? Will I ever get my memory back?"

A ripple of anxiety ran through Jake, leaving him feeling like he'd just ridden eight seconds on a bull that would rather kill him than let him off. The prospect of never regaining her memory must terrify her.

Uncle James laid a hand on her good arm and spoke in a soothing voice. "There's no reason to believe your memory won't return. You hit your head hard. If you rest and let your body heal, I'm sure it will all come back."

Robert stepped closer to the bed. "Can I ask her a few questions?"

Uncle James' brow lowered. "I don't think that's wise. She doesn't need any unnecessary stress right now."

Despite Uncle James' gentle bedside manner, that look of disappointment had always made Robert and Jake obey. Growing up, he'd usually been the one to deliver the lecture they should have received from their father for their antics. Antics that often involved his own son, Ben, and such things as riding steers and jumping dirt bikes, resulting in emergency room visits, casts, and stitches. Their father's usual response was more along the lines of, *"Did you learn your lesson?"* or *"Good, it'll toughen them up."*

"Can I at least—"

Uncle James raised his hand, cutting Robert off. "She needs to rest. Questions can wait until tomorrow morning." He motioned to the door—his way of telling Robert and Jake to leave.

Jake stared at the woman, her plea echoing in his head. A part of him wanted to insist on staying. But if she didn't remember the accident, she probably didn't remember asking him to stay with her.

Robert and Jake left the woman's room while their uncle stayed behind.

Jake sensed his brother's frustration. He wanted answers, and Jake didn't blame him. "Did you find anything out about the driver?"

"Well, Brian Barnes has no record, not even a speeding ticket. No next of kin listed. The car is registered under the same name. His ID and license plate registration both list an address where he hasn't lived for the last six months. I'm beginning to suspect it's not his real name. I sent his crushed cell phone to the state crime lab to see if they can salvage any information from it."

Robert scratched at his jaw. "Barnes' fingerprints are all over the gun, but the computer hasn't found a match in any database anywhere. There's gunshot residue on the gun, which means it was fired recently. We may have a homicide on our hands as well as an abduction."

Jake let out a whistle. "Sounds like she's been through a lot."

"My thoughts exactly," Robert said. "But until she can answer some questions, this investigation is going nowhere."

"Best follow Doc's orders and get a good night's rest. Hopefully, she'll remember something in the morning." Jake headed toward the exit then remembered he rode here in the ambulance. He turned back to Robert. "Can you give me a ride home? I'll ask Lottie to set an extra place for dinner."

"For Lottie's cooking? Sure."

Jake cast one final glance at the woman's door. A sudden chill swept over him, making his hands shake.

Hopefully, Barnes doesn't have an accomplice who will come looking for her.

DELIGHTED TO HAVE Robert home for dinner, Lottie placed an extra-large helping of meatloaf in front of him. "When are you going to find yourself a girl, Robert? And don't give me 'there aren't any good ones around' garbage."

Jake, glad for the reprieve, took a bite of his garlic mashed potatoes. As far as he was concerned, Robert was older and should get married first. At almost thirty-one and twenty-nine, they still had plenty of time to think about marriage. But if Robert was anything like Jake, he'd noticed how happy their cousin, Ben, was with his new wife and their two little girls. Even though Jake didn't feel like he had time to devote to a wife didn't mean he didn't want what Ben had.

"This meatloaf is amazing, Lottie. Man, I miss your cooking." Robert smiled at Lottie, bringing a tinge of pink to her bronze complexion. Then he turned to Zane. "So, how's the herd looking this year?"

Zane swallowed his mouthful of food before responding. "Good.

It's been a busy spring, but we got the herd moved out to summer grazing pastures last week."

And just like that, Robert effectively dodged Lottie's lecture, because Zane, normally a quiet man, always had something to say about the ranch.

Jake scowled at Robert, who winked and snubbed his nose in the air. Robert had a way with women. Their mother and Lottie were no exception. Jake admired his brother's charm and confidence, but he couldn't let go of his serious nature. He worried more about how people felt than what they thought of him.

Talk shifted from the ranch to the accident and the woman's memory loss. Jake and Robert both tried to draw Zane and Lottie's son, Daniel, into the conversation with little success. The twenty-four-year-old had returned home a week ago with a broken femur after wrecking his motorcycle while driving intoxicated.

Jake worried about Daniel—okay, he worried about everyone—but Daniel had him especially concerned. Both his grandfathers were alcoholics, and Daniel seemed to be following in their footsteps. Jake didn't know how to help the kid, since Daniel didn't want help.

Robert carried his empty plate to the sink. "Thanks for dinner." He gave Lottie a hug then turned to Jake. "Are you interested in coming to the hospital in the morning to see if she remembers anything?"

"I probably shouldn't since I have a ton of work to do, but I am curious." A part of him felt guilty for leaving her.

"I bet you are," Robert said with a wink. "Underneath all those bruises and bandages, she's kind of pretty, isn't she?"

"Yeah, she is."

Robert laughed.

Jake had walked right into Robert's trap. He ignored his brother's laughter. "I feel kind of responsible for her. I mean, she was pretty much dumped on my doorstep. Until we find out who she is, she won't have any family around to worry about her."

"Sounds like you're offering to worry about her," Robert said with another chuckle. "You always were a softy for strays."

Jake didn't bother denying it. He'd always had a soft spot for those in need.

Robert sobered. "She sure looked scared when she realized she couldn't remember anything." Jake nodded, and Robert clapped him on the shoulder. "I'm sure she'll appreciate your concern. I'll call you before I head to the hospital in the morning. You can meet me there."

Jake nodded and walked Robert to the door.

Will the woman want me there?

CHAPTER 3

*T*he woman in the hospital bed didn't know whether to scowl or smile when the same doctor from yesterday entered her room. She recognized him. That was good, but she still couldn't remember anything else.

She didn't know who or where she was. They said she'd been in a car accident, but no one had given her any details.

Were others injured too? Was the accident her fault? She had so many questions and no answers.

Everyone expected her to have the answers, but she didn't. Her mind was a complete blank, and that terrified her. Her memories were limited to this doctor and an attractive sheriff—eager to ask her questions. The doctor had prevented that.

She also remembered another tall, broad-shouldered, good-looking man with dark hair and warm brown eyes, who looked a lot like the sheriff. *Should I have recognized him?* She doubted she could ever forget a man as handsome as that. Was he her husband? A pleasant sensation rippled through her abdomen at the thought.

No. He would have stayed and shown more concern if he was my husband.

The doctor checked her vitals. "How are you feeling this morning?"

Despite being middle age, the doctor was a very attractive man. His sandy-brown hair, graying at the temples, lent him a distinguished air. His kind eyes and mouth seemed always on the verge of a smile.

"About the same as yesterday, I guess. I hurt everywhere and I still can't remember anything."

He pulled out a penlight and checked her eyes. "Tell me the last thing you *do* remember."

"I remember you telling me I was in an accident. I remember the sheriff being here and another man. Who was he? Do I know him?"

"That other young man was my nephew, Jake Winters. The accident happened out by his ranch. He rode here in the ambulance with you. The sheriff is also my nephew, and Jake's brother."

That's why they looked so much alike. But why had Jake ridden in the ambulance with her?

The doctor continued asking her simple questions, as he tested her reflexes. She didn't have answers to any of them.

"Do you remember us discussing your injuries yesterday?"

She scowled, causing her stitches to pull. "Yes."

A broken tibia requiring a cast up to the middle of her thigh, a broken radius resulting in a cast that ended a few inches above her elbow, two broken ribs that killed every time she took a deep breath, a head wound that required ten stitches, and a concussion.

No wonder my head hurts so bad.

To top it off, Dr. Young had informed her she needed to wear a neck brace for a week as an added precaution.

"Though your memory loss is complete, the good news is, that's all it is. Memory loss."

That's all?

He pulled a chair close to her bed and sat down, no doubt trying to put her at ease.

It didn't work.

"I double checked the MRI we took yesterday and there doesn't appear to be any damage to those areas of the brain—specifically the limbic system and the hippocampal formations—that are responsible for your memories."

She focused on the doctor's words. "So, you're saying because there is no permanent brain damage, my memories should return?"

Dr. Young studied his hands for a moment before meeting her eyes again. "Theoretically, yes. Your memories should eventually return. Either little by little or in large revelations, but—"

"But head trauma, even severe trauma, rarely causes complete memory loss." She sucked in a sharp breath. *How do I know that?*

"Not by itself, no." The doctor's words were quiet. She focused on what he wasn't saying.

She furrowed her brow and a sharp pain shot across her forehead. "You think my memory loss is a result of something other than head trauma?"

Dr. Young cleared his throat. "Sometimes our body employs defense mechanisms, meaning—"

"Meaning, I am repressing memories that I'm psychologically unable to deal with." She didn't know where the words came from, but she knew they were true.

What happened besides the accident to rob me of my memory?

Dr. Young's eyebrows shot up, creasing his forehead. "It's clear your memory loss hasn't affected your knowledge. I find it interesting you're familiar with such things." He let out a sigh. "Yes, I believe you experienced something very traumatic, and you're having difficulty coping. Your mind has chosen to block everything, because it can't separate it from your other memories."

My memory loss is all in my head? How ironic.

Her brows drew together, causing pain to throb in her eye and forehead again. *I have to stop doing that.* "Like what kind of traumatic event?"

A knock on the door distracted Dr. Young.

The good-looking sheriff poked his head through.

The doctor held up a hand to the sheriff but looked at her. "Do you mind if the sheriff hears the rest of our conversation? He may be able to fill in some of the blanks."

She nodded, and he motioned the sheriff into the room. When the sheriff's equally handsome brother walked in behind him Dr. Young looked at her again, seeking approval.

She gave a quick nod, unsure why the rancher had come. If he was the one who called for help, she needed to at least thank him.

He removed his cowboy hat and gave her a small smile. The concern on his face soothed her anxiety. She took in his plaid shirt, the way his hip-hugging jeans encased his slightly bowed legs, and well-worn cowboy boots. Yep. He looked every bit the rancher. A very attractive rancher.

Doctor Young introduced the two men then turned back to her. He picked up her right hand and pointed at an angry, red welt across the back of her wrist.

"There is a similar ligature mark on the inside of your left wrist. Your hands were bound when Jake found you in the wreck yesterday."

The sting of perspiration pricked her brow. "What?" Her gaze flew to Jake's, seeking confirmation.

He nodded, his eyes full of compassion.

"Why?" she asked.

Sheriff Winters cleared his throat. "May I?" When Dr. Young nodded, he turned to her. "I believe you were initially placed in the car's trunk when you were abducted. I found several strands of hair in there. I've got the hospital doing a DNA test on them to see if they're yours." When she frowned, he lifted one shoulder and gave her an apologetic look. "We're a small-town Sheriff's Office, we don't have a forensics lab here. I figured it would be quicker to have the hospital run the test versus sending it to the state crime lab. Anyway, despite being tied up, you somehow managed to push your way into the back seat. That's where Jake found you after the accident occurred."

Abducted? She only half heard the rest of the words the sheriff said.

"Who?" the word came out a bark of borderline-hysterical laughter, shooting pain through her ribs. This had to be a joke. Some elaborate, well-played-out, sick prank.

"Why would someone abduct me?"

The concern in the sheriff's eyes matched that of his brother. "I was hoping you could tell me."

"But I can't remember anything, not even my own name." She looked at Dr. Young. "I can't remember my name, but I understand that I'm psychologically repressing my memories because I can't deal with them?" Then before he could respond, she answered her own question. "But memory loss, similar to amnesia, rarely affects the personality and prior knowledge, does it?"

"No, it doesn't. That's why I find it interesting you understand such things. I'm guessing you have a medical background."

The surprised look the brothers exchanged expressed exactly how she felt. *I would know if I was a doctor of some sort. Wouldn't I?*

An uneasiness tightened her chest. "I don't know about that, but... I know I could end up fabricating memories, thinking they are real." The knowledge made it hard to draw a deep breath.

"That is a possibility, I suppose, especially if you're trying to force the memories to return. But not likely. I've no doubt your memory will return, eventually." He patted her leg in a gesture of comfort. "The most important thing now is rest. Don't worry about trying to remember."

There was another knock at the door, then a petite, middle-aged woman walked into the room. "Oh, you poor thing." The woman hurried to the side of the bed and took her hand.

Do I know this woman? She studied the blue-eyed woman with hair the color of summer wheat, hoping for recognition.

Nothing.

"Mom, what are you doing here?" asked the sheriff.

"James told me there was a young woman here who needs someone to take care of her until you find her family."

"That's right," Dr. Young said. "We should be able to release this young lady tomorrow." He gave his nephews a pointed look. "Until we find out who she is, and can contact her family, she'll need someone to care for her and a *safe environment* to recover in."

Her chest tightened at the emphasis he placed on "safe environment".

The petite woman beamed. "I'm going to be her nurse, and the ranch will be the perfect place for her recovery."

"You can't do that to Jake," the sheriff said. "He's got a lot of work to do at the ranch."

"Nonsense. He won't have to do a thing. I'll take care of her. Jake can go about his work like always."

"She and Uncle James are right," Jake spoke for the first time, his deep voice firm and confident. He leaned close to his brother and lowered his voice, but she heard every word. "She may still be in danger."

A chill snaked up her spine. *What kind of danger? What were they not telling me?*

"Good, it's settled, then." The petite woman turned back to the bed. "I'm Faith Winters, and these are my two sons if you haven't figured that out yet."

"But Mom," the sheriff tried again, "aren't you taking care of Ben and Amy's girls?"

"School's out for the summer and Hope wants to spend time with them, so I'm free." Faith patted her arm. "I'm going to leave you for a bit however, while the boys are here. The Jensen girl had her baby last night, and I'd like to check on her. I'll come back later to visit with you."

After Faith left, the doctor excused himself, instructing the sheriff to not overdo it with the questions. "Stressing her out won't help. If she doesn't know the answer, she doesn't know."

Silence filled the room for a moment, then the sheriff stepped forward, all business.

"I take it you haven't remembered your name?" When she shook her head, he continued, "I'd like to take your fingerprints if you don't mind. It could help us identify you."

"That's fine."

He pulled keys from his pocket and tossed them to his brother. "Would you mind getting the small gray case out of the back of my Tahoe?"

After Jake walked out, he turned back to her. "Do you know why someone would tie you up and put you in the trunk of a car or where that car was headed?"

"No."

She read the skepticism on his face. She wished she had an answer for him. As scary as the answer might be, it couldn't be nearly as bad as not knowing. *Could it?*

The sheriff showed her a picture of a man in his early twenties with small round eyes and receding dark hair. "Do you recognize this man?"

She studied the picture, giving herself time to remember.

Nothing came.

"No."

"This was the driver of the car."

"Was? He didn't survive?" There was no one else to question.

The sheriff shook his head.

Jake returned with the gray case, and the sheriff took her fingerprints. After asking permission, he snapped her picture, saying he hoped to get facial recognition despite the bruises and bandages.

"One more thing," said the sheriff. "When Jake found you in the car, you said, *'Don't let them kill me.'* Do you remember saying that to him?"

Her stomach clenched, and she pressed her good hand to her abdomen. "Kill me? Them?" She looked at Jake, and he gave a slight nod. Fighting the fear that swept over her, she shook her head, sending pain shooting through her brow. "I don't remember saying that." Her voice came out little more than a whisper.

The sheriff was persistent. "We found a gun on the driver. It was fired recently. Do you know where that might have happened?"

"Robert, that's enough." Jake's voice held a warning.

She suspected the sheriff was the older of the two, but she doubted he'd argue with his brother when he used that tone.

"She doesn't remember. You're stressing her out."

"Was someone killed with the gun?" the tension in her abdomen shifted to her chest. "Did I shoot someone?" Tears blurred her vision.

"No," the sheriff said. "The gun was covered in the driver's finger-prints. We don't suspect you of foul play."

A cold chill swept over her. "But you don't know for sure, do you? And I can't remember. If I did something as horrible as that, I wouldn't want to remember it."

"Hey, it's okay." Jake stepped to the bed and took her right hand. He squeezed. "You're the one in danger here. But don't worry, we'll protect you."

Jake's calloused hand was warm and strong. Comforting. She relaxed as a sense of security blanketed her.

"That's right." The sheriff's gaze rested on her and Jake's hands and a smile tugged at the corners of his mouth. "One of my officers or I will stand guard outside your room at all times. Please have the nurses contact me if you remember anything, no matter what it is."

She nodded, causing another lancing pain to pierce her skull.

The nurse came in with her breakfast tray and the brothers prepared to leave. Jake gave her hand another squeeze before releasing it, taking the warmth and security with him.

She repressed a shiver.

"Jake," she said as he was about to step through the door. He turned back to look at her. "It sounds like you're going to be stuck with me. I'm sorry."

His eyes crinkled at the edges as he smiled, transforming his serious face. "It's not a problem at all. We've got plenty of room, and the ranch really is a peaceful place for your recovery."

Then he was gone, taking his warmth and comfort with him.

JAKE CAME out of the room to find Robert waiting in the hall.

He grinned at Jake. "Looks like you've found another lost cub to bring home."

"Looks like it." Jake walked past Robert. He wouldn't give his brother the satisfaction of riling him. "Although, Mom's bringing this one home, not me."

"Right. And having her there won't disrupt your schedule at all."

"It shouldn't." Then because he knew his mom, Jake groaned. "But it probably will, won't it?"

Robert's laughter turned to a scowl. "Won't Widow Wheeler be jealous when she hears you've got a beautiful stranger recuperating at the ranch?"

Jake bit back a growl. The mere mention of the rich, young widow was enough to set his blood to boiling. "I know this is a small town, but I'm not planning on telling her."

Robert wiggled his brows. "Oh, I'll make sure she hears. This could work to your advantage." He groaned. "But then she'll double her efforts on me. It's been horrible ever since Ben married Amy."

"No kidding. She's been relentless." Jake rolled his suddenly tense shoulders, as he recalled the way Debbie threw herself at him on their date following the Bachelor Auction last Fall.

She stopped by the ranch at least twice a week to check on the mare he boarded for her. He did his best to avoid her, but it wasn't easy.

Married twice, widowed after the second marriage to a much older, wealthy man, Debbie was looking for husband number three. And she'd set her sights on Robert or Jake. Never mind she was five years older than Jake, and he wanted nothing to do with her. Being independently wealthy, and able to buy whatever she wanted, she did not take "no" for an answer.

Before parting ways in the parking lot, Jake tipped his head toward the hospital. "Do you really think she's still in danger?" He wished he knew her name. It would be nice to call her something other than "she".

Robert shrugged. "I don't know. Her *please don't let them kill me* makes it sound like there was more than one captor. Which makes me wonder where the other one is."

"Where would the car have been heading? The only thing out that road is the lake."

"Hmm... maybe I should cross-check property holdings around the lake with the identity of the driver."

"Do you think someone will claim the driver's body once news of the accident gets out?"

Robert nodded. "I'll talk to the morgue and give them instructions not to release Barnes' body to anyone without first contacting me. Too bad you're tied up with the ranch; you'd make a good deputy."

Jake smiled. "Nah, that work's too dangerous for me."

Being an officer of the law in the small town of Providence was more boring than it was exciting. Something as exciting as this accident rarely happened around here. Except for the kidnapping of his cousin's daughter over a year and a half ago, things in Providence were blissfully boring.

"That's right, breaking horses and wrangling steers is much safer."

"Yep."

CHAPTER 4

*V*ince Cooper climbed from his Ford Expedition and stretched. The cool morning breeze carried the song of birds, the rustle of leaves, and the scent of pine trees and the lake. Appreciating the fresh air, he sucked in a deep breath before letting it out in a long, low whistle.

The current boss's lake house was nice—two stories, mostly glass, hanging right over the water. The people who hired him and Frankie always owned nice homes, and cars. Extravagances they usually came by illegally.

I haven't been fishing in ages.

Maybe he and Frankie could wrangle an extended vacation here once they took care of the woman and ensured the evidence disappeared.

Climbing the three steps to the front door, he knocked—three taps followed by another two. He waited for Frankie to open the door, hoping the woman hadn't given him any problems.

When the door didn't open, he pounded on it with the side of his fist. Still nothing.

Cursing under his breath, he rounded the house to the garage and punched in the code the pompous fool, he now called boss, had given them. He popped his knuckles while waiting for the garage door to rise. He couldn't wait to be done with this job. It had gotten complicated yesterday when the target's sister showed up.

Vince hated complications.

He stared into the empty garage. *Where's Frankie's Lexus?*

The instructions had been clear. *Take the woman to the cabin and wait for me to arrive.* But it had taken Vince longer to search the two apartments than he'd expected, so he'd spent the night in Spokane and driven out this morning. He'd called last night but didn't get an answer. Chalking it up to poor cell service by the lake, he hadn't been concerned. Frankie was more than capable of taking care of the woman.

He darted into the house through the garage. "Frankie!" Using his brother's real name was a mistake, but the possibility of something going wrong made him forget the rules. A quick search of the lakefront house told Vince what he already suspected. Not only were Frankie and the woman not here, they'd never arrived.

He pulled out his phone and punched in his brother's number.

It went straight to voice mail, which meant Frankie's phone was off.

Heat filled his body. Cursing, he turned from the windows that overlooked the pristine lake and picked up a lamp. He hurled it against the wall.

Forty-five minutes later, he sat at a table in what appeared to be the most popular eating establishment this nowhere town had to offer. He was starving and clueless. He'd called Frankie a dozen times with no answer. So he did what he did best: blend in and listen.

People always talked, especially in Podunk towns. If something out of the ordinary had happened around here, people would talk about it.

He didn't have to wait long.

One of the two older men at a nearby table quizzed the waitress. "Hey, Amy, what happened out at the Double Diamond yesterday?"

"A car crashed into the ranch's front gate." The pretty blond waitress put a hand on her hip. "But you already knew that, didn't you, Roy?"

Vince's hand stilled with his Coke glass to his lips. He took a gulp, focusing on the conversation at the next table.

"I heard it crushed the driver's side," said Roy's buddy.

A chill swept over Vince that had nothing to do with the ice-cold beverage cascading down his throat.

Roy took a bite of his burger then spoke around the food in his mouth. "Yep, I heard the driver died."

The glass slipped from Vince's fingers as he choked on the sweet syrup that suddenly turned bitter in his mouth. It bounced off the table into his lap, spilling soda and ice down the front of him.

The blond waitress spun around and pulled a bar towel from the waistband of her apron. "Let me clean that up for you."

He grabbed the towel from her when it looked like she was about to give him a frontal pat-down. He did not need her discovering the hard butt of the Glock under his jacket.

It was all he could do to focus on the task at hand as perspiration pricked his neck and the room threatened to spin.

Not Frankie. Vince had promised their father he'd look after his younger, half-brother. Vince had always tried to keep Frankie from going into the family business. But the kid had a gift for stealth and deception, and the family business was simply too lucrative.

"Here's another towel." The waitress mopped up the table as Vince struggled to breathe.

It couldn't have been his brother's car. Sure, Frankie had a lead foot occasionally, but he was the cautious one. He rarely took the risks Vince did. That's why Vince had stayed behind and search the apartments. He figured sending the kid ahead with the woman would be the best way to keep him from getting caught.

The waitress brought another glass of Coke and gave him a broad smile. "Let me get you another burger and fries. It'll be on the house."

He stared at her pretty smile and sky-blue eyes. The woman was a beauty. And Vince loved beautiful women. Any other time, he would have flirted with her, but not today. Today, he needed to find out if his brother was in that accident.

He grabbed the plate she'd picked up. "This is fine. A few soggy fries never hurt anyone." To prove his point, he picked up a fry and shoved it in his mouth.

Roy and his buddy's stared at him as he chewed. Swallowing proved almost as difficult as breathing though. Keeping a tight grip, he picked up his fresh Coke and took a sip to wash down the greasy potato.

Turning toward the men at the next table, he kept his expression neutral. "Did I hear you say something about an accident?"

Both men nodded. Roy was the first to speak. "Sure enough. They weren't from around here though."

"What makes you say that?" His voice came out akin to a squeak.

"Everybody knows everybody around here, and nobody recognized them," said Roy's buddy around another bite of burger. He tipped his head toward Vince. "Where did you say you were from?"

I didn't.

Vince gave a dismissive wave. "Up north. I'm just passing through."

Roy jumped in. "It was a black Lexus. No one around here drives a fancy car like that."

Roy rambled on, but Vince couldn't hear him over the roaring in his ears. *No!* He gripped the edge of the table so tight the Formica dug into his palm. *How did this happen?*

"...said the woman has multiple broken bones, but I guess she fared better than the driver, though, huh?"

The woman? They found her in the trunk? Vince swiped a hand across his mouth to loosen his clenched jaw. Talk about complications. Why couldn't she have died? It would have saved him the work of putting a bullet in her, and it would have wrapped up this whole messy job. He didn't care that there was still evidence out there somewhere of the boss's illegal activities.

Frankie was dead!

He bolted to his feet, knocking the table so hard with his thigh his Coke tipped over again.

Roy's buddy gaped at him. "Boy, you're the clumsiest person I've ever met."

Seeing the pretty waitress headed his direction with another bar towel, he tossed a twenty on the table and bolted for the door.

~

THE WOMAN in the bed traced the weave of the hospital blanket across her lap with a fingernail, trying to determine whether it was gray or blue. The drab color matched exactly how she felt.

The pain meds kept her pain at bay, but a restlessness and helplessness filled her. *How long before the sheriff returns to tell me who I am?*

Would her fingerprints reveal her identity? She doubted the picture he took would help identify her since her face was so discolored and misshapen. She hadn't seen it yet, but if the pain emanating around her left eye and brow were anything to go by, she looked horrible.

A light knock sounded on her door before it swung open. Faith Winters stepped into the room. "Ah, it's much less crowded in here without all those men towering around."

The woman watched Faith as she checked the IV and blood pressure monitor like she knew what all the lights and symbols actually meant. Her visitor was petite and slender with the slightest hint of gray in the blond hair that framed her oval face. She couldn't believe Faith was the mother of the two men who had to be at least six feet tall. *They must get their height from their father.*

Faith turned compassionate eyes on her. "How are you feeling?"

"Pretty good, I guess." She doubted Faith wanted to know the truth; that she felt anxious, scared, and all alone.

"I understand they had to cut your clothes off yesterday. Not that you'd be able to wear them with your casts. I'll pick you up some clothing. Would you rather sweatpants and t-shirts or loose, summer dresses?"

"Um..." *Do I prefer sweatpants or dresses?* She wrinkled her brow, causing her stitches to pull. *Ouch, I really need to remember to stop doing that.* "Maybe, both. If the dresses are long and loose, not confining."

Faith gave her a reassuring smile. "Of course, sweatpants for sleeping in, and dresses for lounging around the house. You'll likely spend the first few days in bed since your body needs rest to heal. Do you have a color preference? Not that Providence has much of a selection of dresses, or sweatpants for that matter. I suppose I could make a trip to Kennewick. It's not like I'm doing anything nowadays."

She detected the wistful note in Faith's voice, but what caught her attention was the name of the town where they were. *Providence.* The knowledge did her no good, though. Not much of a selection meant Providence was a small town. But none of the people she'd met so far recognized her, so she probably wasn't from around here.

Color? What was her favorite color? Shouldn't this be part of her personality? Something she should remember. *Why am I blocking this?* Hiding her frustration, she responded. "Any color will do, I guess. I don't recall... what color I like."

Her consternation must have shown on her face because Faith clasped her hand. "I'm sorry. Of course, you don't. I'll see what I can find."

"I don't want to inconvenience you."

Faith waved her hand. "It's no trouble at all." She pushed the nurse's call button. When a nurse responded, she asked for a piece of paper and a pen. "My kids keep telling me to use my phone to keep notes and lists, but I like tangible things. With technology, it's so easy to accidentally push a wrong button, you know. And then when I lose something, I have no idea how to get it back. Smart-phones are supposed to make things easier, but they make me feel dumb and cause me anxiety."

Smart phones? Do I have a cell phone? I must, but where is it? My whole life would be on that phone. It could help me remember. Hope surged in her breast.

A nurse walked into the room. "Here you go, Faith."

The woman sat up, causing pain to slice through her ribs. "Where's my phone?" At the nurse's confused stare, she attempted to quell her excitement. "I mean... my personal belongings."

The nurse pulled a white bag from the small closet and Faith took it. "There's not much in here. Your clothes are basically rags. What are you looking for?"

Her chest tightened at the words *Jane Doe* written on the bag. "Um... my phone. Maybe it could help me remem—" her words died off when she saw Faith's grim face.

"There's no phone in here. Only shoes and your ruined clothing."

Swallowing the disappointment, she stammered, "C-can I see them? Maybe they'll look familiar."

Faith pulled out a pair of blue suede slip-on shoes. They looked comfortable—dressy, yet casual—but not familiar. She shook her head and looked away.

Faith put the shoes back in the bag and thanked the nurse. After the nurse left, Faith sat on the edge of the bed. "It will come. Don't force it. You'll only make yourself more upset." Then she picked up the pen and continued to talk as she wrote. "I'll get you some sandals or flip flops as well as sun dresses, slippers, sweatpants, and t-shirts. How about underclothing?" When she didn't respond, Faith continued, "I don't suppose you recall your bra size and what type of undies you prefer."

Heat flooded her cheeks at Faith's directness. She shifted uncomfortably in the bed, and pain lanced through her ribs. She closed her eyes, attempting to focus on something else, but her mind was blank. All she recalled was two tall, handsome brothers.

"I'm sorry, dear. I'm causing you to overdo it, aren't I?"

"No. It's okay. I shouldn't have tried to move."

Faith reached for the bag with *Jane Doe's* belongings. "Let me see if they put your underclothing in here."

She stopped herself from nodding and shot Faith a smile.

Faith copied down sizes from the clothing in the bag then asked, "How about makeup and other toiletries?"

Do I wear make-up? She stared at Faith as the question rattled around inside her head. Raising her right hand to her face she touched her cheek. Panic rose in her chest, stealing her breath. She frowned at Faith.

Faith's voice was quiet when she spoke again. "Has anyone brought you a mirror? Do you even know what you look like?"

She shook her head, and Faith said, "I'll be right back."

The other woman walked out of the room, leaving her to wonder if she really wanted to know. She returned a few moments later and held up a mirror. "Here."

She bit back a gasp as her stomach twisted. The left side of her face was purple from the cheek bone to the hairline, her eye partially swollen shut. Stitches ran along her hairline. No wonder her head hurt so bad. Her right eye sported a much smaller, blue bruise. She tried to look beyond the bruises.

Shouldn't the color of my eyes be familiar?

What had happened to make her forget everything so completely that she didn't even recognize her own face?

Faith took her hand. "Every thing's going to be okay. It'll come back. In the meantime, I'm going to take good care of you."

She blinked back the tears that blurred her vision and squeezed Faith's hand. "Thank you, but... why are you helping me? I'm a stranger."

"You won't be a stranger for long, dear. And helping people is what I do." Faith shrugged and picked the pen up again. "Now, let's see... I don't think you need any makeup. As much as you're going to want to hide the bruises, I wouldn't suggest trying to rub much makeup on them. Should I get you some powder foundation?"

She looked back at her reflection. A tear clung to her long, thick lashes. She might as well accentuate the positives, even though they were difficult to see amid the bruising.

"Mascara too, please." Then she touched her dry cracked lips. "And lip gloss."

"Sheer? Or would you like colored gloss?" Before she could answer, Faith continued. "You have beautiful lips, so red and full."

Were her lips naturally this red? Or did they look red because her face was so pale?

"Sheer is fine, or maybe a frost," she responded, wondering if that was her preference.

The room fell silent a few minutes later after Faith left. The woman picked up the mirror again and studied her face. *Jane Doe.*

How long will it take for the sheriff to identify me?

CHAPTER 5

*J*ake pulled his truck to a stop in the hospital parking lot.
What am I doing here?

It was seven thirty in the evening, and unable to get the auburn-haired woman with emerald eyes out of his mind, he'd decided to visit her.

Robert had texted him this afternoon; fingerprints identified the woman as Emily Anderson. Robert was attempting to locate her family.

Emily. It suited her. It was a pretty name, and she was a pretty woman, despite the bruises and cuts on her face.

Robert had also informed him she was thirty years old and not married.

He shut off the engine but made no move to get out of his truck. He wasn't a concerned family member. Concerned, yes, but it wasn't his place to sit at her bedside. That's where her boyfriend or parents belonged. Did she have a boyfriend?

Were her family and friends going crazy wondering where she was?

Pulling the keys from the ignition, he resisted the urge to start the truck and drive away.

Coward.

He'd ridden fifteen-hundred-pound bulls and broken wild mustangs. Why was he so nervous to go visit with a pretty woman?

He slid down from his truck, wincing at the pain in his thigh, where he'd gotten kicked that afternoon by the colt he was breaking.

Feeling empty-handed, he rubbed his palms against his thighs as he approached her—Emily's—room. He should bring flowers or something, but that was probably not appropriate, considering he didn't even know her.

"Hey, Dale." Jake greeted the deputy who sat outside Emily's door, relieved it wasn't his brother who sat there. Robert would never let him live it down. "I'm going to visit with her for a while. You can take a break if you'd like."

"Thanks, Jake. It'll be nice to stretch my legs."

With Dale walking away, Jake rubbed his hands on his jeans again, this time to dry his damp palms.

What is wrong with me? True, he didn't date much, but it wasn't like he was afraid of women. Well, he was afraid of Debbie Wheeler. Ever since she threw herself at him last fall, he was afraid of being alone with her.

He knocked on the door then opened it to see Emily's eyes closed. Her cheeks held more color than this morning. Should he leave or go in?

She opened her eyes and smiled at him. With a dimple creasing each cheek, she looked younger than thirty.

"Hi, Jake."

"Hello." He returned her smile as he entered the room.

"You missed Ben and Amy by half an hour."

Jake's eyebrows shot up at the mention of his cousins. "They visited you?"

"I think they felt bad for me. Ben said his dad told them about me, and Amy insisted they visit."

Amy was thoughtful like that.

"Did they bring the girls?"

"No, they thought it would be too much for me. But they told me about them."

"They're little cuties and they're good girls, but they are busy two-year-olds." Jake shifted from one foot to the other then snatched the hat off his head. His mother would chew him out for being so slow to remove his hat in a lady's presence. "You're probably tired after visiting with them. I should let you rest."

"I've been resting all day. Seriously, these four walls have become very boring." She motioned to the television. "And there's nothing worth watching."

Jake shoved his hands in his pockets. "How are you feeling?"

"A little better, I guess. I hurt everywhere though." She put her right hand against the left side of her abdomen.

"I'll bet. The casts will be on a lot longer than it will take for the ribs to heal, but they'll be the most painful of all."

Emily cocked her head as much as the neck brace allowed and narrowed her eyes. "You sound like you speak from experience."

He nodded. "I've broken a few ribs before. Waiting for them to heal was the longest three weeks of my life, both times."

"How did you break your ribs?"

"The first time was bull riding, and the second time, I was thrown from a headstrong mustang and took a hoof to the ribs."

Emily grimaced. "Ouch. I thought you were a rancher, not a rodeo cowboy."

"I was born and raised on the ranch. But I had to have something to keep me from getting bored at college, so I did the amateur rodeo for fun." He crossed the room and sat in the chair.

"Do I detect a hint of a limp in your walk that wasn't there this morning?"

"You're observant." He pointed at his left thigh. "I got kicked by the spawn of Satan."

Emily laughed then winced, putting her hand to her ribs again.

"Actually, it was the son of Zeus. I'm pretty sure I misnamed his sire though. Zeus is the most stubborn horse I've ever worked with, and his son, Hercules, is every bit as bad." Jake bit his tongue. He wasn't usually this talkative. He'd better change the subject or he'd end up telling her he got kicked because he wasn't paying attention. He'd been thinking about her instead. He cleared his throat. "So, Robert said your name is Emily Anderson? Did the name spark any memories for you?"

She scowled. "No. Before he came, I had almost started to think my name was Leah, because it felt familiar. But apparently, that's my mother's name."

"So, you sort of remembered your mother's name. That's a good sign, isn't it?"

"Maybe. But I don't remember her at all." Her eyes glistened, and she blinked away the tears.

"I can't imagine how frustrated you must feel."

Emily smiled, though it looked forced. "I have learned, however, that I don't like green gelatin." She pointed to the uneaten blob on the dinner tray near her bed.

Jake looked at the tray. The gelatin wasn't the only thing she hadn't eaten.

"I'm not a fan of gelatin either, green or otherwise."

"What's your favorite food? I'd tell you mine, but..." She shrugged.

"Well, I like food in general, but ice cream is my weakness."

"I like ice cream." She wrinkled her brow in concentration then winced. "I think. It sounds good anyway."

He scooted to the edge of his chair. "What flavor do you think you'd like?"

"Hmm... chocolate, but not plain chocolate. I like chocolate with chunks of chocolate, like brownies and stuff." She frowned. "It's weird how I know that, but I have no specific memory attached to the knowledge."

"That is strange. Chocolate with chocolate huh? I'll be back in a few minutes." Jake stood, slipping his hat on as he walked from the room.

He was glad Dale took his job seriously and had returned to the chair outside Emily's room already. It would have felt wrong leaving her unprotected to make an ice cream run.

He smiled at Dale. "I'll be back in a bit."

Jogging out the front door and to his truck, he drove to Providence's one and only grocery store. He quickly selected two pints of the richest chocolate ice cream he could find, then grabbed a third one—for Dale.

He paused at the nurses' station when he arrived back at the hospital to ask for three spoons. Dale gave him a big grin when Jake handed over the ice cream. But Jake's true reward was the smile that split Emily's face when he walked into her room. The depth of her dimples was a dead giveaway to her feelings.

"You bought ice cream?"

"The chocolatiest I could find." Jake took the lid off one and stuck a spoon in before handing it to her. Then he took his and sat in the chair again.

"I like a man who knows what he likes and doesn't hesitate to go for it." She wrinkled her brow, again. "At least, I think I do."

Jake chuckled. "It sounds like you have all kinds of surprises to look forward to."

"That's one way of looking at it." Then changing the subject, she said, "You know, you don't sound like a cowboy."

Jake chuckled. "What is a cowboy supposed to sound like?"

"I don't know. I expected a drawl or something."

"Well, I was born and raised in Washington, not Texas. In fact, my mother grew up cultured and educated. She insisted on raising us the same way. She expected us to speak and act like gentlemen at all times."

"Judging by your horses' names, I assume your education included Greek Mythology?"

Jake grinned. "That was mostly my idea. Mythology was more interesting than most of the great philosophers." Jake continued to talk about his mother's influences: piano lessons, reading the classics, watching musicals. He had a hard time holding back a groan as he talked.

"I'll bet she made you take dance lessons too."

"Of course." It came out a growl, then he smiled. "But the only dancing I do nowadays is country swing."

"What's that saying? You can lead a horse to water, but you can't make him drink?"

Jake chuckled. "Something like that. Anyway, I went to college because my parents insisted. So I left the ranch for four years, not counting summers. They were the longest four years of my life."

"Right, your rodeo years. What did you study?"

"My dad insisted I get a business degree so I wouldn't run the ranch into the ground, and I had a double minor of animal science and agriculture."

"All that in four years? I'm impressed. Tell me more about your family. I would tell you about myself, but…" She shrugged and smiled. "It would all be lies."

Jake laughed. She had an interesting sense of humor, considering her situation.

"Well, you've met my older brother, Robert, and my mother, Faith. I also have a younger sister named Riley, who's twenty-three. She's away at college, completing her nursing degree this summer."

"Does she find it easier to stay away from the ranch than you did?"

He shrugged. "She loves the ranch, but she's driven to get her degree."

"Does Robert live on the ranch too?"

"No. He built a house in town a few years ago. He always says he'd never trade his upbringing on the ranch for anything, but he wasn't interested in taking over. He comes out and rides occasionally or helps with the round-up sometimes, but other than that he's not that involved."

"Your mother came back to visit me after you left this morning. She's very friendly."

"She's a bundle of energy, isn't she? Always on the go, needing to take care of anyone she considers less fortunate than herself, which is everyone. Your accident is timely for her. She used to tend Ben and Amy's little girls, but Ben's mom, who is the high school principal, is free for the summer and wanted to spend more time with them, so my mom is at loose ends." Jake took time to savor a bite of ice cream before continuing. "She's a nurse, or at least she used to be. She retired a few years ago when my father had a stroke. She took care of him for two years until he passed away."

"I'm sorry to hear that."

Jake swallowed the emotion blocking his throat. "Thank you. Losing him was hard, but it was even harder seeing him no longer able to do what he loved. That was when I went from being one of the ranch hands to being the boss. Thank goodness I have Zane. He was my father's right-hand man for my whole life, and now he's mine. I don't know what I would do without him."

"I'm glad you have him. That must have been difficult trying to fill your father's shoes at such a young age."

He nodded. "It *was* overwhelming at first, but I love ranching. It's who I am." Silently, he added, I *could never give it up.*

Two hours later, Jake grinned as he walked to his truck, unsure why he'd been so anxious about visiting Emily. He'd enjoyed the time spent with her. He'd done most of the talking, but she'd been an avid listener and frequently asked questions.

She had a surprisingly positive attitude, considering all she'd been through. Of course, she couldn't remember what she'd been through. Would she be different if she knew what kind of trauma she'd suffered? Would she have acted differently toward him if she knew she had a boyfriend waiting at home, worrying about her?

One thing was certain; he needed to be careful about getting involved with her. He couldn't afford distractions that would pull him away from the ranch. *I know nothing about her. She doesn't even know anything about herself.*

Regardless, he pulled out his phone. It was late, but he found the name he wanted in his call list and hit send anyway.

"Zane," he said when the foreman's deep voice answered. "Sorry for calling so late. I want you to go ahead and hire that other ranch hand we discussed the other day. I'm going to be busy breaking the colts this summer."

Besides, his mother or Emily might need him.

CHAPTER 6

*E*mily carefully pulled the new brush through her hair.

Faith had blown into her room like a mini tornado right after Dr. Young informed her she was being released into the Winter's capable hands. Faith, to take care of her. Jake, to protect her.

Do I really need protecting?

Faith had brought a duffel bag full of what she deemed to be necessities for Emily, then chattered the whole time she helped Emily dress. "I need to leave you for a little while. I'm in the church choir and I can't be late. But Jake will be here with his truck, right after services, to drive you to the ranch. I don't think you'd be comfortable in my little car with your casts."

Church? Do I go to church? Intuitively, Emily knew she believed in God, but she couldn't recall whether she attended church regularly.

With a wave, Faith disappeared, leaving Emily with her thoughts— that quickly turned to Jake.

He'd been a welcome distraction last night. She'd enjoyed Ben and Amy's visit, but her room had grown so quiet after they left, and her frustration over her inability to remember anything had grown. Yes, she'd enjoyed visiting with the handsome rancher who made impulsive ice cream purchases.

The warmth in Jake's brown eyes made her feel comfortable despite her situation, which made her anxious.

Pain lanced through Emily's ribs as she reached for the bag of her personal belongings the nurse had left on the end of her bed. Shifting, she reached again, this time hooking the hairbrush in the bag's edge to drag it closer. Taking out the ruined clothing, she dropped them to the side before pulling out the blue flats.

Do I wear these often?

Wincing, she managed to slip the right shoe on before shoving the left in the duffel bag Faith had brought. She tossed the personal-belongings bag on the bedside table.

Thunk.

There was something in the bag. Emily grabbed it and looked in but saw nothing. Feeling the bottom with her hand, she realized there, in the creased corner of the bag, was a small, hard object. She reached deep inside to retrieve it.

A key.

A flash of adrenalin surged through her body, making her fingers tingle. *What does it go to?* A sense of urgency swept over her. *This key is important,* she knew it.

But why?

It must have been in her pocket at the time of the accident. She pushed the call button for a nurse, then tapped her fingers on the side rail, as she waited for a response.

As soon as a nurse opened her door, she blurted, "Where did this key come from?"

The nurse frowned. "I don't know."

"I found it in my personal belongings."

"It must have been on your person when you arrived. Would you like me to see if the nurse who took care of you in the E.R. is here today?"

"Yes, thank you." Emily fingered the key, willing herself to remember what it was for.

She waited.

Nothing.

She couldn't remember a single thing prior to waking up in the hospital. She blinked away the tears that filled her eyes and took a deep breath.

A young, blond nurse stepped into her room and explained she'd found the key in Emily's bra when they removed her clothing.

Emily's brow puckered. "In my bra? Did my clothing have pockets?"

The girl shrugged. "I was surprised to find the key there, considering your dress slacks had pockets."

"Was there anything else in my pockets? Or my bra?"

Why did I put it down my shirt if I had pockets? Was I trying to ensure someone wouldn't find it?

She gripped the key tighter. Was it a house key? No, it wasn't shaped like a typical house key, nor did it look like a car key.

"Thank you," Emily said after the nurse assured her there was nothing else on her person.

She was still contemplating what the key could be for when Jake showed up, looking as handsome and comfortable in dress slacks, bolo tie, and blazer as he did in his wranglers and t-shirt last night.

Concern filled his eyes. "Are you okay?"

"I'm fine. I just have a headache." It was the truth. Although her headache had less to do with her injuries and more to do with the mystery of the key. Slipping the tiny piece of metal into the bag Faith had brought, she forced a smile. It was bad enough imposing on a stranger, she didn't want to worry Jake any more than necessary.

It wasn't long before a nurse pushed her in a wheelchair to the hospital entrance where Jake's truck waited.

"It's kind of high for you to climb into with your broken leg. I'll lift you in, but I don't want to hurt your ribs, so speak up if I hurt you." He bent down and put one arm under her knees, then gently slid the other behind her back.

When she leaned forward so he could get his arm behind her, a sharp pain stabbed her side and she gasped.

He pulled back. "Broken ribs hurt worst when you bend or lean forward. Maybe it will help if you put your good arm around my shoulders and lift your upper body up to avoid bending." He bent again, waited for her to put her arm around his shoulders, then slowly lifted.

She held her breath. When she felt no pain, she gave him a brief smile. "I'm good."

He guided her casted leg into the truck first then carefully set her on the seat. Closing her door, he walked to the driver's side and climbed in.

Pain pricked her side again as she reached across her body to buckle her seat belt. Wincing, she straightened.

"Here, let me." Jake lifted the center console exposing the bench seat and her buckle. He took the seat belt from her.

She caught a fresh, clean, very masculine scent as he leaned toward her. The man smelled as good as he looked.

Click.

Jake buckled her belt, barely touching her, and disappointment filled her when he leaned away.

He put the console back down. "You can prop your cast on here."

Emily rested her arm on the console, doing her best not to stare at the handsome man behind the wheel as his scent filled the cab of the truck. Instead, she watched out the window as they drove in silence, hoping to spot something familiar.

Anything.

Near what she guessed to be the outskirts of town, she spotted a large, expensive-looking house. The mansion with an unfinished yard, looked pretentious and out of place among the farmland.

After a few more miles, Emily noticed a white, triple-rail fence running along the highway.

Jake pointed out the window. "This is part of the ranch."

"It's big," she said in awe as she realized the fence spanned for miles.

"You're only seeing a small part of it."

Emily wasn't sure what she expected, but Jake had much more acreage than she'd imagined. He probably had a lot more horses and cattle than she'd first thought too.

Jake was a busy man. The last thing he needed was an invalid-stranger imposing on him. Her lack of family and inability to take care of herself created a tightness in her chest.

Jake turned into a long tree-lined lane under a massive gate with the name Double Diamond Ranch across the top. Both ends were flanked with interlocking diamonds. She suspected the insignia was the ranch's brand.

Emily studied the sprawling ranch house with a wrap-around porch. Her gaze shifted to the massive, red stables that stood some distance behind the house.

Jake Winters is a wealthy man.

He pulled to a stop in front of the house. Hopping out, he carried her in and was about to set her on the couch when Faith stepped through a swinging door.

"She needs to go to bed and rest."

Jake straightened and followed Faith down a long hallway to a room where she placed something on the nightstand before pulling down the covers on a queen-sized bed.

Jake laid her down. "I'm sorry," he said when Emily gasped in pain.

Emily tried to smile to assure him she was okay, but it probably looked like a grimace. Her whole body hurt.

Faith slipped her shoe off and tucked the covers around her. After shooing Jake out of the room, she turned to the nightstand.

"Dr. Young prescribed you some pain meds as well as a few sleeping pills in case you find it hard to sleep with your casts. We'll start with a pain pill. It'll probably knock you out as it is."

Emily couldn't muster an argument as Faith handed her a pill and waited for her to slip it in her mouth before handing her the water. She couldn't believe how much getting dressed and making the trip to the ranch had exhausted her.

Faith stepped to the window and closed the Americana-themed curtains that matched the homemade quilt on the bed, darkening the room.

Faith's lack of chatter surprised Emily. She took her nursing responsibilities very seriously. That or Emily looked as bad as she felt.

"Thank you," Emily said as Faith stepped to the door. "I can't thank you and Jake enough."

"Don't you fret, dear. You just rest now."

After Faith walked out, Emily closed her eyes and tried to relax, despite the pain pulsing through her body. How strange that she was at the mercy of strangers, yet she felt welcome and safe, despite not knowing who she was or what had happened to her.

JAKE LEFT Robert's old room, where he'd laid Emily, to pace the great room. He wasn't needed; his mother was capable of caring for her patient, but he couldn't get the concern he'd seen on Emily's face when he arrived at the hospital out of his mind.

She'd quickly hidden it, but by the time they arrived at the ranch, she looked defeated and exhausted.

His mother came out of Emily's room. "Don't you have work to do?"

"I do... I'm just making sure you don't need me for anything else."

"We'll be fine." Faith lifted her chin. "I already got your father's wheelchair and your old crutches out of storage." Jake detected a slight tremor in his mother's voice. "It will be best if she'll let us push her around in the wheelchair, but I suspect she is a strong, independent woman."

Jake put his arm around his mother's shoulders. "I know it's difficult for you to be back at the ranch nursing an invalid again, Mom. I know being at the ranch at all is hard."

She hugged him. "It is hard because there are so many happy memories here." She grew misty-eyed. "But it's not the same without him."

He squeezed her shoulder. "No, it's not."

His mom had moved in with his Aunt Charity after his Uncle Rich died suddenly a little over a year ago. She said it was because she didn't want Charity to be alone, but Jake suspected she needed to get away from the ranch.

Jake didn't blame her. Some days, working the ranch, trying to fill the void left by his father, Jake felt overwhelmed.

She leaned away enough to look up at him. "You should have moved into the master bedroom like I told you to."

"No, Mom. That's your room. This will always be your home."

"It's time for it to become your home, son. It's time for you to find a wife and have a family of your own."

"You can save your breath." Jake dropped his arm and stepped away. "Lottie gives me this lecture on a regular basis. I'm too busy to devote time to a wife and kids."

"You're only as busy as you choose to be, Jake. If you found something... or someone you cared about as much as you do this ranch, you'd find a way to make time."

He'd had someone once, but Lydia had wanted nothing to do with the ranch.

"I can't afford to leave long enough to find someone to care about as much as I do this ranch." He'd invested two years into the last relationship that failed.

"Maybe you won't have to go anywhere. Maybe she'll come to you." Faith looked toward the hall.

"Emily? She's a stranger, Mom. I'm fine with her recuperating here at the ranch, but don't try to matchmake. We know nothing about her."

"You'll have plenty of time to get to know her while she recuperates." When Jake scowled at her, she raised her hands in resignation. "All I'm saying is maybe there's a reason that car wrecked on your property. I think the Lord brought her here for a reason."

Jake shook his head. He should have known his mom had ulterior motives in bringing Emily to the ranch.

"I've got work to do." Jake headed to his room to change his clothes.

CHAPTER 7

*E*mily shifted on the couch, attempting to get comfortable. After sleeping for three hours, she woke up feeling much better and wanted to get out of bed. She hated being pushed around in the wheelchair, but Faith insisted it was the only way she'd allow Emily out of her room.

Sitting with her leg propped up on the large ottoman in the great room, Emily scanned her surroundings as much as her neck brace allowed. Tall windows let in plenty of late-afternoon light, offering a view of a front yard flanked by a pasture where horses grazed. The great room spanned the depth of the house, with double patio doors at the back letting in additional light. A large oak dining table occupied the far side.

Emily liked how the light complimented the room furnished with comfort in mind; leather furniture, a large flat screen television mounted over the fireplace, oak bookcases full of books and DVDs. Emily peered at the shelves from across the room while she listened to Faith talk about the additions they'd made to the ranch house over the years.

She recognized many classic literature titles and the extensive selection of musicals Jake and Robert must have found torturous. She smiled as she pictured a squirming teenage Jake who would rather rope steers, forced to endure the singing and dancing.

A gleaming baby grand piano sat in the corner of the room. *Is that where Jake took piano lessons?* Did Faith teach him? Had she stood over his shoulder to make sure he practiced? Or had she paid someone else to teach her unwilling sons, so she wouldn't have to fight that battle?

Both Robert and Jake towered over Faith, but Emily suspected they respected their mother and wouldn't dream of talking back to her.

Faith sat down beside her with a thick scrapbook. "This was my Robert as a baby. He was the busiest little guy..." she continued to talk as she showed Emily picture after picture. Happy family pictures in which younger versions of Robert and Jake grew to look like their handsome father.

Riley, their younger sister, looked like a younger version of Faith with darker hair. She saw countless pictures of the siblings working on the ranch, riding horses, branding cattle, and hauling hay.

Do I have a scrapbook? One full of happy family memories. Ignoring the twinge of longing and anxiety that swept over her, she focused on a picture of Robert and Jake with Ben.

A few minutes later, Emily studied a picture of adolescent Jake. "Is Jake holding a cat?"

"No, that's a mountain lion cub."

"A mountain lion?"

"Many years ago, our ranch hands kept coming across the carcasses of dead calves. We realized a mountain lion had taken up residence on the northernmost part of the ranch. We managed to trap it and turn it over to Fish and Game to relocate. When they caught it, they realized it was a female and had been nursing cubs. Blake sent Robert and Jake to search the surrounding area to see if they could find the babies. They searched for an entire day but found nothing. Jake insisted on going out again the next day but found nothing. On the third day, his father told him to forget about it, but Jake wouldn't let it go. He hurried through his chores and searched again. He finally found two cubs, but one had died. Jake brought the other one, very sick and weak, home in his shirt and insisted on caring for it until it was strong enough to turn over to Fish and Game."

Emily studied the picture. Jake couldn't have been older than thirteen. There was no mistaking the same warmth in his brown eyes that she saw at the hospital last night. Most teenage boys wouldn't care what happened to a couple of abandoned cubs, but Jake not only cared, he did something about it.

"I thought we would have a battle on our hands when it came time to turn the cub over to Fish and Game, but Jake recognized keeping it wasn't an option. No amount of love and caring could change the mountain lion into something it wasn't."

They were still looking at the scrapbook when Jake came in the back door a few minutes later. His footsteps faltered when he saw them sitting together. He smiled and tipped his hat. "Ladies."

A ripple of attraction for the handsome rancher danced through Emily's stomach.

Continuing toward his office, Jake froze at the door. "Mom, the scrapbooks? Really? I'm sure Emily doesn't care about any of those pictures."

She smiled. "On the contrary, I find them very entertaining." Emily couldn't help herself—Jake's discomfort amused her.

He made a noise akin to a groan and continued into his office.

Faith continued to point out pictures of her children throughout their high school years, commenting as she did so. Robert and Jake went from being attractive boys to handsome young men to gorgeous adults. No awkward, ugly stages for this family.

The way Jake's eyes lit up when he smiled brought a smile to her lips

She tuned back into Faith's voice. "When Jake was a Senior, Providence won the 1A football championship. Jake played defensive end."

It didn't surprise Emily that Jake had played football. It appeared he could do everything and do it well.

"And this was right after he won a high school rodeo championship. It went straight to his head. He thought he was hot stuff that year."

"Mom." Jake came out of his office and hurried around the couch. "Emily doesn't need to see anymore."

Despite Jake's tan, a blush colored his cheeks clear to the tips of his ears.

Emily bit back a laugh.

"It's fine, Jake." Faith tried to push his hands away as he reached for the scrapbook. "She's enjoying herself, and besides, those pictures were a long time ago. There's no point in being embarrassed over them now."

Jake's eyes met hers and Emily smiled. "I promise not to hold anything against you."

"That's nice to know," he said through tight lips. "But I'm taking this anyway." Tugging the large scrapbook out of Faith's hands, he walked over to the shelf where the book belonged, then changed his mind and took it into his office.

"Well bummer," Faith said, shoulders slumping. "We were just getting to the good stuff."

A few moments later, Jake crossed through the room, carrying a checkbook. He made the motion of tipping his hat as he reached the back door but didn't meet their eyes.

Faith smiled. "Actually, there weren't many more pictures of Jake except his winning a blue ribbon in 4H and graduating with honors."

Yep, Jake did everything well. He was good-looking and smart.

"You wouldn't believe the amount of food those boys put away as teenagers, especially when they went through their bodybuilding stage." Faith giggled. "I bet those were the pictures Jake didn't want you to see. They thought they were so buff, even when they were still skinny shrimps. They wrestled each other constantly, trying to prove who was strongest." Faith laughed again. "As soon as one of them won, my husband took the winner down and pinned him. Just to keep them humble."

A truck door slammed, drawing their attention to the window. Robert walked through the front door a few moments later, carrying a file folder.

"Hi Mom. Emily, how are you doing?"

"As well as can be expected. Faith is taking good care of me."

"Mom's the best, isn't she?"

Before Emily had the chance to answer, Jake came through the back door again, a sheen of perspiration on his neck.

He looked at Robert. "Is everything okay?"

"I found out a little more information about Emily and thought I'd come tell her. Can I borrow your laptop, Jake?"

Jake grabbed his laptop from his office and sat on the couch near Robert.

Emily couldn't help but admire the brothers. They were both broad shouldered and fit. *If they wrestled now, who would win?* Emily put her money on Jake.

He looked like he had fifteen pounds on his brother. Though his long sleeve shirt didn't hug his shoulders like the t-shirt he wore to the hospital last night, she suspected it was fifteen pounds of pure muscle.

"I apologize, Emily, for taking so long to find this information. I've been focusing most of my attention on the driver and the car. I've been checking property holdings near the lake, which is where we believe he was taking you. Unfortunately, I've come up empty-handed in that regard. There are no properties registered to Brian Barnes. And it doesn't look like we'll be able to get anything useful from his cell phone. It was too badly damaged." Robert typed something into the laptop then slid to the edge of the couch. "But Uncle James was right. You're a doctor."

Emily's brow wrinkled. Thankfully, the motion didn't hurt as bad today as it did yesterday. "I am?"

Shouldn't that sound or feel right?

"Emily Anderson, Doctor of Psychology. You work for Alpine Family Therapists in Spokane." Robert turned the laptop toward her, and an image stared back at her that looked like her, minus the black eyes and bandage.

The woman in the photo wore more makeup than Emily thought she usually wore, and her hair hung in long loose curls. Emily doubted she normally spent that kind of time on her hair.

Was the photo simply a glamour shot for the website? Taking a deep breath, she fought the panic tightening her chest.

Why doesn't any of it feel familiar?

She reached for the laptop. "May I?"

Wincing at the pain in her ribs, she sat back and let Robert place the computer on her lap. She scrolled to the top of the web page, hoping to see something familiar.

Anything.

Three pairs of eyes watched her. She was almost as concerned about letting Faith and her sons down as she was about remembering something.

The website listed an older man with a goatee and kind eyes, named Dr. Joseph Lewis, as a psychiatrist. A blond woman, who looked to be in her mid-forties, by the name of Dr. Susan Miller came next. There was Emily's face again, followed by Therapist Tyler Hall and Julie Moore, the receptionist.

If she'd worked with these people, shouldn't they look familiar? Emily closed her eyes, willing some memory, any memory, to return.

Nothing.

Fear and frustration built behind her eyelids in the form of tears. She didn't want to cry in front of these strangers. She took several deep breaths before opening her eyes, keeping them downcast. The faces on the computer screen may as well be strangers too. The thought was not comforting.

She looked up to find the two brothers staring at her.

Robert's voice was quiet, compassionate. "Does any of it spark a memory?"

Emily scowled and shook her head. The motion hurt, but she didn't care. She didn't trust herself to speak.

"It's okay, dear." Faith patted her arm. "It'll come."

Robert motioned to the laptop. "I contacted Dr. Lewis and let him know about your accident and your memory loss. He said he'd like to talk to you if you feel up to calling him. I also asked him to review your case files for your clients... uh, patients to see if one of them could be behind your abduction."

Emily looked back at Dr. Lewis' picture. *Call him?* The man was as much a stranger, if not more so, than the three people staring at her.

Robert opened the file he'd brought in with him and pulled out a photo. "So far, the only living relative I've been able to identify is your brother, Cameron Anderson. He lives in Spokane. I've contacted the police there. They'll locate him and inform him of your whereabouts and condition. We should hear from the police, if not your brother himself, in the next day or two."

Emily reached out with a shaky hand and took the photo. *Will it spark a memory?* Surely, she'd recognize her own brother.

She studied the photo. It looked like an enlarged version of a driver's license photo. The young man in the photo was attractive with wavy brown hair, blue eyes, and wore an expression that looked more like a smirk, than a smile.

Emily's chest tightened, trapping the breath in her lungs. *Why doesn't he look familiar?*

"Are you s-sure... this is my b-brother?" She hated the way her voice shook.

"Yes," Robert said. "Your—"

"I can see the family resemblance," Faith said, cutting Robert off. "He's quite attractive."

As she continued to study the picture, she spotted similarities to her image from the website. They had the same wavy hair and shape around the eyes. She couldn't compare the image she saw in the photo with what she saw when she looked in the mirror.

"Why... can't I... remember him?" Her voice grew husky as tears clogged her throat.

Faith squeezed her arm.

Emily blinked away the tears that filled her eyes and took several deep breaths. Setting the picture down, she grabbed the glass of water Faith had placed on the end table earlier and took several long swallows while she composed herself.

She set her glass down. "Is there anything else?"

Her stomach knotted. She wasn't sure she could handle any more right now. She'd hoped something would spark a memory. But when nothing did, disappointment and the fear of her memory never returning made it difficult to breathe. She suddenly felt very heavy and very tired.

Robert looked at the file in his hand then set it on the ottoman. "No, I'm afraid that's all for now. Unfortunately, having to rely on the police department in another city slows things down."

"Thank you, Sheriff. I'm sure you're doing the best you can."

"Call me Robert, please."

"Robert." She attempted to smile. "Do you mind if I keep this photo of my... brother?"

"That's fine."

Emily felt like a child who had disappointed everyone. They all wanted answers, no one more than her, though. But she'd failed and nearly broken down in front of everyone.

She wanted—no needed—to be alone without these concerned strangers staring at her. She looked to Jake for help because Faith would coddle her, and that would be her undoing.

"I could use some fresh air. Do you think I could sit out on the back deck for a while?"

Jake stood. "Absolutely."

"That's a wonderful idea." Faith rose also. "Here's the wheelchair."

"I got it, Mom." He bent over Emily. His breath tickled her cheek as he whispered, "Lean into me so I don't hurt your ribs."

Emily put her arm around his shoulder. A ripple of pleasure skittered through her abdomen as his shoulders bunched beneath her arm. If she wasn't so miserable, she would have analyzed the effect Jake's nearness had on her.

Robert opened the back door for them. "Jake, can I have a word with you before I leave?"

Jake nodded and continued through the door. He knelt on one knee next to a chaise lounge and carefully put Emily down.

Emily gave him a tight smile. "Thank you."

"Are you sure you're all right?" he asked. "Do you want my mom to keep you company?"

"No." Then, because she'd responded faster and louder than necessary, she smiled. "I'd like to be alone for a while. You know, to think."

"And it's difficult to think with my mom's chattering." He gave her hand a quick squeeze before letting go. "I get it. I'll be around. Call out if you need anything."

Emily bit her tongue to keep from calling him back. For some reason, she felt secure in his presence.

~

JAKE CAUGHT his mother headed toward the back door with her bag of yarn, a partially finished baby blanket hanging out. He put out a hand to stop her.

"I think she wants to be alone right now. She said she wants to do some thinking."

"Poor girl. Yes, she could use a little quiet, I suppose. Well, I'll go see if Lottie needs any help, then. Robert, are you sticking around for dinner?"

"Not tonight, Mom. But thanks." He picked up the folder he tossed on the ottoman earlier and shot Jake a look.

Jake followed Robert out to his Tahoe before his brother turned to talk to him.

"Wow, she was upset when nothing sparked a memory." Robert let out a sigh.

Jake rubbed his neck, not wanting to admit how his stomach had sank when Emily didn't remember anything. "Can you imagine how she must feel? I'm amazed at how well she composed herself, though. Most women use their emotions to play on a man's sympathies."

"I agree, but it sounds like we've both been around Debbie Wheeler a little too much."

"A little?" Jake growled. "That woman is out here every couple days."

"I feel your pain. Somehow she got my cell number and now I get calls and texts at all hours of the day and night."

Jake scowled. "Can we change the subject? I'm afraid talking about her might cause her to come driving up the lane."

"Gladly." Robert chuckled. "So, I sort of lied to Emily about not having any other information." He opened the file folder and showed Jake a copy of an obituary. "Her father died in a car accident about ten months ago. I wasn't kidding when I said her brother is the only living relative I've been able to find. When she looked so upset at not being able to remember anything, I couldn't bring myself to tell her more bad news."

A sharp twinge of pain filled Jake's chest for Emily's sake. He sighed. "That's probably a good call. I'm not sure she could handle that kind of news right now. I doubt it would have helped trigger her memory anyway."

Robert shrugged. "Who knows. Either way, I'm not sure this was the right time." Robert climbed in his truck, started it, and rolled down the window. "On the bright side, Little Brother, I've determined for certain there's no husband." He winked at Jake. "Take care of your pretty little cub." He put the vehicle in reverse in time to back away from the punch Jake itched to throw through the open window. Accelerating, Robert called out the window, "Rawr."

Jake scowled at the back of Robert's Tahoe, resisting the urge to pick up a rock and throw it at the back window. His brother never tired of teasing and goading him. Sometimes, Jake gave in and enjoyed the fight; other times, he didn't give Robert the satisfaction. Not reacting when Robert expected him to was his own way of goading his big brother.

As he returned to the house, a small smile lifted his lips. It shouldn't please him that Emily had no significant other, but it did.

CHAPTER 8

*F*aith placed a pill and glass of water on the table beside Emily's plate. "You should try to eat a little more before you take your pain pill this morning."

Emily sat alone at the kitchen table. Everyone had long since eaten breakfast by the time she'd awakened, and Faith had been hovering ever since. She'd wanted to bring Emily breakfast in bed, but Emily insisted on getting up. She hated being an invalid. It was bad enough she needed help dressing, she didn't enjoy having Faith wait on her too.

She pushed her plate away, a half-eaten waffle remaining. It tasted delicious, but her appetite had dissipated. Not knowing who she was and what had robbed her of her memory left a perpetual knot in her stomach.

"I don't want to take another pill yet."

"Your body needs rest, and it can't rest if you're fighting pain." Faith gave her a no-nonsense look.

Emily glanced at Jake, who leaned against the sink holding a glass of water. She might need his help to avoid Faith's smothering.

He looked like he'd put in a day's work already, yet he still caused a strange flutter in her stomach.

"Can I take ibuprofen this time?" She looked at the pain pill on the table. "Those pills make me so sluggish. I'll never remember if I can't think straight."

Faith frowned. "You can't force the memories to return. You know that, right?"

Emily nodded.

Faith grabbed a bottle of ibuprofen from the kitchen cabinet and laid some pills in front of Emily.

She really didn't want to take these either, but she knew she'd be miserable if she let the pain get out of control.

After swallowing the pills, she asked, "Could I sit outside? I'd like to enjoy the fresh air for a while."

Lottie mumbled something about fertilizer and fresh air as she wiped the counter, making Jake chuckle.

Faith ignored them and gave Emily a stern look. Finally, she sighed. "Okay. Jake, please move the lounge chair to the front porch. The back deck doesn't have much shade this time of day."

Jake set his glass on the counter. "Yes, ma'am."

"That's not necessary. I can sit on..." Emily's words died off when Faith shot her a hard look, eyebrows raised, hands on her hips.

No wonder Robert and Jake didn't argue with their mother. Faith looked prepared to scold Emily and send her to her room. That was the last place Emily wanted to go.

She looked at Jake, who smiled and gave an almost imperceptible shake of his head.

Faith dropped her hands from her hips. "It's a lovely day. I'll get my book and join you on the front porch."

This time, the look she shot Jake was a plea for help. Emily respected Faith and she loved her for her hospitality, but the woman liked to talk, and Emily desperately needed quiet.

Jake cleared his throat. "Mom, I'm sure Emily will be fine resting on the front porch. Alone."

"What if she needs something?"

"I've got a mountain of paperwork to do in my office. I'll keep an eye on her."

Faith exchanged a surprised look with Lottie, then her gaze zeroed in on Jake. "Since when do you voluntarily do the paperwork?" Just as Jake looked like he was about to squirm under his mother's scrutiny, Faith smiled. "Actually, I've been itching to go for a ride. I'll leave Emily in your capable hands, then." Giving Lottie a quick wink, she added, "I should change into something more suitable for riding though."

Emily looked at Faith's jeans, t-shirt, and cowboy boots. Something told her Faith had played her and Jake.

Faith paused halfway through the swinging door and looked over her shoulder with a gleam in her eye. "Jake, would you saddle Pearl for me after you get Emily settled on the porch?"

A few minutes later, Jake lifted Emily from the wheelchair. Warmth enveloped her as his strong arms wrapped around her. His heady, masculine scent mingled with horses surrounded her. Her pulse raced as his gaze held hers for a moment before depositing her on the lounge chair.

He cleared his throat. "Can I get you anything?"

Breathe. She smiled at him. "I'm fine, thank you."

Jake pointed to the window behind her. "That's my office. I'll open my window so I can hear you if you need anything." He turned and entered the house.

Emily took a deep breath. Trying to ignore the attraction she felt for Jake, she willed herself to relax. Becoming attached to someone when she didn't even know who she was not a good idea.

Blocking out the ache in her skull and ribs, she laid her head back and focused on her surroundings. A light breeze stirred the hem of her cotton summer dress, carrying with it the scent of fresh-cut alfalfa and the unmistakable odor of animals and hard work. The occasional clank of a metal gate, lowing of cattle, and shout of a man attested to the work taking place behind the ranch house.

She closed her eyes, pondering the peace that permeated her soul. She didn't know who she was or even where she was, but she felt safe in this place with these people.

The window behind her opened and she knew Jake was in his

office. A twinge of guilt gnawed at her. He didn't strike her as the type to be content behind a desk when work needed to be done outside. According to Faith, Jake hated paperwork.

Was he doing it now because she'd sent him a plea for help?

Emily admired Jake's relationship with Faith. His respect and affection for his mother was clear in everything he did. She tried to remember her own parents. *Am I close to them? Are they worried about me?*

Her chest tightened, and a heaviness settled over her. Nothing. She couldn't remember a single thing before waking up in the hospital. What had happened to make her block everything out?

Emily looked toward the highway where a black SUV had stopped near the Double Diamond's front gate. Struggling to see it through the trees near the lane's entrance, she leaned to her right, hoping to get a better look. The SUV backed up a few yards, giving her a clearer view. A large man with dark hair climbed out.

The memory of the gray interior of an SUV hit her. Her breath hitched as a man's voice from the front of the vehicle pierced her consciousness.

"Boss said find out what she knows, then take care of her. We need to destroy the evidence."

Emily's heart thundered against her ribs. *I remembered something. Something terrifying. Something she wished she hadn't remembered.*

"Ja-Jake."

Jake must have heard the panic in her voice because he came through the front door seconds after she called his name.

"What's wrong?"

Emily's hand trembled as she pointed at the black SUV. "I re-remember something a-about that SUV." Her voice shook as badly as her hand.

Jake squinted at the vehicle, then he scooped her up in his arms and carried her inside.

She bit her tongue to keep from crying out at the pain his hasty movements created in her ribs. Before she knew it, he'd deposited her, less gently than usual, on the couch and gone into his office. Moments later, he walked out carrying a hunting rifle with a scope.

"What are you doing with the gun?"

"Taking a closer look," he called over his shoulder as he stepped out the front door.

Emily tensed, waiting for him to return. *He won't shoot the man, will he?* Did the man mean her harm? Relief flooded over her when Jake walked back into the house.

He set down the rifle near the door and pulled out his cell phone.

"Did you see anything?" she asked.

"Not much. The guy was looking at the house through binoculars. When he saw me point a rifle his direction, he got in his vehicle and drove away." Then, speaking into his phone, he said, "Robert, come out to the ranch, quick." He ended the call without an explanation or giving Robert time to argue. He sat beside her. "Are you okay?"

Emily nodded, still shaken.

"Did you say you remembered something?"

"I r-remember being in the back of an SUV, with a gray interior, a-and a man's voice." Her voice shook as she repeated the words. "He said, 'Boss said to find out what she knows, then take care of her. We need to destroy the evidence.'"

"You didn't recognize the voice as someone you know?"

She shook her head, causing the dull ache in her head to pound.

"Do you have any idea who the 'boss' could be or what evidence they were talking about?"

Again, Emily shook her head then regretted it.

"Try to focus on what you saw in the back of the SUV. Is there anything that might help with a make or model of the vehicle?"

She closed her eyes and tried to focus on the memory. "No, nothing."

Robert burst through the front door. "What's going on?"

Robert's quick arrival surprised Emily. He must have been driving fast. He'd made, in a matter of minutes, the drive that had taken fifteen minutes yesterday.

"Emily was sitting on the front porch when she saw a black SUV stop out by the gate. It sparked a memory."

Robert pulled the pen and notebook from his pocket and sat on the edge of the ottoman, facing her. "What was it?"

Emily repeated what she'd told Jake, trying to remember every detail.

"You're sure this was an actual memory? Not something your mind made up, like you feared might happened?"

"She was scared," Jake said. "I doubt a false memory could trigger that kind of fear."

"Can you recall what the man, whose voice you heard, might look like?"

Emily shook her head, again regretting the action. "I don't recall seeing his face."

Jake leaned forward. "My binoculars are in my truck, so I used the scope on my rifle to get a better look. I got a quick glimpse of him. As soon as he saw me, he drove away toward the lake."

"Can you give me a description?"

"Not a good one. He was tall, roughly six two, large build, dark hair."

"What about the SUV?"

"Judging by the shape and size, I'd say it was an Expedition or Excursion."

"Well, that gives us a little something to go on." Then, reading through his notes, he quietly repeated the words Emily had heard.

Emily gasped as something else pricked at her memory. "Say those words again, louder and a little deeper." She closed her eyes and listened as Robert repeated the words.

An additional memory flooded her mind, bringing hope, followed by fear. "I remember the back of the SUV opening and seeing two men standing there. One was tall, the other considerably shorter. I didn't see their faces because the sun was behind them. They tied my wrists." She rubbed her forehead with a trembling hand, concentrating, willing more of the memory to come. "The tall one said, 'Take her out to the boss's property by the lake. I'll meet you there after I take care of things here.' Then they both picked me up and moved me from the SUV to another vehicle. That's when I saw it was black. Then... everything went black."

Emily continued to rub her forehead, trying to remember more. But there wasn't anymore. Everything went black and stayed black until she opened her eyes in the hospital and saw a handsome cowboy sitting by her bed.

Tears of frustration pricked at her eyes. She blinked, hoping to force them away but ended up pushing them onto her cheeks. With a trembling hand, she swiped them away.

Jake clasped her hand in both of his. "It'll be okay. We'll keep you safe."

His hands, though calloused, were warm and strong, giving her a sense of peace and security. Her trembling gradually subsided, and she relaxed.

"Would you mind taking another look at the picture of the driver?" Robert pulled the same photo he'd shown her at the hospital from the file folder he'd carried in with him.

Emily studied the photo, trying to link it to the memory. It looked vaguely familiar, but she figured it was because she'd seen it at the hospital.

"This might be the shorter guy, but their faces were always in a shadow, so I didn't get a good look at either of them."

"Now we know for sure there was more than one assailant, and you're still in danger. I'll try to get one of my deputies out here as soon as I can. Brady's wife had her baby, so I'm down a man."

"Don't worry about it. I've got it covered." Jake continued to hold her hand in one of his as he pulled out his cell phone with the other. Robert and Emily watched as he punched in a number and waited. "Zane, I need Daniel up at the main house right away. He'll be here a while."

"That's right," Robert said. "I forgot Daniel's home. He can stand, or rather sit, guard on the front porch. It will be good for him."

"Who's Daniel?"

Jake squeezed her hand. "He's Zane and Lottie's son and kind of like a little brother to us. He's home recuperating from a broken leg." The two brothers exchanged a tense look that made Emily curious about what they weren't saying.

Five minutes later, a tall, good-looking, although unkempt, young man came through the back door on crutches, swinging a full-length cast.

"Daniel." Jake stood and clapped the younger man's shoulder. "How are you doing today?" Jake studied Daniel's face.

"Fine." Daniel's quiet voice lacked conviction.

As Jake introduced Daniel to Emily, she studied the young man's appearance. His shaggy, unruly jet-black hair looked as though it hadn't seen a comb for a while. His skin appeared flushed despite his tan complexion, and his eyelids drooped. She couldn't see his eyes clearly, but his pupils looked unnaturally small, considering he was indoors.

"How would you like to earn a paycheck?" Jake asked Daniel, his hand still on the younger man's shoulder.

"I'd love to Jake, but you know I can't do anything." Daniel motioned to his cast.

"I have the perfect job for you."

Robert stepped to Daniel's side. "Emily here—"

"Robert." Jake cut him off. "Let's talk about this outside." He motioned with his head before stepping to the door and holding it open for Daniel and Robert. After a quick, concerned glance at Emily, he picked up the rifle near the front door and stepped out, closing the door behind him.

Emily heard the men's muffled voices. She didn't even try to hear what they said. She knew they discussed her and the danger she was in. It was sweet of Jake to take the conversation outside as if that would spare her.

It didn't.

Her hand began to tremble again now that Jake no longer held it, matching the churning in her stomach.

Knowing Jake would keep a guard posted on the front porch calmed her racing heart though. Daniel, however, didn't look well. He looked sick. She trusted Jake, but she couldn't shake the uneasiness she felt concerning Daniel.

As the tension in her body eased, exhaustion overwhelmed her. If Faith was here, she would have asked for help getting to her bed. She knew Jake would help her with whatever she needed, but she didn't want to bother him. The man already did so much for her.

She lifted her cast off the ottoman and rotated her body sideways, shifting her broken leg to the couch. Her dress slid up as she shifted, exposing more than a little of her thigh. She attempted to push it down with her right hand, but a stabbing pain in her ribs brought her efforts to an abrupt end.

It wasn't worth the effort. The amount of skin exposed by her hiked up dress wasn't indecent. She laid back against the arm of the couch, struggling to get comfortable with her neck brace.

After another minute, Jake came back in. He sat on the ottoman, facing her, his brown eyes full of concern. "Daniel will keep a lookout. If the SUV returns, we'll know. Are you okay? Do you need a pain pill?"

"I'm fine, but I'd like to rest for a bit."

"Would you like me to carry you to your bed?"

She fought the urge to say *yes* just so she could be in his arms again. "No, I don't want to bother moving. Do you mind if I stay here?"

"Not at all." He stood and grabbed a throw pillow and a light blanket from the other couch. "Let me put this behind your head. Don't you try to move. Let me lift you." He bent over her and slipped his hand behind her shoulders. His masculine scent hit her full force, and warmth settled in her stomach as he lifted her enough to slip the pillow behind her head and neck. "Is that a good position?"

Her *yes* came out a breathless whisper.

He tugged down her dress, his fingertips barely brushing her thigh, leaving her skin tingling. He spread the throw blanket over her. "I'll either be here in the house or nearby outside. Holler if you need me."

She smiled. "Holler, huh? Now you sound like a cowboy."

"Shucks, ma'am, it's downright hard keepin' up the facade all the time," Jake drawled, smiling as he walked away.

Emily chuckled. Her smile lingered as she closed her eyes. Jake's drawl was almost as cute as he was. The man may have gotten his good looks from his dad, but he had Faith's compassion.

She thought it was the ranch that made her feel safe and gave her a measure of peace, but it was Jake. His promise to keep her safe and his gentleness in making her comfortable made her feel special and protected. Which attracted her to him even more, and that was dangerous as long as she didn't know who she was.

CHAPTER 9

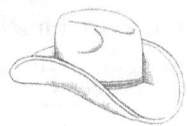

*T*hump, thump, thump.

Emily awoke to a soft rhythmic drumming. She lay still, listening to the noise, trying to determine its source. Faith's voice in the kitchen, and Lottie's softer tones, drifted her way. She looked toward Jake's open office door.

Was he in there?

Poor man.

He hated being stuck inside doing paperwork, but today must feel especially torturous with Emily having interrupted his work.

Thoughts of the SUV, her lone memory before waking up in the hospital, filled her head. Tamping down the fear, she focused on the memory, hoping to recall something more.

She let out a frustrated sigh when nothing new came to mind.

Thump, thump, thump.

There was the soft drumming again. Moving carefully, she sat up and shifted to look out the window. Daniel's right shoulder blocked part of the view.

As she studied him, he swiped at his brow and the nape of his neck. She recalled the pleasant temperature earlier. It was too early in the summer to be that hot, besides Daniel sat in the shade.

He bounced his good leg again.

Ah, the source of the drumming. He swiped at his brow again then scratched at first one arm then the other.

He's not well.

"Have you been awake long?" Emily jumped at Jake's voice near her shoulder.

She'd been so focused on Daniel's behavior she hadn't heard him come out of his office. When he joined her on the couch, she saw he'd taken off his boots. That's how he'd sneaked up on her.

"A few minutes."

"What were you looking at? Did you remember something else?"

"No. I was watching Daniel. Is it safe for him to have a loaded gun?"

"Daniel knows how to handle a gun."

"That may be true before..." she left the words hanging.

Jake's eyes narrowed. "Before what?"

"Before he broke his leg and became dependent on his painkillers."

Jake's eyes widened, and a flash of guilt crossed his face.

"But perhaps the painkillers are masking something else, something bigger."

Jake scratched the back of his neck. "Daniel's a good kid. He went through something difficult last fall. He doesn't want anyone to know about it though. We hoped getting him back to the ranch would help, but with his broken leg..."

"Making excuses for him won't help him with his problem."

"How can you tell he's got a problem just by looking at him?" Jake's tone was skeptical.

"He's bouncing his leg because he's anxious. He's sweating and itching." Daniel scratched his arm again, proving her point. "His skin is flushed, and it doesn't look like he's paid much attention to his appearance for a while now. These are all classic signs of drug addiction."

Jake let out a deep sigh and put his face in his hands, propping his elbows on his knees. "He's only been taking the pills for a couple weeks. Is it possible to become addicted that fast?"

"Addiction might be a strong word at this point, but he appears to be developing a dependency on his pain meds." She put her hand on his arm. "You don't need to tell me anything you don't want to, especially something Daniel wouldn't want you to." She looked at Daniel's back as he bounced his leg again. "I'd like to go talk to him."

"It's not safe out there."

"I'm sure the driver of the black SUV has no intention of returning after you pointed a gun his direction. Get me my crutches, please, and go see if Lottie has a glass of lemonade." She gave him her best determined look.

Jake stared at her for a moment. "Let me at least carry you out."

"I'm a psychologist, Jake. If you carry me out, it will be harder for me to look competent and gain Daniel's trust."

She held his gaze, refusing to let hers waver.

Jake stood and went to get her crutches.

A FEW MINUTES LATER, Jake carried out two glasses of lemonade as Emily hobbled out onto the porch. Mindful of letting her shoulder support her weight on the crutches, she didn't expect the effort of shifting the left crutch forward with her casted arm to be so awkward and painful. Her pride would not let her admit Jake was right though.

"Do you mind if I sit with you, Daniel? It's so hard to stay cooped up inside on such a beautiful day." She lowered herself as carefully and gracefully as she could onto the lounge chair, hiding a wince as she did so. Resisting the urge to wipe the perspiration she felt beading on her brow from that little bit of exertion, she gave Jake a subtle nod, letting him know he could leave.

Daniel rose to his feet then sat again after Emily settled herself. "Are you sure it's safe for you to be out here?"

"I doubt we'll see the SUV again today. If you saw Jake pointing a rifle your direction, would you come back?"

"I'd never go up against Jake in shooting. I'm no match for him." He took a long swig of the lemonade.

"I bet you shoot well, though, don't you?"

He shrugged. "Pretty good, I guess, but not as good as Jake and Robert. They've got impeccable aim."

Emily giggled. "This is comical, don't you think?" When Daniel gave her a questioning look, she explained. "The lame guarding the lame."

"Yeah, kind of." Daniel cracked a smile.

"So, how did you break your leg?"

"I crashed my motorcycle into a tree," he mumbled.

Emily winced as she eyed his leg. "That's a tall cast. Did you break your femur?"

"Yeah."

"I've heard that's the most painful bone to break. Would you agree?" Then rushing on she added, "I guess I should ask if you've broken other bones, so I know if you had a comparison."

"I've broken my arm and my ankle. Yeah, the femur has been the most painful."

"Let me guess; the arm and ankle had something to do with a horse and a bull?"

He smiled again. "A horse and a steer."

"You sound like Jake." Was Jake listening? If he'd returned to his office, where the window was remained open, he could hear their conversation. "Was it as hard for you to leave the ranch to go to school as it was for Jake?"

Daniel looked away as he chewed on his fingernail and bounced his leg.

Come on. Let me in.

"It was hard to leave the ranch the first few years to go to school, but this last year was the hardest."

Yes!

"Why was this year harder?" Emily tried to keep her tone casual.

Again, he took his time answering, his face registering regret. Did he regret engaging in this conversation with her, or did he regret something else entirely?

"Jake's sister, Riley, and I dated last summer. I liked her... a lot, but

73

we were both going to different colleges. We decided it wouldn't be fair to each other to try to maintain a long-distance relationship."

"I imagine that was hard. Was the break-up mutual?" At his nod, she continued. "Jake said you're like a brother to him, so I would think Riley was like a sister to you. Was it weird dating someone you were so close to?"

He shrugged. "It was a little at first. But it just felt right. She was my best friend. There was no one I would rather be with."

"How did Jake react when he found out you were dating?" Emily tried to keep her tone conversational, but she hung on every word he said and studied his body language.

"We kept it hidden from him for a while, but he knew all along." Daniel smiled. "When we told him, he said it was about time."

"You still care about her a lot, don't you?"

He nodded as he scratched at his arm. "As much as I'd love to see her again, I'm glad she didn't come home this summer."

"Why?"

"I don't want her to see me like this." Daniel's voice grew quiet.

"Like what?" Emily waited for him to answer. When he didn't, she asked, "How long ago did you break your leg?"

"Two weeks," he mumbled, swiping at his brow again.

"Does it still hurt?"

He nodded but didn't meet her eyes.

"Were you given pain meds?" When he responded with a nod, she asked, "Enough to last you two weeks?"

Daniel gave her a sharp look then looked away when she held his gaze. "They... um... didn't last that long, but Dr. Young gave me another half of a prescription a few days ago."

"How many pills do you have left?"

"Three." His response was so quiet Emily barely heard him.

"Are you in pain now? When did you take your last dose?"

His bouncing leg created a steady drumming on the wooden porch. He scratched his arm again before consulting his phone. "Almost five hours ago."

"You're becoming addicted to your pain killers. You realize that, don't you?"

Daniel glared at her then lowered his eyes. "I've tried not to. I've only taken more than the prescribed dose a couple times."

"But you used them to help you deal with other addictions, didn't you?"

~

JAKE HELD HIS BREATH, waiting for Daniel's response. He didn't mean to eavesdrop, but Emily and Daniel's voices carried through the open window. Emily's did, anyway; Daniel's mumbles were harder to pick up.

But the kid was talking. Since Daniel had come home with his broken leg, he'd barely said a word. He didn't want help or interference. Zane, Lottie, and Jake all knew he had a problem, but Daniel got angry anytime they tried to talk to him about it.

The drumming from Daniel's bouncing leg stopped.

He couldn't believe Emily had drawn Daniel into conversation so quickly. He remembered how easy it had been to talk to her at the hospital. There was something special about her.

"Daniel, I can help you. If you'll let me."

Emily's offer was met with silence. Then, so low Jake barely heard him, Daniel said, "I developed a drinking problem last fall... after..."

Again, Jake held his breath. Would Daniel tell Emily what had driven him to drink? He insisted he didn't want anyone to know, especially Riley. Jake was the only one, besides Daniel's parents, who knew what happened last fall.

"I was involved in an accident," came Daniel's quiet murmur.

Jake let out his breath. Well, it wasn't the whole truth, but it was more than he expected Daniel to volunteer.

"Do you want help with your drug and alcohol addiction?"

"Yes." It was a hoarse whisper.

Jake sucked in a deep breath. He wanted to kiss Emily's strawberry-red lips. He couldn't believe she'd gotten Daniel to open up to her, let alone ask for help. He hadn't told her everything, but Jake was sure, with time, Emily could get him to trust her.

Daniel asked for help. That was huge.

"It will be difficult and extremely unpleasant." Emily's serious tone, serving as a warning to Daniel, came through the open window. "It would be much easier if you could do the things you enjoy, like working and riding."

"Being at the ranch and not able to do anything is killing me."

"You need something for your mind to focus on while keeping your hands busy."

"What... like puzzles?" Daniel's voice was full of doubt.

"That might help if you enjoy that kind of thing, but I think you need something more engaging." After a lengthy silence, Emily laughed. "I'd suggest you have Faith teach you to crochet, but I doubt you'd enjoy that."

"No." Daniel's response was emphatic.

Jake considered suggesting Daniel take up whittling, but then wondered whether the kid was in a safe enough mental state to have a knife in his hands. Of course, he wasn't about to let Emily and Daniel know he was eavesdropping.

"Do you play a musical instrument?"

"I've still got the guitar I had back when I was in junior high. Robert gave me a few lessons, but then he went away to college, and I never really learned to play it."

"Sounds like we've found the perfect challenge. Jake!"

Jake jumped when she called his name. Heat crept up his neck. He shouldn't have eavesdropped, but he still wanted to kiss Emily.

He stood and went to the front door.

"Everything okay?" he asked as he stepped out on the porch, trying to act nonchalant.

"Not at the moment," Emily said. Then she smiled at Daniel. "But it will be." She looked back at Jake. "Do you think you and Lottie could bring Daniel half of one of his pain pills and find his guitar?"

Jake looked at Emily for a long moment. He smiled and winked at her. "Absolutely."

He hoped Emily was as good of a counselor as she was pretty.

CHAPTER 10

*J*ake yawned and stretched. It was after eleven, and he'd spent most of the day in the house doing paperwork. Trying, anyway. He'd had difficulty focusing even before Emily had interrupted him from the front porch this morning.

He'd tried working again while she rested, but he'd been worried about her and what she'd remembered. Then he'd been tense the entire time Emily talked to Daniel.

Finally, after Daniel had his medicine and guitar, and Emily helped him search for guitar tutorials on-line, Jake escaped the house. After checking in with Zane, he saddled Thor and went for a badly needed ride.

It helped clear his head and ease the tension, but he'd been in his office, ever since dinner, working on the blasted paperwork for the solar power project. He contemplated sleeping for a couple hours before going out to bale hay. Sometimes it was easier to go without sleep.

A strange noise caught his attention; a bump followed by a thud, then it repeated. He stepped out of his office to find Emily shuffling down the hall with her crutches.

"Can I help you with something?"

"I'm fine," she said with a sigh. "Can't sleep. I keep thinking about that SUV and wondering what it is I'm supposed to know, and what kind of evidence the men are looking for. And how did I get mixed up in this?"

"Would you like some hot cocoa?" Jake asked. "That's what my mom used to make for me when I couldn't sleep."

"Sounds good, but I don't want to bother your mom."

"We won't bother her. I'll make it. Let me get your wheelchair."

She scowled at him. "No."

He thought about arguing with her, but she stared him down. His mom was right. Emily was independent and stubborn. He couldn't blame her though. It was difficult being so dependent on others.

Biting back a smile of admiration, he led her to the kitchen, pausing to hold the swinging door for her. He guided her to the counter where she sat on a barstool. Getting out a small saucepan, he poured milk into it and set it on the stove on low heat. Then he set out cocoa powder and sugar.

Emily's eyebrows rose. "When you suggested hot cocoa, I thought you meant stirring store-bought hot chocolate powder into water."

"No, that stuff is fine when you're camping, but it's not as good as the homemade stuff. I may be a bachelor, but I've learned how to do a few things for myself."

"A few? Do you cook anything besides cocoa?"

"Well, Lottie leaves me leftovers when she won't be around to cook, and I'm competent with the microwave." He shot her a cheesy grin.

"But do you actually cook?"

"I can make spaghetti and chili. Sometimes, I make soup and grilled cheese sandwiches."

"Grilled cheese? That's complicated. Let me guess, your spaghetti sauce, chili, and soup all come from a can?"

"I did mention I'm a bachelor, right? A very busy bachelor I might add." He waved a whisk in the air as he defended himself. "I can grill a mean steak, though."

"Steak, huh? I'd like to try your steak sometime."

"You will. Tomorrow. He went to the magnetic white board on the side of the refrigerator, wiped off the lasagna listed for Tuesday's dinner, and wrote steak. Then he returned to the stove to stir the sugar and cocoa mixture into the steaming milk.

Emily had hardly touched her dinner. Had her injuries affected her appetite? Or was it concern about the memories she couldn't recall? Of course, the memories she'd recalled today were enough to affect anyone's appetite.

Turning to the fridge, he retrieved a jar of salsa and poured some into a bowl then grabbed a bag of tortilla chips from the pantry.

"Try Lottie's homemade salsa." He placed both in front of her before returning to the stove again.

"Is it spicy?" Emily hesitated before putting the chip she'd dipped in her mouth.

"A little." Jake grabbed a chip, scooped up some salsa, and shoved it into his mouth.

She took a bite. "Mmm." She grabbed another chip. "Do you always eat dinner with Zane and Lottie?"

"They're like family. We've shared dinner a lot over the years. It was pointless for Lottie to cook here then go home to fix another meal for her family."

"They're nice, and Lottie is an amazing cook. Daniel seems like a good kid too, despite his struggles."

Jake pulled two mugs from the cupboard. "He is a good kid. Thank you for what you are doing for him. I didn't realize how bad his problem had become until he came home with his broken leg. Whenever I tried to talk to him about it, he got defensive. I'm impressed that you got him to open up to you so fast."

"Apparently, I've had a little practice. Don't get too excited. Daniel's got a long, hard road ahead of him. He agreed to let me help him, but he hasn't fully confided in me yet. Hopefully, with time, he'll come to trust me."

Jake rubbed his neck. "I promised him I wouldn't tell anyone what happened that caused him to start drinking, but I'd tell you if I thought it would help him."

"If you tell me, it won't help him. It needs to come from him."

Jake placed a steaming mug of hot cocoa in front of her. "Be careful. It's hot."

Emily blew on her cocoa then took a sip. "Delicious. I'm impressed."

"I'm glad you like it." His chest swelled as relief filled him.

Why am I trying so hard to impress her?

Emily winked and flashed her dimples at him. "It could do with a bit more chocolate."

"Right, you like chocolate with chocolate."

He stood and looked through the cabinets. Finding what he searched for, he returned to the counter and sprinkled a few chocolate chips into her mug. Grabbing a spoon, he stirred it until the morsels melted.

"You will make a wonderful husband for some lucky woman someday." Emily said, a twinkle in her eyes.

Jake held her gaze. Her eyes were the most beautiful shade of green, like fresh cut grass. She licked her lips, and his eyes dropped to her mouth. He wanted a taste of those strawberry-red lips.

Whoa. Where did that come from?

Emily cleared her throat. "Provided she likes chocolate."

Jake chuckled and took a sip of his own cocoa, tearing his gaze away from her lips.

"So, your mom used to make hot cocoa for you when you couldn't sleep? Did that happen often?"

Nice. Change the topic. Now maybe he could concentrate on something other than her beautiful emerald eyes and enticing red lips.

Jake shrugged. "Sometimes, I had difficulty sleeping. I had some ADHD tendencies, which working on the ranch helped with, but I had anxiety too. I'd often get stressed out over things. Usually, things I could do little about, like world hunger and social injustices."

"Things like abandoned mountain lion cubs?"

"She told you about that?" Then before she could answer, he continued. "I hate to think what all she told you about me."

"Don't worry, it was all good." Emily took a sip of her cocoa. "I imagine being cooped up all day doing paperwork and keeping an eye on an invalid creates plenty of anxiety and pent-up energy." Emily gave him a knowing look.

He took a sip of cocoa while debating how honest he should be. "Maybe a little."

He considered adding how distracting the beautiful invalid was but figured he'd better keep that thought to himself. No need to make things awkward again.

His cheeks warmed as he admitted, "I heard my mom tell my fifth-grade teacher I was tender-hearted. I didn't know what that meant, but I didn't like how it sounded. I looked it up, and I didn't like the definition either. It made me sound like a wuss." He chuckled. "I picked a fight with the school bully to prove her wrong. I busted his front tooth, and I felt so bad about it I was extra nice to him after that. He became one of my best friends."

Emily chuckled. "And as an adult, how do you feel about being called tender-hearted?"

Not much had changed about his personality. He couldn't help caring about people, but it was the least masculine adjective to describe a man.

Ignoring her question, he raised his mug. "Hot cocoa always did the trick when I couldn't sleep."

"You sure it wasn't talking things out with your mom?"

"Nope. It was the cocoa." Jake put his mug to his lips.

Emily chuckled. "Right, because men don't like to admit they have feelings, let alone talk about them."

"Yep." And Jake had no intention of telling his mom, or anyone else, how Emily made him feel.

CHAPTER 11

*E*mily tapped her nails on the table. She was almost as fidgety as Daniel, although for different reasons. She wasn't sure why she felt so antsy, but it drove her crazy.

"Can I take a shower?" Emily pushed away her half-eaten plate of biscuits and gravy and looked at Faith, who loaded dishes into the dishwasher.

Faith had assisted her with sponge baths the last two days, but Emily desperately wanted to wash her hair and feel clean.

"We'll need to protect your casts. Let me see what I can come up with."

She hoped a shower would help dispel the anxiety and frustration that filled her. She'd slept well after her late-night visit with Jake. Had the delicious hot cocoa done the trick, as Jake claimed, or was it the enjoyable conversation they'd shared? It had effectively rid her mind of yesterday's memories. For a while, anyway.

Despite a late but good night's rest, she couldn't get the words she'd recalled yesterday out of her head this morning. Nor could she recall a single other memory, and that frustrated her.

She couldn't stop wondering what the key she kept in the night-stand might go to. Many times, she considered telling Robert about it, but it was her only link to her memory, and she wasn't ready to relinquish it yet. She'd held and fingered it so many times she had every groove memorized.

Twenty minutes later, Emily assured Faith she could manage on her own as she hobbled into the walk-in shower of the master bathroom. With casts covered in trash bags, she turned on the water and sat on the handicap chair.

She willed herself to relax as the hot water ran over her bruised body. Without warning, tears mingled with the beads of water. She made no effort to stop them. For the first time since waking up in the hospital, she allowed the emotions raging inside her free reign. Helplessness. Anxiety. Fear.

This was the fourth day since her accident. Robert had said he was working to find her brother, but so far, they hadn't located him. Why wasn't her brother looking for her? Were they estranged?

Why can't I even remember my brother?

Emily took her time in the shower. Heat filled her face when she caught sight of her red eyes in the mirror. At least the bruise around her right eye had faded to an ugly shade of greenish-yellow. Her left eye had changed from purple to blue.

She couldn't bring herself to make eye contact with Faith while she helped her dress and braided her hair. Gratefully, Faith pretended not to notice her red eyes. Instead, she talked non-stop about the challenges and joys of being a rancher's wife.

Emily was too emotionally exhausted to analyze if Faith talked about being a rancher's wife simply because she liked to talk or if she had ulterior motives.

When Faith helped her settle on the couch, Emily heard Jake's deep voice out on the front porch. A strange fluttering assaulted her stomach. He came into the house a few minutes later and greeted her with a smile as he tipped his hat.

Emily's heart stuttered. Such a gentleman. And handsome too, whether he was sweaty and dirty or making hot cocoa. There was something pure male about him, tender-hearted or not.

"Mom, I'm heading back out to the stables. Do you need anything from me before I go?"

The respect and affection he showed his mom made him even more attractive.

As Faith took a moment to contemplate, Emily did her own contemplating, surprised that Jake working outside disappointed her.

"I think we're fine," Faith said.

Jake tipped his hat and turned to the back door.

Emily sat up a little straighter. "Jake, could I borrow your laptop?"

"Sure." He disappeared into his office and brought the laptop and set it on her lap. As he bent over her, he whispered, "How'd you sleep last night?"

Emily's breath hitched. "Great. That hot cocoa did the trick."

Jake winked at her. "I told you."

She smiled. "Yes, you did. Thank you."

Jake's gaze held hers for a moment, then he was gone.

For fifteen minutes, she searched the Internet for keys. Convinced her mystery key was not a car or a house key, she searched for safety deposit keys. If it was for a safety deposit box, how would she find out which bank it belonged to? After ten more minutes of searching with no concrete answers, she changed her search.

She brought up the family therapist website Robert had shown her, hoping it would spark a memory this time. When nothing came, she changed her search again. She'd indulged in enough self-pity today.

She saw Daniel's fidgeting through the window as she looked over the symptoms of opioid and alcohol withdrawal. He clearly struggled with many of the symptoms she reviewed.

"Faith, could you get me my crutches? I'd like to sit on the front porch."

Faith stood. "I'll push you out in the wheelchair, dear, but you shouldn't be out on the front porch. Why don't I help you out to the back patio? There's not a lot of shade this time of day, but—"

"No." Emily hadn't had the energy to argue with Faith when she'd insisted on bringing her to the great room in the chair, but Daniel needed her now. And she wouldn't go out there in a wheelchair. "Daniel is standing guard. I'm sure I'll be fine, and I prefer the freedom the crutches give me." She tried to keep her tone kind yet firm.

Faith chuckled. "I told Jake, the day we brought you home from the hospital, you were the stubborn, independent type. Although, Jake can be stubborn too. I wonder who would win in a battle of wills between you two." She continued to chuckle as she walked out of the room.

Win? Between Jake and me? Why did Faith think there would ever be a battle of wills between them? Then, because Jake occupied too many of her thoughts and limited memories, she forced him out and focused on Daniel, whose bouncing leg recreated yesterday's familiar drumming.

"I can see you're struggling, Daniel," Emily said a few minutes later, after settling on the lounge chair. "I'd like to tell you it will get easier soon, but the truth is this will take time and you'll likely feel much worse before you feel any better."

"Wow." Daniel let out his breath in a quick huff. "That's not what I want to hear right now."

"Talk to me about something pleasant. Tell me what it was like to grow up on the ranch."

And so went Emily's afternoon. She spent hours talking to Daniel, alternately distracting him from what he was going through and preparing him for what he would experience. She encouraged him to focus on learning to play his guitar and suggested frequent walks down the lane.

They discussed how heavy his alcohol use had been prior to breaking his leg, and Daniel confided that both of his grandfathers were alcoholics, which meant Daniel's addictions would be that much more difficult to overcome.

"In some regards, you're lucky. The drugs have masked some of the initial alcohol withdrawal, but your dependence on the alcohol caused you to form an addiction to the pain killers faster than most people would. The drug withdrawals will be strong even though you've only been on them a few weeks."

Before long, Daniel felt achy, nauseous, and needed to go to the bathroom frequently. All symptoms Emily had warned him about.

Deciding she needed to talk with Jake and Daniel's parents, she suggested Daniel take a walk down the lane, hoping movement would be good for him. Though he looked miserable, Daniel didn't argue. He slung the strap of the hunting rifle over his shoulder, picked up his crutches, and took off.

Picking up her own crutches, she followed the wrap-around porch in search of Jake. Reaching the back patio, she looked toward the stables and corrals. There was little activity. Crossing the back patio that spanned the length of the house, she entered through the mudroom, hoping to find Lottie in the kitchen.

The housekeeper stood by the counter peeling potatoes.

Emily shuffled to stand on the opposite side of the counter. "I need to sit down with you and Zane, and probably Jake as well, to discuss Daniel's recovery. I know this may not be a good time for the men, but it is important."

Lottie dropped the potato she'd been peeling. "Absolutely. Whatever you say. I'll find them. But first..." She wrapped her arms around Emily, hugging her so tightly she winced. "Thank you so much for helping Daniel."

Then Lottie was out the door, leaving Emily alone in the kitchen. She made her way to the table and sat down to wait for the others.

She didn't have to wait long. While Zane washed up at the basin in the mudroom, Jake washed at the kitchen sink. Judging from the dirt and perspiration that clung to their clothes, they had been working hard.

She watched the play of muscles in Jake's back under his long-sleeved work shirt, and that familiar warmth settled in her stomach.

When they joined her at the table, Emily explained the symptoms Daniel was beginning to experience and how bad they would get before they improved. She explained how the drug dependency and withdrawal would affect the alcohol withdrawal symptoms. She warned of things they needed to watch for, especially throughout the nights.

"He needs a lot of fluids and as much exercise as possible, despite his broken leg. He needs worthwhile distraction—something he can focus on, especially since he can't be physically active."

Jake looked at Zane. "Let's have him take over the repair and cleaning of the tack. Maybe that will help a little."

"That's good, but if he didn't have a broken leg, I would recommend heavy exercise."

"He can do upper body workouts. There's still that bar in the stables where Robert and I used to do pull-ups."

Pull-ups? Emily's gaze settled on Jake's solid shoulders then roamed down over his chest. His shirt, though not snug, sure fit nicely. Her heart rate kicked up a notch. Pull-ups could only do so much. Jake had done a lot more than pull-ups to get those muscles. The way he carried her around so effortlessly attested to his strength.

Does he still work out?

"Will he be able to wean off the pain killers with the remaining pill and a half he has left? Will he need a few more?" Lottie asked concerned.

Emily jumped. She'd been studying Jake's shoulders so intently she'd forgotten there were others in the room. Her eyes jumped to his.

His eyebrows raised, amusement lighting his eyes.

Heat filled her cheeks. Had he been looking at her the whole time she'd been studying his shoulders?

Focus. You're a professional. Act like it.

"He's trying to spread them out. We should applaud him for that. He's only been on the meds for two weeks, so he should be able to do it, but it won't be pleasant. I'm afraid the alcohol dependency will kick in once the drug withdrawals slow down. He'll need a lot of support and attention, which he'll hate. Being confined to the porch, while he's going through this, is not ideal."

Jake nodded in acknowledgment then turned to Zane. "Work up a schedule with all the ranch hands. Have everybody take turns standing guard each day to give Daniel a break unless they're working the outskirts. We'll give them regular pay." He looked at Emily for a long moment before turning back to Zane and lowering his voice. "It might be best if everyone is carrying."

Jake's words caught her off guard. *Is he saying he wants all the ranch hands armed?* Was that a good idea? It did provide a sense of comfort, knowing Jake took her safety seriously, but it also sounded dangerous.

"Do we tell them why they are guarding the house?" Zane asked Jake, with a quick glance at Emily.

Jake regarded her for a moment before answering. "No. Tell them we've received threats against the ranch."

Emily appreciated his effort to protect her from the reality of her situation, but all this cloak and dagger stuff made the fear and uncertainty hanging over her heavier, darker. "Jake, if you feel you need to tell them, I don't mind."

"It's best they don't know. These guys often leave the ranch to get drunk. The less they know, the less they can blabber."

"He's right, ma'am," Zane said.

Deciding to let it go, she returned to the reason for this discussion. "Daniel needs to take his turns. It will be the easiest way for me to work with him. Getting him over the withdrawals is only the first step. Recovery is not an event, it's a process."

Jake looked at Zane, and his foreman acknowledged with a nod. Then Jake cleared his throat. "Listen, Emily, I don't want you going out on the front porch while any of the other ranch hands stand guard. Some of these guys have... serious baggage."

"If they're struggling with something, maybe I could help them too. It's not like I've got any—"

"No!" Jake said, then, as though he regretted shouting, he softened his voice. "Please, promise me you'll avoid the front porch unless Daniel's out there."

"Some of these guys are pretty rough characters, ma'am," Zane added.

"Okay, I'll stay away."

She trusted Jake. He'd made her safety a priority. She'd respect his decision, but she couldn't quite let his bossiness go.

"Can I spend time on the back patio? I can't stand being cooped up inside all the time."

"Yes, you can go out on the back patio, and hopefully they won't bother you there. But if any of them do, you call for me, Lottie, or my mom, and tell us you'd like to rest, got it?"

Emily bit back a smile. *Jake's cute when he's being bossy.*

Something inside her wanted to argue with him, to see how he'd react. Faith had said he was stubborn, but she'd seen Jake treat his mother and Lottie with reverence and respect, and the gentle way he carried her around told her he was a softy. He was strong, but he was indeed tenderhearted and compassionate.

Instead of arguing, she let out a dramatic sigh. "Got it."

Jake held her gaze. Was he angry she'd mocked him? No. The pinch of his lips looked like he fought a smile. Regardless, she squirmed under his direct scrutiny and dropped her eyes to his broad shoulders. That was a mistake, because she had an even harder time tearing her gaze away from them.

Jake cleared his throat, and Emily's gaze jumped back up to his. Amusement filled his eyes again, and his lips quirked upward. "Are we done here?"

Trying not to look guilty, Emily smiled. "Yes, we're done." Then with a feigned air of superiority, she added, "for now."

Jake raised his eyebrows in a challenge. He waited for Zane and Lottie to leave the table before standing. Planting his palms on the gleaming oak surface, he leaned toward her, lowering his head until his face was inches from hers. "Does Daniel know his psychologist gets easily distracted?"

Emily's face burned, but she met his gaze. "Oh, we all have our vices, Jake. I'm looking forward to figuring out your weakness."

Jake's eyes widened, and he gave an uncomfortable chuckle. His gazed stayed locked with hers for a long moment before he turned away. He paused on his way out of the kitchen to snatch a chunk of potato from the bowl Lottie had been filling before Emily distracted her.

Lottie stood behind him. "What do you think you're doing, young man?" In one fluid motion and with a dexterity that said she'd done this a thousand times, Lottie pulled the dish towel from her shoulder, swirled it in the air, and flicked it at Jake's backside.

Jake laughed as he shoved the potato in his mouth. Face full of guilt, he ducked while attempting to hop out of her reach. He wasn't quick enough. The towel hit its target with a sharp snap.

Emily laughed. The emotion felt foreign, yet so wonderful. Jake looked at her, color creeping up his neck, his eyes twinkling.

Emily couldn't help herself—she laughed again. She didn't know what made Jake more adorable—the blush or the fact that he enjoyed teasing his housekeeper.

"Jake," Lottie said, pulling Emily from her thoughts. "Looks like you're up for dinner tonight." She pointed at the menu he'd altered last night, then with a mocking voice she mumbled under her breath, "Have I ever changed the menu?"

"Right." A sheepish looked crossed Jake's face as he glanced at the clock then at Zane and back to Lottie. "Give me thirty minutes. Then I'll get showered and fire up the grill."

Emily stared at the door long after he walked out, praying she'd recover her memory before she completely fell for the rugged cowboy.

VINCE PULLED off the road at the turn to the lake and smacked the steering wheel of his cousin's Nissan. Pulling the cell phone from his pocket, he punched in the boss's number.

"Is it taken care of? Do you have the evidence?" came the boss's clipped voice.

The sharp, domineering attitude grated on Vince's nerves. He grit his teeth to keep from giving the *Boss* a piece of his mind.

The arrogant jerk hadn't even expressed condolences a couple days ago when Vince had called to tell him Frankie was dead. He'd simply reminded Vince he'd screwed up by leaving a witness and insisted he clean up his mess and get the evidence.

Vince itched to remind him he was the one who'd started this whole thing with his nefarious activities.

"I can't get to the woman."

He'd gone by the hospital before she'd been released, but there had been a cop sitting outside her room. He'd hightailed it out of there before anyone got a good look at him.

Thanks to another visit to the diner, he'd learned the lady from the accident was staying at the Double Diamond Ranch after being discharged from the hospital. Fortunately, he hadn't crossed paths with Roy and his Buddy or the pretty blond waitress again.

He'd also overheard that the lady from the car accident apparently had amnesia. He should be thankful. That was probably the only reason a wanted poster sporting his face wasn't plastered everywhere. He'd already considered cutting his losses and disappearing, but he needed the remainder of the fifty grand the boss owed him.

"What do you mean you can't get to her?" Alarm filled the man's voice, pulling Vince from his musings. "You must take care of her. Need I remind you she has seen your face?"

"I know, but they have her under armed guard at a ranch the size of Texas. Every time I turn around, the sheriff or one of his deputies is patrolling the area."

His Excursion had been spotted near the ranch. That's why he'd borrowed his cousin, Ralph's, car. And though he'd glimpsed the woman on the front porch, verifying she was still there, he couldn't get close enough to get his hands on her.

"Do whatever it takes. Don't contact me again until you've taken care of the woman and have the evidence in hand." With that, the pompous jerk hung up.

Vince muttered a string of curses and tossed his phone on the passenger seat. He never allowed a "boss" to talk to him like that. Normally, he didn't hesitate to take out any man who didn't show him the respect he deserved, but he needed to finish this. He needed the rest of the money to bury Frankie. Then maybe he would slip away to some tropical island and disappear.

Besides, the pompous jerk was right. Vince *had* messed up. He'd jumped the gun. He figured Cameron Anderson would tell his sister everything if given the chance. Vince had been determined not to let that happen.

But Anderson had already talked to his sister. And if her memory returned, she could identify Vince.

CHAPTER 12

*J*ake bit back a smile when Emily's eyes widened as he walked into the kitchen wearing his favorite, well-worn jeans that fit like a second skin, and an equally snug white t-shirt.

He was acting like Robert, which was so unlike him. But he'd caught Emily studying his shoulders earlier and he intended to give her something to look at.

In fact, he contemplated working out with Daniel. Not because he needed to tone-up but rather to get—and keep—Emily's attention. And to support Daniel, of course.

Despite his words to his mother about not knowing anything about Emily, he found he wanted to know everything about her.

Where is this coming from?

He was too busy to get involved with a woman, especially one with a possible murderer after her. But those emerald eyes and red lips distracted him at every turn.

Jake watched Emily from the corner of his eye as he seasoned the steaks Lottie had thawed. Her gaze repeatedly drifted his way, filling him with satisfaction.

He smiled at her. "Would you care to join me outside while I grill?"

"I guess I'd better if I want to make sure you actually do it yourself."

Jake set the steaks and grilling tongs on the table and prepared to pick her up, but Emily grabbed her crutches and held them in front of her like a shield. She gave Jake a stubborn look.

He smiled, grabbed the steaks, and held the door for her. He dragged a lounge chair closer to the barbecue for her to sit on, and they visited while Jake grilled the steaks.

"How do you like your steak?" Jake asked after talking about the ranch for some time.

"Medium well."

"This one's yours, then." One by one, Jake pulled the remaining steaks off the grill and headed inside. "Stay put, I'll bring you a plate."

He returned a few minutes later and handed her a plate loaded with steak, potato salad, and baked beans. He pulled another lounge chair near hers and sat.

"It sounds like Daniel is having a tough time. He's feeling pretty sick and doesn't have much of an appetite."

"Poor guy. This is likely to go on for a while. Should we sit out front with him?"

"He's not out there. Zane got a plate of food and took him home. Lottie and Mom decided to eat in the kitchen."

He'd caught the look his mom exchanged with Lottie before insisting they wanted to stay in the cool, air-conditioned house. He didn't bother telling them he hadn't turned the AC on yet this summer. Despite his warning for her not to matchmake, she was doing it anyway. He should be angry, but the truth was he looked forward to spending time alone with Emily.

He watched Emily take her first bite of steak. A look of surprise crossed her face, followed by appreciation.

"Mmm... Not bad for a bachelor. That is some good meat."

Jake gave her an I-told-you-so look.

"It's nice to know you won't go hungry, as long as you raise beef."

Hungry? No. Lonely? Definitely.

∼

EMILY ENJOYED the food almost as much as she enjoyed the company. She made it a point to eat every bite of steak, but she couldn't finish the salads.

Jake finished off her food like he'd done with her ice cream at the hospital.

Faith came out on the patio wringing her hands. "Margaret Turner fell and broke her hip today."

Jake cringed. "Wow, that's not good at her age. How old is she? Ninety?"

"Ninety-two. No, it's not good. I feel like I should go check on her. Jake, are you going to be around this evening?"

"I'll be here, Mom. Go be with Ms. Turner."

"Are you sure? Emily, do you need anything before I go? It's been a while since you've had any pain medicine."

"I'm fine, Faith. Don't worry about me. I hope your friend can heal from this." She contemplated having Faith get rid of the rest of her pain pills so they wouldn't be a source of temptation for Daniel. But she still needed them at night, and she knew Faith kept them tucked away somewhere in her room.

Faith frowned. "I feel bad leaving you." Then her eyes lit up. "Jake, you should take Emily for a drive up to the bluff and show her the ranch."

"Sure, okay. Emily will be fine. Don't worry."

Faith disappeared, and Jake took their empty plates inside, returning a few minutes later.

"Are you ready?"

"For what?"

"Mom will chew me out if I don't take you for a ride."

She held up a hand as he reached down to pick her up. "I can walk with my crutches."

"Not out here you can't. The ground is too uneven. It's not safe for you to cross it on your own." Again, Jake bent to pick her up, giving her barely enough time to put her arm around his shoulders before slipping his arms under her.

Jake's fresh, zesty scent tickled her nose. He smelled so good and entirely masculine. She'd caught a hint of it a couple times earlier this evening and had thought it was nice. But now, as it hit her full force, her breath caught, and her stomach turned somersaults. Oh yeah, she liked the way Jake smelled.

She also liked the way his jeans and t-shirt hugged the muscles she'd searched for under his work shirt. *Did he dress like this on purpose? To get a reaction out of me.*

She was reacting all right, but she refused to show it. It was all she could do not to rub her hand across his shoulders as he carried her.

Relief, followed by disappointment, washed over her when he set her in his truck. He leaned over to buckle her seat belt before closing her door. He'd hardly touched her, but his proximity and scent caused her mouth to go dry and her temperature to rise.

When he closed her door, she sucked in a deep breath and licked her lips. She was glad to have a little distance between them, even if it was only the center console. She couldn't believe how everything about him affected her.

Have I ever responded to a man like this before?

She had no idea. But deep down, she had a feeling the intensity of what she experienced, here with Jake, was a first for her. She wouldn't be single at thirty if she'd felt this electricity with another man. She was sure of it.

So what did that mean where Jake was concerned?

Jake put the truck in gear and drove up the lane. He turned onto the highway and headed toward town.

This surprised Emily. When Faith mentioned the bluff, Emily had assumed that meant the hills toward the north end of the ranch. She was doubly surprised when several minutes later Jake pulled up to a low building full of windows that looked like a quaint restaurant sporting the name Charity's Diner.

"This is the bluff?"

Jake laughed. "Nope, this this my Aunt Charity's diner. I thought I'd get us some pie to take up to the bluff. Unless you'd rather go to the Tasty Freeze at the other end of town. I think they have chocolate ice cream, and I could ask them to mix in some brownies or something."

A warm flush swept over Emily. If Jake's teasing tone hadn't led Emily to believe he was flirting with her, the twinkle in his eyes sure did. She liked that he remembered her ice cream preferences and she liked him. More and more with each passing hour.

"I'll settle for pie, this time." She smiled so he'd know she was teasing. "I mean, your aunt's pie must be pretty amazing if this is where you bring me when you're trying to impress me."

Jake's eyes widened, and the tips of his ears turned pink as she stared him down, daring him to deny he was trying to impress her. Finally, after a lengthy staring contest, Jake's lips turned up. "What kind of pie do you want?"

Smart man. He'd neither denied nor admitted he was trying to impress her. For some reason she found that wildly attractive.

She matched his smile. "Surprise me." It was the only response she could come up with, since her mind was a little muddled by the unexpected flutter of desire that rippled through her. Besides, the man was full of surprises.

EMILY WATCHED Jake enter the diner and approach the counter. She appreciated the way he walked. Not cocky like a strut but a little more than a swagger. And boy did his backside look good in those jeans!

A slender yet busty redhead approached Jake as soon as he placed his order.

Curious, Emily's gaze stayed glued on Jake through the window.

Jake took a step back, but the redhead advanced again, leaning in a little closer this time. Jake didn't move. Was it because he was backed up against the counter, or did he welcome the pretty woman's proximity?

Jake cast his gaze around the diner. Was he looking for a way out of the situation? Or checking to make sure they didn't have an audience so he could take advantage of the opportunity the redhead clearly offered? When he didn't push away from the counter, Emily suspected it was the latter.

A chill swept over her. If he had a thing with the redhead, then why was he flirting with Emily and leading her on? Okay, maybe he hadn't exactly been leading her on, but he hadn't denied he'd been trying to affect her.

And it had worked, if the knot that formed in her stomach when the redhead put her hand on Jake's arm was anything to go by. Emily told herself to look away, but she couldn't tear her eyes from the couple.

Jake's head snapped up, and he turned to look across the diner. *Is that relief on his face?*

Emily watched as he extricated himself from the redhead and hurried over to a table where a familiar man in a blue button down sat.

Dr. Young. And was that Faith sitting beside Jake's uncle?

Confusion swept over Emily. Faith didn't strike her as the type to lie about going to see an elderly friend who broke a hip so she could meet up with... her brother-in-law? Emily tried to remember if she'd heard anything about Dr. Young's wife. Was he a widower, left alone at much too young of an age like Faith?

Emily continued to stare as Jake pulled out a chair and sat down by his mom and Dr. Young, looking perfectly at ease. Doctor Young pushed his empty plate away and put his arm around Faith's shoulders. Faith leaned into him.

Emily sighed, feeling mildly embarrassed to be gawking at the older couple yet pleased for them. *What does Jake think of his mom dating his uncle?*

Brassy red hair passing in front of the truck pulled Emily's attention away from the diner. She watched the woman who had been sidled up to Jake a few moments ago climb into a red Porsche and drive away.

Is she compensating for something with the flashy car? Emily wasn't sure whether the question arose out of an occupational hazard or her own jealousy.

Jake climbed into the truck a few minutes later, a to-go bag in hand.

"Was that your mom with Dr. Young?" Emily didn't mean to blurt it out like that, but curiosity had been eating at her ever since Jake sat down at their table.

Jake's face registered surprise, then he laughed. "No, that's my aunt Hope."

"Oh." Emily's heart dropped a little. She was happy for Dr. Young —that he hadn't lost his wife, but she kind of liked the idea of Faith finding love again. She was too young to spend the rest of her life alone.

"So... your mom and Hope are twins?"

"Triplets, along with my Aunt Charity, the owner of the diner." He motioned out the window toward the building as he backed the truck up.

Triplets? Faith, Hope, and Charity. What wonderful names for amazing women, assuming Faith's sisters were as caring and compassionate as she was.

Emily caught sight of a large dark-haired man behind the wheel of a silver car that pulled into the parking lot of the diner as they pulled out. An unexplainable chill shook her body.

"Are you okay?" Jake asked. "What was that all about?"

She tried to look over her shoulder at the car but couldn't turn her head far enough, thanks to the neck brace. "I don't know. Deja vu, I guess."

"Did you remember something?"

Emily pictured the glimpse she'd seen of the man's face, trying to recall more. But there was nothing. No association, no context of time or place.

"No, I didn't remember anything." Emily shook her head, trying to dispel her odd reaction to a stranger. Tell me more about your aunts. Are they as kind and giving as your mom?"

"Definitely." Jake continued to talk about his aunts and extended family as he drove toward the hills.

Still feeling unsettled, Emily kept an eye on her side mirror, making sure they weren't being followed. Seeing no lights behind them, she told herself to let it go. She listened to Jake share memories of his childhood surrounded by cousins, and longing filled Emily's chest. She wished she had memories like that. Jake's family sounded amazing.

At this point though, she'd settle for meeting her brother.

RELIEF FILLED EMILY when they finally arrived at the bluff. The road had grown rough, and Emily's pain medicine had long since worn off.

Jake handed her a pair of binoculars before pointing across the valley in front of them. "The Double Diamond."

Emily had no problem spotting the ranch house and the surrounding out-buildings without the binoculars. She used them anyway as he pointed out the bunk house and Zane and Lottie's small home flanked by a large garden and an orchard.

"Lottie insists on growing our fruit and vegetables. The ranch hands are required to take turns working in the orchard and garden."

"Does Lottie cook for the ranch hands too?"

"Goodness, no," Jake chuckled. "She would quit on me if I asked her to do that. I have an ornery old codger named Hank who fixes the meals for the ranch hands and manages the bunk house. He's pretty good at keeping the hands out of trouble while they're here on the ranch."

Emily's heart gave an odd little flutter at the affection in Jake's voice as he spoke of Hank. She reminded herself he'd been sidled up to a pretty redhead not long ago. Time to change the subject.

"Lottie's a gem. I hope you realize how lucky you are to have her." Emily liked the no-nonsense, sometimes sassy, housekeeper. Her cooking was amazing. Emily wished she had more of an appetite lately. She took another bite of the chocolate mousse cheesecake Jake had gotten her. *Mmm... It* was delicious, but she'd probably have to let Jake finish it.

"She is amazing. She's been like a second mother to me. I think she is the reason my mother felt comfortable leaving the ranch to go stay with my Aunt Charity after Uncle Richard passed away. She knew I would be taken care of."

Emily gave him a teasing grin. "Most people learn to take care of themselves."

"We had this discussion last night, remember? I *can* take care of myself, but not as good as Lottie can." He gave her a heart-stopping grin, and wild horses raced through her stomach.

Jake continued to talk about the cattle and crops they raised. The number of calves born each spring and the amount of cattle Jake sold and shipped across the U.S. every year astounded Emily. This was a much larger operation than she'd originally guessed.

"When you say you put the cattle out on the range, do you mean on government rangeland?" Emily asked.

"No. We keep all of our cattle on our own land, which means we maintain miles and miles of fence line."

"How much land do you own?"

"About forty thousand acres."

Emily whistled. "Wow."

Despite having ranch hands to help, Jake must be extremely busy. Guilt swept over her for imposing on him. She sensed that because she was here, Jake wasn't doing near the work he usually did.

Jake continued to share information about the ranch. He motioned toward the gently rolling hills to the left. "That's where the cattle graze for the summer."

Emily looked where he pointed, spotting black blobs on the low, green hillsides. "I'm surprised they're so green, considering this area of Washington is a desert."

Jake pointed further north. "A tributary of the Snake River crosses our land, and we've dug a series of ditches across portions of the land to make good use of the water. We've also dug two additional wells to ensure the cattle have plenty of grass for grazing." Then he pointed in the opposite direction. "Over there we raise the hay we need to feed the animals during the winter."

Raising the binoculars, Emily studied a series of green circles, each with a silver pivot line. One field had a striped pattern in light and dark green hues.

"Why is that field striped?"

"I cut the alfalfa there today. And I baled the one to the right of that last night."

Emily's brow furrowed. "You made me hot cocoa last night."

"After you went to bed, I went out and baled."

"That was after midnight. Did I keep you from your work? Couldn't it have waited until morning?"

"We always bale at night. We have to do it while the dew is on the hay to help hold the bales together."

She noticed he didn't comment on her keeping him from his work.

"And how long did you bale?"

"Until almost dawn."

According to Faith, Jake usually got up with the sun. "Did you get any sleep at all last night?"

Jake shrugged as he looked away. "I slept on the couch for an hour or two this morning."

"How are you even awake right now?"

He winked at her. "Stimulating conversation with a beautiful woman does wonders."

Emily's cheeks warmed. She'd hardly call herself beautiful, especially with two black eyes and stitches in her head.

"If I work through the night very often without catching up on my sleep, I'll fall asleep in a heartbeat if I sit still too long."

As enjoyable as this was, maybe she should hurry this tour up. She pointed beyond the house and stables in the one direction he hadn't mentioned.

"What about that area over there?"

"That area has sandy soil. Nothing has ever grown well on it, so I'm leasing it to the government for a solar project."

Emily's eyebrows shot up. "A solar project?"

"If I can ever get the mountain of paperwork finished," he said through gritted teeth. "It should provide a number of additional jobs here in the area for a few years while it's being built."

"That's admirable. Won't it cause a lot of unwanted traffic on your ranch?"

"I'll build a separate access road this fall. So it shouldn't disturb the workings of the ranch much."

Emily shifted her body to stare at him. "I've only known you a few days, but I have to say, you amaze me."

"What do you mean?"

"I look at all you do, all you are responsible for, and I'm amazed at your hard work, determination, and compassion."

Jake waved a hand as though brushing off her praise. "You want to know what amazes me?"

"What?"

"That." He pointed out the windshield to the setting sun shooting golden rays upward from the horizon. The underside of the scattered clouds had a pink tinge to them. "When I look at the beauty of God's creations, I feel so insignificant yet grateful to be a part of it all."

Emily stared at him a moment longer before appreciating the sunset. "It is beautiful."

As Emily admired the beautiful landscape that resembled a patch-work quilt and the setting sun with its golden rays, a comforting warmth settled over her. She'd been trying so hard to remember who she was and where she belonged it had created a constant tension in her.

As the tension slipped away, it dawned on her—at this moment, despite all she didn't know about herself and the danger she was in—this was where she wanted to be. Right here, on this ranch, with Jake, knowing he would keep her safe.

As hard as it was to accept the way things were, she was grateful for this amazing, handsome rancher and his mother.

She pulled the elastic from her braid and separated the strands. She ran her fingers through her hair and shook it out, gently massaging her scalp, willing herself to let go of her worries.

At least for a little while.

CHAPTER 13

*J*ake had grown so relaxed talking to Emily he risked falling asleep. Until the scent of strawberries filled the cab of the truck. He recognized the scent as the same shampoo Riley used. But it had never smelled like this on his sister.

He studied the horizon, trying to analyze his attraction toward Emily. Was it because she was in danger or because she was so easy to talk to? Maybe it was her beautiful green eyes and full red lips.

Emily continued to shake out her waves, and the scent grew stronger. So did his attraction. Her hair brushed his arm below the sleeve of his t-shirt, setting his skin afire.

Had she done that on purpose to make sure he noticed? Like he'd worn this tight t-shirt to get her attention? He glanced at her face.

Her eyes were closed. For the first time since she'd awakened in the hospital, her features were relaxed.

She's beautiful. Despite the bruises.

The hair thing had been unintentional, but she had his attention. Were her auburn tresses as silky as they looked? He balled his hands into fists to keep from finding out.

He didn't need this kind of distraction. He knew nothing about her and the danger she was in. He had too much work to do on the ranch, and he could never devote the time to a woman, which she deserved.

Isn't that why I hired another ranch hand? So I could have time?

Yes, he'd been around when needed, but the inactivity drove him crazy. He wanted to be out riding, roping, and working hard. He needed to exhaust himself each day so he could sleep at night.

That's why he'd baled hay last night. If he'd gone to bed, thoughts of Emily's emerald eyes and strawberry-red lips would have kept him awake half the night, like they had the previous night.

He started the engine. "We'd better head back. If I sit much longer, I'll fall asleep." Or *run my hands through your hair.* He doubted that would go over well.

Emily continued to ask questions about the ranch as they drove back, making the ride back pass quickly.

When he lifted her from the truck to carry her into the house, Jake couldn't help himself. He inhaled deeply to see if her hair still smelled like strawberries.

It did. And it smelled so good.

He was allergic to strawberries, so he rarely thought about them. But Emily reminded him of strawberries, from her full red lips to her strawberry-scented auburn hair. He had a feeling he was going to forever feel differently about strawberries.

When they got in the house, Jake hesitated near the couch, reluctant to put Emily down. After smelling her hair one final time, he set her on the couch.

He straightened and cleared his throat, his mouth suddenly dry. It must be from all the talking he'd done on the drive. "Would you like a drink of water?"

"Yes, please."

Jake escaped to the kitchen where he downed a full glass, then refilled it and filled a glass for Emily. When he gave it to her, she took a few swallows then set her glass on the end table and stared at the baby grand piano in the far corner of the room.

She looked tired, but his mother wasn't home yet, and it wouldn't be appropriate for him to offer to help her get ready for bed. He was about to suggest they watch a movie when she scooted to the edge of the couch.

"Will you find my crutches, please?"

"Sure." He wanted to insist on carrying her wherever she needed to go but decided he should let her have what little independence he could. No need to make things awkward if she needed to go to the bathroom. He retrieved her crutches from the back patio, where they'd left them earlier.

"Thank you." Without another word, Emily shuffled to the piano. She sat down and plucked a few keys. She eyed the sheet music that lay open on the piano then played the top hand.

Jake stood behind her. When she stopped playing, he asked, "Did you remember learning to play? Or was it instinctual?"

"I don't know. I got this feeling that maybe I could play. It's strange that I felt it tonight when I have been looking at this piano for three days without feeling anything."

Emily's fingers glided over the ivory keys again as she played. Slowly. Thoughtfully.

Jake checked the music in front of her. He was rusty, but he could tell she wasn't playing from the sheet music. He didn't recognize the notes she played. Glancing at her face, he watched her eyes close. He listened to the beautiful melody, appreciating her talent.

Emily stopped playing and lowered her head as much as her neck brace allowed.

Jake looked at her face again.

Tears streamed down her cheeks.

He perched on the edge of the bench and pulled her into his arms. "You remembered something, didn't you?"

She nodded.

When she didn't speak, he waited a few moments then asked, "Who taught you to play?"

"My mother," she whispered.

"Why does remembering your mother make you sad?"

"She died when I was sixteen after a lengthy battle with breast cancer."

"Oh, Emily, I'm sorry." He hugged her tighter against him, resting his chin against her hair. Emily's pain overshadowed all thoughts of appreciating its scent. "That music was beautiful. What was it?"

"My mom wrote that. She was incredibly gifted. She had the most beautiful voice." Her tone grew wistful. "I loved listening to her sing."

"I'm glad you remembered her."

Emily twisted a lock of hair around her fingers. "She used to brush my hair whenever I was upset. She'd brush and sing until I calmed down. Then we'd talk, sometimes for hours. It sounds selfish, but that's what I missed the most when she died." Fresh tears slid down her cheeks. "It was one of the last things she did for me before she passed away. I tried to refuse because she was so weak, but she insisted."

Jake tightened his arm around her shoulders and pressed his cheek against her hair. "I can't sing worth a darn, but would you let me brush your hair?"

He was asking for trouble, but he didn't know how else to comfort her right now. And more than anything he wanted to comfort Emily.

She pulled back and looked at him, her brow creased.

He tucked a lock of hair behind her ear. "I'd like to brush your hair, Emily. Will you let me do that for you?"

Her lips lifted in a slow smile, and she nodded.

Releasing her, Jake stood and went to the bathroom to find her hairbrush. All the way there and back, he asked himself what he was doing. He couldn't allow this woman to be a distraction. And he couldn't allow himself to become interested in her.

His stomach sank as he acknowledged it was too late. On both accounts.

When Jake returned to the great room, he found Emily sitting on the couch. He grabbed the TV remote and took a moment to get Pandora on the television. "I was serious when I said I don't sing, so what would you like to listen to?"

Emily suggested an artist that played instrumental music, and Jake created a new play list. Then he looked at her, realizing how awkward this situation was.

"How did your mother brush your hair?"

She gave him a small smile. "You don't have to do this, Jake."

"I want to." It was the truth. He wanted to touch her hair to see if it was as soft as it looked.

"Well, I usually laid my head on her lap, but I don't think I can lie on my left side," she said, subtly pointing out that they were in the wrong position for her to lay her head on his lap.

Taking the hint, Jake stood and helped Emily shift to the other end of the couch before sitting again. Carefully, Emily laid down, resting her head on his thigh, then she shifted, searching for a more comfortable position for her neck. She finally relaxed with her shoulder pressed against the outside of his thigh.

Jake shifted her hair to the back as she situated herself. He pulled the brush through her locks, careful of tangles. After the fourth stroke, he felt as much as heard her sigh. Emily needed this. Encouraged, he continued.

Her hair was softer than he'd imagined. The tantalizing strawberry scent he liked so much drifted up to him. After a few more strokes, a warm dampness permeated his jeans where Emily's cheek rested. She was crying again.

Am I doing it wrong? He stroked her shoulder. "Am I hurting you?" Or did she just hurt?

She tried to shake her head, but between her neck brace and his thigh her head hardly moved. She sniffled. "It's strange. I can remember some things about my mom now, but I can't remember my father and brother. My memories are isolated to her. I see a few shadowy images in my mind, but they don't feel as real as my memories of her. I don't understand why I can't remember more."

Remembering what Robert said about her father, Jake chose his words carefully. "Maybe your mind isn't ready to accept or process memories concerning your father and brother yet."

"You think so?" She was quiet for a moment. "I bet you're right. Robert said my brother is my only living relative." Her voice grew quieter as she continued to speak. "That means my father is dead... and my mind is not ready to accept that... knowledge again."

Fresh tears soaked Jake's leg. He continued brushing, attempting to soothe her the best he could.

After a few more minutes, she apologized for getting his jeans wet and lifted her head, but Jake shushed her and gently pushed her back against his leg. "Relax." He continued to brush with rhythmic strokes until she relaxed again.

He enjoyed brushing her hair. More than he should. What had started out as awkward had become intimate, natural, and soothing. For both of them.

Jake set the brush aside and ran his fingers through her long silky hair. He let himself relax, enjoying the feel of Emily's head against his leg. Resting his hand on her shoulder, he laid his head back against the high back of the couch and closed his eyes. He should go to bed, but he didn't want to disturb Emily.

Not yet.

~

JAKE WASN'T sure how long he'd been asleep, but he awoke when his mother walked through the front door. She took one look at him and Emily, and her eyebrows shot up. She didn't even bother trying to hide her amusement.

"I'm sorry I'm so late," she whispered. Her tone sounded apologetic, but the smile on her face said otherwise. "I stopped by Charity's to pick up a few things, and Hope stopped by. We lost track of time while we visited." She let out a sigh and smiled again. "I haven't laughed with my sisters like that in a long time. It was nice." Then a frown crossed her face. "But I should have been here to help Emily to bed."

"It's fine, Mom." Jake kept his voice low. "I'm glad you had a nice visit. Emily had a difficult time for a while tonight. She remembered her mother who died when Emily was sixteen."

Faith sighed. "The poor girl. I should help her to bed."

"I'll carry her in." Jake put his hand under Emily's head to support it while he slid his body out from under her. She sat up as he slid his arms under her. "Shh... be still," he whispered with his lips against her hair. The strawberry scent wasn't as strong now, but he enjoyed the feel of her in his arms.

He carried her to her room and gently laid her on the bed. He was reluctant to leave, but his mother walked in, carrying Emily's crutches. Emily didn't need him anymore. His stomach dropped at the thought. He turned to leave.

"Jake." Emily grabbed his hand. "Thank you." She let go and reached up to stroke her hair, letting him know exactly what she was thanking him for.

He curled his fingers into a fist to prevent himself from reaching out and stroking her hair one last time. "You're welcome."

He returned to the great room and turned off the music. He picked up the hairbrush from the end table, intending to return it to the bathroom but decided to lock up first. His mom came out of Emily's room as he locked the back door.

"Poor girl, she's exhausted."

"She was upset. She finally remembered something, but it was a sad memory."

His mother got a twinkle in her eyes. "You two looked comfortable on the couch. I have to say you make an attractive couple."

"Mom don't make more of it than it is. She was upset, and I did my best to comfort her."

She looked at the hairbrush in his hand and gave him a knowing look.

"I was just... she likes... her mother used to brush her hair to soothe her."

"You did good, son." She patted his arm. "Keep in mind you're capable of doing more than comforting."

Jake's eyes narrowed. It was bad enough he felt a strong attraction toward Emily; he didn't need his mother pushing her on him or vice a versa. He couldn't get involved with a woman like her. Someone who would leave the ranch as soon as her memory returned, and she was able.

"Jake, you have so much to offer a woman. You're a handsome, successful rancher with a large house that needs a family to fill it, *and* you're patient, giving, and compassionate."

"I told you; I'm too busy for a wife and children."

"Nonsense," Faith chided. "You've been around plenty the past couple of days."

"Because I hired an extra ranch hand to help in case you or Emily needed me."

"Exactly, and you can afford to do that all the time. So what makes you think you don't have time for a wife and family?"

"Fine. I can afford it, but that doesn't mean I'll always put a wife and children first. I don't want to turn out like dad." Jake regretted saying the words when his mother's expression turned to shock.

"What do you mean? Your father was a wonderful husband and father."

As much as he'd like to, Jake couldn't take back the words. He forged ahead, hoping he didn't hurt his mother any worse than he already had. "Come on, Mom, Dad neglected you, and he would have neglected us kids if we hadn't always been by his side, working with him."

Her eyes grew troubled. "Your father never neglected me."

"He worked long hours on the ranch, and you always buried yourself in dozens of projects to stay busy. So you wouldn't get lonely."

She grabbed his arm. "I did do a lot of things to keep myself busy, but that was my way of coping with how fast you all grew up. Besides, helping others is what matters to me. You know that. I need to be needed. I know your father loved this ranch and his animals, and it may have felt like he put it all first, before me. But I never felt that way." She squeezed his arm. "I never doubted his love for me. I never wanted for anything. I know he wasn't the most patient man when it came to getting the work done and making sure it was done right, but when he spent time with me..." She smiled and her voice softened, taking on a dreamy tone. "I never felt like I took second place or that his mind was elsewhere. He focused solely on me when we were together. He often brought me bouquets of wildflowers to let me know he thought about me when he was away. Occasionally, with

Lottie's help, he even surprised me with a picnic." Faith's smile deepened. "You were conceived on one such picnic."

"Okay." Jake put up his hands to ward off any more information. "I don't need details."

His mother chuckled.

"Wait, my birthday is in November, so that means I was conceived... in January." A chill swept over Jake. *That must have been one cold picnic!*

"Your father was a very resourceful man." Faith chuckled again, her cheeks growing pink. "But I won't bore you with the details."

"Thank you."

"Honey, my point is, you are a wonderful man and a hard worker, but you shouldn't avoid marriage because you're afraid you won't be a good enough husband and father. None of us are ever good enough. That's what God's grace is for." She grabbed his other arm as well to make sure she had his full attention. "But as long as you deny yourself the privilege of loving a woman and having a family, you're forfeiting so many wonderful blessings. I know your father would be proud of the man you've become and how successful you've been with the ranch, but you know he'd be the first to tell you to 'git the lead out, and git 'er done.'"

Jake chuckled. His mother was right. His father would be disappointed that Jake thought only about himself and whether he was man enough to run the ranch *and* love a woman.

Jake's chest tightened. Had he exaggerated his perceptions of his father's shortcomings because of his own anxiety and self-doubts? If he didn't allow himself to fall in love, he wouldn't get hurt again.

His love hadn't been enough to make Lydia happy. So, why did he think it would be enough to make another woman happy?

A woman like Emily.

CHAPTER 14

*E*mily pushed the eggs and bacon around on her plate. Once again, she didn't have an appetite. Her heart was heavy after last night's recollections of her mother.

Jake sat across the table from her. "You don't like eggs?"

She gave him a wan smile. "I guess I'm not very hungry." She let out a deep sigh. "I wish I could remember more, you know. I wish I could remember happy things."

"Poor Margaret. I'm not sure she'll recover from this." Faith's voice, from the other side of the kitchen, interrupted their conversation. "She was so down last night and not making much sense, thanks to the morphine." Faith crossed the kitchen. "Speaking of pain medicine, how are you feeling, Emily? You haven't asked for your medicine this morning. Would you like ibuprofen, or do you need something stronger?"

Emily still had a lot of pain, especially when she did too much or moved too fast, but she hoped if she avoided the stronger medicine, eventually her memory would return. She was just glad to be rid of the neck brace. Technically, she should have worn it another day, but she'd worn Faith down with her insistence that her neck felt fine.

"I'm fine for now. I'll take some ibuprofen later."

"We'll see how you feel after you get dressed. I know that's exhausting. Would you like me to braid your hair again today? Or maybe we can do one of those messy buns the girls like to do nowadays. You have such long thick hair. The possibilities are endless."

Faith's enthusiasm and energy exhausted Emily. She loved the woman and was grateful for her kindness, but Faith's energy was almost more than Emily could handle today.

She bit back a smile and looked at Jake. His pinched lips looked like he fought a smile of his own.

Jake gave her a wink, setting her stomach aflutter. "Mom, I think you should check on Ms. Turner this morning. I'll bet she's pretty down."

"I can't leave Emily again."

"I thought I'd give Amy a call and see if she'd like to come visit with Emily for a while."

"That's a wonderful idea." Faith turned to Emily. "Amy is always fun to visit with. Her girls are the cutest things ever. And I should spend more time with Margaret. I'm not sure how much longer she'll be with us."

"It's settled, then." Jake stood and pulled his cell phone from his pocket.

Thirty minutes later, Emily was relaxing in the great room when Amy arrived with her daughters. The beautiful two-year-olds didn't look like twins as Emily had expected. Both had curly blond hair—one golden and the other platinum—and beautiful blue eyes that were on opposite ends of the spectrum; one deep, sapphire blue and the other sky blue.

"Oh, there are my little cherubs." Faith knelt and hugged the girls, who enthusiastically returned her embrace, nearly knocking her over. "I've missed you girls so much."

Faith continued to gush over the girls until they became interested in a basket of toys Amy pulled from a cupboard. Then Faith fussed and hovered over Emily again.

"Are you sure you don't need some pain medicine before I go?"

When Emily shook her head, she continued. "Would you like me to get you a glass of water? Or a pillow or blanket?"

"I'm fine, Faith. You're spoiling me. I'll let Amy know if I need anything. You go visit with your friend."

Faith continued to hover until Amy spoke up. "I'll make sure she takes it easy, Faith."

Faith nodded and left through the kitchen. The room fell quiet.

Amy smiled. "Wow. She's a ball of energy, isn't she? I'm not sure if I'll ever get used to her enthusiasm. She's such a sweetheart, though. She was a lifesaver for me when I first came to Providence. The girls love her."

"How long have you lived in Providence?"

"About ten months. My car broke down as I passed through in the middle of the night last August."

Passed through? This wasn't Amy's home.

"Why were you driving in the middle of the night?"

Amy chewed on her bottom lip. "I was... running away... from a bad situation."

Emily noted Amy's reticence to talk about herself. Was she shy? Or did she not want to talk about the situation she'd run from?

"I guess we kind of have that in common." Emily frowned, and her brow creased. "Except I don't know what I was running from. Technically, I wasn't running... by choice."

"I wasn't running from anything as serious as what you are going through." Amy bit her bottom lip again.

"You don't have to tell me if you don't want to. I was only trying to make conversation. I'm afraid I can't share much information about myself, so it makes the conversation one-sided." Emily gave her an apologetic smile.

"It's okay." Amy shrugged. "I don't really like talking about myself. I didn't exactly have a normal, happy childhood." Amy paused then seemed to shift gears. "Kallie's father was... unfaithful and abusive when he drank." Amy fingered the hem of her shirt and gave what looked like a forced smile. "I left with Kallie in the middle of the night after catching him with—" Amy bit off her words. "When I decided I'd had enough."

"It takes a lot of courage to leave an abusive relationship."

"If I'd truly been courageous, I would have left a lot sooner."

"The important thing is you got out." Emily gave her a confused look. "You took only Kallie? Aren't both girls yours?"

"No, Cassey is Ben's daughter from his first marriage."

Again, Amy bit her lip, as though reluctant to share information about Ben's first wife.

Curiosity got the better of Emily. "Is Ben divorced?"

"No, his wife died in a car accident a little over a year and a half ago."

Died in a car accident.

The words echoed in Emily's mind. Icy fingers gripped her heart as she remembered opening her door to find two police officers on her doorstep. "Oh no."

Her heart sank. She knew why they were there. She didn't know what had happened, or to whom, but she knew they had bad news. It was always bad news. That's the only reason police officers show up on doorsteps late at night.

"Are you Emily Anderson?" the older officer asked. Emily nodded. "The daughter of Adam Anderson?"

Something had happened to her father. But how? She'd seen him last night when she'd gone out to dinner with him and her brother to celebrate Cameron's birthday.

"What happened?" she choked out.

"I'm afraid he died in a car accident," the officer said, his eyes full of sympathy. "He fell asleep at the wheel and drove off the road, down a steep embankment. I'm sorry."

"You're sure it was my father?" Emily's voice caught on a sob. "And you're sure he's dead?"

"Yes, ma'am. I'm terribly sorry."

The officers' faces swam in front of her as her legs gave way. She would have sunk to the floor if it hadn't been for the officers' quick reflexes. They caught her and guided her to the sofa.

"Emily." A hand touched her arm. "Are you okay?"

Two blurry, angelic faces stared up at Emily with concerned looks. She swiped at the tears and blinked to clear her vision.

"Are you okay?" came Amy's voice again.

Emily couldn't answer. She tried to nod but couldn't even do that because she wasn't okay. Her father was dead.

Jake walked in the back door. "There are the little cuties—" His voice abruptly died off when he saw Emily crying. "What's wrong?" he whispered to Amy as he approached the couch where Emily sat with Amy beside her.

Amy shrugged and moved away.

Jake pulled a handkerchief from his pocket and took her place. Remembering how patient and gentle Jake was last night caused Emily's tears to increase.

"Emily?" His voice was tender, like a caress. He pressed the handkerchief into her hand and placed his arm around her shoulders, gently pulling her toward him.

Shifting so leaning against Jake wouldn't hurt her ribs, she rested her head against his shoulder. She needed Jake's strength right now. As much as she wanted her memories to return, the pain that accompanied each memory was almost more than she could bear.

"I mentioned that Ben's first wife died in a car accident." Amy's quiet voice pierced her anguish. "Then she said, 'Oh no,' and started crying. She had this funny look, like maybe she remembered something."

"My father," Emily said without lifting her head from Jake's shoulder.

"What?" Jake asked.

"I remembered the night two police officers showed up at my door to tell me my father died in a car accident."

"Oh, Emily." Jake's arm tightened around her.

"Remembering it was like experiencing it for the first time. This is not something my mind is making up. It can't be. It hurts too bad." Emily sniffed, fighting more tears.

"Can you tell us about it?" Jake asked after a moment.

"He fell asleep at the wheel and rolled his car down a steep embankment." Emily lifted her head from Jake's shoulder. "It happened almost ten months ago."

"Were you alone when the police notified you?"

"Yes, but they stayed with me until the officers brought Cameron to my house." Emily gasped as a weight lifted from her chest and some of her sadness dissipated. She lifted her head and grabbed Jake's hand. "I remember my brother. I remember Cameron."

"That's great." Then more soberly he added, "I'm sorry about your father, Emily."

"I remembered." Excitement crept into her voice. Then her smile faded as the familiar heaviness returned.

"What's wrong?"

"I remember I have a brother but not much else. I can see a few hazy pictures in my head of what I think is my childhood, but like last night, I'm not certain if they are real or not."

"Don't force it." Jake stroked her hair. "It'll come. Give it time. Once you see your brother, I'm sure everything will come back to you."

"I hope so. Why do you think it's taking so long to locate him? Do you think he's away on a trip or something?"

"It's possible."

"I'm glad you remembered something," Amy spoke up. "I'm sorry it wasn't a happy memory."

Emily attempted a smile. "Thank you. Me too." She looked at Jake. "I'd like to remember something happy."

His arm tightened around her. "Would you like to go rest for a while?"

No doubt Jake intended to carry her to her room. As tempting as the thought of remaining in the security of Jake's arms was, she pushed herself away, attempting to shake off her somber mood.

"No. I don't want to rest. I need a distraction. I need happiness and fresh air." She looked at Amy. "Would you mind if we continue our visit outside?"

Amy exchanged a concerned look with Jake, who shrugged then nodded. "That's a great idea."

"I saddled Honey," Jake said. "I came in to see if you'd let me give the girls a ride." Then turning to the toddlers, he asked, "Who wants a horsey ride?"

"Me, me, me," they sang in unison, bouncing up and down.

"That's not fair, Jake." Amy scowled at him. "I can't say no now."

Jake grinned. "You could, but you'd be the meanest mother ever."

"Very well, we'd better go outside so I can keep an eye on the one who isn't riding."

Jake stood and bent to scoop Emily up in his arms.

Emily scowled. "I can walk on my own. Hand me my crutches."

"I know you can, but you take forever." He gave her a teasing grin. "It's quicker this way."

"Save your breath, Emily," Amy said. "Jake, Robert, and Ben are the most stubborn men I've ever met. You won't win there."

Jake smiled at Emily. "See. Thank you, Amy."

Within moments, Emily found herself on the lounge chair on the back patio. Amy sat on the nearby swing with Cassey as Jake walked away with Kallie on his shoulders. He put a skip in his step, bouncing up and down, causing the toddler to giggle.

Emily tried not to think about what a wonderful father Jake would make. She couldn't afford to think like that. Not when she knew so little about herself.

She turned back to Amy. "Why do you say Jake, Robert, and Ben are the most stubborn men you've met?"

Amy smiled. "You probably haven't met Debbie Wheeler yet. She owns the mansion outside of town. She's a young, wealthy widow who's looking to marry again. She has her sights set on Providence's most eligible bachelors, and she'll do just about anything to get their attention."

"Let me guess, Robert and Jake?"

"Bingo. Ben used to be on that list too, but I took him off the market, so she's doubled her efforts on Robert and Jake."

"What does she do?"

"She frequently calls the Sheriff's Office requesting Robert come investigate a break-in at her house, or she locks her keys in her car and wants Robert to jimmy it for her."

"How does she try to get Jake's attention?" Emily wasn't sure why, but she was more than a little curious to hear Amy's answer.

"She bought an expensive horse and asked Jake to stable it for her. She rarely rides it, but she drops in all the time to 'check' on her horse." Amy made air quotes as she said check. "I'm pretty sure she spends more time checking out Jake than she does her horse. She's come onto him strongly a few times. Poor guy. They try to be civil to her, because they are gentlemen, but she can get annoying."

An odd twisting sensation swept through Emily's stomach. *Am I jealous? Over a stranger who Jake doesn't even like?* No, it was possessiveness. Emily didn't want someone else vying for Jake's attention. She wanted it for herself.

"Anyway, I first met Jake when I came to the ranch with Ben's family last Labor Day." Amy's voice put an end to Emily's musings.

Good thing too. She wasn't sure she liked the direction her thoughts had taken.

"I offered to be widow repellent when Debbie showed up uninvited."

"Widow repellent?"

"I stuck close to Jake's side and flirted with him. I did everything I could to keep his attention on me. Debbie hated it. Especially when I fell off the fence and landed in a heap at Jake's feet," Amy giggled. "She was so fed up with me she took off. But I broke my toe in the fall. As soon as Jake realized I'd hurt myself, he insisted on carrying me back to the house. Robert ended up carrying me to Ben's truck so he could drive me to the hospital for an X-ray. Then Ben carried me into the house when we got home from the hospital." Amy lifted Cassey off the swing so she could play with the dog.

"So, Jake isn't the only one who insists on carrying women around?"

"No, all three of them are like that. They're complete gentlemen. Which surprised me because I didn't think men like that existed anymore." Amy grinned and in a mock whisper said, "Honestly, I think they do it to boost their own egos."

Emily laughed. She thought about the tight jeans and t-shirt Jake wore last night. She doubted he had a confidence problem. *No. He wanted to make sure he had my attention.*

He'd succeeded.

Their conversation came to a halt when Jake brought Kallie back and took Cassey to ride the horse.

After Jake left, Emily asked Amy questions about her life before coming to providence, hoping to spark conversation again. Amy's reticence to talk about herself slowly subsided as Emily gently encouraged her. She shared snippets of her life, giving Emily glimpses of working at a young age in a restaurant and bar. Gradually, she opened up about abusive stepfathers and her mother's live-in boyfriends.

Kallie wasn't content for long on the swing with Amy and soon climbed down. She now ran around the back yard with the dog following her.

Emily was glad Amy felt comfortable enough to share things Emily suspected she'd shared with very few. She sensed Amy held things back, though. Maybe someday, Emily would earn Amy's full trust, so she'd feel comfortable truly opening up.

Someday? Would she be here long enough for someday to arrive? If Robert found her brother, she could go home soon.

Jake returned with Cassey then disappeared with Honey.

Emily and Amy continued talking while the girls played with the dogs. Emily enjoyed getting to know Amy and learning more about Jake and his family.

Amy sat up straighter and looked toward the stables. "Speak of the she-devil."

Emily's gaze followed Amy's. She spotted a red Porsche coming to a stop outside the stables.

"That's Widow Wheeler," said Amy.

Both women watched in silence as a slender, but busty, brassy redhead stepped out of the car, wearing high heels and glittering jewelry.

Emily recognized the woman from the diner. So, Jake really had been looking for an escape last night. And his uncle had taken mercy on him and given him one.

"She comes to check on her horse dressed like that?"

Amy rolled her eyes. "She's obviously not here to ride."

"I doubt she could climb on a horse in those tight pants, not to mention the heels."

After a few minutes, Debbie came out of the stables and looked around. Catching sight of Amy and Emily on the back patio, she walked their direction, stumbling in her high heels as she crossed the uneven grass.

As she grew closer, Emily took in her form-fitting blouse, manicured nails, and flawless hair. The woman accentuated her assets well. Despite a few fine lines around her eyes, Debbie was a very attractive woman.

"Hi, Debbie," Amy greeted.

"Hello." Debbie's voice held an air of disdain. Her eyes roamed over Emily.

Amy made introductions. "Debbie, this is Emily Anderson. Emily, Debbie Wheeler."

Debbie smiled, though the curve of her lips looked more like a smirk than a smile. She propped a hand on her hip. "So, the rumors are true. There *is* a strange woman recuperating at the Double Diamond."

"Guilty." Emily smiled. She could see why Jake's family didn't care for the woman. "It was so kind of Jake to open his home to me." Then because she couldn't help herself, she added, "Isn't he amazing?"

Amy smothered a giggle, and Debbie scowled first at Emily then Amy.

"Do you know where he is?" she asked, tapping her toes.

"I'm not sure," Amy hedged. "He said he had a lot of work to do today."

"Well, will you tell him I stopped by?" Debbie studied her nails. "I need to talk to him."

"I'll be leaving soon. I doubt I'll see him before I go," Amy said with poorly feigned regret.

Emily gave Debbie an innocent smile. "I'm sure I'll see him this evening, if not sooner."

Debbie glared at Emily. "Tell him to call me please." Then she spun on her spiked heel and marched away.

Amy waited until Debbie was out of earshot before speaking. "Nicely done. I'm sure it chafes her to think of Jake spending his evenings with you. I wish I'd had your confidence when I first met her. She intimidated me for the longest time."

"Goodness gracious. I can see why nobody likes her. And I can see why you were intimidated by her, but I bet she has much lower self-esteem than you think."

Self-esteem aside, Emily was glad Jake wasn't interested in the beautiful young widow. The tension between her and Jake was taut enough. Emily didn't want to be jealous of another woman.

CHAPTER 15

*J*ake walked out of the stables, Zane at his side. "I don't know. Hercules isn't responding to my normal training methods. He's as stubborn as his sire."

"Then you be equally as stubborn. But don't give up. He'll come around."

Zane didn't talk much, but when he did, Jake listened. As usual, Zane was right. Jake couldn't give up on the stallion no matter how stubborn he was. He needed to be patient.

Patience.

His gaze shifted toward the house as his thoughts turned to Emily. She was being incredibly patient, waiting for her memory to return and word from her brother. *Not that she has a choice.*

His pulse kicked up a notch when he spotted her on the back patio, relaxing on a lounge chair. "Hold off saddling Hercules, Zane. I'll be back in a few minutes."

It wouldn't do to have Emily occupying his thoughts while he worked with the stubborn colt. *I'll just say hi, see if she needs anything, then get back to work.*

Thirty minutes later, Jake stretched his legs out in front of him as he told Emily yet another story of Robert convincing him to do something stupid.

He couldn't remember the last time he'd sat on the patio in the middle of the afternoon drinking lemonade. *I've got work to do, so why am I still here?*

Except for their late-night hot cocoa and their drive two nights ago, Jake hadn't talked to Emily much. She slept late most mornings, napped in the afternoons, and went to bed early.

Her body needed the rest to heal, and it was time for her nap now, but Jake didn't want her to go in any more than he wanted to get back to work. He was grateful his mother hadn't returned yet from her ride, or she would insist Emily go rest.

Emily must be one heck of a therapist.

She was so easy to talk to. When he was with her, he felt like he was the only person in the world that mattered and everything he said was important to her.

Jake set down his lemonade and studied her. The worry lines etched between her brows had become permanent features. From a distance, she looked at ease here on the back patio, but the way she twisted her hair around her fingers showed the tension she tried to hide. It had been a week since the accident with no word from her brother.

A bad feeling settled in Jake's gut. *Why was it taking so long to find him?*

The unmistakable purr of Debbie's Porsche reached his ears moments before it appeared near the stables.

Jake groaned.

"What's the matter?" Concern laced Emily's words.

"That car belongs to Wid-... uh... Debbie Wheeler. I keep a horse stabled for her."

"Ah, Widow Wheeler. Amy told me about her. Oops, I forgot to tell you she stopped by yesterday looking for you." Emily pressed her fingers to her smiling lips. "She didn't stay long. When she couldn't find you, she left a message with me to tell you to call her. Sorry, I forgot." Emily didn't look one bit sorry. In fact, she had a mischievous twinkle in her eyes.

A flush warmed his neck. "I saw her coming, and I hid."

"I thought you disappeared rather quickly. So, do you need some... widow repellent?"

Jake shot her a questioning look. Would it deter Debbie if she found him enjoying Emily's company in the middle of the afternoon when he was usually too busy to pay Debbie any attention? Or would Debbie double her efforts to get his attention in the afternoons?

He had no desire for Debbie to find him, with or without Emily. Jake's palms itched with the urge to hide or at least look too busy to spend time with Debbie. He picked up his hat and stood, contemplating hiding in the house.

"Jake." Emily's urgent voice snapped his attention back to her. "Come here, I need you."

Jake tossed his hat back on the table and dropped to one knee by her lounge chair. "What's wrong?" He searched her face for signs of pain or alarm. Had she remembered something?

Emily's emerald eyes showed no signs of pain or fear, rather they shimmered with humor, making them look like precious gems.

She shifted her legs to the side and patted the edge of her lounge chair. "Sit here."

What is she up to? Jake looked toward the stables where Debbie had disappeared. He didn't have much time to hide.

"Sit!" Emily commanded.

Jake's eyes narrowed. There was nothing wrong with Emily. She was preventing him from hiding on purpose. Was this some psychological exercise? Would she tell him he needed to face Debbie and tell her how he felt, or rather didn't feel, about her? He'd been there, done that, and it hadn't worked.

Emily obviously didn't know Debbie well enough to know she didn't take no for an answer, but the thought of sitting close to Emily for a moment was a little too tempting. He perched on the edge of her chair, hoping he wouldn't tip them both over.

"Good. Now put your hand over here." She grabbed his wrist and placed his hand on the armrest on the other side of her body. The movement turned his back to the stables and brought him closer to Emily. "Okay, lean toward me, like we're having a serious conversation."

His gaze focused on the faint freckles sprinkled across her nose, and once again he acknowledged how beautiful she was. The smell of strawberries drifted over him, and he inhaled deeply as his eyes drifted to her glossy, red lips that glistened like iced strawberries.

He sucked in a sharp breath through his suddenly dry mouth and chuckled. "What are you doing?"

"I'm your widow repellent."

Jake jerked away, but she grabbed the front of his shirt and pulled him toward her. His breath caught in his throat.

"The last woman who acted as widow repellent for me ended up with a broken toe."

She rolled her eyes and held up her cast. "Don't worry, I'll stay off of the fence."

His voice dropped to a whisper. "You don't have to do this."

Jake's heart rate tripled as he looked into her eyes, mere inches from his. The discoloration around her right eye had disappeared, and the bruising around her left had lightened up. He hardly noticed it anymore, instead, his gaze lingered on her thick lashes and the golden flecks in her emerald eyes.

"I want to. It might help deter Debbie if you kiss me."

"I'm not going to kiss you."

Idiot. Why did he say that? His eyes dropped to her lips again and his mouth moistened. He wanted to kiss her. Badly. He'd been wondering what it would be like to taste her full red lips, and she was giving him the perfect opportunity, but he was turning her down?

What is wrong with me?

"You don't want to kiss me?" Color flooded her cheeks, and disappointment clouded her eyes.

Did she *want* him to kiss her?

"No. I mean yes, I want to, but..."

Her eyes lit up again. Her face was so close her breath tickled his cheek.

His fingers itched to bury themselves in her silky strands. He only needed to lean in a bit more to close the gap between his lips and hers.

"But what?"

Jake blinked. "I don't use women like that." He'd never make that mistake again.

"I never thought you did but thank you for the clarification." Emily's voice dropped to a whisper. "Debbie's coming this way." She grabbed the front of his shirt again when he turned to look over his shoulder. "No, don't look. Just kiss me." She tugged on his shirt, closing the gap between their lips.

Her lips, warm and every bit as soft as he imagined they would be, sent an electric shock through him. Stunned, he pulled back and searched her eyes. He'd never had a woman insist he kiss her quite like that.

Did she only do this for Debbie's benefit?

He recognized a desire in her eyes that surely matched his own and regretted pulling away. He slipped a hand behind her shoulder and pulled her to him, careful not to hurt her neck or ribs. His lips met hers again, this time with more pressure.

Emily sighed, and he tasted lemonade... and something sweet.

Strawberries?

She tasted like strawberries and lemonade. The combination of tart and sweet was intoxicating. He wasn't sure which of them deepened the kiss, but another sigh escaped her lips, or maybe he was the one who sighed.

Emily's right hand released his shirt and crept up to the back of his neck. The gentle pressure she exerted prevented him from pulling away. Not that he had any desire to do so.

As his lips melded with Emily's, he was vaguely aware of Debbie calling his name followed by a cry of exclamation. Still the kiss continued. Jake felt powerless to break contact with Emily.

Electricity shot through his veins, and he had a momentary

thought that kissing Emily might have been a mistake. Something told him he'd never be the same after kissing her strawberry-flavored lips.

She loosened her hold on the back of his neck but made no move to pull away.

The sound of Debbie's Porsche roaring to life brought him back to his senses, and he broke off the kiss but kept his face close to hers. He studied Emily's face as he tried to catch his breath.

Her eyes shone with a light he'd never seen there before, and her face was flushed. Was she feeling the effect of the kiss as much as he did?

He wanted to kiss her again, but he didn't dare. That kiss had rocked him. There had been something about the feel and taste of her mouth against his that superseded anything he'd experienced with any other woman.

Debbie's tires squealed as she turned onto the highway and gunned it. Jake let out a breathy chuckle, and Emily joined him. He pulled a little farther away but remained on the edge of her chair.

"You didn't have to do that," he whispered, short of breath.

"You didn't like it?" A mixture of hurt and embarrassment shadowed her eyes, but her voice held the same breathless quality as his.

"Are you kidding? I meant kissing me wasn't necessary."

Emily shrugged. "It was effective."

"It was, but..."

The kiss they'd shared felt like a lot more than just a public display of affection. He'd felt an emotional connection to this beautiful woman who had shown up at his ranch a few days ago, bloody and broken.

But he hardly knew her. She didn't even know herself right now. He couldn't take advantage of that.

She must have seen the doubt in his eyes. "Please don't think I'm a tease. I've never done anything like that before." Her brow wrinkled. "At least I don't think I have."

"Then why did you insist we kiss?"

Her cheeks grew rosy and she lowered her eyes. "I don't know. I guess, I was trying to do you a favor. It's the least I could do, considering all you've done for me."

Jake shot to his feet, heat coursing through him. "You don't have to repay my generosity with physical favors. I'm not *that* kind of man either."

He grabbed his hat and shoved it on his head. Emily hadn't felt the same connection he did. The thought disappointed Jake more than it should have.

"I know you're not that kind of—"

"No offense Emily, but there's a lot we don't know about each other."

Feeling the need to put some distance between them before he said or did something he would regret, he stepped to the edge of the porch.

"I need to get back to work. Do you need me to help you back inside?"

Emily stared at her hands. "No. I'm perfectly capable of getting around on my own."

Taking long strides, Jake walked to the stables where the tool room door stood open. He stepped inside and planted his hands on his hips. *Why did I come in here?*

He felt bad walking away from Emily like that, but it was a good thing he had, because if he'd carried her into the house, he probably would have kissed her again.

How had she gotten under his skin so quickly? He needed to strengthen his resolve not to get involved with her.

What resolve? It's too late, and you know it.

He'd done it again. Fell for a woman he hardly knew. Kicking a feed bucket, he sent it skittering across the room where it knocked over a shovel.

At least he thought he'd known Lydia. But with Emily, he had to admit he didn't know a single thing about her. Except that she was beautiful, and he loved talking to her. Oh, and her mother and father were both dead, which did nothing to help him steel his heart against her.

Needing something to do, he grabbed a pitchfork and went to the closest stall and started fluffing the fresh laid straw. Robert found him there less than a minute later.

"Hey," Robert said.

"Hey," Jake grunted, avoiding Robert's gaze. He pushed the straw to one side of the stall, then knowing that wasn't where it belonged, he flung it back across the floor.

"So, when was this stall last cleaned?"

"This morning," Jake grunted again, slowing his actions.

"And what exactly are you doing?"

Jake froze. "I don't know."

"Is something wrong?" When Jake didn't answer, Robert went on. "I passed Debbie on my way here. Did she throw herself at you again?" Robert bit back a smile.

"No." Jake leaned the pitchfork against the wall and hooked his thumbs into his pockets. "She didn't get the chance. I was... busy."

Robert's eyes narrowed. "Busy?"

"I was..." Jake cleared his throat. "I was with Emily. I kissed her. I mean, she kissed me. Actually, she forced me to kiss her."

Robert laughed. "She forced you to kiss her? I'd love to see exactly how that went down."

Jake shot him a watch-it-or-I'll-punch-you look.

Robert's eyes sparked with amusement. "So... are you bragging or complaining about kissing Emily?"

"Neither," Jake growled.

"Was it that bad?"

Jake gave him an incredulous look. His mouth watered at the memory of strawberries and lemonade.

"It was that good?" Robert guessed.

Jake nodded, unable to stop the grin that pulled at his lips.

"It must have been amazing to fluster you like this."

All Jake could do was smile and nod again. He looked at the straw he'd been shuffling around and chuckled at himself.

"So, what exactly is your problem?"

Jake's smile faded. "It was only for Debbie's benefit. Emily said it was the least she could do after all I've done for her."

"Oh." Robert's face grew serious. "That's not what a guy wants to hear after an earth-shattering kiss."

Earth-shattering was a good way to describe the kiss he'd shared with Emily. "Yeah."

"Well, did you tell her you enjoyed it?"

"Yeah, sort of." Jake scratched the back of his neck.

"What did she say?"

Jake pushed his hands into his pockets. "All she said was it proved effective in driving Debbie away."

"Ouch!" Robert patted Jake on the shoulder. "In my experience, a woman doesn't invite—or force—a man to kiss her if she doesn't want to be kissed."

"You think?"

Jake hadn't dated anyone seriously for a long time, and it had been even longer since he'd kissed a woman, unless he counted Debbie throwing herself at him last fall. He fought the urge to shudder and cringed instead. That was an experience he'd rather forget.

He'd never had a woman insist he kiss her like Emily had. Surely, she wouldn't have forced him to kiss her if she didn't want to be kissed.

He pulled his hands from his pocket. As much as he hated to admit when Robert was right, his brother's words made sense.

"Hey, bro." Robert scratched his head, his face serious. "As amusing as I find your love life, this isn't a social call. I'm afraid I have some bad news for Emily."

Jake's muscles tensed at Robert's grim tone. "What?"

"The Spokane police finally found Emily's brother." Robert chewed the inside of his lip a moment before adding, "He's dead. Murdered. Most likely the day Emily was abducted."

A vice closed around Jake's chest, sucking the air from his lungs. He doubled his right fist and punched the wooden wall of the stall, letting loose a string of words his mother would have scolded him for.

Pain ripped through his knuckles, mirroring the pain in his chest. Emily had lost everyone. Couldn't the poor woman get a break?

"Dude. I know you hate seeing others in pain but hurting yourself won't bring her brother back or help Emily."

Jake flexed his fingers and clenched his teeth. Robert was right again.

"He was shot in her condo. She likely witnessed it."

"No wonder she didn't want to remember."

"I'm guessing the driver of the car shot her brother," Robert said. "I've spoken with the Spokane Police Department and reminded them of Emily's whereabouts and her memory loss. They agreed to let me continue to investigate on this end. But that also means I have to break the news to Emily."

"I'm sorry, man." Jake had envied Robert many times throughout his life, but this was not one of those times.

"The police said it looked like her condo was tossed as though the killer searched for something. They want her to come to her place as soon as possible to see if anything was taken that may give us clues as to who killed her brother." Robert scratched his jaw. "Do I tell her he was killed in her condo?"

Jake sighed. "I don't know."

"If I don't tell her, and she goes home, then maybe her memory will return, and she can tell us exactly what happened. On the other hand, if I tell her that's where he was killed, would she subconsciously block the memories from returning because she doesn't want to remember it?"

"Ironic, isn't it? Emily's the psychologist. She could tell you the right answer. Do you want me to come in with you to talk with her? Mom's not here right now."

Whether Robert wanted him there or not, he wanted to be there. For Emily.

Robert sighed. "Please."

CHAPTER 16

$\mathcal{E}$ mily waited until Jake entered the stables before making her way into the house. Pain sliced through her ribs as she plopped down on the couch. Leaning her head back, she closed her eyes and groaned.

Jake wasn't a man who used a woman for his own selfish purposes, yet that's exactly what she'd done. She used Jake's desire to avoid Debbie to get him to kiss her. *I practically forced him to kiss me.* Her cheeks burned at the memory.

Disappointment had been swift when he'd pulled away, but when he drew her to him and claimed her lips again...

He'd stolen her breath and sent her pulse racing.

She'd meant it when she said she didn't think she was the kind of woman to lead a man on like that. She didn't know much about herself, but she was certain that was not normal behavior for her. So why had she done it?

I wanted Jake to kiss me.

She had a feeling he'd wanted it too, but he would never take advantage of her. She should have told him the truth, instead of using gratitude as an excuse.

Communication is key.

The words rang in her head. Was that the psychologist in her talk-ing? Emily groaned. *Why can't I remember?* Even simple details that had been a part of her everyday life eluded her.

Jake was a part of her life now, and she needed to be honest with him. And with herself. She needed to tell him the truth, soon, or she would lose her nerve, and it would create a wall between them.

She wanted nothing to affect her relationship—if you could call it that—with Jake. With her whole life in limbo, Jake was the one thing that felt right. He was strong and confident and made her feel safe. She needed that right now.

It was more than that, though. He made her feel special. If the backyard leading to the stables wasn't so uneven, she would have gone in search of Jake.

At that moment, as though her thoughts had conjured him, Jake walked through the back door, followed by Robert.

"Jake, I need to talk to you," she blurted. "Alone. Please."

"Okay, we'll talk later. Robert has something he needs to tell you." Jake's voice was quiet, somber.

Catching sight of his bloody knuckles, her eyes flew to his face. Jake looked away. She'd seen the tension in his shoulders when he left her on the back deck. Was he upset enough to punch something?

Of course, he is. They had shared an amazing kiss and she'd brushed it off. She needed to make this right.

She gave him a pleading look. "Please, let me say what I need to say. Robert, would you give us a minute?"

"Sure." Robert shot Jake a grim look, then went to the kitchen.

As soon as Robert left the room, Jake sat beside her, his eyes meeting hers. His sudden closeness made her stomach somersault.

Why had she thought it would be a good idea to clear the air between them? She fidgeted with her dress and swallowed the lump in her throat.

"What happened to your hand?"

Jake moved his bloody knuckles out of her line of sight. "Nothing."

She took a deep breath. "I wasn't entirely honest with y-you a little while a-ago." She hated how her voice shook. When she decided she needed to talk to Jake, she didn't realize how vulnerable she'd feel at admitting how much she'd wanted him to kiss her.

"Whatever it is. You can say it."

Encouraged, she blurted, "I shouldn't have made you kiss me for Debbie's benefit. And I shouldn't have said it was the least I could do because of my gratitude. I did it because..."

Jake's eyebrows raised, and his lips curved upward. "Yes?"

"The truth is I wanted you to kiss me, okay? I used your predicament with Debbie to get you to kiss me. I'm sorry."

Jake's smile broadened, but he didn't say anything.

Why was he making this so awkward?

"I think you wanted to kiss me too," she said in a mildly accusing tone. Jake's eyebrows rose another notch and he continued to smile at her. She crossed her arms over her body—the best she could with a cast on, anyway. "Aren't you going to say something?"

Jake's smile never faltered. "What makes you think I wanted to kiss you too?"

He's teasing me. Well, two can play this game.

"I don't know. Maybe because of the way you smell my hair."

Jake's smile slackened.

"Or because you act reluctant to put me down every time you carry me."

"You noticed all that?" Jake asked, unguarded, as color crept up his neck. "Your hair smells so good—like strawberries. Your kiss even tasted like strawberries." He mused with a smile as his gaze lingered on her mouth.

Emily licked her lips. "I caught you smelling my hair because I was noticing how good you smelled at the same time." Jake's smile broadened, and she forged ahead. "Seriously, Jake, we'd have to be dense not to recognize the attraction between us."

Jake cleared his throat. "Are you always this direct?"

She chuckled. "I don't know. I feel like honesty and communication are important, I guess."

"They are important, but that doesn't always make it easy." Jake scratched the back of his neck. "I'm not sure I'm as comfortable with being direct as you are."

"I won't force you to kiss me again, but if you want to... it won't be unwelcome."

Jake held her gaze as he bit back a smile. "Does that mean you enjoyed it as much as I did?"

Her cheeks warmed, and she nodded.

"Good to know. As much as I'd like to kiss you again, I'm afraid this isn't a good time. Robert has something he needs to tell you."

Something in Jake's tone turned Emily's blood cold.

"ROBERT!" Jake shouted. He remained beside Emily as he waited for his brother to join them.

Robert entered the great room with his hands full. He handed a glass of water to Emily, who accepted it with a confused look, took a sip, and set it on the end table. Then he handed the paper-towel-wrapped ice pack in his other hand to Jake.

Jake scowled at his brother as he accepted the ice pack. He dabbed at the blood on his knuckles and set the ice pack aside.

"What did you do to your knuckles, Jake?" Emily asked.

"Nothing."

"He punched a wall," Robert said.

Jake itched to punch his brother. Instead, he shot him a hard glare.

"Because of me? Because I—"

"No. Not because of you." He took Emily's hand in his. He couldn't let her think he'd punched a wall because of the kiss they had shared.

He glowered at Robert. His mom and Lottie were bad enough. He didn't need his brother meddling in his love life too.

Love life? What love life? Sharing a kiss with Emily did not create a relationship. But something in him longed for a relationship with her.

He gave himself a mental shake and shot Robert a get-on-with-it look.

Robert sat on the corner of the ottoman in front of Emily and tugged at the collar of his uniform. "Emily, the Spokane Police Department found your brother yesterday."

Emily's brow creased, and her voice shook when she spoke. "What do you mean found?" She gripped Jake's hand, causing the broken skin on his knuckles to pull.

Jake welcomed the pain. Too bad he couldn't take away the pain Emily was about to experience.

"I'm afraid he's dead." Robert's voice was gentle, but the words carried a harshness that could never be softened.

"No!" Emily gasped. She pulled her hand from Jake's and covered her mouth. "He can't be. I finally remembered I have a brother and he's gone?"

A fist squeezed Jake's heart at the anguish in her voice. He put his arm around her shoulders and pulled her against him.

She resisted, shaking her head. "He can't be dead. I can't lose him, too." Then the tears came, but Emily continued to talk through them. "It's not fair... every time I remember... someone... it turns out... they're dead." Emily doubled her fist and pounded it on Jake's thigh, punctuating her words. "Why? Why can't there be one, single, happy memory?" She leaned against Jake then and sobbed into his shirt.

He looked at Robert over Emily's head.

Robert returned his gaze with a sober expression. He needed to tell Emily the rest, but Jake shot him a pleading look to wait a few minutes.

His brother either understood or he didn't want to share the rest with her yet. Robert sat back and waited for Emily's tears to subside, then he handed her the glass of water from the end table.

"Thank you," she whispered, taking the water from him. "You knew I would need this, didn't you?" She drained the glass, then set it on the end table again. "It's crazy how fast c-crying dehydrates you."

Robert leaned forward. "I know this is hard, Emily, but there's more I need to tell you."

She shook her head as tears filled her eyes again. "Not more bad news. Please."

Her voice was so small Jake wanted to pull her onto his lap and never let her go. He wanted to protect her from every bad thing in the world. He settled for tightening his arm around her.

Robert cleared his throat. "Cameron was murdered."

"Murdered?" Emily asked in disbelief.

Robert rushed on. "On the same day you were abducted. The Spokane Police think you may have witnessed his murder."

"And they planned to kill me too." Her voice, now flat, sounded as though she tried to distance herself from what she was hearing. From what she may have seen. She repeated the words she'd remembered a few days ago. "Find out what she knows, then take care of her."

"Yes, they killed your brother, and probably planned on killing you."

"Why? Why would they kill Cameron? He wouldn't hurt a soul." She pounded Jake's leg again with her fist. "Why can't I remember any of it?"

For a small woman, she had a deceptively strong punch. He'd let her continue punching his leg all day if it would take away her pain.

Unfortunately, it wouldn't. She needed comforting. But she had no one left to do that for her. Jake tightened his arm around her, pulling her toward him again. He clasped her hand in his, interlocking their fingers.

"This is likely the trauma Uncle James suggested might be affecting your memory," he said.

"You think?" she said, her voice heavy with sarcasm. Then her tone softened. "It has to be, right? If I did witness it, I don't want to remember it."

Robert's eyes met Jake's, then he looked at Emily and cleared his throat. "You may know more than the identity of the man who killed your brother. The Spokane Police said someone searched your condo."

Emily gasped again. "What were they looking for? What do they think I know?" She put her hand to her chest. "Was I involved in something illegal? Something that would get me killed but got my brother killed instead?"

"No." Jake squeezed her hand. "You are a victim of circumstance."

Robert gave Jake a sharp look—a warning.

Robert's right.

Jake knew next to nothing about Emily, other than he loved the smell and feel of her hair, the taste of her lips, and the feel of her in his arms.

No, there was more than that. Something he couldn't explain but he knew Emily was a good person.

Emily's sudden gasp pulled him from his thoughts. "Maybe I do know something, except I don't know what it is."

Robert looked at her with raised eyebrows.

Emily scooted to the edge of the couch. "Jake, hand me my crutches."

Jake helped her to her feet and handed her the crutches.

"I'll be right back," she said before shuffling down the hall.

Robert rubbed the back of his neck. "Man, that never gets easier."

"I'll bet it's especially hard when it's murder, and it the last living relative." Jake's throat tightened.

"Listen, Jake, you—"

Jake held up a hand to cut him off. "I know what you're going to say. You're right, I don't know much about her, but I know she is good. She would never get mixed up in something illegal. Didn't you see the horror on her face when she thought that's what might have happened?"

"I'm inclined to agree with you, but wait until there are no more mysteries before you get involved with her."

"I know," Jake said in a low growl. Low, because Emily was returning and a growl, because he was afraid it might already be too late.

Robert held his gaze a moment longer. *He knows.* Robert knew Jake was losing the battle to keep himself from falling for Emily.

Emily sat beside Jake again and opened her hand, revealing a key.

"I don't know where this key came from or what it goes to, but it was among my personal belongings when I left the hospital."

Robert took the key and examined it. "In your personal belongings?"

"Yes, the nurse found it..." Emily cleared her throat. "In my bra when she removed my clothing."

"Why was it in... there?" Robert asked.

"I asked myself and the nurse the same question since my clothing had pockets. The only reason I would have put it there... was if I didn't want someone to find it." Emily paused for a moment, then continued, "I don't think it's a car or house key. It might belong to a safety deposit box, but I don't know which bank. There isn't any identification on the key besides that number."

"Do you mind if I hang onto the key and do some checking? Maybe I'll have Ben help me out."

"If that key is the reason... my brother was... killed—" her voice broke. "I don't ever want to see it again."

"I'm sorry, Emily, I know this is hard," Robert said. "But can you tell me what your last memory of your brother was?"

Emily stared at the floor as she spoke. "My only clear memory is when the police brought him to my house after my father died. There are a few other faint and fuzzy memories from my childhood, but that's it."

Silence filled the room for a moment, then Emily asked, "If Cameron was killed the day I was abducted, why am I only now hearing about it?"

Robert looked at Jake, who shook his head. He didn't think Emily could handle any more difficult news today.

Robert rubbed his jaw and hedged, "His body wasn't found until yesterday."

"He laid dead somewhere for a whole week and no one knew? No one even cared?" Emily grew emotional again.

"I hate to admit it, but I think there was some incompetence in Spokane's investigation and a lack of communication within the police department."

"Where was his body found?" She asked.

Robert gave Jake a strained look and cleared his throat.

Emily raised a hand before Robert could speak. "You know what? I don't want to know. I don't want to be able to imagine it."

Robert let out a sigh.

"Cameron's apartment and your condo have both been searched. Police are hoping you can identify what's missing. It might provide a clue to who killed your brother. Do you feel like going to your apartment and taking a look?"

"Tomorrow," Jake said before Emily could speak. Robert and Emily both looked at him. He clasped her hand. "It's getting late in the day, and it will take a while for her to go through both apartments. Besides, she needs some time to process this latest information."

Emily looked down at their hands. She nodded. "I would like a little time. I've been so anxious for my memory to return, but now, I'm not sure I want to remember."

"Do you think you'll feel like going in the morning?" Robert asked. "I'd like to go along if you don't mind. I want to make sure there is no more lack of communication."

Emily nodded, then looked at Jake, her eyes questioning.

He squeezed her hand. "I'm coming too."

He hoped his support would be enough to help her through what she needed to do.

CHAPTER 17

*J*ake stopped his truck in front of Emily's condo. He glanced at her sitting silently beside him, unease twisting his gut. He wished she didn't have to go through this.

A man climbed from a dark sedan on the opposite side of the road. Robert climbed from his Tahoe and met the man in the middle of the street. He'd arranged for the detective working Cameron's case to meet them, hoping Emily would remember something and could give a statement here rather than down at the police station.

When Robert left yesterday, Jake had walked him out and expressed concern about Emily's condo being the crime scene and what she was likely to see. He wasn't sure she could handle seeing evidence of her brother's murder.

Robert had assured him the crime scene had been cleaned by professionals. "They removed a blood-soaked rug. The wood floor beneath it was stained, but they covered it with a different rug. We'll see if she notices."

Emily didn't want to be here. Jake could see it in the slump of her shoulders. Her bruised, red-rimmed, emerald eyes were filled with dark shadows. She'd hardly touched her dinner last night before asking his mom for a sleeping pill and turning in earlier than usual. She'd had little appetite this morning again and had barely said two words on the drive.

Jake's chest tightened. He hoped she could make it through this.

"Does it look familiar?" Jake asked.

Emily's brow wrinkled. "Not particularly."

"I wish you didn't have to do this. But you know this is the best way to catch the people who killed your brother."

She nodded.

"When you're ready, I'll carry you in."

"I don't need you to carry me. I can walk." She reached for the door handle.

Jake climbed out and hurried to her door. He walked patiently beside her up the short walk. When they reached the five steps leading to the wide front porch shared by Emily and her neighbors, Jake wanted to sweep her up in his arms and carry her up. For Emily's pride and because Robert and the detective stood at the top, he followed closely behind instead.

When they reached the porch, Robert introduced Detective McIntyre. The tall, slender detective, who looked to be in his mid-forties, held a key he'd gotten from the neighbors.

"Dr. Anderson," Detective McIntyre said, "Sheriff Winters tells me you have been through a lot. I'll take your statement when you're ready. Do you mind if I record you?" He held up a small recording device. "It's the best way to ensure we get all the information we need."

Emily nodded. "If I don't remember, there won't be much to record."

The detective opened the door to Emily's condo, and the three men stood back to let her enter. Jake tried not to hover, but he stayed as close to Emily as he could without getting in her way. He didn't know where her brother's body had lain, but his eyes fell on the only rug in the front room.

Would it stand out to Emily? If she remembered what happened, how would she react?

Everywhere Jake looked, things were in disarray. Cupboards and drawers hung open, cushions lay scattered across the room, and papers littered the floor near the desk in the corner. Emily wandered through the living room then to the kitchen and back to the living room again.

"Is it familiar?" Robert asked, from his position near the front door.

Her brow furrowed. "A little."

Jake's gaze followed her as she shuffled into a bedroom where clothes lay piled on the floor near a dresser whose drawers all stood open. Someone had been very thorough. Would the state of disarray help or hinder Emily's memory?

Jake remained outside her bedroom but stayed near in case she needed him.

A few minutes later, Emily stepped out of her bedroom and froze. Leaning against her crutches, she pointed at the center of the living room floor. "That rug..." Then she gasped, and her hand flew to her mouth to cover a scream, letting her crutches fall to the floor. "Cameron!"

Jake's heart plummeted. He'd half-hoped she wouldn't remember and have to face that pain. Catching her as she sank to the floor, he lifted her into his arms.

"They killed him!" she screamed hysterically. "He's dead!"

Jake held her close while he waited for Robert to fix the cushions on the couch. Then he sat with her on his lap and held her tight.

Robert sat in a nearby armchair, nodding pointedly at the detective, who sat at the opposite end of the couch from Emily and Jake. He got the hint and started the recording device.

Emily said nothing for quite some time. She simply sobbed uncontrollably in Jake's arms.

His heart ached for her. He wished she could have recovered her memory without having to remember she'd witnessed her brother's brutal murder in her own living room.

As Emily's sobs subsided, Robert got her a glass of water from the kitchen. Emily thanked him and downed it, then handed the glass back to him. She leaned away from Jake's chest and put her hand on the wet spot on his shoulder.

"Robert, my water bearer and Jake, my handkerchief."

Her voice was so small and broken Jake's throat constricted. "It's fine."

His arms tightened as she shifted to move off his lap. He wanted to insist she stay there, but just because he needed to comfort her didn't mean she needed that kind of comfort from him. Relaxing his hold, he helped her shift to sit beside him, keeping an arm around her shoulders.

He pulled the handkerchief from his pocket and handed it to her.

She gave him a weak smile as she accepted it. Then she leaned into him, and something inside of him relaxed.

"Can you tell us what you remembered?" Jake asked.

"They shot him!" Her voice broke again, but no more tears came.

"Who?" Robert asked.

"Two men. One was tall, the other shorter. I didn't see the short one's face, but I think he was the driver of the car, whose picture you showed me, Robert."

"Can you tell us why your brother was in your condo and why those men killed him?" Detective McIntyre asked.

Emily thought for a moment as though trying to put the pieces together in her mind. "Last Friday, Cameron called me at work and insisted I meet him here. He said it was an emergency. He sounded frantic, which concerned me because he was the most level-headed guy I know. I told the secretary to reschedule my afternoon appointments and hurried home." She twisted Jake's handkerchief around the fingers of her casted hand. "I thought I had beat him here because I didn't see his car out front. But when I came into the house, he was already inside."

Emily paused, her brow creasing. "When I asked him what was wrong, he talked really fast, saying he was in serious trouble, and he was afraid he'd brought the trouble to me. He kept pacing back and forth. The blinds were closed, but he kept peeking out the front window. When I asked what kind of trouble, he said the car accident that killed our dad was not an accident." Her voice broke again, and Jake tightened his arm around her shoulders. "I asked him what he meant, and he told me he found a key among Dad's personal belongings that the police gave him after the accident. We were both so distraught, neither of us could deal with any of that for a long time."

"What did the key go to?" asked Detective McIntyre.

"To a safety deposit box where he found a thumb drive."

Robert leaned forward. "Did he say what was on the thumb drive?"

"No, but he said he double-checked and confirmed the files on it. He told me Dad knew his life was in danger. Then he said, 'But they know I know, and they're after me.' Then he apologized again for putting me in danger."

She ran a shaky hand through her hair. "After one of his many times looking out the window, he said, 'They found me.' Then he pulled a key from his pocket and said he'd moved the evidence."

"Did he say where he'd moved it?" Detective McIntyre asked.

"No. And he was so panicked he scared me. He shoved the key into my hand and told me to hide it where no one would find it. Then he pushed me into my bedroom and shoved the screen out of the window. He told me to run and call the police." She paused, her voice growing quieter. "I didn't want to leave him because he was so agitated. Before I made it out of my bedroom though, two men came through the front door. Cameron told them he didn't have the information they wanted anymore."

The tears came again as she continued. "They didn't even give him a chance to explain. They just shot him. There were two loud pops, and then... he fell to the ground."

"They must've had suppressors," Robert said. "You said you heard two shots?"

"Yes," Emily said without hesitation. "Two, close together."

Detective McIntyre confirmed her words. "He was shot once each with a Colt .38 and a 9 mm. Glock."

Judging by Robert's clenched jaw, the information was news to him. Why had the police left that detail out? Was this the kind of miscommunication Robert meant?

"I found the .38 on the driver of the car," Robert said. "That means the driver of the SUV carries a Glock, and Emily saw the men who killed her brother, so now we know why they're after her."

"That, and for whatever evidence the key leads to," Jake added.

"Where is the key?" McIntyre asked.

"In Providence." Robert's voice was tight. "There's no identification on it. It appears to be for a safety deposit box. Emily gave the Sheriff's Office permission to track down the bank. I've got one of my men working on it."

Robert gave Jake a sly look. Ben didn't work for the Sheriff's Office, but Robert trusted Ben more than he did the Spokane Police Department right now. Jake saw it in his brother's eyes.

Robert looked back to Emily. "Did Cameron say which bank?"

Emily's brow wrinkled in concentration. "No, he just said it was the key to where he'd hidden the evidence."

"Did your father have a safety deposit box in any of the local banks?" Jake asked.

"Not that I know of. To my knowledge, he only banked at U.S. Bank."

Robert made a note in his notebook. "I'll make sure Ben checks with them."

"Can you think of anything else that might help us find who killed your brother? Did he mention what was on the thumb drive, or who was after him?" Detective McIntyre asked.

"No, I don't remember anything else," Emily said, rubbing her brow. "I do remember being shocked when he said Dad's death was not an accident. He could have said something right after that I may have missed, because I couldn't believe someone intentionally killed my father and wanted to kill my brother." She laid her head against Jake's shoulder and squeezed her eyes shut.

Jake stroked her hair and shoulder. Robert's eyes bore a hole through him, but he didn't care. Emily needed him. And he needed to comfort her.

He wanted to find the man responsible for her pain and beat him to a pulp, but he didn't know how to do that. He'd leave that to Robert and the police and do the one thing he could right now—comfort Emily.

"What happened after they shot your brother? What did you do?" Robert asked.

"I don't think they realized I was here at first. I felt like I stood there forever, frozen in fear and shock, waiting for Cameron to get up, but it was probably only a few seconds. Then I climbed out the window and ran toward the back alley. They must have heard me." Her voice shook. "One of them followed me out the window and chased after me. Then out of nowhere, the big one stepped in front of me. He hit me, and everything went black." Emily touched the right side of her face that hardly showed any bruising now.

Jake balled his fists. Oh, how he wanted to get his hands on the man who had hurt her.

"Emily, will you tell Detective McIntyre what you remember when you came to in the back of the black SUV?" Robert asked.

Emily repeated everything she'd told Robert and Jake a few days ago.

"The driver of the SUV may be hiding out near the lake located twenty minutes from my brother's ranch. We've cross-checked property holdings around the lake with the license plate and driver of the car, but we've come up empty-handed so far. The black SUV was spotted near the ranch several days ago but hasn't been seen since."

"Dr. Anderson, did you get a good look at either of the gunmen?" the detective asked.

"Not the shorter one, and I only got a glimpse of the taller one, but everything happened so fast. I'm not sure I could give a very accurate description."

"Would you be willing to try?"

Emily shrugged. "I guess."

Robert leaned forward. "Your brother said he double-checked the files on the thumb drive. Any idea what kind of files they were?"

"No clue, but he and my dad both worked for Andertech Solutions. Maybe it was something to do with work."

Robert and Detective McIntyre both made notes in their notebooks, then McIntyre turned off the recording device and suggested she look around her home and determine if anything was missing.

Jake helped Emily to her feet as Robert picked up her crutches near the bedroom door. Emily wandered from room to room. Jake insisted on carrying her upstairs, where she checked the guest bedroom and extra bathroom. They appeared to have hardly been touched.

While she was in her bedroom, Robert lifted the corner of the rug in the center of the living room. Jake's stomach clenched at the sight of the stained hardwood. He didn't want Emily to see the stain, ever.

The only way to get rid of a stain like that would be to sand it out. He checked with the detective to see if he'd be returning the key to the neighbors, explaining that he wanted to arrange to have the floor fixed.

"As far as I can tell," Emily said, walking out of her room. "My laptop and my cell phone are all that's missing."

"Both electronic devices," Robert said. "The gunmen probably thought your brother forwarded whatever was on that jump drive to you. And they took your phone and computer in case there was evidence on them."

"But there wasn't anything, as far as I know."

Detective McIntyre pulled his phone from his pocket. "Until we identify and arrest the second gunman and have the jump drive in hand, you're in danger. I'll arrange to have you taken to a safe house."

Emily shot Jake a look of panic.

Jake took a step toward Emily. "That won't be necessary. She'll be returning to the ranch with us." He looked to Robert for backup.

"That's right. We've got an armed guard posted at the ranch around the clock." It wasn't entirely true, but it would be now they knew the full extent of the danger Emily was in. "We've kept her safe for the past week. We'll continue to do so until we catch whoever is after her."

The detective glanced at Emily with eyebrows raised.

"I'm sure I'll be perfectly safe at the ranch."

McIntyre shrugged. "I hope my captain doesn't give me grief over it. With the accident occurring in your jurisdiction, dumping the girl, er... Dr. Anderson, there I guess that makes her your responsibility."

"I'll talk to your captain," Robert said.

As they prepared to leave, Jake asked Emily if she wanted to pack some clothing. Emily nodded and shuffled to her bedroom. Jake absently listened to Robert and Detective McIntyre discuss the case as he paced her front room.

McIntyre informed them Cameron's vehicle had been located at the park half a block away. Evidently, he'd tried not to lead whoever was after him to his sister.

Jake's eyes went to Emily's open bedroom door for the dozenth time. *Should I check on her?*

No. She needed some space and privacy. With nothing else to do, he continued to pace.

When she finally came out of the bedroom with fresh tears glistening on her cheeks, she carried one small bag. "I don't have many clothes that will fit over my casts, so I guess I'm stuck with these dresses." Her voice was quiet, frail.

Jake stepped in front of her, cupped her face, and wiped her tears away with his thumbs. "You look beautiful in dresses." He lifted the bag from her hands. "Is there anything else you'd like to take with you?"

Emily looked around. She collected the contents of her purse, strewn across the table, then walked over to a bookshelf. She tapped a large book on the bottom shelf with the end of a crutch. "Would you mind grabbing that scrapbook, please?"

Jake retrieved the book, and they headed to the door. When they reached the steps outside, Jake handed the bag and book to Robert so he could carry Emily down the steps.

Emily protested with a scowl, a weak one at that.

Jake climbed into the truck after helping Emily in, but before he could start the engine, Emily asked in a quiet voice, "Did Robert know? That Cameron was killed in my home? Did you know?"

Jake's gut twisted. He didn't want to lie, but he also didn't want to cause her more pain. *Will she feel betrayed that we didn't tell her?*

"I'm sorry, Emily. We weren't sure if we should tell you. We were afraid if you knew, it might hinder your ability to remember."

Emily dropped her eyes to her lap. "You were right not to tell me. If I had known, I probably would have repressed the memories." Then she pressed her hand to her eyes. "I wish I could have gotten my full memory back without having to see what happened to him."

Jake squeezed her shoulder. "I'm so sorry for everything you've been through."

She patted his hand. "Thank you for being here for me." She pulled his hand from her shoulder and lightly touched his scabbed and bruised knuckles. "Why did you punch a wall, Jake?"

Jake's first instinct was to pull away, but he liked her gentle touch, so he left his hand in hers. "I was mad, sad, angry, whatever you want to call it, when I found out your brother was dead."

"You were upset for my sake? So, it *was* because of me..."

"But it wasn't—"

"It wasn't because of our kiss." She looked at him and new tears filled her eyes. "Don't ever think being tender-hearted is a bad thing, Jake. Your compassion is my lifeline right now."

And she was becoming a big part of his.

VINCE SWORE as he watched the dually, king-cab truck from the Double Diamond turn down Dr. Anderson's street. *They've found Anderson's body.*

Not that he needed to follow them here to know that. He'd had his cousin Ralph keeping an eye on the place in case the pretty psychologist or one of her friends showed up. According to Ralph, the good doctor's condo had been crawling with police since late in the afternoon two days ago.

Vince figured it was only a matter of time before Anderson's sister regained her memory. What better place to do that than here in her apartment where she first saw Vince's face?

He drove past the street, not bothering to turn in. He needed to make some quick plans, and he needed his SUV. He couldn't do what needed to be done in Ralph's wimpy little Nissan.

CHAPTER 18

*a*fter a stop at Cameron's apartment, where Emily frequently grew emotional and determined only Cameron's laptop and cell phone were missing, they drove to the police station.

Jake studied Emily's face as she described her brother's killer for the sketch artist. Grief and exhaustion lined her features, and her frustration over not being able to give a better description became evident.

He wanted to tell them she was finished so he could take her home.

Relief filled Jake when they finally came up with a basic sketch. He tried to lead her out of the police station, but she insisted on speaking to Detective McIntyre again.

"I'd like to see my brother."

McIntyre avoided Emily's gaze and scratched his neck. "Um... that's not a good idea."

Robert stepped forward; his face filled with sympathy. "Emily, I know this is difficult, but your brother has been dead for a whole week."

Emily swayed as Robert's meaning hit her. Jake stepped up behind her and put a hand on her shoulder.

She leaned into him.

How much more can she take?

"Ma'am," McIntyre scratched his neck again, "Considering one of the men who killed your brother is still out there, it's not wise to hold a memorial service right now. It'll put you in more danger."

Emily nodded then turned away, her face stoic. "I suppose you're right. I guess I need to make some decisions." With that, she hobbled out the door.

After a quick stop for food, Jake hoped would put some color back into Emily's cheeks, but she only picked at, he took her home. He asked questions about Cameron, thinking it might help to talk about him, but after several monosyllabic responses, he stopped trying. It wasn't long before Emily fell asleep. Or pretended to be asleep.

As Emily's subtle, feminine, strawberry-tinted scent filled the cab of the truck, memories of losing his father flooded Jake's mind. That had been hard to accept because his dad was only fifty-eight. But he'd lived a full life, even if it ended too soon.

Cameron, on the other hand, was three years older than Jake and had his whole life ahead of him. Had he ever married or wanted a family? Had he ever considered he might not get to enjoy all the things he thought he still had plenty of time for?

Jake contemplated his own life. Would he miss out on the most important things in life, like a wife and kids, because his priorities weren't what they should be?

Some things are worth making changes for, aren't they?

After catching sight of a black SUV three cars back, Jake kept a close eye on traffic. Could it be the SUV Robert had been searching for? He continued to watch as it dropped back a few cars.

Anxiety knotted his stomach. They should have waited for Robert to drive back with them. But he'd stayed behind to review Emily's father's file, hoping to go over her father's car.

The knot in Jake's stomach tightened as traffic lightened and the SUV sped closer. Passing two cars, it changed lanes, pulling in behind Jake's truck. He considered speeding up but going any faster would put them at greater risk of an accident. A quick glance at the nonexistent shoulder of the road and the steep drop-off beyond the guardrail ruled out pulling over.

Jake eased off the gas.

The sun glinting off the windshield of the SUV drawing closer in his rear-view mirror, momentarily blinded him. *It's going to ram us!*

The realization squeezed the air from Jake's lungs and drove the temperature in his truck up. He spared a glance at Emily to make sure she was buckled.

The jolt and surge from behind when the SUV hit them rocked them both forward.

"What's going on, Jake?" Alarm filled Emily's voice.

Jake swore and gently pressed the brake, keeping an iron grip on the steering wheel. "I'm afraid our friend in the black SUV found us." He couldn't keep the tension from his voice.

As Emily strained to look out the back window, the SUV hit the left side of Jake's rear bumper, pushing them toward the guardrail that didn't look strong enough a keep a V.W. bug on the road, let alone a one-ton pick-up. The truck swerved as he struggled to maintain control.

Again, Jake tapped his brakes. They pulled, then suddenly the pedal released and sunk to the floor. Trying again, he pumped the brakes. Nothing.

No. No. No. This isn't happening.

"What's the matter with your brakes?" Panic laced Emily's words.

Clenching his teeth so hard his jaw ached, Jake didn't bother to respond. Hearing the truth—his brakes were useless—wouldn't make Emily feel any better.

Jake's pulse kicked into overdrive. Had the driver of the SUV cut his brake line? Maybe while they were eating? But that didn't make sense. His brakes had been fine until now. Jake glanced at the ravine beside them again. This whole thing had been carefully orchestrated.

Jake cursed under his breath again. He should have realized bringing Emily out in the open would make her a target. He'd been so worried about her regaining her memory and comforting her he'd forgotten to be vigilant.

The SUV rammed them again and Jake pulled at the wheel with a white-knuckled grip, his sweaty palms making the steering wheel slippery. Checking his mirrors, he surveyed the surrounding traffic. Thankfully, the other vehicles had dropped back to avoid the lunatic behind them. Jake kept his truck in the center of the two-lane highway to prevent the SUV from coming up on his left and forcing him off the road.

"Jake!" Emily's voice bordered on hysterics.

"It'll be okay, Em. I won't let anything happen to you."

Jake hoped he could keep his promise. He remembered the handgun he'd stashed in the glove compartment. Would he need to use it to keep Emily safe?

He shifted to a lower gear, grimacing at the groan of the engine. It wasn't good for his transmission, but it was the best way to slow his truck enough to safely use the emergency brake.

Another powerful shove caused his truck to swerve, and his chest to tighten. He pulled his truck back to the center of the road. It's a good thing he drove such a big vehicle. If he'd been driving anything smaller, the SUV would have pushed him off the road by now.

Jake again shifted down a gear, his engine grinding in protest. Then he slowly pushed in his emergency brake, knowing that pressing it too fast would stop them too suddenly. That's the last thing he wanted with the SUV bearing down on them.

The SUV struck again. A loud pop punctuated the scrape of metal. Jake's truck pulled to the left. *Great! A blown tire.* Checking the shoulder of the road, Jake heaved a sigh of relief. They were past the ravine.

He pulled the coasting truck to the edge of the road, knowing they'd be sitting ducks. Unbuckling, he grabbed the handgun he'd stashed in the glove box that morning. Ignoring Emily's gasp, he checked to make sure it was loaded and slid the safety off.

Lowering his window, he made sure the gun was in full view as the SUV came to a stop beside them. Jake wanted their stalker to know he meant business.

I won't let anything happen to Emily.

The beefy, dark-haired driver's murderous eyes widened in shock before he lowered his own gun and sped away.

The breath Jake hadn't realized he'd been holding came out in a sudden rush. He'd never shot at another human being before, but he would have if it meant keeping Emily safe. Glad he hadn't been forced to make that decision today, he slid the safety on and tucked the gun under his seat.

Emily's quiet sobs brought his head up. "That was him, Jake. He killed Cameron."

Jake lifted the center console and pulled her into his arms.

"And that ravine back there is where my father died."

And where we nearly died.

CHAPTER 19

*J*ake shifted in the lazy boy, crossing one ankle over the opposite knee. His gaze drifted to the clock again.

It had been almost three hours since they'd returned to the ranch, and Emily had asked his mother for a pain pill. There wasn't a pill strong enough to dull the pain she felt, but the pills tended to make her sleep. And she needed the rest.

But Jake couldn't help but wonder whether she was actually sleeping. Or did she simply want to be alone with her grief?

After getting Emily settled in bed, his mother had flitted around the house, cleaning things that were already clean. Her nervous energy confirmed she was as concerned about Emily as he was. That's why, after checking in with Zane, he'd stayed in the house.

In case Emily needs me.

She needed so much more than the shoulder he could offer, but he was powerless to do anything more. The one thing he'd accomplished this afternoon was a series of phone calls to arrange to have Emily's floor sanded and refinished.

Hearing her bedroom door open and the familiar bump and thump of her cast and crutches, he jumped to his feet and met her in the hallway, eager to help her in any way he could.

Her red swollen eyes were so full of pain, his heart broke for her.

"Can I make a phone call in your office?"

He had to strain to hear her quiet voice.

"Absolutely." He opened the office door for her.

She closed the door behind her, but it didn't latch tight.

Jake stood close to the door until she was safely settled in his office chair. As he turned away, he heard her choked voice. "Joe, they killed him! Cameron is dead!"

Jake stepped away from the door. *Joe?* Did she remember she had a boyfriend after everything came back to her? A burning sensation filled his chest. Emily must have a close relationship with Joe for him to be the first one she contacted.

He returned to the great room and picked up the paperback western he'd been looking at for the last three hours—looking at, but not reading. For the life of him, he couldn't concentrate enough on the words to make sense of them. He threw the book across the room in disgust.

One thing occupied his mind. A beautiful, grieving woman, who sat in his office pouring her heart out to another man.

A short knock on the front door followed by his cousin Ben walking in drew his attention. Relief swept over Jake, and he welcomed the distraction. Despite being a lawyer, Ben was an excellent mechanic.

"Hey, Jake." Ben gave Jake a quick bear hug. "I'm glad you're okay. How's Emily doing?"

"She's having a hard time."

"I'll bet. What happened to your truck?"

"I'm not sure. One minute my brakes worked fine and the next they didn't. I thought the driver of the SUV must have cut my brake lines while we were eating lunch. But when Robert and the police arrived, I checked them, and they looked fine as far as I could see. I can't figure out why they failed."

"Should we go take a look?"

Jake looked toward his office. He didn't want Emily to be alone when she came out, but he needed to get out of this house.

"Yeah, go on out. I need to change my clothes and talk to my mom."

By the time Jake joined Ben in the equipment shed, where he'd had the tow truck leave his truck, Ben already had the hood of his truck up and one tire off.

"I need more light here, Jake," Ben called from under the truck.

Jake ran an extension cord and plugged in a work light.

"Well, I'll be..." Ben said after a few moments.

"What did you find?"

Ben slid out from under the truck. "I took the brake line off, and after wiggling it, I managed to bleed brake fluid through it. Apparently, there was an air pocket blocking the flow of fluid. That's what caused the brakes to fail."

"How did I get an air pocket in my brake line?"

"After you brought the light over, I found a pinhole in the tubing. It looks like someone pierced the tubing and forced air into the line, so your brakes would fail when the flow of fluid stopped."

Jake's jaw dropped. "Who would know how to do something like that?"

"A professional." Ben's grim expression caused a chill to sweep over Jake.

"You think the guy that killed Emily's brother, and is now after her, is a professional hit man versus someone who doesn't want whatever Cameron knew to get out?"

"Think about it." Ben stood up. "Robert hasn't found any information on the driver of the car that wrecked. They searched Emily's place and her brother's. The driver of the SUV calculated his attack today at a specific, potentially lethal time. Any amateur worried about incriminating evidence getting out wouldn't have been so calculated, he would have been desperate and sloppy."

Jake pushed off his hat and scratched his head. "You're right."

Ben leaned back against the truck, folded his arms across his chest, and studied Jake.

"Robert said you insisted on bringing Emily back to the ranch when the detective suggested taking her to a safe house."

"Of course, I did. I mean, it took the police department a whole week to find Emily's brother. Robert wasn't particularly confident about the department's skills, and neither was I."

"In their defense, they were simply filling a request to locate the next of kin from our Sheriff's department. They didn't know they had a homicide on their hands."

Jake squirmed. Ben was right, and Jake knew better than to argue with a lawyer.

"Is your lack of confidence in the Spokane Police Department the only reason you insisted on bringing Emily back here?" Ben stared at him, eyes narrowed, and Jake fidgeted. Ben was the most perceptive person Jake knew. He had a way of looking at you, like he could see right into your soul.

He hated when Ben looked at him like that.

"The woman has lost her entire family." Jake's words came out more forceful than he'd intended, but he continued anyway. "I wasn't about to let her go to who-knows-where to be guarded by strangers. I know she hasn't known us long, but I'm sure she'll be more comfortable here. Besides, she's helping Daniel with his problems. He needs her here."

"And it's much easier for you to keep an eye on her if she's here at the ranch."

"Exactly," Jake agreed.

Ben smiled, and Jake realized he'd walked right into Ben's trap.

"Are you sure Daniel is the only one who needs her here?"

Jake scowled at Ben.

"It's amazing how fast a pretty woman can get to you, huh?"

"She's totally gotten under my skin," Jake admitted with a sigh, slumping back against the truck. No use keeping up the pretense with Ben when he could see right through Jake. "Like an itch I have to scratch."

Ben nodded. "Like a mosquito bite. You know you shouldn't scratch it, but it feels so good when you do."

"I'm getting in over my head, aren't I?" Jake asked, scratching the back of his neck.

Ben smiled. "Is that a bad thing? Head over heels, that's a fun place to be."

"Spoken like a true newlywed. Is this how you felt with Amy?"

Ben rubbed absently at his chest. "Something happened to me the first time I saw Amy. It's hard to describe. It wasn't necessarily a physical attraction, although I did find her attractive. It was more like she poked a hole in the clouds that had darkened my life for so long and allowed the sunlight to break through. I didn't realize she was getting under my skin, until she was so deep, I knew I couldn't go on if I lost her."

Jake wasn't sure he could bear to lose Emily.

"I can't deny I'm attracted to Emily, and not just physically. I mean, when I see her hurting, which has happened a lot, I want to take her pain away."

Ben shoved his hands into his pockets. "Take it from someone who knows great loss, there's nothing you can do to take her pain away. But you can help her endure it. If she'll let you."

"I want to help her anyway I can."

"That's always been your nature, Jake. And you're good at it."

"But I'm afraid I'm getting in too deep."

"By 'in too deep,' I assume you mean falling in love with her? Why are you *afraid* of falling in love?"

"I'm too busy for a relationship. I'm running one of the largest ranches in the state. I don't have time for a wife or kids. It wouldn't be fair to any woman to saddle her with this." He waved his arm in a wide-sweeping circle. Despite his talk with his mother two nights ago, he still had doubts he could make a woman happy and continue ranching.

Would Emily leave as soon as her brother's killer was caught? If she felt as strongly about him as he did her, would she ask him to give up his ranch? He didn't want to be forced to choose again.

Lydia's words echoed in his head. *"You're always working. You never have time for me. I don't want what's left of you after you're done with the cows and the horses. I won't play second fiddle to animals."*

Ben chuckled, pulling Jake out of his musings. "Believe me, when you get a wife, you'll find it's easier to make time for her than you think." When Jake rolled his eyes at Ben, he continued talking. "I hate to break it to you, but you don't run one of the largest ranches in the state." Jake was about to argue with him, but Ben rushed on. "Zane does. And he's doing a mighty fine job. You simply own the ranch. You can do that and have a family. From what Robert tells me, you've been around plenty in the past week while Emily has been recuperating."

"I had to hire another man to make sure I wasn't dumping too much on Zane by my stepping back a little."

"So? You can afford it, can't you? Let me tell you, spending your time with a woman is much more enjoyable than spending it with cows or money."

"Of course, I can afford it, but that's not the point."

"What is the point?"

"It drives me crazy to hang around the house, doing so little. I couldn't do this forever."

"Are you sure it's the inactivity that's driving you crazy and not a certain someone?" Ben eyed him knowingly.

Jake chose not to answer. Ben was right. When he was away from Emily, working, he thought about her constantly. He was also right that as long as Zane was around, the ranch would function fine without him.

Maybe he shouldn't fight his attraction for Emily so hard. He didn't want to miss out on loving a woman—Emily—because he wasn't willing to take a chance. Maybe he needed to alter his priorities.

Despite his desire to be out working hard all day, spending time with Emily brought a different kind of fulfillment. Warmth crept through him as he remembered the feel of her silky soft tresses slipping through his fingers and the taste of lemonade and strawberries on her lips.

Then he remembered Emily called someone named Joe, and his spirits dampened.

Time to change the subject.

"So, you think it's a professional that's after Emily?"

"I do. And you insisting she come back here concerns me."

"Why? We're keeping a guard posted."

"The fact that he already knows where she is, puts her, as well as everyone else on this ranch, in danger. There are a lot more ways to the ranch house than by the front gate."

"You think I made the wrong choice by bringing her back here?" Jake would never forgive himself if he failed Emily or the rest of his family.

"I think you made the choice Emily needed you to make. There's nothing wrong with that, but you need to be vigilant."

Jake's stomach bottomed out. *What have I done?*

JAKE TURNED off the television and tossed the remote on the couch. It was almost eleven, and everyone had gone to bed some time ago. He doubted he'd sleep, since he'd done no physical activity today, but it was time to turn in. All he'd done today was worry about Emily.

When he'd come into the house after working on his truck with Ben, the others were finishing dinner. It didn't look like Emily had eaten much, again. Shortly after dinner, she expressed a desire to go to bed, asking his mom for a sleeping pill.

It would take her a long time to come to terms with her loss, but he hoped she could indeed deal with it. He remembered how long it had taken Ben to accept the loss of his wife and daughter. Ben shut everybody out for months.

Would Emily do the same thing? She had no family, but she had friends. Would she let them help her through her grief? *Will she let me help her?*

Duke, the Australian shepherd, who slept on the back porch, barked, followed by Ace, the border collie who slept on the front porch. The hair on Jake's neck stood up. The dogs only barked when a stranger came around.

Jake pulled a shotgun and a handful of shells from the gun safe in his office. He loaded the gun on his way out the back door. He stepped out on the patio, scanning the yard. By the light of the full moon, he spotted Duke at the side yard, near the stables.

Staying in the shadows against the house, he worked his way toward them. Both dogs barked at the trees that lined the far side of the lane, where it curved toward Zane and Lottie's house and the bunkhouse.

Jake shushed the dogs and listened for any sign that someone was out there. The faint snap of a twig set the dogs barking again. They inched closer to the trees.

"Go get it," Jake commanded.

Both dogs took off into the trees. Though not trained attack dogs, they were good with cattle and knew when Jake said "go get it" they were to drive whatever he sent them after back toward him.

Jake waited for the dogs to return, which they did, but not before Jake heard an engine start near the highway. The black SUV, no doubt.

Ben was right. *I've put everyone in danger.*

Jake worked his way around the house and back to the patio. Both dogs returned to their spots on their respective doorsteps. The threat must be gone.

His mother opened the back door as he stepped up on the back deck. "What's going on, Jake?"

Jake's heart jumped into his throat.

"Geez, Mom. You scared me to death. You shouldn't startle someone carrying a loaded gun."

"And why are you carrying a loaded gun around in the dark?"

Jake didn't want to worry her by telling her they'd had a prowler, but he'd never been good at lying, especially to his mom.

"There was someone out there, wasn't there?" She saved him the trouble of having to come up with a convincing lie.

"Yeah. The dogs scared him away. I heard an engine starting up out by the highway."

"Oh dear. You'd better call Robert and get me a gun."

"I'm not giving you a gun, Mom."

"Why not? I'm perfectly competent with guns, you know that."

"It's too dangerous. You are not standing guard with a gun. This guy is a murderer."

"Well, at least let me take a gun to my room so I'll be able to sleep tonight. If I have one in my room and you have one in your room, and Emily is between us, then we can keep her safe."

"I'm not taking a gun to my room."

"Well, whether you do or not, I am."

"Mom, you don't need to take a gun to bed with you. I'll stand guard."

His mom stepped so close Jake looked down his nose at her. "You can't stand guard all night. You won't be any good for Emily tomorrow."

Am I that transparent?

His mother said the one thing she knew would make Jake change his mind. He needed to be there in case Emily needed him. Not just for her, but for himself.

"Fine." He sighed as he put the safety on the shotgun and handed it to her. He pulled out his phone as he walked into his office to get another rifle.

When Robert arrived fifteen minutes later, he was glad his mother had returned to her room. He didn't need a lecture from his older brother about letting their mother take a gun to bed.

Jake explained to Robert about the dogs barking and hearing an engine start. He also told him about what he and Ben had discussed. Not the part about Emily getting under his skin. He was sure Robert already knew that.

"Yeah, Ben called me," Robert said. "I hate to say it, but I agree with him. It worries me because we don't know to what lengths this guy will go and what or who he might consider acceptable collateral damage."

"You think I should have let Detective McIntyre take her to the safe house?"

"No way," Robert said. "Guys like this know how to take out their targets, even in safe houses. We'll keep her safe here. I doubt he'll come back tonight. But we need to take extra precautions. We'll work out a schedule with Zane in the morning for your ranch hands to provide 'round-the-clock guard. My deputies will patrol this stretch of highway regularly too. Now, find me a blanket and pillow."

"You don't have to stay here. I'll stand guard tonight."

"No way. I need you alert tomorrow, and Emily will need you."

Jake looked away from Robert's knowing gaze. *Apparently, I am that transparent.*

"I know you haven't known each other that long, but she trusts you, Jake. She needs someone she can count on right now, and I think she'd like that person to be you."

"You think so?"

"Yeah, and I'm pretty sure you want to be that person." Robert gave him a sly smile. "You know these homeless kittens need a lot of TLC."

"She's not homeless," Jake growled, doubling his fists.

"I'm kidding, bro," Robert said, taking a step backward. "Don't wake up Mom, she'll put us to work."

"She's awake. Or she was." Jake rubbed the back of his neck. "She took a shotgun to bed with her."

"You let Mom take a gun to bed?" Robert said, voice raised.

"I'd like to see *you* tell her no!"

"Hmm... good point."

"Emily's in your old room. You can sleep in my bed or Riley's. You don't have to sleep on the couch."

"I'll be more alert out here."

Jake got a pillow and blanket out of the hall closet and tossed them at his brother, then after strapping on a handgun, he picked up his rifle and headed toward the back door.

"Where are you going?" Robert asked before he made it out.

Jake stopped with his hand on the doorknob. "It's a full moon."

Robert would understand the draw for Jake to take a ride in the light of the full moon. He'd done it often as a teenager when he couldn't sleep. Long rides in the moonlight and his mother's hot cocoa. That's how he'd learned to cope with his energy and anxieties.

"It's been a long day. I need some fresh air."

Robert would also know Jake wouldn't sleep a wink until he knew that whoever had been out there was indeed gone.

"Well, give our old knock before you come back in so I don't shoot you," Robert said as he pulled off his boots.

Jake went to the stables and saddled Thor, who seemed to have missed him as much as he'd missed riding the past few days.

As he and Thor set off at a gallop toward the front fence line, Jake let out a deep sigh. This was exactly what he needed.

After following the fence line for a mile, Jake turned Thor in the direction of an open meadow, where he could let him run. He still needed to release some tension.

As he rode, Emily weighed heavily on his mind. He marveled at the depth of his feelings for her. He'd known her such a short time, but the thought of losing her made it hard to breathe.

Would he be able to be everything Emily needed him to be? Would she let him be there for her?

He sent a silent prayer heavenward for Emily, then he sent another one for himself.

CHAPTER 20

"*L*ila Cooper called 911 yesterday requesting help to get into her car." Robert sat at the breakfast table entertaining Emily, Faith, and Lottie. "She claimed she'd locked her keys in her car. When Brady arrived to jimmy her car door, he realized the car she wanted to get into wasn't hers. It was the same color, but that was all. It was an entirely different make and model. She got so mad at Brady for refusing to help her she hit him over the head with her purse."

Faith and Lottie burst out laughing. Emily smiled, unable to help herself.

"I don't know why her kids haven't taken her license away," Faith said. "She's the scariest driver on the roads,"

"She can hardly see over the dash," Lottie added.

Robert gave his mom a stern look. "Some moms are stubborn and don't take 'no' for an answer."

Faith pointed her finger at him. "Robert Blake Winters don't you dare sass me. I can handle a gun better blindfolded than senile Lila Cooper can drive a car."

Emily smiled again as Robert's ears turned red, and he ducked his head. She'd heard enough whispers among Lottie, Faith, and Robert this morning to know Robert had spent the night here because there had been a late-night prowler.

And though the news, on top of her brother's death, made her already heavy heart heavier, Emily loved the life and energy in the house this morning. She needed distraction and entertainment.

Then it dawned on her, she would never share breakfast with Cameron again, like she'd done almost every Saturday since their dad's death. She would never again experience the joy and fun of family. Tears filled her eyes, and she lowered her chin to blink them away. She couldn't believe she could still cry after all the tears she'd shed yesterday.

Her gaze drifted to the mudroom door as Jake and Daniel came in. They were both very sweaty and looked especially buff this morning. Jake wore a plain gray t-shirt that hugged his torso and loose basketball shorts. Besides jeans, Emily had only ever seen Jake in a pair of dress slacks.

The man looked good, no matter what he wore. Sweat and all.

Jake paused on his way to the sink and made eye contact with her. She looked away, embarrassed that he'd caught her staring at his shoulders, again. Her stomach rolled. She'd eaten little, but what she had eaten threatened to come up. How could she admire a man moments after lamenting that she'd never see her brother again?

I'm the worst sister ever.

Thoughts of turning to Trent, her brother's best friend, for comfort after her father's death, and where that had led, filled her mind. There were some things she wished she hadn't remembered.

One after another, Faith, Lottie, and Robert all stood and took their empty plates to the sink. After washing up, Daniel sat at the bar where Robert engaged him in conversation, and Jake sat across from Emily.

She studied her uneaten food. With her emotions so raw, she felt exposed.

Her face warmed as she remembered the tears she cried in Jake's arms yesterday. She should feel embarrassed, but mostly she felt grateful. Having him close had been so comforting, but had she taken advantage of his compassion?

"Emily."

Jake's voice was soft, like a caress. He may as well have reached out and stroked her cheek.

She met his eyes, so full of tenderness. It was almost her undoing. She wanted him to wrap her in his arms and hold her until she didn't hurt anymore. Tell her it would all be okay. She had to look away again.

"How can I help you make it through this day?"

Emily caught her breath.

Wow. Where had Jake learned such empathy? Faith was kind and compassionate, but there was something about Jake that made him... special.

Emily closed her eyes and took several deep breaths, trying to quell the emotions that pummeled her. Attraction. Loneliness. Grief. Pain. Fear.

It was all too much. She'd been through this before, and she didn't think she could do it again.

"I assume you've recovered your full memory?" When she nodded, he said, "You probably have a list of people you need to call. Would you like some help?"

She would love to hand him a list of names and let him shoulder that burden, but she couldn't do that. No. This was something she needed to do herself, for Cameron.

"Or maybe some moral support?" Jake added when she didn't answer.

"Thank you, Jake. That's very kind of you."

"You're welcome to use my office." Jake squeezed her hand that lay on the table. "I'm here, Em. Anything you need... I'm here for you."

Emily nodded. She didn't dare speak for fear she would start crying again.

Anything I need? Emily had to bite her tongue to keep from saying she needed him.

~

DANIEL WAITED PATIENTLY for Emily to settle into the chaise lounge on the front porch before taking his seat again. "I'm sorry about your brother, Emily."

"Thank you. How are you doing today? You looked good after your workout with Jake this morning."

After breakfast, Emily had taken her time showering, trying to delay the inevitable. She'd been about to enter Jake's office when she realized Daniel stood guard on the front porch. Dreading the phone calls, she decided to postpone them a little longer and join Daniel. She didn't talk to him at all yesterday.

Daniel shrugged, but Emily could see the tension in his shoulders. "It's rough but getting a little easier each day. I know you're going through a lot. Don't feel like you need to talk with me."

"I need to talk with someone and do something. When I'm alone, I think too much about what I've lost... about what I've seen."

"Death is hard to unsee, isn't it?" Daniel's voice was quiet.

Emily caught the tone of his voice and knew Daniel had seen someone die. Was it a violent death, like her brother's? Someone close to him? Was that why he started drinking?

"It is hard." She wracked her brain for the right words to say in this moment. Could she get him to talk to her? "How did it make you feel when you experienced death?" She held her breath.

Daniel was quiet for so long, Emily wondered if he would answer, or if she would have to try another tactic.

"Guilty."

Guilty? That was not what she expected. "Will you tell me why?"

Daniel's eyes remained fixed on a horse in the pasture. He shifted in his seat before answering. "Because I killed a kid."

Shocked, Emily fought the urge to gasp. She wasn't supposed to react emotionally or pass judgment on the things her patients told her. "I'm sure you didn't do it on purpose. Will you tell me what happened?"

Daniel chewed on his fingernail before speaking. "I was living in

Portland last fall. Finishing up my degree and starting an internship at an architectural firm. But I missed the ranch... and Riley. One day, I saw an advertisement for a motorbike for sale. It reminded me of the ranch, and I decided to buy it." He propped his elbows on his knees and hung his head.

Emily leaned forward, straining to hear him.

"When I drove through the subdivision looking for the seller's house... this teenage driver came barreling out of his driveway right at me. He didn't even look where he was going. I swerved to miss him then looked over my shoulder to make sure he didn't hit me." Daniel plunged both hands into his hair. "I didn't see the little boy riding his bike down his driveway... right into the street... in front of me."

Emily bit her tongue to keep from assuring him it wasn't his fault. It's not that she couldn't be compassionate and professional at the same time. She just wasn't sure she could do it without getting emotional.

Besides, Daniel didn't need to hear it wasn't his fault. He needed someone to validate the guilt he felt and his struggle to deal with it.

"What happened to the little boy?" she asked, although, she was sure she already knew.

"He lay there... unmoving, with his eyes closed. He looked like he was sleeping." Daniel's voice shook as he continued. "I called 911... then waited for what felt like an eternity for the ambulance to show up... I can still hear his mother's screams." He buried his face in his hands.

"I'll bet that was difficult." She squeezed her eyes closed, remembering how she'd waited for her brother to get up.

"I didn't even run over him." Anguish filled his voice. "I stopped... but not in time. I knocked him off his bike, causing his head to hit the road... so hard..." Daniel swiped tears from his eyes. "There wasn't even any blood... but he never opened his eyes. After I finished talking to the police, I went to the hospital... I had to know if he would be okay. I tried to keep my distance from his parents... but I saw his mother... when the doctor came to talk to them—" Daniel's voice broke, and his Adam's apple bobbed repeatedly.

Emily reached over and put her hand on his knee. He looked up at her. She let him see the tears flowing down her own face.

Encouraged, he continued, "She just sank to the floor."

"You've carried such a heavy burden, Daniel. Who did you tell? Who did you talk to?"

"I told my parents what happened, and they came to visit me for a few days, so Jake knows. But other than that, I never told anyone. I couldn't because it meant reliving it. Besides, my roommate wasn't exactly the sensitive type. He could see I struggled with it though. He's the one who persuaded me to drown my guilt in Jack Daniels." He gave a pained smirk before burying his face in his hands again. "I hated it. I hated the taste and how guilty I felt for turning my back on the way I was raised. But I liked how numb it made me, so I didn't feel the guilt over killing that kid."

Emily had no desire for alcohol, but she would love to feel numb for a while. *Focus on Daniel's problems, not your own.*

"Do you feel the accident was your fault?"

Daniel was quiet for a long time before speaking. "I wasn't even going that fast, and I would have been able to stop... or at least avoid hitting him... if I hadn't swerved to miss the other car." He paused for a moment, then continued, "But it never would've happened if I hadn't gone to buy that motorcycle."

"Maybe not. But it did happen. It's how we deal with life's challenges that defines who we are." Emily tried not to dwell on what that meant for her.

Daniel gave a sad smile. "I turned to alcohol. What does that say about me?" He continued before Emily could say anything. "And I bought the motorcycle anyway. I think I did it to punish myself. I rode it all the time and was rather reckless."

"Were you hoping to get in an accident? Did you think if you injured or killed yourself, you'd be getting what you deserved?"

He shrugged. "I don't know. Maybe. To tell you the truth, I didn't think clearly about much of anything. I kept drinking because I liked how it masked the pain."

"Did you drink because you wanted to? Or because you had to?"

When Daniel didn't respond, she went on. "You know your family's history will make your fight to stay sober much harder, don't you?"

Daniel hung his head and nodded.

"What could you have done differently to help you cope with your struggles?"

He shot to his feet, grabbing the railing for support. "It doesn't matter. I made the wrong choice, and I'll pay for it for the rest of my life."

"Recovery from an addiction is not a single event, Daniel. It's a process. In your case, a life-long process. But recovery is possible."

"Maybe, but I've got a record now." He sunk, defeated back into his chair. "That's not something that will go away."

"Why do have a record?"

Daniel took his time answering. "I was drunk when I... wrecked my bike and broke my leg."

"Was anyone else injured in the accident?" Emily asked, fearing the answer.

"Not seriously, no. But their car was totaled. Jake covered what the insurance didn't to replace their car so there wouldn't be a lawsuit. But I go to court in two weeks, for the drunk driving offense. Ben has agreed to represent me, but I can hardly look him in the eye."

"Why? If Robert and Jake are like brothers to you, I would think Ben would be like a cousin."

"Because, Ben's first wife was killed by a drunk driver," he groaned.

"I see. I understand why you would feel uncomfortable about that. Are you afraid Ben won't give you a fair representation?"

"No, it's not that. I plan on pleading guilty to all the charges. I feel bad, you know. That I turned out like the guy that killed Ben's wife."

"I don't know anything about the man responsible for Ben's wife's death, but do you want to know what I think?" When Daniel looked at her, she continued. "I see a young man who has been through something difficult and made some poor decisions. But I see your remorse, and I've seen you work hard over the past few days to overcome your problems. You're surrounded by people who care about you and will help you succeed. You can do this, Daniel."

He lowered his gaze.

"Think about it. How hard must it be for Ben to agree to help you? He's doing it because he cares about you, and he sees a young man who is worth the effort. Like Jake does, and so do I."

Emily twisted a lock of hair. *I hope I'm strong enough to help you through this.*

CHAPTER 21

*E*xhaustion consumed Emily by the time she shuffled back into the house. She wanted to crawl into bed and hide away from everyone and everything, but she needed to make some phone calls. Dreading the task, she headed toward Jake's office.

Before she made it there, Jake walked in the back door. He gave her a tender smile and stepped close.

"Is there anything I can do for you, Emily?"

His voice, so tender, was almost her undoing, again. Would it ever get easier? After her father died, her grief had been horrible, but she'd had Cameron. And Trent.

She didn't want to think about Trent right now. But she had to. He needed to be told about Cameron's death.

"Does that offer of moral support still stand?" Maybe if she had a handsome rancher nearby, distracting her, she wouldn't get so emotional talking to Cameron's friends.

Not likely.

"Absolutely. I take it you haven't made your phone calls yet?"

"No, I've been talking to Daniel. We had a good talk." She turned toward Jake's office. "As much as I would like to, I can't let myself get sidetracked again."

Jake followed her into his office and closed the door. "Would you like to sit on the couch? It might be more comfortable."

It wasn't a couch, it was a love seat, but there was no need to make it sound so intimate. "Yes, but I need your laptop to look up some numbers since I don't have Cameron's contacts."

Jake grabbed the phone and his laptop and sat beside Emily.

She pulled the computer onto her lap and searched for the numbers she needed. Once she found the first number, she took a deep breath and mumbled, "I'll do the easiest one first."

She called Cameron's landlord. She didn't tell him her brother had been murdered, only that he'd died unexpectedly. He expressed his surprise and condolences and assured her that Cameron's lease was paid until the end of the month. That gave Emily two and a half weeks to clean his apartment out.

When that phone call ended, she debated who to call next. She had two more people she absolutely needed to call. Neither of which she wanted to talk to. Three, if she counted Trent. But she was hoping she could get Kiera to notify Trent. She found the next number, closed her eyes, and took a deep breath before she punched it in.

"Mr. Garrison's office, please," she said, when the receptionist answered.

"May I ask who's calling?" the receptionist asked.

"Emily Anderson."

"Hi, Emily, how are you doing?"

Emily sucked in a sharp breath. "I'm fine Gloria, thanks for asking. Is Maxwell available?" Emily had never cared for Gloria, or Max for that matter. But her father's close association with them forced her to see them regularly.

She closed her eyes and took another deep breath. Thinking about her father made this harder.

"Emily," Max's booming voice came over the phone. "How are you sweetheart? I haven't seen you in forever." Before Emily could respond, he continued. "Have you seen Cameron? He hasn't come into work for a week. I know he prefers working from home, but we haven't had any communication from him. Which is not like him. And his phone goes straight to voice mail."

"Cameron's dead, Max." Emily's voice broke. Would she ever be able to say those words without the stabbing pain accompanying them?

"Oh no," came the still too loud, sympathetic voice. "How? What happened?"

"He was murdered—" Those words were even harder to say.

Jake slipped a comforting arm around her shoulders, and she leaned into him, drawing strength from him.

"Oh, Emily, I'm so sorry. Cameron was such a good kid. I can't believe someone would want to hurt him. Was it a mugging or something?"

"No. Two men shot him in my house."

"In your house? Did you two get messed up in something illegal?"

Heat rushed through Emily's veins. "No, of course not." Why had Max jumped to that conclusion?

"Sorry," Max's voice sounded contrite. "This is such a shock. I don't understand how or why this happened."

"Me either," she lied. She'd never really liked Max, but today in her heightened emotional state, she found him especially irritating.

"I can't imagine how difficult this must be for you, Emily. You shouldn't be alone right now. Why don't you come stay with Denise and I?"

"That's very kind of you, but I'm not alone. I'm staying with... friends." Jake squeezed her shoulder, and once again, she was grateful for his comforting touch. "I'd appreciate it if you would let the co-workers he was closest to know. And have someone clean out his office and send his things to my home address."

"Of course, of course. Do you know when the funeral will be?" His voice finally quieted.

"The police won't release his body, while the investigation is still open."

Why did she feel the need to lie to Max? Was she trying to avoid the concern she knew he and Denise would shower on her if they knew she was in danger? She doubted they could protect her any better than Jake and Robert.

"Do they have any idea who shot him?" Max's booming voice asked, full of concern.

"No."

"That's too bad. Listen, honey, I know this is a difficult time for you, and I want you to know there's no rush. But you need to consider what you want to do with your father's half of the company. Do you want to continue to keep it as residual income like you and Cameron were doing, or are you interested in selling out to me?"

"I'm not sure I can think about that right now. I'd like to keep it as is for the time being. I may have a lawyer contact you sometime in the future to discuss it. I don't think I can deal with it." Tears clogged her throat again.

"I understand. Take care of yourself and let me know if there's anything Denise and I can do for you."

"Thank you." Emily hung up the phone and, once again, closed her eyes and took several deep breaths to calm her emotions.

"Why did you lie to him? It sounded like he was more than your brother's boss."

"He is... was. I don't know why, but I've never really cared for the man. He rubs me the wrong way, and I always feel so tense after talking to him." She rolled her shoulders.

"I'll be right back." Jake stood and walked out of the office. He returned less than a minute later, carrying her hairbrush.

A smile crept to her face. Jake was the sweetest man in the world.

"This love seat is not big enough for you to lie down, but if you want to move to the office chair, I'll brush your hair to help you relax, and you can tell me why you don't like him."

This man was quickly claiming a large piece of her heart.

183

JAKE SHIFTED the laptop back to the desk and helped Emily to her feet. Once she'd settle in his chair, he took out the braid from her still damp hair.

Emily sighed and relaxed almost immediately as he brushed.

Jake inhaled the tantalizing strawberry scent. He would always and forever think of Emily any time he smelled strawberries.

"Your hair smells so good." A blush heated his neck when he realized he'd spoken aloud. Thank goodness she couldn't see his face.

"Like strawberries. I like the scent too."

Jake doubted she liked it for the same reasons he did. Surely, the scent didn't create the same powerful attraction in her as it did in him.

He cleared his throat. "So, tell me about Maxwell. What, besides his loud voice, rubs you the wrong way?"

"You noticed, huh? He's always been that way. Too loud. Too flashy. Too... fake. I've never felt like he was sincere about anything. Except at my father's funeral. He took my father's death hard. He and my father had been friends since they were roommates in college. My mom told me once, Max cheated off my dad throughout the Chemistry class they shared. Maybe that's why I don't like him. I guess I grew up with this preconceived notion he wasn't a nice guy. But he was always nice to me and Cameron. So nice, sometimes, that it seemed odd. He always called me sweetheart and honey, which bugged me, even though he never did anything inappropriate. It just felt weird.

"He's kind of like an uncle, I guess. After my mom died, we often spent holidays with him and Denise and their son, Jeffery. He and my father started a computer software company after college. My dad did the programming, and Maxwell had the business degree, so he did the marketing, and he did a good job too. But, maybe because of the Chemistry thing, I always felt that without my dad's skills, he never would have succeeded on his own."

"He mentioned you selling your father's half of the company. I assume you decided not to do anything with it after your dad died?"

"No. Cameron was a programmer for the company, and though he never said so, I think he was interested in someday stepping into my father's position, which I would like to have seen. When we decided not to sell out to Max, he set it up so that we got a dividend check every six months. I opened a special account for it. I don't even know if any money has been deposited yet. But now, with Cameron gone too..." her voice grew husky. "I'm not sure I want to deal with any of it. It's a painful reminder of my father and brother. Do you think Ben would represent me? Maybe I can let him take care of negotiations."

"I'm sure he would be happy to work with you."

"I know it's a successful company, but I honestly have no idea how much it's worth." Then with a sigh, she added, "I don't care either. I just want my dad and Cameron back." Her words ended on a sob.

Jake knelt to the side of the chair and pulled Emily into his arms. He continued to stroke her hair while she wept. Her tears were short-lived, and she soon pulled away, apologizing for crying on him again.

Jake cupped her face. "Hey, consider me your handkerchief. You need someone to share your grief with, Em. I'd like to be that person... If you'll let me."

Emily studied him for a long moment before nodding and giving him a weak smile. "Would you mind getting me a glass of water? All these tears are making my throat hurt."

"Sure." Jake put the hairbrush on the desk and headed to the kitchen. He got a glass of ice water and was heading out of the kitchen when his mom caught him. "How is she doing?"

"She's struggling, but that's expected, I guess."

"It is," Faith agreed. "I'm glad she's letting you share her grief."

"Me too."

"You're a hard man to say no to, with your warm brown eyes, strong arms, and caring nature." His mom gave him a one-armed hug.

"I'm not sure if I should feel complimented or embarrassed."

"Oh, it was all meant to be a compliment." She patted his arm. "Now, go take care of your girl."

"She's not my girl," he protested.

"Mm-hmm," his mom hummed, as she walked away.

When Jake returned to his office, Emily was on another call. She gave him a quick smile before she spoke into the phone.

"Keira, I know you and Cameron haven't been seeing each other lately, but I have some bad news about Cameron, and I felt you should know."

Jake heard the woman's high-pitched cries after Emily broke the news.

Emily did her best to comfort Kiera while fighting her own tears. When Kiera asked for more information, Emily admitted that Cameron was killed. No, they didn't know why or by whom. She downplayed as many details as she could, probably not to make Kiera more upset.

"Listen, Kiera, I don't have Cameron's contacts, but your friends with the same people. I know this is a lot to ask, but could you spread the word?" Then after a short pause she said, "No, we don't know when the funeral will be, but I will let you know when I have more details."

Sensing her tension, Jake picked up the hairbrush and brushed Emily's hair again.

"No, I haven't talked to Trent. I was hoping you'd call him."

Emily's shoulders rose at the mention of Trent, and so did Jake's curiosity.

"I don't think I can talk to him right now. Not with the way I left things with him." Emily's voice was strained. She waited for Kiera to say something, then she responded, "I know, but I'm not sure I can face him yet. I can't deal with that right now. Besides, I'm not at home. I'm out of town, staying with friends."

Jake was glad Emily considered him and his family friends, but questions raced through his mind. Who was Trent and how had Emily left things with him? Why didn't Emily want to see him?

"Thank you, Kiera. I appreciate it. I'll be going through Cameron's apartment in a couple of weeks, if you'd like, maybe you... and Trent... can help me."

After ending the call a few moments later, Emily propped her elbow on the desk and dropped her head into her palm. Jake squeezed her shoulder in a comforting gesture.

"Wow. That's so exhausting, I want to curl up in bed."

"Maybe you should go rest."

"No, because I'm afraid I'll have bad dreams. What I need is some fresh air."

Jake crouched down and looked into her eyes. "Would you like to go for a ride?"

"You mean a drive in your truck? Is it fixed already? I'm not sure I'm too keen on getting back in your truck again."

"I have another truck, though not as nice as that one. But no, I didn't mean a drive. I said ride, and I meant ride." Jake gave her a mischievous smile.

"Like on a horse? I'd love to ride a horse, but I'd never stay on with these casts."

"I'll work it out. Trust me."

Emily put her hand on his cheek and looked in his eyes. "I do trust you, Jake." Then after a lengthy silence, during which Jake struggled to breathe, she continued. "But if I fall off a horse and break another bone, you might be stuck with me until you're sick of me."

The thought of Emily staying here forever caused his heart to race like a runaway stallion.

Easy now.

"I don't think that's possible."

CHAPTER 22

*J*ake let Emily walk as far as the back patio before he insisted on carrying her to the stables. She couldn't deny being in his strong arms felt good, but she couldn't take advantage of Jake simply because she craved the comfort and security he provided.

She couldn't make that mistake again.

Emily laughed as they entered the stables, and she saw how Jake intended to take her for a ride. "You've got to be kidding."

Two horses, a bay and a chestnut, stood hitched to an old-fashioned buggy meant to carry two people plus a driver. Jake deposited her in the back seat of the buggy and climbed in beside her.

"You're driving this thing from back here?"

"I've got long arms." Jake smiled and winked at her.

Long, strong arms. Emily's breath caught in her throat as she admired the way Jake's shirt molded to his muscular arms. Some days, he wore lightweight, long-sleeved shirts—probably the days he knew he'd be in the sun all day—and other days, he wore t-shirts. Today was a t-shirt day, and she was glad.

Stop it. The man is trying to help you through a difficult time, stop ogling him.

Jake snapped the reins and led the buggy out of the stables and down the lane toward Zane and Lottie's house. Before reaching their house, however, he turned down another lane. Emily spotted Daniel standing beside an open gate. Jake drove the buggy through, and Emily turned to see Daniel close the gate.

Emily looked at the man beside her. He looked every bit the part of a tough rancher, but he had a sensitive side that was in-tune to what she needed. How could one man have two so drastically different sides?

Jake relaxed back in the seat and looked at her.

No doubt he had a million things to do and would rather be working, yet he made her feel like she was all that mattered to him. He couldn't possibly look more handsome than he did in this moment, driving this silly, old, very cozy buggy.

"You're staring at me." Jake's voice was quiet and playful.

"I'm trying to figure you out."

Jake's ears turned red. "What do you mean?"

"Why do you own a buggy? Who even owns a buggy anymore? I can't imagine you use it regularly on the ranch. So, why do you keep it around?"

Jake chuckled. "I prefer to call it a carriage. It sounds much more romantic than buggy."

"I see. Are you trying to be romantic?"

Jake studied her face for a moment. "I would like very much to take you on a romantic carriage ride, Emily. But I know now is not the time for that."

Emily's stomach took flight. Did Jake admit to being romantically interested in her?

Jake gave a nervous chuckle. "How's that for being honest and direct?"

Emily's cheeks flushed. "Well done. But I agree, this is not the right time."

Before Jake looked away, Emily thought she saw a flash of disappointment in his eyes.

"The carriage came with the ranch. It's been passed down for generations. Besides parades and such, we only ever use it to impress the ladies."

"Impress the ladies, huh? Is that what you're trying to do?"

"Depends. Is it working?"

Oh yeah, it's working. Big time. Emily bit back a smile. "Maybe, a little."

"I'll remember that. Today, I was aiming for distraction."

She laughed. "It's working in that regard too." Everything about Jake impressed and attracted her, and he wasn't even trying.

Was he?

She closed her eyes and tipped her head back letting the sun warm her face. Any woman, in the past two centuries would have envied her —riding in a carriage beside this handsome man. She should feel special, privileged. Unfortunately, she felt sad. She couldn't forget the reason she needed a distraction.

"Would you like me to put the top up. It provides a little shade." Jake's deep voice pulled her from her heavy thoughts.

"No, I love the sun."

They rode in silence for a time. She felt Jake's eyes on her, no doubt concerned about her.

He finally broke the silence. "Have you regained your full memory?"

"I think so."

"Did you find some happy memories?"

She didn't miss the hopeful tone in Jake's voice. She closed her eyes again and thought of picnics and family vacations, time spent with grandparents.

"Yes, there are a lot of happy memories."

"Will you tell me about some of them?"

There were so many, she didn't know where to start. Gratitude for this incredible man struck her, and without warning, her eyes filled with tears.

"I'm sorry, I didn't mean to upset you." Jake's voice was full of remorse. "You don't have to tell me, if it's too painful."

Emily smiled and put her hand on his arm. "These are happy tears.

Thank you for making me remember the happy things. I'd love to share some of them with you."

For the next half hour, while Jake drove the carriage across his ranch, she shared stories with him of her family.

"My mom's parents were both teachers, who couldn't have children of their own. They were close to forty when they adopted my mom. By the time Cameron and I came along they were advanced in years. We lived close to them, so I saw them often. I remember them always reading to me. I attribute my love of learning to them. They both passed away when I was in my early twenties."

"What about your dad's parents? Did you spend much time with them?"

She twisted a lock of hair round her fingers as she continued to talk. "Yes, but they lived in Montana, so we didn't see them as often, but that's where my happiest memories are from. My Grandpa Anderson had a small ranch. Nothing like the Double Diamond."

Jake brought the carriage to a stop at the top of a hill that afforded them a view of much of the ranch. Amid the rolling hills lay fertile, irrigated farmland interspersed with wooded areas and desert grazing lands sprinkled with black, grazing cattle.

Emily smiled as she recalled swinging on fence gates, fishing, and catching tadpoles. Then she remembered helping brand and vaccinate the three or four dozen new calves each spring and riding horses.

"Grandpa gave me a horse when I turned eight. She was a sorrel, and she had the most beautiful red coat that glistened in the sun. I wanted to call her Ruby, but Cameron thought that was a stupid name for a horse." The memory of her argument with her brother brought a smile to her face and a pain in her chest.

She and Cameron had always had plenty of arguments throughout their lives, but they had always been close. They would have done anything for each other. The realization she'd never have another disagreement with her brother hit her hard, and Emily couldn't breathe.

Jake clasped her hand and squeezed. She hung on to him for the lifeline he'd become. She shouldn't let him comfort her like this. The man filled a very large hole in her heart. The last time she let a man do that while she grieved turned out disastrous.

She couldn't let herself think about that right now. Sucking in a deep breath, she gave Jake a weak smile and pulled her hand from his. "I named her Jewel. It was so hard to leave her every time we came back to Washington."

"Do you still have family in Montana?"

"No. About eight years ago, my grandma convinced my Grandpa to retire and move to Florida. Said she was tired of Montana winters." Emily played with her hair as she continued to talk. "Dad, Cameron, and I traded in our family vacations to Montana for trips to Florida. I had to say good-bye to Jewel. She was sold with the ranch to a neighboring rancher. She was getting on in years, and I figured she'd be happier on the ranch where she'd spent most of her life. Besides, I was in college and had no place to keep her."

"Do your grandparents still live in Florida?"

She smiled as she remembered how much her grandparents had enjoyed retirement. "Grandpa was never one to sit still. He tried surfing and parasailing, ran day-boat trips, but golfing became his true love. He died from a heart attack on the ninth hole about five years ago. My grandma died in her sleep six months later."

"I'm sorry to hear that, but I'm glad you found some happy memories."

"Me too. I've been blessed by the people I've had in my life, but life isn't the same without them. There isn't a substitute for family and home." A heaviness settled over Emily.

She'd had her condo for two years now, but it had never felt like home. It took family to make a house a home, and she'd never have that again. Maybe she'd marry someday, but that wasn't something she could consider for a long time. Not until she could come to grips with being alone.

Sensing her sadness, Jake put his arm around her and pulled her to him. A part of her knew she should resist him, but a larger part of her needed the comfort he offered. She relaxed her head against his shoulder.

Just because I need comforting, doesn't mean I need the man offering it.

She couldn't fill the holes in her life with the nearest man. As much as she wanted to do exactly that.

WITH RELUCTANCE, Jake pulled the carriage as close to the back patio as he could. He was disappointed to have this time alone with Emily come to an end.

He worried about her.

She'd let him hold her and comfort her for a while out on the hill, but then she'd pulled away and acted tense ever since. She'd hardly spoken for most of the ride home. As he lifted her from the carriage, he read the exhaustion on her face, and she didn't argue when he insisted on carrying her into the house.

He hesitated after stepping in the back door.

"Would you like me to take you to your room so you can rest?" In truth, he didn't want to put her down at all. He wanted to continue to hold her in his arms until all her pain and sadness went away.

Emily didn't look at him. "No, thank you. Just put me down, please."

"Are you okay? Are you upset about something? I mean, something besides... your brother."

Emily took a shaky breath. "I need to make a phone call... I need to call Joe."

Jake carried her to his office and sat her on the love seat with her leg across the cushions, then handed her the phone.

"Would you like me to stay with you?"

"No." Panic filled Emily's face.

Okay. She didn't want him anywhere around while she called Joe.

Jake backed out of the door and closed it.

Why was she so upset? And who was Joe?

Her boyfriend? If that was the case, then who was Trent? An old boyfriend, maybe? One she didn't want to talk to right now.

A burning sensation settled in Jake's gut, as he acknowledged his jealousy. Emily had regained her memory, but there was still so much he didn't know about her.

❧

EMILY CLOSED her eyes as she waited for Joe to answer his phone.

"Emily? How are you holding up?"

The familiar, low timber of Dr. Joseph Lewis's voice calmed Emily, and she reminded herself Jake wasn't the only one she could turn to. True, Jake's embrace provided the physical comfort she longed for, but she also had Joe. He'd been there for her through so many of her struggles. He would always be there for her. That's why he'd been the first person she called yesterday. Of course, she'd thought Cameron would always be there too.

Emily swallowed the tears clogging her throat. "I'm a wreck, Joe."

"You have every right to be. You've been through so much."

A brief silence stretched between them and Emily pictured Joe stroking his goatee as he pondered what to say.

"Em, I can't see your face, so I don't know what you're thinking. I need you to talk me. Tell me what you're feeling, what you need from me."

"I need you to tell me I shouldn't be attracted to Jake while I'm grieving Cameron."

"Jake? Is he the rancher whose house you're staying at?"

"Yes. He's the most compassionate man I've ever met."

"You're grieving. Compassion is a good thing right now."

"I know, but the man has mastered the art of compassion, and I swear he's not even trying."

Joe's voice took on a wary note. "What kind of compassion is he showing?"

He probably thought Jake was trying to seduce her while she was vulnerable.

"Nothing like that," she assured, but then she thought about the things Jake *had* done.

Few people would see brushing her hair and taking her for a

carriage ride as seduction, but they had made her intensely aware of him and strengthened her attraction to him.

"So, you're attracted to Jake because of his compassion?"

"Yes. No. I don't know." She let out a frustrated sigh. "It's not solely his compassion. It's everything. He's handsome and strong... and I feel safe with him." She moaned. "I can't do this again, Joe."

"Emily, you lost your brother, and your father not long ago. You're hurting, and your life is in danger. It's okay to seek safety and security. Attraction to the person providing that is common. It will undoubtedly bring a level of bonding."

"I know." Emily's voice dropped as guilt flooded her. "And I know such bonding won't be enough if I later realize I don't feel that same level of attraction anymore."

Joe let out a sigh. "You need to be careful. You know when you're hurting you don't think clearly enough to make the right decisions."

"That's what I'm afraid of," she said with a groan.

CHAPTER 23

*J*ake yawned and stretched, rubbing his dry eyes. He'd forced himself to spend the evening working on the paperwork for the solar project, again. Unfortunately, progress had been slow because it had taken him forever to focus on the task at hand.

He was about ready to pay Ben or someone to get this darn paperwork finished. The one thing he hated worse than paperwork was having to do it when his mind was elsewhere.

Tonight, his mind was on Emily, as it had been every night since she arrived at the ranch. She'd hardly looked at him during dinner and had avoided him after dinner, so he had come to his office.

He couldn't figure out what had happened this afternoon. One minute she was sharing stories of her childhood and letting him comfort her, and the next she was pulling away. Had his admission of wanting to take her on a romantic carriage ride scared her?

His heart had hurt for her ever since he found out her brother was dead. Why did such a beautiful woman have to suffer such loss? Such pain? He knew God had a plan for each of his children, and he trusted in that. At least he tried to.

Why did His plan for Emily have to be so difficult?

He yawned again and debated going for another ride since it was still a full moon. But he rode for a long time last night and didn't get much sleep. He should go to bed. He was tired enough, he'd probably crash, if he could get his mind off Emily.

Shutting down his computer, he picked up the boots he'd pulled off earlier. After double checking the ranch hand on guard duty was by the front gate in one of the ranch's trucks, he locked up and headed down the hall. Halfway to his room, a noise stopped him in his tracks.

It came from Emily's room. She was crying. Hard. The sobs coming from the other side of the door reminded him of how Riley had wept when their father died. A vice squeezed Jake's heart, and his throat constricted.

He hesitated with his hand on her doorknob and glanced at his mother's closed door. Should he wake her? He wasn't exactly comfortable entering a woman's room in the middle of the night.

But Emily needed him.

Setting his boots down, he opened her door, slowly so as not to alarm her. With the help of the moonlight streaming through the open curtains, he spotted her laying with her back to him. Another sob wracked her body.

"Emily?" She didn't respond. He crept closer and touched her shoulder. "Emily?"

She turned in alarm, attempting to quell her sobbing.

"Jake?" She swiped at her tear-soaked cheeks. "I'm sorry if I woke you."

"You didn't wake me." He sat on the edge of her bed facing her. "Come here." He pulled her to a sitting position and into his arms.

She leaned into his embrace, pressing her head against his shoulder. Her slight frame melded against his body brought out every protective instinct Jake possessed.

"I keep having nightmares. I see them shoot Cameron again and again. And I keep... waiting for him to get up... willing him to be okay... to not be dead." Her voice broke, and a tremor shook her body.

Jake's arms tightened around her. "Oh Emily, I'm so sorry."

"And then... then they're... chasing me."

Jake picked her up and moved her to the middle of the bed, making room for him beside her. He pulled her back into his arms and pressed his lips to her hair. Its faint strawberry scent acted as a balm to soothe his anxiety for Emily.

"You're safe. I won't let anything happen to you."

"Thank you." She took several shuddering breaths, and her sobs gradually subsided. "I do feel safe with you." She was quiet for a few moments, and he wondered if she'd fallen asleep. Then she let out a moan, grabbing the front of his shirt in a tight fist, she curled deeper into his embrace. "I keep seeing it over and over." She looked up at him with imploring eyes. "Please, help me forget. Help me think of something else."

The tears clinging to her long lashes, glistening in the moonlight, twisted Jake's heart. He'd do anything for her. At that moment, with her eyes so full of pain, Jake ached to take away her sorrow.

But he couldn't. He couldn't take away her pain any more than he could bring her brother or her father back. And he couldn't make her unsee the horrible things she'd seen.

He could help her think of something else, though.

Wiping the tears from her cheeks with a gentle caress, he told himself he was doing it to distract her. Not because he'd been dying to kiss her again.

It was a bad idea, one she might misconstrue as him taking advantage of her, but he lowered his lips to hers anyway. He kept the kiss light, letting her know there was no expectation. After a moment, he lifted his head enough to gauge her reaction.

She let out a sigh as her eyes fluttered open. "That's a nice distraction." She strained upward until their lips met again.

Jake pressed his mouth to hers again and tightened his arms around her, being mindful of her ribs. Her right hand crept up his neck.

Warmth flowed from her body to his and back again as his heart raced. Her full lips moved with his, and Jake claimed more of her mouth when she offered. She didn't taste like strawberries tonight, but she tasted so good—sweet and inviting and slightly salty. He could become addicted to the taste of her mouth.

This was why he shouldn't have come into Emily's room in the middle of the night. Kissing her was an even worse idea. But he didn't regret it one bit.

Jake had always prided himself on his self-control. But he felt it slipping now.

Kissing Emily like this was dangerous. The electricity between them was explosive.

He didn't want either of them to regret a kiss that somewhere along the line had ceased to be a means of distraction and become a source of temptation.

With monumental effort, he groaned and pulled his lips from hers, his chest heaving.

Emily's breathing was as labored as his. Disappointment replaced the desire in her eyes.

"Don't look at me like that," he whispered with a ragged breath. "I'm a strong man, but I'm not that strong. At least not where you're concerned."

Emily sucked in a deep breath then let it out again. "If I want more than that it will have to be in my dreams, huh?"

"It gives you something else to think about."

"Yes, it does." She smiled and laid her head against his chest. "But will you stay with me a little longer, please?"

"For a few minutes." He shifted to a more comfortable position, propping an extra pillow from the other side of the bed, behind his head.

He should leave. But holding her felt so good, so right. Besides, Emily needed him, for a few minutes anyway. When she'd pushed him away this afternoon, he'd wondered if she'd ever let him comfort her again.

And now she had.

His elation plummeted. She'd turned to him, and he'd taken advantage of her. He'd been much more of a gentleman than some men might have been, but he'd be lying if claimed he'd only kissed Emily for her benefit.

Emily's breathing grew steady, and her body relaxed in his arms. At least she didn't seem upset about the kiss. Tonight anyway. Would she feel differently tomorrow? Sometimes, regret took a while to sink in.

He didn't want his relationship with Emily clouded by something they'd end up regretting. Yes, he wanted a relationship with her. But she wasn't ready for that. She was dealing with too much and needed time to heal.

Besides, he knew very little about her still. But he wanted to know. He wanted to learn every little thing about her. Would she ever trust him enough to fully confide in him?

Not if he kept kissing her and taking advantage of her when she was so vulnerable.

He would have to be careful around Emily. He wanted to comfort her, but he couldn't keep kissing her like that. Because like their first kiss, this kiss, had left him wanting more.

So much more.

JAKE AWOKE WITH A STRANGE, heavy sensation in his arm. It took him a long, drowsy moment to figure out why. He'd fallen asleep. In Emily's bed. With her in his arms.

He looked toward the window. The gray light coming through curtains told him it was almost dawn. He'd spent the entire night in Emily's bed.

He looked down at her peaceful face and remembered her anguish of the night before. Then he remembered the kiss they'd shared. His pulse sped up as he remembered the feel and taste of her mouth against his. He waited for the guilt and regret he was sure he would feel this morning to hit. But they didn't come.

Having been raised with old-fashioned values and high morals, he knew he should feel guilty. But nothing inappropriate had happened, and Emily had needed him last night.

He could never comfort her like this again, though. It would be playing with fire. And they would both get burned.

He wasn't sure he'd be able to stop with a single kiss next time. Emily was too pretty, and he cared too much for her to hurt her. She was too vulnerable for him to be toying with her emotions.

Although nothing had happened, he did not want his mother to find him in Emily's bed. He slid his body backward as he slowly pulled his arm from under Emily. She rolled toward him, and he paused to make sure he didn't wake her. She had a peaceful, serene smile on her face.

A smile crept to his own lips. *Man, she's beautiful.*

He continued to disengage himself from Emily and her bed. Taking one last look at her, he fought the urge to press his lips to her forehead. Silently, he slipped from her room, picking up the boots he'd left in the hallway last night.

Going to his room, he closed a second door between him and Emily. He took a deep breath and frowned. Still no remorse. That wasn't a good sign. He'd enjoyed holding Emily too much.

And that was a problem.

Finally, a twinge of guilt hit him. But it was guilt for not feeling guilty. Reminding himself he'd already determined he couldn't allow it to happen again, he pushed it from his mind.

As he changed into work clothes, the muscles in his back protested. He had many stiff spots this morning from how he'd spent the night.

It served him right. He needed a physical reminder he shouldn't have slept with Emily.

He would have to work extra hard to work off this frustration.

CHAPTER 24

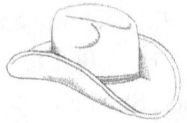

$\mathcal{E}$mily awoke feeling content and peaceful. Then reality crashed down on her, stealing the air from her lungs. The sadness settled over her like her grandmother's heavy homemade quilts, and she rolled onto her side to let the tears wet her pillow as she struggled to catch her breath.

She remembered Jake's comforting embrace last night. He'd smelled so good when he pulled her into his warm embrace, and his kiss had made her forget all the bad things in her life. It also made for some very pleasant dreams.

Heat flooded her cheeks.

She'd done it again. She'd practically forced Jake to kiss her. She hadn't said the words, but she'd begged him to help her think about something else.

And he had.

She should regret it, but she didn't.

Then she remembered his words, *"I'm not that strong, at least not where you're concerned,"* and the guilt hit her. Even after Jake had admitted what a temptation she was, she'd begged him to stay. She used Jake to help her feel better, like she'd done with Trent after her father's death.

How long did he stay with me?

She recalled his arms tightening around her when she'd had another nightmare. His comforting embrace had calmed her, and she'd been able slip back into a peaceful slumber.

A soft knock sounded on her door, followed by Faith poking her head in. Emily swiped at the remaining tears on her cheeks and sat up. Faith stepped into the room and studied Emily.

"Oh, dear." Faith's voice was full of compassion. "Having a tough morning already?" She smoothed Emily's hair back.

Faith's concern brought a fresh wave of tears. Jake gets it from his mom all right. Emily couldn't answer—she simply shrugged and blinked away the tears.

"I wish there was something I could say or do to take away your pain. But I'm afraid it's going to take time."

Time? The way Emily felt now, she didn't think time could heal her broken heart. Time wouldn't bring back her brother or her father. It had never brought back her mother.

Of course, her mother's death had been different. She'd seen her mother deteriorate right before her eyes. She'd begged God to take her mother so she wouldn't have to suffer anymore. But the revelation that her father had been killed and to have witnessed her brother's murder... She couldn't see how time would help that.

Remembering how she'd felt in Jake's arm last night, she focused on the comfort his embrace gave her. She'd felt like everything would somehow be all right. It was ridiculous to think Jake's embrace could fix everything with her world, but somehow, it did.

If only for a little while.

But it couldn't last. A man's embrace when she was grieving was comforting, but it carried with it a whole slew of problems.

Like attraction.

Attraction led to relationships and relationships led to commitments. And Emily was not in a good emotional state to make a commitment.

Though Emily didn't feel like getting out of bed, didn't feel like eating breakfast, didn't feel like facing anyone, she let Faith persuade her to get dressed.

A short time later, Emily sat at the kitchen table, having only eaten a few bites of her omelet before losing her appetite. Joe would not be happy with her.

Faith and Lottie had eaten with her, but they had finished, and Faith now loaded the dishwasher while conversing with Lottie. Emily heard the door in the mudroom on the far side of the kitchen open, and her heart skipped a beat.

Would Jake walk through the doorway or would it be Zane or Daniel? She wasn't sure how to act after last night's kiss. How long had he stayed in her bed? Would he regret staying with her, kissing her?

Jake stepped through the doorway and Emily's breath caught in her throat. His steps faltered when he saw her sitting at the table. Then a slow smile spread across his face.

"Have a seat, Jake," Lottie said. "I'll bring you a plate."

Jake stopped to wash his hands, then he sat across from Emily. She couldn't meet his eyes. She was glad to see him, but she should never have made him kiss her and stay with her last night.

"Emily." Jake's voice was low.

She met his gaze.

Jake studied her face. "You look like you've had a rough morning."

If she didn't feel so guilty, she would take offense to his comment. "How long did you stay with me?" She kept her voice low, not wanting his mother and Lottie to hear.

Jake glanced over his shoulder before answering. "A heck of a lot longer than my mother would approve of." Then a slow smile spread over his face, and he winked at her. "But not as long as I would have liked."

"Okay, you two," Faith said, smiling as she and Lottie walked past on their way out of the kitchen. "Lottie and I will leave so you don't have to whisper."

Heat filled Emily's cheeks.

Jake chuckled. "She always disappears when I'm around, doesn't she?"

"I'm sure she wouldn't walk away if she knew what we were talking about." Emily frowned. "Jake, I'm sorry about last night."

Jake's smile disappeared.

"I should never have encouraged you to kiss me, I mean I practically forced you to kiss me again. And it wasn't fair of me to ask you to stay... after... after that ki—"

"I'm not sorry." Jake cut her off. "I don't regret a single moment from last night. Except for the part where I had to make myself stop kissing you. And for the record, you didn't force me to kiss you. I did it because I wanted to. Please don't tell me you didn't enjoy it. I'm not sure my ego can handle that."

A smile curved her lips. "I enjoyed it." Probably too much. "But I shouldn't have made you do that, because I know you're not that kind of guy."

Jake speared a bite of omelet with his fork. "What makes you think I'm not that kind of guy?"

"Because you checked to make sure your mother wasn't listening before you admitted to spending the night with me."

His smile faded, and he cleared his throat. "You're right, I'm not that kind of guy. I believe complete commitment should accompany intimacy."

"Me too." Emily lowered her eyes. "That's why I feel so bad about asking you to stay with me."

Jake took her hand that lay on the table, and she looked at him again. "Look, Emily nothing inappropriate happened. You needed someone to comfort... and distract you. That's what I did. But I'd be lying if I said that's all it was, because it meant much more to me than that." Then he gave an uncomfortable chuckle. "I can't believe I admitted that out loud, considering we've known each other such a short time, but it's true. How's that for being direct?"

Emily smiled, but it was full of sadness. "You're getting the hang of it, but we can't do that again. I'm not capable of commitment right now."

Jake let out a sigh. "No, we can't." He squeezed her hand. "Despite the attraction between us, now is not the time to start a relationship." When she nodded, he continued. "I know this is a difficult time for you, so I'll try not to confuse things for you by kissing you again. The last thing I want is to take advantage of you when you're vulnerable, but I'm here for you. If you need a shoulder to cry on or someone to chase away the bad dreams, I'm here for you. For as long as you need."

"Thank you." She squeezed his hand.

He held her gaze for a long moment before Emily broke the silence. "Eat your breakfast. It's probably cold by now."

He gave her a sharp look. "Is that why you're not eating? I know you don't have much of an appetite, but you should try to eat a little more."

Emily picked up her fork and forced herself to take another bite. Joe would like this man.

Lottie pushed through the swinging door with a laundry basket on her hip as Jake took his last bite. "Jacob Andrew Winters! Since when do you make your own bed?"

Jake's face turned beet red, and Emily couldn't help herself, she busted out laughing. Fortunately, Lottie didn't wait for an answer, but continued right on through the kitchen to the combined laundry and mudroom.

Jake glared at Emily. "What's so funny?"

"You're not very good at being sneaky." She smothered another chuckle. "You obviously haven't had much practice at this kind of deception."

Jake stood and leaned close to her ear. His breath tickled her cheek when he spoke. "Let's hope she doesn't notice my clothes from last night smell like you. We'll never hear the end of it."

Emily's smile faded, and Jake was the one chuckling as he deposited his plate in the sink and walked out.

"RILEY HAD an unexpected schedule change and is coming home for a couple of days," Faith announced over lunch. "She says she needs a break."

Jake's face paled, and he gave his mom a pointed look. "I'm not sure that's a good idea."

Emily knew why Jake was concerned about his sister coming home. He didn't want to put her in danger.

"Maybe, it's not a *good* idea, considering all that's going on." Faith patted Emily's arm. "But how would you have felt if we had told you 'no' when you wanted to come home from college for the weekend?"

Emily bit back a smile. Faith knew exactly how to push Jake's buttons. The muscle in Jake's jaw tensed.

"Okay, but she doesn't ride out on her own," Jake growled.

"I'll let you tell her that."

"Unless, she's carrying," he amended.

"I'm sure she'll agree to that."

"I'm sorry, my being here is putting everyone in danger," Emily said.

Jake and Faith both looked at her and spoke at the same time.

"It's hardly your fault, dear," said Faith.

"No more apologies today." Jake gave her a stern look.

Her cheeks turned hot at his reference to her apology this morning. Faith gave her a curious look. Emily did not want to explain to Faith, so she let it drop. Apparently, Jake knew how to push Emily's buttons.

"Good. It's settled. She'll be here in a few hours."

Emily welcomed the distraction Jake's sister might provide. Was she as sensitive and compassionate as Jake?

"IT'S HORRIBLE, Joe. I'm in limbo, knowing my life is in danger, waiting for something to happen. Everyone on the ranch is carrying guns, and it's all my fault." Emily sat in Jake's office, twisting a lock of hair around her finger. She hoped he wouldn't mind, but he hadn't been around to ask, so she'd gone in any way to call Joe.

They had been talking for half an hour, with Emily doing most of the talking, or rather venting. She'd cried, she'd yelled, and Joe patiently talked her through her avalanche of emotions. When she sat down to make this call, she'd promised herself she would tell him about what happened last night, but she hadn't been able to bring it up.

"Let the others worry about your safety. The important thing is to take care of yourself, Em. Are you eating?"

Emily went quiet. She knew Joe wouldn't let her go without answering.

"Emily?"

She let out a sigh. "I'm trying."

"Which means you're not eating enough."

She knew she should consume more calories than she was, but knowing and doing were two different things. Like she knew she shouldn't have asked Jake to stay with her last night, but she'd done it anyway. *Because I'm weak.*

"I slept with him last night, Joe." The words flew out of her mouth at the same moment the door opened.

Jake was three steps into the room before he registered her sitting on the love seat and the words she'd said. He froze and stared at her, a mixture of emotions crossed his face. Shock. Anger. Hurt.

"Jake?" Emily and Joe said in unison. Joe questioning and Emily exclaiming.

"Joe, I've got to go."

"Emily. Wait. We need to talk about this."

Jake spun around and walked out of the room.

Emily hung up on Joe's protests. "Jake, come back. Please."

Jake stopped. It was a long moment before he turned around. He stepped into the office and slammed the door behind him. He planted his feet and folded his arms. "Why did you tell him we slept together?"

"We did... sort of."

"He'll think I took advantage of you."

Joe probably thought exactly that. Jake had every right to be upset. Emily rubbed her forehead. Why hadn't she kept her mouth shut?

"I'll call him back and explain."

Jake's jaw clenched, and his nostrils flared. "Who is Joe, anyway? And why would you tell him that?"

Emily thought about all Joe had helped her through. "He's all I have left. I tell him everything."

Hurt filled Jake's eyes, and he turned to leave.

"Jake."

He froze with his hand on the doorknob.

"Let me explain, please."

Jake turned back and sat beside her, setting his hat on the arm of the love seat. "I'm listening." He didn't look at her and his shoulders remained hunched.

"I met Joe when I was sixteen and going through... some... difficult things."

"Isn't that when your mother died?" Jake's voice sounded contrite.

"Yes, and I didn't handle her death well. Joe helped me through all of that and... other things since." She wanted to tell Jake everything, but she wasn't ready to bare her soul to anyone new. Especially with her brother's death bringing back those struggles.

"So, you've known Joe for what, fourteen years?"

"Yes."

"And you tell him everything? You just talk?" Jake scratched the back of his neck.

"Yes." Emily hid a smile.

Was Jake trying to get information about Joe because he was jealous? How would he react if he knew Joe was married and old enough to be her father?

She liked the idea of Jake being jealous over her.

"Do you have feelings for him?" The words exploded from Jake.

"I love him dearly." Emily smiled, and Jake's face fell. "But I'm not *in love* with him."

"You're not?" Relief swept over Jake's features. "Good. I mean, so he's not your boyfriend?"

Were those beads of sweat on his brow?

Emily shook her head, enjoying Jake's discomfort. Then her lips curved up. "His wife, Beth, would be concerned if she heard you ask that."

"Do you have a boyfriend?" Jake shrugged, as though the answer didn't matter. "I mean... it might be good to know if I have to worry about a jealous boyfriend, since we... slept together... and all."

Emily laughed. "No, I don't have a boyfriend. What about you? Do I need to worry about any jealous girlfriends, besides Debbie?"

Jake let out a growl at the mention of Debbie. "No girlfriend."

"Good." Emily smiled and met his eyes. "I think what we're dealing with is complicated enough, right now."

"What exactly are we dealing with?" Jake asked with a twinkle in his eye, his confidence returning.

"A powerful attraction we can't give in to."

"Right." Jake tore his eyes away from hers. "And sitting this close to you, staring into your gorgeous emerald eyes, is not helping." He stood and put his hat on. He walked to the door and opened it, then with a sheepish look, turned back to his desk and shoved a checkbook and pen into his back pocket. He stopped again in the doorway. "When you call Joe back, make sure he knows I would never hurt you, Emily."

Emily stared at the door for a long time after it closed. *No, but I might hurt you.*

CHAPTER 25

*V*ince aimed his rifle toward the ranch house and peered through the high-powered scope. He wished he had a better view of the back patio.

His pulse kicked up a notch as he zeroed in on a woman with long, dark hair leaving the house. *Is it Dr. Anderson?* No. It couldn't be. The woman he wanted had two casts.

This woman, with a holstered handgun on her hip, walked with long purposeful strides toward a fence. A horse trotted over and nuzzled her shoulder in response to her whistle.

He heard the whistle because the breeze carried it his direction, just as it carried his scent away from the ranch house. If it hadn't been working in his favor, the dogs who'd nipped at his heels the other night would have caught his scent hours ago.

He lowered the gun when the woman entered the stable. Shifting, he attempted to find a more comfortable position on his perch in a cottonwood tree. In the last four hours, he'd tried every position possible in this tree and others within the copse of trees a hundred and fifty yards from the ranch house. This one afforded the best view, but he wasn't sure how long he could last up here.

He'd been here since before sunup and grown increasingly more discouraged over the hours. Every ranch hand he'd spotted carried a gun. Between the dogs and the guard, posted by the front gate at night, it was impossible to get close to his target.

He contemplated grabbing the woman who now saddled a horse. He could hold her ransom for Dr. Anderson. But he wasn't prepared to take her right now. He had no disguise to hide his identity. The last thing he needed was another witness. Nor did he have the drugs with him to immobilize her. Judging by the gun on her hip and the confidence with which she saddled her horse, she'd be a fighter.

He watched through the scope, his spirits sinking deeper, as she climbed on her horse and galloped away in the opposite direction.

EMILY TURNED the page of the book she'd been reading for the past hour then immediately turned it back when she realized she had no clue what she'd just read. Faith had recommended the novel to take her mind off things.

It wasn't working.

She couldn't stop thinking about her final conversation with her brother. She played his words over and over in her mind, trying to remember something she might have missed. Something that would give her a clue concerning the key.

It's futile.

The harder she thought the more her head hurt, and the more her head hurt the darker her mood became. She wanted to get outside and go for a brisk walk.

This stupid cast!

She'd been jealous when Riley, who looked like a taller, darker-haired version of her mother, had packed a lunch, and announced she was taking a long ride. Before walking out the door, she'd talked to Faith. "By the way, I'm going out to dinner with friends this evening."

"You should invite Daniel to join you," Faith had said. "He doesn't leave the ranch much."

"I did. He said he has guard duty again this evening. To tell you the truth, I was relieved. I mean it would be awkward, don't you think?"

"It's hard to go back to being friends when you've been more, isn't it?" Faith gave her a comforting hug.

Riley nodded, then she was gone, and Emily wished she could go with her. She would've loved to ride a horse and visit with Riley. She had a feeling Jake's sister was having as hard of time over the break-up as Daniel was.

Riley's gaze had strayed to Daniel during breakfast almost as much as his had drifted to her.

Emily recalled the comments Riley made after visiting with Daniel yesterday afternoon. "Something is different about him. He's changed."

"What do you mean?" Faith asked.

Riley shrugged. "I asked him how he broke his leg, and all he said was he wrecked a motorcycle. Daniel has been riding dirt bikes and four-wheelers since he was four. I don't understand how he wrecked a motorcycle."

Faith and Riley had gone on to speculate whether Daniel had been dating someone in Portland, and Emily wondered if Daniel and Riley would ever be close enough again for him to feel comfortable telling her what he'd been through.

Riley had left hours ago, and Emily was going crazy.

She jumped at the sound of the mudroom door slamming. "Mom!"

It was Jake, and there was a tension in his voice that said something was wrong. Very wrong. Faith sat aside her crocheting and stood, but Jake burst through the swinging door carrying a first aid kit and a dish towel in one hand. He held a bloody handkerchief to his brow with the other.

"Jake," Faith gasped. "What happened?"

"I came off a horse and got kicked before I could get myself off the ground." The words came out a growl.

Emily watched, mesmerized as Faith took the towel and first aid kit from him and pushed him toward the lazy boy. She spread the towel on the back of the chair before he laid his head back. Then she opened the first aid kit on the nearby end table. Jake's calmness and Faith's efficiency impressed Emily. This was not the first time Faith had dressed Jake's wounds.

How many times had something like this happened? And what would Jake have done if his mom wasn't here? Did Lottie ever dress his wounds?

"Oh, Jake, you grabbed one of Lottie's good towels."

"So, I'll give her a raise," he growled.

"You pay her plenty," Faith said. "Now let me look at this." She peeled back the handkerchief. "Oh dear, it's a bleeder. You should go get stitches."

"No. Stitches will leave a scar."

"You're as stubborn as your father was."

"Why, thank you," Jake said, a semblance of a smile on his face. Until Faith touched his wound, then he grimaced.

"That wasn't a compliment. Now hold still." Faith eyed the wound for a moment then pulled clean gauze from the first aid kit and pressed it to his wound. "Hold this. I've got to get something to clean it with."

Faith left the room, and Emily continued to stare at Jake.

He opened one eye and looked at her. "Looks like we'll have matching black eyes."

"Are you sure you're okay? Shouldn't you go to the hospital?"

"Na. They haven't got anything I don't have here. Besides, Mom's the best nurse in the county."

"And you have a well-supplied first aid kit."

"Yep."

"Okay," said Faith returning with a glass of water and a bowl of soapy water. She set the bowl down on the end table and handed Jake some tablets from the first aid kit and the glass. "For the headache."

He took them without complaint.

"Now, let's get the bleeding stopped."

Faith took a small bottle from the kit and squeezed some liquid on the wound. Jake sucked in a sharp breath and clenched his jaw. After a few moments, she cleaned the wound. Faith tried to be gentle, but Jake's hands balled into fists as he repeatedly winced.

"Jake, this really should have stitches," Faith said. "It's right on the bone."

"No, just put some glue on it and a butterfly bandage."

Faith made sounds of exasperation as she followed Jake's instructions, and Jake groaned and winced.

"These butterfly bandages are too long, and the cut is too close to your eye."

"Cut them smaller then," he growled. His patience was obviously wearing thin.

A few moments later, as Faith finished, Zane walked in carrying Jake's hat.

"You all right?" Zane asked.

"Yep. Did you get him settled down?"

"Yeah, he should be good to go."

Emily leaned forward, ignoring the twinge of pain in her ribs. "You're going to get back on the horse?"

"Of course he is," Faith said in a disapproving tone, as she cleaned up. "Zane, talk some sense into him, will you?"

"Come on, Faith, you know any common sense the boy had got kicked out of him a long time ago," Zane said straight-faced.

Emily laughed out loud. Jake turned the scowl he'd been giving Zane on her.

She sobered.

He put his hat on his head and headed for the door.

Emily sat up straighter. "Jake." When he turned to look at her, she asked, "You're seriously getting back on?" At his nod she asked, "Can I come watch?"

He grinned. "Wow, that'll put the pressure on." He called to Zane, who was almost out the door. "Grab a chair for Emily, will you?"

Emily scooted toward the edge of the couch and reached for her crutches.

"If you're going out there, I'm carrying you. The ground is much too uneven for you to walk." Jake came and swept her up in his arms before she could argue.

"You got bucked off a horse. You shouldn't be carrying me."

"Exactly, I got bucked off in front of my men and my pride took a big hit. If I return carrying a pretty woman, they won't dare give me a hard time about being bucked off."

Emily laughed.

Jake stepped out onto the back porch and waited for his mom to close the door behind him. Then he looked at Emily, his face full of concern.

"You've lost weight."

"What?" Emily laughed self-consciously. She knew she'd lost weight, but had she lost so much that it was noticeable to Jake?

"I can tell you've lost weight."

"I think you're getting stronger since you've been working out with Daniel." She couldn't resist squeezing his shoulder where her hand rested.

"Emily, this is serious. You're hardly eating."

Emily lowered her eyes. *I'm trying.*

"I know you're suffering right now. But you can't afford to not eat. Your body needs nutrition to heal."

"Can we talk about this later, please?" she asked, uncomfortable with Jake's scrutiny. "Your horse is waiting, and I can't wait to see him buck you off again." She forced a smile.

He studied her face for a moment. "Fine, we'll talk about this later. But we will talk about it."

Jake carried her across the yard and past the stables to a corral where a saddled, young, black stallion waited. He sat her in the lounge chair Zane had carried out. With furrowed brow, he studied her face for a moment before straightening and entering the corral.

Emily looked at the ranch hands gathered to watch Jake ride the freshly broken—or perhaps not-quite-broken colt.

Daniel, who had been leaning against the fence, made his way over to stand beside Emily. "Hey."

She looked up at him. "I'm nervous for him. Do I need to be? He's done this before, right?"

"A million times. Jake's the best at breaking horses. That's why everyone's watching."

"But if the horse is broken, it shouldn't have bucked him off."

"Someone slammed a gate right as Jake climbed on, and it startled the horse. This one is more stubborn than most though. Dad calmed him down, but it will probably still take Jake for a ride."

Emily held her breath as Jake approached the colt. She couldn't hear what he said as he talked to the horse in a low, soothing voice. He took his time, stroking the horse's neck, front withers, then hindquarters. Finally, he prepared to lift himself into the saddle.

Emily bit her lip.

Jake settled in the saddle and relaxed. The colt reared up, and Jake leaned into its neck. Emily held her breath as she continued to watch the horse rear again then buck and rear a third time. Jake managed to stay on the horse, appearing calm in the saddle, waiting for the stallion to settle down.

Jake was the epitome of grace in the saddle. Art in motion. So incredibly beautiful it took Emily's breath away.

After bucking and rearing a couple more times, the horse stilled, sides heaving.

Realizing she'd balled the fabric of her dress in her clenched fist, Emily relaxed her hand and smoothed out the material. If she didn't have a cast on her left hand, she would have applauded.

But applause might break the magic happening in the corral, and Jake would get bucked off again. She glanced around at the other spectators. They were as in awe as she was.

Now that the horse had exhausted itself, Jake took control and taught the colt to obey his commands. Nudging the horse in the flanks, he rode around the corral a few times then turned and rode the opposite direction. He led the horse through a series of figure-eights, starts, and stops with the slightest movement of his wrist. Jake's muscular thighs did most of the work, giving the horse directions. Man and beast moved together as one.

Weightlessness filled Emily's chest as she kept her eyes glued on Jake and the stallion. The scene was every bit as beautiful as the sunset she and Jake watched the other night. It was a performance she could watch again and again.

Finally, Jake dismounted, and Emily fought the urge to applaud. Once again, Jake spoke softly while stroking the horse's neck, withers, and hindquarters. Eventually, he led the colt over to a ranch hand. "See that he gets a good rub down and give him some oats."

A few moments later, Jake sauntered over and crouched next to her chair. "Sorry, you didn't get to see me get bucked off."

Feeling the magic of what she'd witnessed, Emily showed Jake how glad she was he hadn't gotten bucked off. She reached out, grabbed the front of his shirt, and pulled him toward her. She pressed her lips to his in a firm kiss. Caught off guard and off balance, Jake dropped to the edge of her chair. Recovering quickly, he slipped one hand into her hair and deepened the kiss, setting her body aflame.

Cheers and catcalls from the ranch hands pierced Emily's consciousness, and she released his shirt and his lips.

Her face burned.

"He tames the beast *and* gets the girl," Daniel shouted. "And that, men, is why he's the boss."

"That's right," Jake yelled over his shoulder. "Now get back to work."

He stood, picked Emily up, and walked back toward the house. He didn't say a word until he sat on the back-porch swing with her on his lap, her cast laying across the swing. Emily wanted to protest but realized there was no other chair on the back porch.

"What was that all about? I thought we agreed we shouldn't kiss anymore. For the time being anyway."

"You promised not to kiss me when I'm vulnerable. But I didn't agree to that." Emily's cheeks warmed again. "I'm sorry. I shouldn't have kissed you like that in front of your men. I was so worried about you. Then I was so excited for you. Then so touched by how beautiful it all was. I guess I couldn't contain myself."

"Are you saying you get amorous when you're excited?" He raised his eyebrows at her.

"Apparently, I do with you." She knit her brow in concentration. "I'm certain I've never done that before to a man."

"So, are you still excited?" he asked, wiggling his eyebrows, his voice hopeful.

Emily weighed her emotions. *Yes.* His nearness and that look in his eyes excited her, and that was dangerous. "Nope, afraid not. The moment has passed." She wasn't about to tell him her pulse had risen, and she struggled to keep her breathing even.

"Pity." His voice was filled with disappointment. "I suppose it's for the best, though. I've already been knocked for a loop once today."

Emily studied his face. She took in the bruising around the bandage his mother had applied over his left eyebrow. It must hurt like crazy, but Jake acted like it wasn't even there. She spotted a faint white line at the end of his right eyebrow and another on his left cheek bone, below his eye.

"What are you doing?" He gave a self-conscious chuckle.

"I'm trying to figure out how many times you've had your face cut open, like you did today."

"Probably too many to count, but this..." he pushed back his hat and lifted his hair, where Emily saw an inch-long, white caterpillar-like scar along his hairline. "And this..." he lifted his chin and pointed under his left jaw, where Emily spotted another scar amid the stubble. "Were the only ones I had stitched up and they left noticeable scars."

"Interesting. And how many broken bones have you had?"

"Several," he hedged, "and yes, I went to the hospital for them. Although, I ended up waiting for a full week before I went in for a broken wrist."

"A full week?"

"I was busy. We had a lot going on. Besides, it was a hairline fracture. It's not like my hand was dangling or anything."

"Of course not," she said, her tone full of sarcasm. "But you love it don't you?" Her tone change to one of reverence. "You love the ranch, the animals?"

"I do," he said with conviction. "I think I would go insane if I could no longer work with my hands, work with animals, and work the land."

An unexplained sadness crept over her. The story of her life lately. There were so many things she wanted to do but couldn't.

Jake must have noticed a change in her countenance because he stroked her hair in a gesture of comfort. "Hey, what just happened? Are you thinking about your brother?"

"No, actually I was thinking about my life. I'm trying to remember if I've ever felt that kind of passion for anything."

"You got a doctorate degree, which I'm sure wasn't easy. I imagine you feel passionate about helping people work through their problems."

"Maybe. I guess I don't really view it the same. I mean, watching you with that horse. That was amazing."

"I think what you are doing with Daniel is amazing. When everything is resolved, and life gets back to normal, I bet you'll realize how much your work means to you."

Emily didn't welcome trying to find a normal without her brother. "I hope you're right. It's hard to deal with this grief and not be able to physically work off its effects."

Jake lifted her chin and held her gaze. "You had a nightmare last night, didn't you?"

She looked away. Last night's nightmare had been especially bad, and she'd wished Jake had been there to hold her and chase away her fears. But she couldn't run to him every time she had a hard time.

"Why didn't you tell me?"

"You know why," she whispered.

Emily pushed backward to get off his lap. Though he acted reluctant to let her go, he helped her shift, keeping her legs across his lap when she attempted to lower them. She looked at his face to see if he was teasing her. The intensity of his gaze surprised her.

"I want to help you through this difficult time, Emily."

"You can't spend the night in my bed every night to keep the nightmares away."

"I wish I could," he said, his voice low. "It hurts me to see you struggling, and there is nothing I can do to help you."

"You are helping, Jake. Knowing you care, helps."

"I do care, Emily. More than you know."

Emily's breath seized in her chest, and millions of tiny winged creatures took flight in her stomach. Jake held her gaze for a moment before she tore her eyes away.

Boy, am I in trouble!

She couldn't fall in love with Jake, not while she was mourning. She expressed false emotions when she grieved. She couldn't make Jake a casualty of her grief like she had Trent.

Jake stroked her hair again. "I wish there was more I could do." He let out a frustrated sigh. "I'd love to find whoever is responsible so you can get some closure."

"Me too."

"But, Emily, you need to eat. You are too slender as it is."

"I know, but food has no appeal."

"If you could have anything you want tonight, what would you have. What's your favorite comfort food?"

Emily thought for a moment, then a slow smile spread across her face. "Pizza from Gordiano's. It was mine and Cameron's favorite Italian restaurant. They make the best pizza."

"Then let's go, tonight. I'll take you to Gordiano's."

"Do we dare? The last time we went to Spokane, someone messed with your truck and tried to force us off the road."

"Good point." Frustration filled Jake's voice. Then he snapped his fingers. "Robert said something about going to Spokane today to consult with the police there. Should I call and see if he's still there?"

At Emily's nod. Jake pulled out his phone. After connecting with Robert, he looked at Emily and smiled, "We caught him just in time. He was getting ready to head home." He covered the phone and whispered to Emily. "If he's bringing the pizza, should we invite him to join us for dinner?" At her nod, he asked, "Would you like a little more company? We could invite Ben and Amy."

Emily shrugged and nodded. She didn't feel like having company, but Jake was trying so hard to help her feel better; she couldn't tell him no. Besides, maybe having people around for the evening, would help distract her and she could avoid the nightmares tonight.

Jake relayed information from her to Robert, telling him what to order and to be sure to get take-and-bake; so it wouldn't be cold by the time he got back. Then he texted Ben and Amy.

He chuckled when Amy responded. "You're in luck. Amy made one of her chocolate cakes. It's kind of famous around here. I think you'll like it."

Emily smiled. "Chocolate, huh?"

"Chocolate with more chocolate."

His eyes lingered on her face and heat coursed through her veins. "Hmm... yes. And you like strawberries. Too bad I didn't put my strawberry lip gloss on after lunch."

The fire in Jake's eyes intensified, and he let out a quiet groan.

They heard the hum of Debbie Wheeler's Porsche, and Jake's groan grew louder.

"Too bad I'm not still sitting on your lap, huh?"

Jake looked at her and smiled, "Yeah, wouldn't that irritate Debbie?"

"You can kiss me again," she said with a grin.

"I don't—"

"I know, you don't use women like that, but I'm offering, so you wouldn't be using me."

"Stop tempting me," it came out a low growl as Debbie approached them.

"Jake, I'm so glad I caught you when you weren't busy," Debbie said in a syrupy-sweet voice.

Emily spoke up before Jake could. "He is busy. He's acting as my counselor and helping me deal with some personal things."

Debbie's brow wrinkled. "Counselor?"

"That's right," Jake agreed, fighting a smile. "It's going to take a while. Emily has a lot of issues." He patted her thigh. Unfortunately, it was the leg with the cast, so Emily doubted it had the effect on Debbie that he hoped for.

"Well, do you think you'd have some time later this evening? I'd like to talk to you about Lady."

"Lady is fine, Deb—"

"Actually," Emily cut in as she reached up and played with the hair at the nape of Jake's neck. She smiled when he twitched, reacting to her touch. "We have plans with Ben and Amy tonight, don't we?" She intentionally left out Robert's name, so it sounded like a double date.

"We do."

"I see. Well, maybe I'll try to catch you tomorrow." Debbie looked dejected, and Emily almost felt bad for her. "I'm glad to see you're not working quite so hard anymore, Jake."

"Oh, I'm working harder than ever. I have to because I keep getting distracted." He looked at Emily again, not tearing his eyes away as Debbie walked away in a huff. He reached up and pulled Emily's hand away from his hair. "You little liar." At Emily's look of confusion, he continued. "You said you weren't a tease and a flirt, but you are. You'd better be careful, or you'll make me break my promise."

"Promise?" Emily's voice squeaked.

"My promise not to kiss you anymore when you're upset. You're not acting too vulnerable at the moment, though."

Leaning over, he slipped his arm behind her, pulling her to him. He lowered his lips to hers, and a shiver of pleasure rippled through her followed by a warmth that caused her body temperature to skyrocket. He took his time exploring her mouth in a lengthy and very thorough kiss.

Emily grabbed a fistful of his shirt and kissed him back. She shouldn't allow this, let alone encourage it. But heaven help her, she liked the feel of Jake's lips on hers.

When he ended the kiss, Emily's heart continued to race, and she struggled to catch her breath.

Breathing heavily, he held her gaze. Then he smiled and, without a word, lifted her legs and slid out from under them. Without looking back, he walked into the house. A few moments later, he returned with her crutches. He leaned them against the side of the house within her reach.

"I'd better get back to work. I have a feeling it'll be a whole lot safer to climb on another skittish colt than to stay here with you. If you're lucky, maybe I'll get bucked off again." He leaned down to whisper in her ear, his breath caressing her cheek. "You taste good, even without the lip gloss." Then he walked away.

Emily willed her heart to stop racing.

Jake stopped at the steps and looked back. "Have you figured it out yet?"

"Figured what out?"

"What my weakness is?" He winked, placed his hat on his head, and walked away without a backward glance.

So much for slowing her racing pulse.

CHAPTER 26

*D*inner with Robert, Ben, and Amy proved to be a nice distraction. Jake took plenty of good-natured ribbing from Ben and Robert about his black eye and getting bucked off.

Amy even joked about it. "There are better ways to impress a woman, Jake."

Jake's gaze found Emily's. "I figured that out today."

Emily scowled at him as her cheeks heated. She searched for a way to shift the conversation. Everything that came to mind only made her attraction to Jake more obvious. That this had turned into a double date didn't help, since Robert loaded two plates with pizza and joined Daniel on the front porch. Nor did it help that Jake had pretty much told her she was his weakness. The thought both excited and terrified her.

Now was not the time to fall for Jake. She would end up hurting him, like she had Trent.

When Jake told his mother of their plans, Faith immediately made plans of her own to spend the evening with a friend who had recently been diagnosed with cancer and insisted Zane take Lottie out.

Emily felt Jake's eyes on her frequently, and though the pizza tasted good, her appetite had waned. She forced herself to eat the last half of her slice.

Jake had given her the largest piece; she was sure of it.

Robert rejoined them as they finished up, and Emily was grateful for the distraction his energy provided, until he singled her out. "So, Emily, you're a psychologist, huh? Have you got Jake all figured out?"

Emily's cheeks warmed. She'd heard enough stories from Faith and seen enough of Robert to know he like to joke around. Knowing he was teasing, she didn't plan on answering, but everyone waited for a response. She looked at Jake, who paled.

"I've figured out a few things about him," Emily hedged. When Jake raised his eyebrows, and Robert prodded her to elaborate, she continued. "Jake is a rock. He is solid and secure. He's passionate."

Ben coughed to hide his laughter, and Robert laughed outright. Jake's eyebrows rose even higher, questioning.

"He never does anything halfway. He is passionate about the ranch and skilled with horses. He's also gentle, patient, and selfless." Her gaze locked with his. "He'll sacrifice himself for the sake of others." Then smiling she added, "He has a high tolerance for pain. He's horrible at deception, and he likes strawberries."

Jake's ears turned red, and he propped his elbow on the table and planted his chin in his hand to hide his smile.

"Jake's allergic to strawberries," Robert and Ben said in unison.

"He still likes them." She looked at Jake, daring him to disagree.

"She's right, I do. Strawberry flavor, anyway." His lips quirked up at the corners.

Emily figured he was glad they had picked up on the strawberry part, and not the deception part. That would have been harder to explain.

"He never was good at telling a lie," Robert agreed, obviously having heard all her words, but didn't bother asking for an explanation. Then he chuckled. "Passionate, huh?"

"Are you sure Robert's not the passionate one?" Amy chimed in. "I mean he's the one who made out with twins—" Amy clapped her hand over her mouth as though she'd said something she shouldn't have. She looked at Jake, an apologetic expression on her face.

"Amy!" Jake growled.

"I'm sorry, Jake." Amy took her hand off her mouth long enough to apologize before covering her mouth again.

Robert turned to Jake. "You told her?" Not giving Jake time to respond, he punched Jake on the shoulder.

"Ow!" Jake rubbed his shoulder. "See Amy, that's why we're afraid of Robert."

"But you're bigger and stronger than he is."

"Well, he hits harder. Ben you need to teach Amy to think before she speaks," Jake said, still rubbing his shoulder.

"There's really only one way to shut her up," Ben said with a smile. "Unfortunately, I haven't learned to anticipate when she's going to say something someone will regret."

Amy turned to Ben; eyebrows raised. "Oh, really? And what exactly is the only way to shut me up?"

Without warning, Ben pulled Amy off her chair, onto his lap, and kissed her. Amy recovered from her surprise and wrapped her arms around his neck.

"Okay, you two, break it up." Robert threw a wadded napkin at them, hitting Ben in the cheek. When they separated, Robert turned to Jake. "Why did you tell her about the twins?"

"He felt bad about that horrible high-recoil buckshot you insisted he have me shoot on our date." Amy defended Jake. "So I convinced him to tell me something you and Ben wouldn't want me to know. You guys were always giving me such a hard time, I—"

"You better kiss her again, Ben, because she's about to get me into more trouble." Jake buried his face in his hands.

"I'm sorry, Jake. I'll shut my mouth." Amy grimaced then pressed her lips together.

"What else did you tell her?" Robert and Ben asked in unison.

Jake glared at Amy. "Nothing she wouldn't have heard eventually."

Ben and Robert both looked at Amy as though tempted to pry whatever it was out of her.

"Oh, for Pete's sake, I told her how Ben broke his ankle his senior year of high school," Jake said. Then he turned to Ben. "Please don't hit the same arm Robert did. I need to use that arm tomorrow."

"I won't take it out on you, Jake." Ben gave his wife a seductive look. "I'll take it out on her. I know how persuasive she can be. She's very good at getting what she wants."

Amy giggled and flushed under his gaze.

A smile tugged at Emily's lips as she watched the exchange between brothers and cousin. They were close and cared a great deal about each other, even if they had a strange way of showing it.

Without warning, her chest tightened, stealing her breath. She and Cameron had been close, especially after their dad died, but they had also enjoyed teasing each other. She'd never experience this kind of sibling camaraderie with her brother again. She would never know this sense of togetherness, of family.

She blinked the moisture from her eyes. She hadn't shed any tears today, and the pressure had built behind her eyes, screaming for release.

Jake's leg pressed against hers under the table, and she met his gaze. That was a mistake. When he looked at her like that—with his eyes so full of tenderness—it was all she could do not to break down and fall into his arms.

She looked away and thought about what Amy had said. Something about dating Jake. How long ago was that, and how long had they dated?

Did Jake ever kiss Amy the way he kissed me this afternoon?

That's better. Jealousy was much easier to handle than grief. Although it only took one look at Ben and Amy to see they were deeply in love.

Robert pulled her out of her musings. "Amy, why did you say Jake is bigger and stronger than I am? We're the same height."

"But Jake's shoulders are broader, and he does more physical labor than you do."

"I work out regularly on my home gym," Robert said, squaring his shoulders. "Besides, I taught Jake everything he knows. I bet I can still take him." He gave Jake a challenging look.

Emily noted Robert's ego. Was it simply his personality or was he hiding insecurities?

Emily had noted some time ago that Jake's shoulders were broader than Robert's. She also knew Jake had been working out twice a day with Daniel. How would Robert react when Jake beat him at the arm wrestle they were already preparing for by clearing the end of the table?

By unspoken agreement, Ben stood as moderator. Emily and Amy watched, amused as Robert's and Jake's veins stood out on their temples, and their biceps bulged with the effort.

Jake won the first round.

"That's not fair," Robert said. "You have positional advantage. Trade me seats."

Robert and Jake switched seats, and Robert won round two. Jake won round three, but Robert wasn't ready to concede.

"Left-handed this time," Robert said, bracing his left elbow on the table."

Emily couldn't help herself, she cheered when Jake won.

"Fine," Robert grumbled. "I admit it, my not-so-little brother is stronger than I am. Ben do you want to have a go? My ego needs a boost."

"No way, I've gotten soft since going back to the law office. I should come workout with you."

"As much as I hate to admit it, you could probably beat me right now. Jake wore me out." Robert rubbed his shoulder.

"By the way," Ben said to Robert, "everyone knew about the twins. The girls told the whole school."

"Is that why I had no problem getting a date that year?" He smiled. "And why most of the girls wanted to make out?"

"Do you want to know what I've figured out about you, Robert?" Emily asked.

The room fell silent, all eyes darted back and forth between Robert and Emily.

"I don't know," Robert said with an uncomfortable chuckle. "My ego is already bruised, I'm not sure I can handle you telling me I'm cocky and self-centered."

"Sometimes, the truth hurts, doesn't it?" Ben said.

"Some might call it egotistical and cocky, but I call it confident and self-assured. Unlike many who are self-centered, I can tell you care for those closest to you. You would do anything for them." Emily held Robert's gaze, but she saw both Jake and Ben nodding out of the corner of her eye. "You have a protective and caring nature. That's probably why you chose law enforcement. But you know you can't always be there to protect the ones you love." She glanced at Jake, then back to Robert. "So you taught them to be strong. You encouraged Jake to work out, and you wrestled with him to test and motivate him. What little I've seen of Riley, I recognize that you've encouraged her to be strong and independent also, in different ways. You did a good job." She paused for a moment. "I can tell you have loved deeply, but you've been hurt in that regard, haven't you?" Out of the corner of her eye, she saw Jake and Ben exchange an incredulous look. She wouldn't tell them she had learned that tidbit of information from Faith. "You try to hide it, but for someone like you, who cares so much, it left scars. I wonder if she has any idea what she walked away from."

The room was quiet when Emily stopped talking. Robert's eyes narrowed, but he smiled. He was clearly uncomfortable with what Emily said yet acted pleased. Trying to diffuse the tension she'd created, she shrugged. "But I could be wrong."

"You aren't," Jake and Ben said simultaneously.

Amy stood. "Who's ready for cake?"

Obviously, the tension needed more diffusing.

Emily had just taken her first bite of the decadent chocolate cake with layers of chocolate mousse and ganache, when Jake spoke. "I love your cake, Amy, but I'll always associate it with Debbie."

Ben chuckled, Robert snorted, and Emily looked at Jake, confused.

Robert leaned forward. "Last fall during Providence's Fall Festival Amy had this *great* idea to raise money."

Emily caught the sarcasm in Robert's voice.

"She suggested a bachelor auction. You know, where the women bid on the bachelors to win a date with them?" Jake said.

Emily nodded. She could see where this was going. Of course, Debbie with all her money won the bachelor auction, but what did Amy's delicious cake have to do with the auction?

"In my defense," Amy broke in, "all I did was suggest it. The other women loved the idea and ran with it."

Jake pointed his fork at Amy. "To me, it will always be your fault."

Robert held up a forkful of cake. "She used this chocolate cake to bribe Jake and me to agree to the auction."

"Then they blackmailed me into going out on a date with each of them before they agreed," Amy said.

So Amy only went out with Jake so he would agree to the auction. And she'd gone out with Robert too. The knowledge pleased Emily. She like Amy and didn't want to be jealous of her.

"I see," said Emily, "and Debbie won the auction, of course."

"It was bad," Robert said. "She was all over Jake during that date."

Jake groaned. "She's been pretty relentless since."

"I don't know," Emily said with a teasing grin. "She didn't stick around long today. Nor did she bother you the other day."

Jake smiled back at her, his eyes twinkling. "No offense, Amy, but Emily is better Widow Repellent than you were."

"I'll bet she is. I saw her put Debbie in her place with a single comment."

"You should see what she does to Jake with a single kiss," Robert said with a laugh.

Jake's fist shot out lightning fast, striking Robert's shoulder.

"Ouch!" Robert rubbed his arm. "I did not hit you that hard."

Emily couldn't help herself. She laughed until she had tears in her eyes.

CHAPTER 27

"I'm sorry I haven't been able to locate the bank the key belongs to, Emily." Ben sat perched on the back-porch swing while Emily relaxed on her usual lounge chair.

Relaxed didn't really fit how she felt, though. Especially not on the inside. Grief and anger ate at her. Each day that passed that she couldn't lay her brother to rest tied her stomach in knots, and knowing her life was in danger, kept her throat tight with fear.

"I'm sure you're doing everything you can."

"I should look outside of Spokane. I mean, if he didn't want anyone to find it, maybe he put it in a bank in another city."

"You might be right. I keep replaying my last conversation with him, trying to remember exactly what he said but..." Choking back the tears that clogged her throat every time she replayed how that last conversation ended, she sucked in a steadying breath.

Ben studied his clasped hands, letting her compose herself. Why had he come to the ranch today? He could have told her he hadn't had any success last night when they were here for pizza, or he could have called. Did he have some other reason for coming? Out of everyone Emily had met since the accident, Ben was the only one who truly understood what she was going through.

"How did you cope, Ben?" The words were out before she could stop herself.

He looked up at her, eyes narrowed, jaw clenched. Emily considered clarifying, but she was sure Ben knew what she meant.

He raked both hands through his hair and let out a sigh. "I didn't cope. Not well, anyway. And not for a long time. Not until Amy forced me to confront my grief." He studied the wooden planks of the patio floor for a moment. "It took a whole year. A year full of darkness." He lifted his eyes and met Emily's. There was an intensity to their sapphire depths. "Don't fight your grief. Share it with those around you. I hope you know you're surrounded by people who care about you. Faith and Jake. Amy and I are here for you, and I'm sure you have friends and coworkers in Spokane you can talk to. Let them help."

Is that why he'd come? Had he somehow recognized she was trying not to over-burden anyone with her grief? Especially Jake.

"Thank you, Ben. I appreciate that."

The corners of Ben's mouth turned up. "I think Robert established last night that Jake is strong enough to handle it."

Emily's face warmed as her own lips turned up. "You're as bad as Faith and Lottie."

Jake again. She always turned to Jake. Was she taking advantage of his compassion? Was she becoming too emotionally attached?

"Perhaps, but keep in mind we hurt the ones who care about us when we don't let them help carry our burdens. And I think you know Jake cares about you."

Emily looked away from Ben's intense gaze. She knew. She saw it in the way Jake looked at her, in his gentle touch, in the intensity of their kisses.

She cared about him too. But would allowing Jake to continue comforting her forge a bond that wasn't genuine? A bond she couldn't handle when she'd healed a little, like she'd done with Trent after her father's death?

"I know it's hard to believe, but it will get easier. It will take time. Maybe a long time, but someday..." Ben looked out toward the pasture for a moment before his gaze returned to hers. "Someday, you'll find happiness. It will be different from the happiness you experienced in the past, but you will be happy again."

Ben's words sounded like something Emily would say to her patients but being on the receiving end of those words felt different.

Could she really be happy again?

It had taken years for the pain of her mother's death to subside, and now, losing both her father and her brother so close together, Emily wasn't sure she would ever be able to fill the void their absence had left in her life.

As usual, when this pain filled her, she longed for Jake to hold her. Comfort her. Tell her everything would be okay.

Jake.

It always came back to Jake. She had no other outlet for her grief. Following Ben's gaze to the pasture where horses grazed, she recognized the longing in his eyes. Did he long for a brisk ride to help chase away the loss that still haunted him? She had no doubt he loved Amy, but Emily knew you could never let go of someone you'd loved and lost. What she wouldn't give to climb on a horse and attempt to outrun her demons. For a little while at least.

"You look like you could use a ride." She kept her voice quiet, but Ben startled at her words.

He gave her a half smile. "I could. You know, I love Amy, and my life is fuller than I ever thought possible, but sometimes..." He twisted his wedding band. "Sometimes, I need to let go and remember and mourn a little more."

Will I ever reach a point where my life is full of happiness? Where I only need to mourn a little more?

JAKE SPOTTED Emily on the lounge chair with her head back and eyes closed. He slowed his steps. Was she sleeping? Had she had nightmares again last night? She'd looked well rested at breakfast. But he knew Emily kept much of her inner turmoil hidden.

The fact Ben had borrowed some of Jake's clothes and boots and headed out for a ride after talking with Emily, told him Emily probably experienced the same unrest he'd seen in Ben's eyes.

He stepped up onto the patio, studying her face. She possessed a natural beauty and gracefulness he hadn't seen often. Her dark auburn hair framed an almost flawless face. The bruises were fading, leaving long dark eyelashes resting on smooth, rosy cheeks. Her full red lips, that tasted as good as they looked, turned up in a slight smile.

"If you keep staring at me like that, you'll creep me out."

Jake startled. She'd opened her eyes while he'd been studying her lips. The tips of his ears grew warm. "Just admiring the scenery. It's beautiful." He pulled the other lounge chair closer to her and perched on the edge.

Emily rolled her eyes and smiled, flashing her dimples, and his heart stumbled. She ignored his comment. "Did Ben send you?"

Jake shrugged. Ben hadn't said Emily needed him—he hadn't needed to. Jake couldn't seem to stay away.

"Do you want me to leave?"

"No." She looked down at her hand that gripped the fabric of her dress in a tight fist. "But I shouldn't ask you to stay."

"Why shouldn't I stay?" Jake asked, shifting to sit on the edge of her seat, bringing him almost as close as the day they first kissed.

"Because... I can't... think straight when you're near." She pushed at his chest to prevent him from coming closer. The warmth of her hand through his t-shirt caused his pulse to speed up. "Because... I want things I shouldn't, like last time. I can't do this again." She scooted away from him and reached for her crutches that lay on the floor beside her chair. "I'm sorry Jake, I'm not strong enough to do this."

Confusion filled Jake as he helped her get to her feet. "Do what? Grieve? Of course, you're not strong enough. That's why I want to be here for you."

"I can't Jake. I can't do that to a man again." She started her awkward shuffle into the house.

Jake stared after her. *What just happened?* He felt like he'd missed something. Something important. But he didn't understand what.

He went after her. "Can't do what again? This is about more than grieving for Cameron, isn't it? Why won't you talk to me?" He caught up to her inside the house.

She was pulling away from him. He'd sensed her pulling away physically the last couple days, but now she'd distanced herself from him emotionally.

A single tear fell on her cheek. "You have been my rock, Jake, but I need to separate myself from you a little. I need to do this by myself, so I don't get too caught up in... in... you." She leaned on her crutches and waved her hand toward his chest.

He put his hands on her shoulders. "Emily, you don't need to go through this alone. Please talk to me."

She took a deep breath. "I need to make a phone call."

Jake's stomach dropped. She didn't want to talk to him. She wanted to talk to Joe, like she had every day since regaining her memory.

With a sigh of disgust, Jake raised his hand toward his office. "Be my guest. Go call your precious Joe. I don't understand why you'll let him help you through this and not me. I'm right here, Em. Flesh and blood, and I want to help you. Why won't you let me?"

"Because..." Her voice shook. "Because... you're part of the prob-lem." She turned away as she said the words.

Emily may as well have slapped him. Shocked, he turned and walked out the door. *How did I become part of the problem?* He'd tried to keep things platonic. Sure, he'd gotten a little carried away with that kiss yesterday, but she'd kissed him back without complaint.

The knot in his stomach blossomed as he admitted he was insanely jealous of Joe. What was Joe to Emily, anyway? He wasn't a boyfriend, so why was Emily always turning to him?

He strode to the corral and grabbed the fastest horse he owned, an all-black Friesian stallion. Normally, when he needed to rid himself of frustration, he rode Thor. But Zeus was stronger and faster. Jake needed more than speed and power right now. He needed the chal-lenge of keeping this headstrong stallion in control.

The similarity between Emily and Zeus was not lost on him.

Except where his relationship with Emily was concerned, Jake felt like he'd lost any control he may have had.

Questions continued to race through his mind as he saddled the anxious stallion. Where had he gone wrong? What was Emily so upset about doing again? What man had she hurt before?

Once he had the horse saddled, he set off at a thundering pace, hoping he hadn't made a mistake in taking Zeus. It would serve him right if the horse dumped him off and left him stranded miles from the house.

Wouldn't that please Emily.

CHAPTER 28

*E*mily sat in Jake's office chair. Her mind on the man. A heaviness settled in her chest. She'd seen the hurt in Jake's eyes, before he stomped out the back door.

She hadn't meant to hurt him. *So why did I?*

Jake had been wonderful, but she couldn't deny how she felt about him. Every thought, every emotion, it all led her to Jake. She hadn't even been able to talk with Ben without thinking about Jake.

She didn't make rational decisions when she was mourning, she knew that from experience. Punching in the familiar number, she waited for Joe to pick up.

"Joe—" her voice cracked as soon as she heard her dear friend's voice. "It's happening again."

"Emily, tell me what's going on," came Joe's confident and gentle voice over the phone.

"I'm falling in love with him."

"I assume you're talking about the rancher?" Joe asked when she didn't elaborate.

"Yes."

"And you feel like this is the same thing that happened with Trent?"

"Yes, but it's worse this time. Why do I keep doing this?" She groaned into the phone.

"Correct me if I'm wrong, but I believe you told me you were never in love with Trent."

"No. I liked how having someone care for me made me feel. I confused it with love, but I was never in love with Trent."

"Why do you think what you are experiencing with Jake is really love?"

Emily let out a sigh as she thought about how her pulse raced every time Jake looked at her with those warm brown eyes. How comfortable she felt in his strong arms, and how breathless she became every time he kissed her. The constant desire to be near him. "Trust me, there's plenty of dopamine, oxytocin, and physical reactions present."

"But you never felt these things with Trent?"

"No," she said, not sure where he was heading.

"So why are you comparing what is happening with your rancher to what happened with Trent? It sounds like you feel differently—more strongly—about your rancher than you did Trent."

Emily thought about his words. He'd called Jake "her rancher" twice. She liked that, yet something inside her screamed it was wrong for her to feel that way. She'd found comfort in Trent's arms after her father's death, but she had never felt the longing, the shortness of breath, and racing pulse she experienced with Jake.

"I'm supposed to be mourning my brother, not finding myself constantly attracted to a handsome, compassionate rancher," she said with self-loathing.

"We can't dictate how or when our heart falls in love, Emily."

No she couldn't. She'd tried so hard not to fall for Jake. *Am I really in love with him?* Or was it just physical attraction born of her need to not be alone? When she no longer mourned Cameron, would she still find Jake attractive and react the same way?

"Jake has been so wonderful since I remembered..." She closed her eyes and sucked in a sharp breath, trying to block out the scene that gave her nightmares. "But what if he's a different person than I thought he was once I'm no longer mourning and don't need his comforting? You know, I couldn't handle the things I learned about Trent later." Emily's heart grew heavy as she remembered the hurt in Trent's eyes when she told him to leave and never come back.

"Give yourself some credit. You recognized you weren't in love with Trent and couldn't help him with his problems. Don't go throwing your rancher in the same lot as Trent because you met him during another difficult time in your life."

"But how do I separate the need to be loved and the desire to belong with someone from the man? I'm afraid I'm confusing my psychological desires with my emotional needs."

"Give yourself time, Em. There's nothing that says the two can't be fulfilled by the same means. Don't make rash decisions. Give yourself time to mourn your brother, then get to know your rancher. Find out what else you love about him besides his compassion."

Everything. There wasn't a single thing about Jake she didn't like. She smiled as she thought about his gift with horses, the way he supported Daniel through his struggles, and the respect he showed his mother and Lottie. She even loved the great—sometimes volatile— relationship he had with Robert.

Emily's stomach sank. "What if... what if when he gets to know the real me, the me who's not needing a shoulder to cry on, what if he can't handle that? What if he doesn't like the stubborn, opinionated me with all my issues?"

"If he can't love the real you when you are ready to share that part with him, then he doesn't deserve you." Joe's voice was vehement, bringing a smile to her face. "Don't let yourself get drawn into another situation you will regret. If things get to be more than you can handle, say the word, and Beth and I will come get you. You know you always have a place with us. We think of you as family, I hope you know that."

"Thank you, Joe. I do consider you family. I love you and Beth dearly. But I think it's safer for everybody if I stay where I'm at for the time being."

"I understand. You take care of yourself." After a brief pause, Joe asked, "Are you eating?"

"Yes, I'm eating," she said with a sigh.

"Are you eating enough?"

If Jake had recognized her weight loss after only a few days, then the answer was no.

"I'm trying."

"Remember to set your limits and stick to them. This applies to your relationship with Jake too. Set clear boundaries and keep them."

After she ended the call, she remained in Jake's office for some time. Talking to Joe had calmed her fears. It wasn't fair to compare Jake to Trent, but it was hard to separate the two. She kept turning to Jake for comfort, like she'd turned to Trent, after her father's death.

The things she felt for Jake were stronger than anything she'd felt for Trent, and that scared her, because she was completely alone now.

She didn't want to make the biggest mistake of her life simply because she didn't want to be alone. More than anything, she wanted a family. She wanted someone to love as much as she needed someone to love her.

Was that someone Jake? Could he be the man she was meant to be with?

Her heart skipped a beat at the thought. *Yes.* He could be, but she couldn't make such decisions and form such close relationships when she was so emotionally unstable and so desperate for a family.

IT WAS LATE, and the house was dark by the time Jake came through the mudroom door. He wasn't eager to see Emily again after blowing up at her the way he had.

But he couldn't wait to see her gorgeous emerald eyes again and make her tantalizing lips turn up in a smile, revealing her dimples. She was all he could think about.

Man, I've got it bad.

He washed up and found the plate of food Lottie left in the fridge for him. After eating a solitary dinner, he headed to the shower.

Fifteen minutes later, he went to lock up and found Emily sitting on the sofa illuminated by a single lamp. His pulse kicked up a notch.

Knowing he owed her an apology, he sat on the edge of the ottoman, facing her.

"Emily, I'm sorry for the way I spoke to you this afternoon." It was all he could do to meet her eyes.

Her eyes filled with remorse. "I'm the one who should apologize. The way I acted was unfair to you. I'm an emotional wreck. Please don't take anything I say, or do, personally." She was quiet for a moment then asked, "Where were you all evening?"

Jake let out a sigh. "Riding, then I spent a couple hours cleaning out the equipment shed."

"Did you stay away because of me?"

He shrugged. "I didn't want to make whatever you were struggling with harder."

"Apparently, it doesn't matter whether you're off riding or sitting beside me, I feel... things. Things that are hard for me to process right now. You've been wonderful, Jake, but I need you to not be quite so wonderful and compassionate." She gave him a weak smile as if she knew her words didn't really make sense.

His brow creased. "I'm not sure I understand."

"Of course you don't, because it's part of your nature." She pointed a finger at him and gave him a stern look. "Don't kiss me anymore. I like it too much, but I can't handle that kind of distraction right now."

Jake's heart tried to jump out of his chest. He bit his lip to keep from laughing. It was nice to know she enjoyed the kisses as much as he did. "No more kissing," he acknowledged with a nod. "Can I brush your hair? And make you hot cocoa?"

Emily sighed. "I guess so, but I should say no to the hair brushing, because I like that too much too."

So do I.

He bit back another smile. "Can I hold you when you're upset?"

"That's like all the time." Then recognizing he was teasing, she smiled. "Only when I'm crying. That will cut the holding in half at least."

Relieved she wasn't completely pulling away from him, he leaned forward. "So, did you have a bad dream? Is that why you're up? Should I get the hairbrush? Or would you rather the hot cocoa?"

"Neither." She gave him a scowl that made her look adorable. "I didn't have a bad dream. I haven't been to sleep yet." Letting out a deep sigh, she rubbed her brow. "I need to write Cameron's obituary."

"Oh." Jake took in the over-sized sweatshirt she wore—the one she'd taken from her brother's apartment—along with another scrapbook that sat on her lap. He shifted from the ottoman to sit beside her on the couch. "I'd offer to help, but since I didn't know him, all I can offer is moral support."

"That's what I mean by not being so compassionate." She shook her head and smiled. Then she scowled again. "Why do you always have to smell... and look... so good?"

Jake didn't even try to hide his smile this time. "You can thank Lottie. She buys my soap and deodorant."

Emily scowled. "I will do no such thing. The last thing she and your mother need is encouragement."

Agreeing, he pointed at the scrapbooks. "Will you tell me about Cameron?"

A sad smile lit her face. "He was the best big brother. He always looked out for me. He was brilliant, but rather naive and gullible at times because he didn't have a malicious bone in his body. He was handsome in a computer geek sort of way." She continued to talk as she opened the first of the two scrapbooks she held on her lap.

Jake saw pictures of Cameron winning spelling bees and science fairs. Occasionally, there were family photos among the snapshots and pictures of Emily and Cameron as young children and preteens. He saw photos of smiling, happy children on their grandpa's ranch and family vacations.

Emily lifted another page, then shut the book before Jake saw what was on the page.

"Is something wrong?"

"I'm... not sure... I want you to see anymore right now."

Something in her face told Jake she was embarrassed by the pictures, but he sensed a deeper emotion than just embarrassment. He wanted to know more about her, but was it wise to press the issue?

He kept his tone light when he spoke. "Come on, you got to see my pictures."

"But you were always good looking. You never had braces or went through any ugly stages."

"Are you trying to tell me you had braces and felt awkward as a teenager?"

"Glasses, braces... I was definitely... awkward, and I got teased plenty."

"Can I see? I promise I won't hold anything against you."

Emily debated for a long time. Finally, she opened the second book and turned the pages, letting Jake see pictures of her as a young child. The beautiful emerald eyes were a dead giveaway that this was indeed Emily.

"You were cute. Even without your two front teeth."

After a few more minutes, she stopped turning pages. "When my mom got sick... I stopped... doing everything. I spent every minute I could at her bedside... and I became a stress eater." Jake heard the self-loathing in her tone. "Food was the one thing that brought me any comfort."

"I can't imagine how difficult losing your mother must have been."

She turned the pages again, as she talked. "I put on about thirty pounds while my mother battled cancer."

As the pages turned, Jake saw the beautiful young girl with the emerald eyes morph into a person that saddened him. It wasn't only the weight gain. Glasses hid her beautiful eyes, and the long auburn hair he loved had been cut into a pageboy style.

"When my mom became too sick to brush my hair, I chopped it off. Not because I couldn't brush my own hair, but because I was angry. I was mad at God and the world, and I showed it by doing the most drastic thing I could think of."

"Know what I miss in these pictures?" Jake tilted her head with his fingers under her chin to look into her eyes. "I miss your dimples. I'm sorry you didn't have a reason to smile." Then he lightened the mood by joking, "I really wanted to see your braces."

Emily elbowed him in the ribs. "My face was so round my dimples hardly showed when I smiled." Then she turned another page. "You're in luck. The school photographer wouldn't take my picture until I smiled."

"Look at that." Jake smothered a chuckle. "Dimples and braces. At least you took off your glasses so I can see your beautiful eyes. I know you're self-conscious about your pictures, but even in these I can see your inner beauty."

"Whatever." She elbowed him again. "You don't need to butter me up."

Jake frowned. *Did she not understand how beautiful she was? How beautiful she still is.*

Letting it go, he asked, "Do you wear contacts now?"

"No, I had corrective surgery years ago. I was so glad to ditch the glasses for good." Then she grew serious again. "After my mother died, food no longer held any appeal to me, and I couldn't bear to be at home where my mother's absence was so profound. I spent hours everyday walking, pretending my mother wasn't gone."

"So, the loss of appetite when you're mourning isn't a new thing?" Jake asked.

Emily took her time answering. "Food was the one thing I had control over when everything went wrong. For months after my mom died, I still struggled to make myself eat more than a few bites, if I ate at all."

"You became anorexic?" *Is that why she ate so little?*

"Not technically. I didn't have a distorted image of my body. I was simply too distraught to eat because I didn't process my mother's death properly. I didn't really have anyone to share my grief with. My brother left for college, and my father was so wrapped up in his own grief I was afraid talking to him would make things harder for him. So, I kept it all bottled up, and didn't eat because I was too sad."

"Wow, I had no idea you went through that." Jake couldn't fathom the pain Emily must have experienced. Losing his dad had been hard, but he'd had his family and the ranch to focus on, which helped with his grief.

"I went from somewhere around one hundred and fifty pounds down to ninety-five pounds within six months."

Jake sucked in a sharp breath. That was too slender for someone her height.

"My counselor at school became so concerned she insisted my dad get me professional help. Joe saved me. He broke through my defenses and forced me to confront my anger and bitterness over my mom's death. He made me talk about my feelings. He helped me see that not eating wouldn't bring my mother back and that I was hurting those that loved me. Cameron even dropped out of school and moved home so he could be there to give me moral support."

Jake clasped her hand. "I'm sorry for what I said about Joe this afternoon. When you said he helped you through some difficult things... I didn't understand... I thought you meant your grief."

She lowered her eyes. "That's what I wanted you to believe, but Joe has helped me through more than you know. He's the reason I became a psychologist. I wanted to help other people the way he helped me."

"Understanding the extreme you went to when your mother died, you realize I'm going to encourage you eat, don't you?"

Emily smirked. "You want to be my accountability partner?"

The thought of being Emily's partner warmed Jake like nothing else ever had, and a flush rose up his neck. He'd love to have her as his partner for life. He cleared his throat. "Yes."

"You'll need to actually show up for dinner if you're going to make sure I eat my food."

"I'll be there. Every meal." Jake wanted to help Emily anyway he could, and if this is what she needed, he'd be there.

Emily groaned. "Oh, brother."

They looked at the scrapbooks a little longer then Emily grew serious. "Can I ask you something?"

Jake nodded. "Anything."

"When I offered to act as widow repellent for you, you were quick to tell me you weren't the kind of man who uses a woman for his own selfish purposes. Why did you feel the need to clarify that?"

Jake tensed. He didn't want to discuss these things with Emily. But she deserved to know everything about him, like he wanted to know everything about her.

"Who accused you of using them, Jake?"

Here we go. Time for me to face my past.

EMILY FELT Jake's body tense before he shifted away. He ran his finger along the seam of the leather sofa. His lack of eye contact caused a knot to settle in her stomach, and she feared what little food she'd gotten down at dinner might come back up.

Jake's gaze drifted to the windows on the far side of the room. "During my Junior and Senior year at college, I dated a woman named Lydia. She was in several of my business classes, and we spent a lot of time together in study groups and collaborating on projects. When it came time to complete my Senior project, my business plan, I outlined all the things I wanted to do with the ranch. I planned to expand our herds by improving the bloodlines and doubling the size of our hay fields by putting in pivot lines. I backed it all up with research and itemized the expenses that would become investments and projected revenue, including government grants. I was so excited about improving this ranch."

"I sense a big 'but' coming."

"When I showed the preliminary plans for my project to my professor, he told me ranching wasn't a legitimate business, especially since the ranch was already established."

Emily scowled. "I bet you'd like to show him exactly how legitimate of a business your ranch is."

Jake laughed. "I would. I was so angry. The deadline for the projects was only a few weeks away, and I had no desire to start over creating a plan for a business I never intended to build. He told me I could join with another student as long as I did my share of the work." Jake studied his hands for a moment.

"Lydia invited me to join her, so I did. I worked hard and did my share of the project, though my heart was never in it. By the time we finished the project—which we got an A on—I had decided she was the woman I wanted to marry. She was a brilliant businesswoman, and I thought we'd make a great team running the ranch together. I planned on proposing before school ended."

Jake in love with another woman? A vice squeezed Emily's heart, and jealousy crashed over her like a giant, slimy, green wave.

"I brought her home to the ranch for spring break. I thought she would be eager to ride horses and four-wheelers with me." Jake's voice dropped. "That she would be willing to at least hang around while I worked even if she didn't want to get dirty with me. But she refused to even try. She hated everything about the ranch. She was bored stiff, even though my mom tried to entertain her."

A smile pulled at Emily's lips. "You mean your scrapbooks weren't enticing enough?"

Jake smiled, but it didn't reach his eyes. "When we returned to school we got in a huge fight. She said she wanted to marry me, but not if I planned on going back to the ranch. She figured since I had a business degree, I could get a job anywhere. When I told her I intended to take over the ranch eventually, she got so angry. I had always been very open about that. I couldn't understand why she wasn't willing to give the ranch a try." Jake looked off in the distance again. "I had no idea my dad would have a stroke a few months later and I would end up taking over so soon."

Emily gave his arm a gentle squeeze.

"She was furious with me for wasting her time and making her think we had a future together. She accused me of using her to get a grade... which I had." Jake looked at her, and Emily saw the self-loathing in his eyes. "I used the woman I loved for my own selfish purposes. And the moment things didn't look like they would work out between us, I walked away."

Emily took Jake's hand in hers. She was both angry at Lydia for forcing Jake to choose between her and his ranch and relieved Jake hadn't married the selfish woman.

"I promised you the first day I came to the ranch I wouldn't hold anything against you, and I meant it. I'm sure you didn't go into that project intending to hurt Lydia. And I doubt walking away from her was as easy as you made it sound." When Jake's only response was the flexing of the muscle in his jaw, she continued. "It sounds like it was a painful break-up."

"It was."

His confirmation made Emily question whether Jake was really over Lydia.

CHAPTER 29

"Good news," Faith said as she walked out onto the back patio where Emily dozed in a lounge chair. "Ben found the bank that your safety deposit key belongs to."

Every muscle in Emily's body tensed. Relief warred with fear. Finally, this would all be over soon, but what would she find in that box?

A few minutes later, Emily sat in the great room with Faith on one side of her and Jake on the other. "In Kennewick?" Emily asked. "Why did he rent a box over two hours away from Spokane?"

"My guess is he thought it would be harder to find, which it definitely was," Ben said.

"He probably hoped it would lead them away from you," Jake added, then shook his head. "But then he came back..."

Remembering the fear on Cameron's face that day in her condo, Emily hugged herself. She wished he'd told her what he'd found sooner so they could have gone straight to the police. What had he and her father found that got them killed?

The thought terrified her. *Do I want to know?*

"I wasted my time looking for boxes rented in Cameron's and your father's names." Ben held the key out to her. "This key goes to a box rented in your name."

"Why did he put it in my name?"

Jake and Ben shared a somber look and Emily's heart sank. *Because Cameron knew he wouldn't be around long enough to come back to it.* She swallowed the tears that clogged her throat and fought to draw air into her tight chest.

Jake clasped her hand, and she hung on for dear life.

JAKE PULLED to a stop in the parking garage near the bank in Kennewick. He turned off the engine and looked out his window as Robert parked next to him. He hoped they didn't need the back-up, but it was nice to know Robert was there.

He turned back to Emily. She'd been quiet during the drive here, and worry lines furrowed her brow.

Jake put his hand on her shoulder and squeezed. "You okay?"

She shrugged. "I'm scared."

"Don't worry. I'll be right beside you. I won't let anything happen to you. And Robert will be here to make sure no one messes with my truck."

"What if something happens to you? When we get out of this truck, we're both targets. Whoever is doing this has killed twice to protect their secret. By asking you to protect me, I'm putting your life at risk. Besides, you won't be able to take your gun into the bank." Tears filled Emily's eyes, and she tried to blink them away, causing a single tear to fall on her cheek. "I'm sorry for getting you mixed up in all of this."

Jake wiped the tear away with his thumb. "Hey, don't do this to yourself. In case you haven't figured it out by now, I would do anything for you."

"I know you would, and I feel like I'm constantly taking advantage of you."

"You've hardly taken advantage of me, Em." Jake studied her face. "Something else is bothering you. What is it?"

Emily looked away from his probing gaze. "I'm worried about what we'll find in the safety deposit box. Did Cameron and my father get themselves messed up in something illegal? I don't want to find anything disparaging about either of them."

"I think you knew your brother well enough to know that's not likely the case. Cameron would want you to have faith in him."

"You're right," she admitted with a sigh. "If it is something bad, I'm sure he didn't get involved knowingly." She looked past Jake's shoulder to Robert waiting in his Tahoe. "Robert probably thinks I'm such a basket case."

"I can almost guarantee he's thinking 'kiss her already and get on with it.'" Jake leaned over and planted a quick kiss on her forehead, then he climbed out and walked around to her door.

She smiled as he helped her down. No doubt she'd seen the thumbs up signal Robert gave him.

Before they left the parking garage, Jake stepped to Robert's window and had a quick word with him. "I'll text you when we're on our way out."

Hopefully, that would be soon and with no complications.

Vince backed Ralph's Nissan into the far corner of the parking garage and lowered the window. The odor of rubber and oil combined with the noise of traffic outside the garage grated on his already frayed nerves. Perspiration pricked his brow, and his shoulder muscles bunched. He popped his neck, weighing his options.

He'd hated having to borrow Ralph's car again, but his Excursion was too well known. He also hated conducting business in public. He didn't have a choice anymore, though. He hadn't been able to get close to Dr. Anderson on the ranch, but he'd tailed her and the rancher here easily enough, thanks to Ralph's car.

If she handed the evidence in that box over to law enforcement, it was game over for the boss.

He couldn't help the smile that pulled at his lips. In Vince's opinion, the arrogant fool had gotten away with too much for far too long. He pressed his mouth into a tight line. But the pompous jerk wouldn't hesitate to throw him under the bus for her father's and brother's murders, and he couldn't have that.

He leaned forward in his seat to get a look at the sheriff parked next to the rancher's truck. There was no way Vince could get his hands on the woman near the truck. And picking them off from across the garage was too risky. He couldn't guarantee a clear shot. Besides, the sheriff would be on him before he could retrieve the evidence.

No. I've got to get them before they get back to the sheriff.

~

"I'M NOT sure I want to see what's in there," Emily whispered, dread seeping into her bones.

Because Cameron had put Emily's name on the safety deposit box, they had no problem getting access once she showed her ID.

"It's time to find your answers." Jake put his arm around her shoulders and gave a gentle squeeze.

Emily nodded. *It is time.* She turned the key and Jake pulled out the box and set it on the table in the center of the room. Emily shivered as she lifted the lid. Why do *they keep this room so cold?*

Inside the box, lay a single sheet of folded paper and a thumb drive.

"That's it?" She took out the paper and read it. Pain filled her chest, and she gasped for air. "He knew. He knew they would kill him."

Jake looked over her shoulder. She held the paper so he could see Cameron's scrawled cursive.

I, Cameron Adam Anderson, being of sound health and mind and fearing for my life do hereby leave all my worldly possessions, investments, and wealth to my sister, Emily Anderson.

It was signed and dated the day Cameron was killed. He'd even had it notarized. In a postscript across the bottom of the page was written, *I'm sorry, Emmy.*

"I'm so sorry," Jake whispered against her hair as he held her close.

Emily wanted to sink into Jake's comforting embrace and let him push away her pain. But she couldn't do that. She couldn't continue to be the victim. Needing to find the strength to take control of her life again, she picked up the thumb drive.

"Two people are dead because of this?" Heat filled her chest, radiating through her body. What secrets did it hold that were worth the lives of two good men?

As if reading her thoughts, Jake said, "Hopefully, it holds the answer to who killed your father and brother and why. Would you like me to carry it for you?"

Emily nodded. She was all too happy to hand over the thumb drive. Besides, her dress had no pockets and she needed her hands free to maneuver on her crutches.

Jake replaced the box and removed the key. While Emily canceled the safety deposit box and returned the key, Jake texted Robert to let him know they were on their way out.

A sense of foreboding filled Emily as they rode the elevator down to the parking garage. Would the information on the thumb drive lead them to the man trying to kill her before he succeeded?

It'll all be over soon. Then she could go home and try to pick up the pieces of her life. The thought of leaving the ranch and Jake was almost as painful as losing her brother. But she needed to leave before she got in too deep.

As they exited the elevator and rounded the corner, a large, hooded figure in a dark sweatshirt charged them and shoved Jake to the ground.

Emily watched in shock as his head slammed into the concrete. She teetered, losing her balance. A strong arm yanked her upright before she could hit the ground and snaked around her neck, jerking her back against a solid chest. The cold barrel of a revolver pressed against her temple.

"Jake!" Emily cried out, her voice weaker than she'd intended. Her crutch fell to the floor as the hooded man dragged her backward.

He's going to kill me. Emily's good leg trembled, and her breath came in sharp, short bursts. The pulse pounding in her ears muted Jake's groan.

He staggered to his feet, shaking his head. "Stop!"

The hooded man halted their backward motion. "Stay out of this, and you won't get hurt."

An icy chill snaked up Emily's spine. She'd heard that voice before, from the back of the SUV. This was the man who killed her brother. And he now pointed his gun at Jake.

"Sorry, I can't do that." Jake pulled the thumb drive from his pocket and held up his hands, palms forward. "I've got what you want."

The rock-hard chest pressed against Emily's back rumbled with a growl. *Did the big ox honestly expect me to be carrying the thumb drive?*

"Let her go, and I'll give you the drive." Jake's voice was hard as flint.

Emily had never heard that tone from Jake before. All gentleness was gone, replaced by anger and something else. Fear, maybe?

Her eyes never left Jake's face as the tension in the ox's body shifted while he weighed his options. *What are you thinking, Jake? Please don't do anything stupid.*

"You can't give it to him, Ja—" The arm tightened around her neck, cutting off her air supply.

Her mind ran wild as she struggled to breathe. If Jake handed over the drive, then the person responsible for her brother's death would go free.

Would the ox let her go? Or would he take the thumb drive and kill both her and Jake anyway?

The thought made her entire body shake. Shadows crowded the edges of her vision, and she focused on Jake's brown eyes, willing herself not to pass out.

Jake's eyes met hers. "I won't let him take you, Emily."

In his eyes, she saw the same determination Jake showed after getting bucked off the colt. Too bad a soft touch and gentle voice wouldn't tame a lunatic with a gun like it did the colt.

"Give me the drive, and I'll release her."

"I don't think so. Let her go, and when she's by my side, I'll toss you the drive."

The arm around her neck loosened, and she sucked in the badly needed oxygen that smelled like body odor mingled with oil and rubber.

"Don't do anything stupid. I won't hesitate to shoot her, or you." The arm around her neck slackened, and he poked her between the shoulder blades with the gun to nudge her forward.

She wanted to feel relieved, but she knew he didn't intend to let her live.

"Wouldn't dream of it," Jake said in a low voice.

Expecting to be shot in the back any second, Emily hobbled forward. She never took her eyes off Jake's face, who never took his eyes off the ox. As soon as she neared Jake, he stepped between her and the gunman.

She turned in time to see Jake toss the thumb drive. Daniel had told her about Jake's impeccable aim, so she knew it was no accident that the drive sailed two feet over the ox's right shoulder. The same arm that held the gun.

The man attempted to catch the drive with his left hand, bringing the gun upward.

Jake rushed him, grabbing the hand with the gun, and tackling the man to the ground.

The ox's hand slammed into the concrete, sending the gun clattering across the floor.

Emily's heart leaped to her throat. *I knew he was going to do something stupid!*

Having the advantage, Jake landed a punch to the ox's jaw. Then the ox punched Jake in the stomach, ripping a grunt from him. The ox growled and grabbed Jake's shirt in both hands and rolled, tangling their arms and legs.

The ox now had the advantage, and he used it to pummel Jake.

Fear for Jake seized Emily, blurring her vision. She couldn't let this man hurt another person she loved. She froze for a moment at the realization that she loved Jake. Then her fear turned to anger.

White-hot heat filled her. She hobbled forward and swung her crutch at the ox's back as he punched Jake a third time. It barely fazed him, but it drew his attention long enough for Jake to land a punch to the man's jaw.

Putting all her anger and grief into the motion, she swung again, bringing the crutch down on the man's head.

The big ox groaned and dropped on Jake's chest.

Jake shoved the man off him and rolled over. After a long moment, he pushed to his feet. He staggered then dropped to his knees again.

"Jake." Emily registered the sound of boots on concrete approaching as she reached out to Jake.

"Don't move! Police!" Robert forced the slowly stirring ox onto his stomach and planted a knee in his back. His eyes cut to Jake. "You okay, man?"

"Took you long enough," Jake grunted as he staggered to his feet again, this time managing to stay upright. He rubbed the side of his head with one hand as he steadied Emily with the other.

Relieved, Emily sunk into him.

"What are you bellyaching about? Looked like Emily had every-thing under control." Robert gave her a quick wink before cuffing the ox and pulling him to his feet. He turned him to face Emily and pulled the hood off the man's head.

Steel gray eyes and a sneering face sent a chill through her.

"Is this the man who shot your brother, Emily?"

EMILY BRACED herself as she studied the man. His was a face she'd never wanted to see again. The face that haunted her dreams.

"Yes." The word came out as little more than a whisper.

Jake's arm tightened around her, and she turned into his embrace. *Jake.* He understood her so well and was quick to offer comfort.

And every time, she accepted that comfort. Except for yesterday afternoon when she'd pushed him away and been miserable afterward. Not only because she'd hurt Jake but because she'd felt so alone.

She let Jake lift her into the truck, where she sat silent during the short ride to the Kennewick police department. Dealing with the legality of jurisdictions before transporting Robert's prisoner to Spokane took forever. At least it gave Jake time to ice his head—where it had hit the concrete—and his jaw that received multiple punches, before making the long ride to Spokane.

She'd tried to insist he not drive, but he'd pointed out if he didn't drive, they would have to ride with Robert and his prisoner. Emily did not want to go anywhere near the man who killed her brother and probably her father, so she'd dropped the argument. She kept a close eye on him as he drove though. The man was tough as nails, but he probably had a concussion.

When they arrived at the Spokane police station, Detective McIntyre met them out front. Robert turned his prisoner over to officers for booking on charges of murder and assault. A short time later, they crowded around the detective's desk as he inserted the thumb drive into his computer.

Emily didn't want to know what was on it, but she couldn't look away. She had to know what had gotten her father and brother killed.

Four sets of eyes stared at the computer as Detective McIntyre opened the single file on the thumb drive. Emily's brow wrinkled in confusion as a series of documents opened.

Robert was the first to speak. "What are we looking at?"

It was a few moments before anyone answered. Finally, Detective McIntyre spoke up. "They look like financial records for..."

"For Andertech Solutions," Emily gasped and covered her mouth with her hand. From the few things she'd seen on the computer, it was clear who was responsible for her dad's and Cameron's deaths, and it made her stomach turn.

How could he? He'd been her father's best friend for over thirty years. She'd eaten dinner at this man's house and spent holidays with him and his family. He'd expressed such heartfelt condolences at her father's funeral and at the news of her brother's death.

Emily's chest tightened, and she struggled to breathe. Her stomach churned again. "I think I'm going to be sick."

Jake knelt beside her chair and pulled her against him. "Take a deep breath." He rubbed his hand up and down her back. "It's Maxwell Garrison, isn't it?"

She nodded, with her cheek pressed to his shirt. After a few moments, she pulled away but covered her face with her hand. She couldn't bring herself to look at the screen again. She didn't need to. Robert's and the detective's quiet murmurs of personal financial records, embezzlement, and gambling penetrated the buzzing in her ears.

Unable to take anymore, she grabbed Jake's arm. "Take me home, please?"

Jake helped her to her feet as Detective McIntyre and Robert gave Emily a compassionate look. The walk to Jake's truck took an eternity. He paused before starting the engine.

"We're still not sure you're out of danger, Emily. By home, I assume you want me to take you back to the ranch?"

"Yes, I want to go the ranch."

The ranch had become her refuge. She felt safe there. Even though no one had said the words, Emily felt loved at the ranch. Faith had been so kind and taken such good care of her. And Jake. Jake had become her rock.

She knew she couldn't stay at the ranch forever, but while her life continued to crumble down around her, she wanted to be in the one place where no one would hurt her.

But that wasn't true.

She cared for Jake so strongly, that if he ever rejected her, it would devastate her. Could she bear that kind of pain on top of everything else she'd lost?

Yet, she would end up hurting him when she left the ranch.

And she needed to leave. Soon.

THAT EVENING, Jake sat beside Emily once again as Robert filled them in on everything the Spokane Police Department had learned.

"Maxwell Garrison has been embezzling from Andertech Solutions for the last ten years, hiding the money in a shell corporation. A corporation that coincidentally owns a property by the lake. That's where Barnes was taking you, Emily. Not only has Garrison purchased multiple vacation homes and lived a lavish lifestyle, he's also racked up some massive gambling debts."

Emily's body stiffened next to Jake. She groaned and leaned her face against her hand. She kept her elbow propped on her cast and her face hidden while Robert told them about Maxwell Garrison's arrest.

Jake worried about Emily. She'd been quiet all evening. He knew she was upset, but she refused to show it. There had been no tears, no shouting, nothing. She'd hardly touched her dinner, even though she knew Jake watched her. He didn't have the heart to insist she eat more since he hadn't had much of an appetite himself.

"We also brought Max's son, Jeffery, in for questioning." Emily's head came up at this. "But we determined he had no knowledge of his father's illegal dealings. Garrison admitted to hiring Vince and Frankie Cooper—a.k.a. Brian Barnes—to kill your father and Cameron. Since Frankie is dead and Vince—who also has multiple aliases—is in custody, you're no longer in danger. You're free to make funeral arrangements for your brother."

"Thank you, Robert." Scooting to the edge of the couch, Emily grabbed her crutches. "If you'll all excuse me, I'd like to go to bed now."

Jake helped her to her feet. "Would you like to call Joe?"

She shook her head and walked out of the room.

His mother followed her but came back almost immediately, her face etched with worry. "She doesn't want help tonight."

Did she seek the privacy of her room to cry? Not wanting to do it in front of him, knowing he would want to comfort her? Or was she in some sort of denial?

Either way, she'd shut Jake out. A deep-seated ache settled in his chest.

At least he wasn't the only one. She hadn't even called Joe tonight. The thought wasn't comforting because it meant Emily was shutting down. She needed Joe. As much as Jake didn't want to accept that, it was true.

"Do you think she'll be okay?" Robert asked, looking at Jake.

"I don't know. This is not how I expected her to react. Finding out Maxwell Garrison was behind this must be devastating. The man had been her father's best friend since college. He was like an uncle to Emily."

"Emily must feel so betrayed," his mom said. "I can only imagine how bad she must be hurting."

Robert shook his head. "Looking at those financial records, the man was taking home a substantial six-figure income. How did he get himself in a position of needing to embezzle millions?"

Jake rubbed his bruised jaw. "Gambling can be very addictive. And desperate people do desperate things."

Robert and his mom both nodded in agreement. Then Robert stood, yawning as he did so. "I'm going to head home. Let me know if there's anything I can do for Emily."

After Robert walked out the front door, Jake's mom gave him a quick hug. "I'm going to turn in too."

Finding himself alone and much too concerned about Emily to sleep, Jake went to his office and picked up the phone. He deliberated for a full minute before searching the call history for a regularly-occurring unfamiliar number. Determining he had the right number by the frequency of the calls, he pushed the talk button.

He glanced at the clock as he listened to the line ring. It wasn't extremely late, but it was later than was considered polite to call a stranger.

"Emily, how are you doing?" The voice on the other end of the line did not sound like someone Jake should be jealous of. It reminded him of his grandfather.

"I'm sorry, Joe, this isn't Emily. This is Jake Winters, and Emily is not doing well."

CHAPTER 30

*J*ake came in the next morning for breakfast to find Emily had already eaten and was now in his office making arrangements for Cameron's burial.

"Did she eat much?" he asked.

His mom shook her head and Lottie frowned.

He didn't want to bother Emily while she made her phone calls, so he ate and went back out to work with one of the young colts. He itched to go for a ride, and he wanted to work hard and get dirty. But he needed to stay close to the house. In case Emily needed him.

Would she ever turn to him again?

He replayed his conversation with Joe last night in his head while he circled the colt on his lead rope.

"What's the matter with Emily?" Joe asked.

Jake explained what they found on the thumb drive and Garrison's admission of hiring the men to kill Emily's father and brother. "She's no longer in danger, but I'm concerned about how she's been acting. Except for her initial reaction, she has shown no emotion. No tears, no crying, screaming, nothing."

"She's processing right now. Losing someone like she did is difficult, but to discover someone you know and trusted, someone you thought cared about you, is responsible... that takes longer to process. She'll go through stages of denial, anger, acceptance, and depression, but she may not manifest them emotionally."

"But I've seen her cry and be angry at the same time," Jake said, remembering how Emily had pounded his leg when she got news of her brother's death.

"I have too," Joe said.

"She told me about what she went through after her mother died."

"She told you about her struggle with...?" Joe's surprised voice died off as he realized he was about to say something he shouldn't.

"About not being able to eat because she didn't mourn her mother properly? Yes. I'm worried about her. I can tell she's lost weight. And she hardly ate a thing this evening. Talking with you helps, but she didn't even want to call you tonight."

"She's struggling with more than the loss of her brother and betrayal by her father's partner right now."

"Like what?" Jake asked, confused.

Joe took his time answering. "I'm not at liberty to say." Then after another brief pause, he spoke again. "She needs you Jake, but she doesn't want to admit to herself that she needs anyone. Emily is a strong, independent woman, but she knows she's alone now, and she's trying to process how she's going to make it all alone."

"She doesn't need to do it alone," Jake said, trying to hide the fervency in his voice. He wasn't sure he was ready to admit how much he cared about Emily to anyone, least of all to a stranger who was a shrink.

"I've told her the same thing. But Emily feels the need to prove it to herself. She doesn't want to repeat past mistakes."

"What past mistakes?"

Again, there was a long silence on the phone. "Never mind." Then letting out a sigh, Joe continued. "This is not the first time Emily has lost a loved one. Although, I dare say, this is the most difficult loss. Something happened after her father died that makes Emily hesitant to rely on others. There are more issues here than dealing with her grief."

"I'm part of the issue now, aren't I?" Jake said, remembering how upset Emily was yesterday.

"You can't take it personally. Her pulling away is an act of self-preservation. She's trying to avoid getting hurt, nor does she want to hurt anyone else."

What exactly did Emily go through after her father's death? He had a feeling it had something to do with a man. Was it the Trent fellow she didn't want to talk to when she notified Cameron's friends of his death?

"So, I'm supposed to let her pull away and watch her starve herself to death?" Jake hadn't intended to let his frustration make him sound so angry.

But he was angry. He was angry at Max Garrison for putting beautiful, sweet, Emily through the heartache she was having to endure.

"No, Jake, you don't need to sit back and do nothing." Joe's voice was forceful now. "Make her confront her feelings. Make her admit her anger, encourage her to cry and yell, but whatever you do, respect the boundaries she has set."

Boundaries?

Last night, Emily set clear boundaries to protect herself. The first and foremost no more kissing. He was such an idiot for having kissed her when he held her in her bed. He knew she was vulnerable, but he'd done it anyway.

Jake talked with Joe for a few more minutes, deciding if Emily hadn't eaten or talked to Jake by the next afternoon, Jake needed to encourage her to confront her feelings. Either way, Joe promised to call the next evening.

Jake watched the bay colt, wondering what he could do to get Emily to talk to him without driving her away.

He wished he could hold her because he liked the feel of her in his arms, but also because she took such comfort from his embrace. How could he comfort her without the physical contact? He wouldn't kiss her anymore. She'd set that boundary and he would respect it, no matter what. It wouldn't be easy, but he respected Emily, and if it made it easier for her to handle everything she was going through, then he would avoid that kind of contact.

It wasn't lunchtime, but Jake returned to the house, hoping to see Emily. He found his mom and Lottie visiting in the kitchen.

"Lunch will be ready in an hour," Lottie said as she folded dish towels.

"It's fine," he said, with a dismissive wave. "I'm not even hungry."

"You're worried about her, aren't you?" his mother asked.

He sat down beside her at the counter. "Yeah." He worried about so many things, and lately, all of them had to do with Emily. As much as he'd like to talk things out with his mom over a cup of hot cocoa, he wasn't about to divulge confidences.

His mother must have read his mood, because she rubbed his shoulder.

"Has she come out of the office?"

"No. Poor girl. She's dealing with so much."

Jake raked his fingers through his hair. "I wish there was some way I could take her pain away."

"I know you do."

Lottie set aside the dish towel she'd been folding. "Is there something you could do that would help her feel better, distract her maybe, for a little while at least?"

He shrugged. "I'm open for suggestions."

"She enjoys being outside. Maybe she would like to go for a ride in the carriage again," Faith said.

"I could make a picnic lunch," Lottie added.

Jake smiled at his mom and Lottie's enthusiasm. Did Emily have any idea how much everyone cared about her?

He wasn't sure Emily would want to spend time with him in such close proximity. But if she agreed to go, it would give him the chance to see if he could get her to open up.

"It's worth a try."

As Faith and Lottie discussed what they could put in the picnic lunch, Jake poked his head out of the kitchen to see that his office door was still closed. He decided to hitch up the carriage before talking to Emily.

Whether she liked it or not, it looked like they were going on a picnic.

~

AT THE SOUND OF A KNOCK, Emily lifted her head from the arm of the love seat in Jake's office. The door opened, and Jake poked his head in. She'd finished her phone calls, but she'd stayed in here because she couldn't face anyone right now.

Jake stepped into the room with such a tender look in his eyes that Emily had to swallow hard to fight the emotions that clawed at her chest. She'd shed so many tears, most of them in this man's arms.

Somehow, she needed to find the strength in herself to deal with her loss.

"I'm sorry I've been monopolizing your office." She pushed herself to a sitting position on the love seat.

"It's fine. It's one of my least favorite places to be because it means paperwork." He rolled the chair over so he could sit in front of her. "Have you taken care of everything you needed to?"

"Yes," she said with a heavy sigh. "It's so much harder dealing with it all myself than it was with Cameron's help."

Jake reached out and took her hand. "You don't need to do it by yourself, Em. I would be more than happy to help you with anything you need."

Emily squeezed his hand then pulled her hand from his. "I know, Jake, and I appreciate that. But I can't do that to you... or myself right now."

"I'm not sure I understand why you feel the need to pull away from me, but I'm trying to give you space. I promise I'll try not to be too compassionate." He gave her a teasing smile.

Emily rolled her eyes. "You're not capable of partial compassion. It's not in your nature."

Jake's brow furrowed, then he shrugged.

Emily bit back a smile. Jake had no idea what she was talking about.

"Mom and Lottie ganged up on me and insisted I get you out of the house." Jake turned pleading eyes on her, and she caught her breath. He looked so adorable. "Would you like to go for a ride in the carriage? We can take a picnic lunch." As Emily debated whether to go with him, he added, "I promise it's not meant to be a romantic ride."

"Is this your way of making sure I eat?" she said, ignoring the comment about romance. She couldn't afford to think along those lines right now.

"I'm worried about you, Em. We all are."

Emily let out a sigh of resignation. "I'd like to go for a ride, and I am kind of hungry, so I'll even try to eat."

"I have the carriage ready, but I need to grab something real quick."

A few minutes later, Jake lifted Emily into the carriage—his strong arms wrapped securely around her.

She tried not to relish how good it felt to be held by him.

Jake headed the team of horses in a different direction than they had previously gone. While they rode, he attempted to make small talk, but Emily only gave brief responses. She didn't feel like talking.

"Have you called Joe?" he finally asked.

"No."

"Are you going to?"

"I don't know." She let out a deep sigh. "I keep telling myself I shouldn't bug Joe or you. I should be strong enough to make it through this on my own. I need to get used to doing things alone."

Jake's knuckles turned white as he tightened his grip on the reigns. "No, Emily. You don't need to do any of it alone. You've got people all around you that care about you. We'll help you through this, and we will be there to help you through other things too if you'll let us."

"I can't, Jake." Then in a quiet voice, she added, "It hurts too bad to let people in, especially when they let you down."

"Are you talking about Max? Or have others hurt you too?"

Emily looked away. She'd been hurt by too many people, and she'd hurt others. "I don't want to talk about it."

"You need to talk about it. You can't keep it all bottled up inside. It will only make you more miserable."

"What am I supposed to do?" she said, raising her voice. "Come running to you every time I feel sad, or have a bad dream? I can't do that, Jake. I won't do that."

"At least talk about it. It'll help you let go of the pain and start the healing."

Emily glared at him. "What? Are you the therapist now?"

"You told Debbie I was acting as your counselor the other day, so let me be your counselor. Talk to me."

"And tell you what?" Emily's throat grew tight.

"Tell me what you're feeling. You've been betrayed by someone you trusted, but you haven't talked about it. You haven't shed a single tear."

"Right, because crying means I'm dealing with it?" Pain seized Emily's chest and she gasped for air.

Jake tried again. "Tears can be healing."

"I could cry a river of tears and not find any solace!" she shouted. Heat rushed through her body. "Is that what you want to hear? Do you want to hear me say I'm angry? Fine. I'm furious with Max. I hate him for taking everyone away from me. My dad was his best friend. He was the reason Max was so wealthy, but it wasn't enough for him. And I'm angry at God. He could have protected those I love, but he didn't. He took them away—" Emily's voice broke, and the tears that had been screaming for release burst through their dam. She was powerless to stop them. "Why?" she wailed. "Why did he take my whole family away from me?"

Jake brought the carriage to a stop and wrapped his arms around her. "That's exactly what I want to hear," he whispered into her hair.

Her tears soaked Jake's shirt as he held her, encouraging her to let it all go. And she did, repeatedly asking "why" as she sobbed, wishing Jake could explain why all this had happened to her. She continued to cry until she couldn't cry anymore.

Finally, she lifted her head from Jake's shoulder and scrubbed at her face, unable to make eye contact with him.

"So, as a counselor, do I just listen or am I supposed to respond?"

She shrugged. "Whatever you feel like."

"Okay, then I'd like to say this: I think your anger toward Max is justified, and I understand why you're angry with God. But He is the only one who can truly help you through all of this. If you'll let Him."

"I don't know if I can," she said, her voice barely above a whisper.

EMILY BREATHED in the fresh air and took in the small purple and yellow wildflowers surrounding the blanket Jake had set her on. She closed her eyes and listened to the water rushing over the small waterfall twenty yards upstream. Even the bark of the pine tree pressing into her back made her feel so alive.

Every time Jake took her for a ride, Emily didn't think she'd seen anything quite so beautiful, especially amid the desert landscape of Southeastern Washington. But the location of today's picnic was the prettiest yet.

They sat in a small grove of Pine and Aspen trees next to a crystal-clear stream, secluded from the rest of the world.

"This is our own little piece of heaven on the ranch." Jake's voice was tinged with pride.

"It's beautiful." She drew in another deep breath and let it out. "And peaceful."

If only she could forget about all she'd lost. *Will I ever truly have peace again?*

Jake spread out enough food to feed a small army. Lottie and Faith had thought of everything—sandwiches, crackers and cheese, chips, vegetables, and assorted fruits, including a separate, small container of strawberries. Packed just for her, since Jake was allergic.

She opened the container and picked out a plump berry. Holding it by the leaves, she took a bite. The sweet juice burst in her mouth. *Delicious.* She closed her eyes savoring the flavor.

How allergic is Jake to strawberries?

If he kissed her after she ate the strawberry would he be able to taste it on her mouth? Would it be enough to cause an allergic reaction?

Heat flooded her cheeks. She shouldn't be thinking about kissing Jake. Kissing was off limits.

She opened her eyes to find his eyes on her mouth. Self-consciously, she licked her lips to make sure there was no juice left on them.

The muscle in his jaw clenched as he tore his eyes away from her face.

Knowing she shouldn't, but unable to stop herself, she cleared her throat and asked, "So, how allergic are you to strawberries?"

Jake's eyebrows rose as he looked at her lips again. Had he read her thoughts?

Planting a hand on the blanket between them, he slowly leaned toward her.

Emily's pulse accelerated, and she forgot to breath.

Jake drew closer, until his cheek almost touched hers. His warm breath against her ear sent a shiver down her spine. "I *should* tell you I'm deathly allergic, so you'll stop teasing me." Then he shifted so his lips almost touched hers.

Her lips parted, and her mouth grew moist.

"But the truth is... I'm only mildly allergic."

His breath brushed across her lips, light as a feather. He pulled away, and she drew in a shaky breath. She'd never felt so relieved and disappointed at the same time. She'd wanted that kiss.

Thank goodness he had the strength to resist kissing her, because kissing would have complicated things further. She needed to find the strength to do this on her own, but she wasn't even strong enough to resist Jake's kiss.

This is the worst possible time in my life to fall in love. She needed to remember that.

"I'm sorry, Jake. I didn't mean to tease you. When I ate the strawberry, I couldn't help thinking..." she let her voice die off, realizing she wasn't making it any easier, for either of them.

"The same thing I was thinking about, obviously." The smile Jake gave her, made her heart stutter. "Serves me right for thinking I need to watch every bite you take to make sure you eat enough."

"I'll do my best to eat," she said. "So, you don't have to watch me."

"Good." The word was little more than a grunt.

After a few minutes of silence, while they each nibbled at their food, Jake asked, "What do you think will happen to your father's company?"

Emily put the cracker she'd been eating on her plate and set her plate down.

Jake's eyes followed her actions, and the look on his face said he regretted asking since she hadn't eaten much yet.

"I don't know," she said. "That company was my father's whole life. But it has taken his life and Cameron's. It kills me to say it, but I'm not sure I want anything to do with it. I'm not qualified to fill my father's or Cameron's shoes. I assume Max's wife and son will continue to benefit from his share."

"If it'll always be a painful reminder, it might be best to sell it."

She nodded. "I should ask Ben to contact Jeffery and the shareholders to see what my options are." She rubbed her forehead, trying to ease the building tension.

Jake reached in his back pocket and pulled out her hairbrush. Holding it up, he arched an eyebrow at her.

She chuckled. "You had to grab one thing, huh? You came prepared, didn't you? You were determined to break down my defenses."

"Just trying to help."

"You're being too helpful, which is not helpful at all." She reached out to snatch the brush away from him, but he pulled it out of her reach.

"Trust me, this is purely selfish. I like your hair."

She looked at him for a long moment. Would it make things harder? For her? For him? She should keep her distance from Jake, but she felt like an invisible magnet pulled her toward him. A magnet stronger than she was.

Jake wanted to help her relax, and he knew how relaxing it was to have her hair brushed. He was a good man. She liked everything about Jake. But she'd end up hurting him if she later realized her feelings for Jake weren't genuine? She didn't want to hurt him like she did Trent when she couldn't help him with his problems.

Why are you comparing your rancher to Trent? Joe's voice echoed in her head. Deep down she knew Jake didn't have the kind of problems Trent did, and she cared more for him than she ever had Trent. But soon she'd need to walk away from Jake to prove to herself she was strong enough to be on her own.

But did that day have to be today?

"Now who's being the tease?" she asked.

Jake looked down at the hairbrush in his hand. "Sorry, I didn't stop to think it might make things harder for you." He was about to put the brush back in his pocket when she grabbed his arm.

"I'd like you to brush my hair, Jake."

His eyes jumped to hers. A slow smile spread across his face and he nodded. "If you can rotate your body and lean your good shoulder against the tree, I can kneel behind you. That'll be more comfortable than lying on the hard ground."

Emily did as he suggested, and Jake knelt behind her. Warmth emanated from his body so close behind her, and her scalp tingled. She inhaled his scent; the fresh soap scent was barely discernible, but he smelled masculine, strong, and perfect.

Letting Jake brush her hair was a mistake.

"You still have food on your plate."

Emily could tell Jake tried to make his comment sound casual and not accusing.

"Is brushing my hair today's form of bribery?"

"I prefer to think of it as a distraction."

It's distracting alright.

She turned her head and scowled at him. She picked up a strawberry and took a bite. At least he wouldn't be watching her face as she ate it. Jake's soft chuckle behind her made her smile. She would have elbowed him if she hadn't been leaning against her good arm. Instead, she let out an exaggerated "Mmmm."

"Lottie will be glad you enjoyed her strawberries."

"These are from Lottie's garden?"

"Picked fresh this morning."

"They're delicious."

"I'll take your word for it," he said in a husky voice, making another shiver of awareness skitter down her spine.

I am so in over my head.

CHAPTER 31

*J*ake sat beside Emily facing Cameron's casket. His heart hurt for her as silent tears rolled down her cheeks. He wasn't sure she'd welcome his arm around her in front of Cameron's friends, but he ached to pull her close. Finally, he reached out and clasped her hand.

She didn't look at him, but she squeezed his hand with a fierceness that surprised him.

His mother, on Emily's left, put an arm around her shoulders. Jake looked around at the crowd of Cameron's closest friends and co-workers, their grief written on their faces. Emily had arranged a simple graveside service because Cameron hated funerals.

Jake appreciated the support of his family. Not only had his mother and Robert come, Zane, Lottie, and Daniel were here, as well as Ben and Amy. Uncle James had brought Aunt Hope. He wasn't sure Hope had ever met Emily, but he was grateful she'd come.

Robert stood, in his Sheriff's uniform, off to Jake's left. He knew Jake worried Emily might still be in danger, so he'd come to the funeral armed. Robert's presence gave Jake some piece of mind.

Concern for Emily consumed him. She'd been quiet and with-drawn the last few days. Not pushing him away, but not seeking him out either. She waited for him at mealtimes, making sure he saw her eat, though he didn't think she ate nearly enough. At least she tried. She'd even talked to Joe a couple of times, but Jake wished he could do more for her.

Following the service, Jake was about to step away—so Cameron's friends could pay their condolences—when Emily grasped his hand again. Warmth flooded him. That Emily wanted him by her side meant the world to him.

He stood close enough for her to lean against him, so she wouldn't need to support herself with her crutches, enabling her to return the hugs from Cameron's friends. She introduced Jake to many of them since everyone eyed him with curiosity.

"Joe—" Emily's voice caught, and tears clung to her lashes.

An older, gray-haired man stepped up and wrapped his arms around Emily, and she clung to him. When Emily finally released Joe, the plump, silver-haired woman beside him embraced her.

"Jake, I'd like you to meet Dr. Joseph Lewis and his wife, Beth." Jake extended his hand as he and Joe shared a meaningful look. Joe looked exactly as Jake had pictured him. Like a loving, caring father.

Joe squeezed Jake's hand. "Thank you for taking such good care of our Emily."

Jake nodded. He bit back the words *it was my pleasure*. They wouldn't sound appropriate. Not with everything Emily had been through.

The couple talked to Emily for a few minutes, then Beth said, "Remember Em, you're always welcome to come stay with us."

"Thank you, Beth. I may take you up on that. I'm not sure I'm ready to go home yet."

Something gripped Jake's chest.

Of course, Emily would want to go home or return to Spokane at least. She needed more time to heal, physically and emotionally, but from the way she'd been distancing herself from him, he had a feeling she didn't want his help anymore.

She'll leave the ranch. The vice gripping his chest tightened.

Would she ever come back?

As the Lewises moved away, a blond with a high-pitched voice approached Emily followed by several of Cameron's co-workers. Then, Emily grabbed his hand and gave it a quick squeeze before releasing it again to greet the tall good-looking blond man who approached next.

Jake put a steadying hand on her low back.

"Emily, I'm so sorry." The man wrapped Emily in an embrace that caused Jake to have to lean away.

Emily tensed, and Jake itched to push the man away. Finally, the blond released her, and his eyes rested on Jake.

"Thank you for coming, Trent," Emily said.

So, this is Trent. What was Emily's history with the man, and why did it make her so tense?

"Aren't you going to introduce us?" The blond asked, still sizing up Jake.

"Trent, I'd like you to meet Jake Winters. Jake, this is Trent Olsen. He's been my brother's best friend since before I can remember."

"Really, Em?" Trent looked at her, eyes full of hurt. "We were engaged for five months, and you introduce me as Cameron's friend?"

Engaged? A hoof to the diaphragm couldn't have knocked the wind out of Jake any more effectively than Trent's words did. With everything she'd shared with him about herself, he thought he knew Emily. He knew there was a man in her past, but he didn't know she'd been engaged. What other things had she neglected to tell him?

"Emily, can I talk to you? Alone?" Trent asked, shooting Jake another glance.

"I'm sorry Trent, I can't." Emily leaned into Jake.

Trent bent and whispered in Emily's ear, but Jake caught the words. "I want you to know I'm getting help. I'm working on my... problem."

"I'm glad. I'm sorry I couldn't be the one to help you," Emily said.

Trent's eyebrows raised as he looked at Jake again. "So, you got to be the lucky guy to comfort her this time, huh? I hope you didn't let those beautiful green eyes suck you in."

"Trent!" Emily gasped, and a tremble shook her body.

Fighting the urge to punch Trent's smug face, Jake put a comforting arm around Emily. "I was fortunate to be there for her during this difficult time," Jake said, not liking Trent's tone or his insinuation.

Emily's green eyes certainly had sucked him in. Her eyes, her silky hair, her strawberry-flavored lips. They had all sucked him in. But he wasn't about to let this jerk know it.

"You know my number, Em. If you need anything," Trent said before departing.

"Goodbye, Trent." The words were filled with sadness.

Jake's family paid their condolences, and the crowd thinned, leaving Robert, who stood off at a distance, and the two of them.

Jake guided Emily back to her seat. "Take all the time you need."

He stepped away to have a quick word with Robert and Ben before they left. Then he leaned against his truck, watching Emily.

She was engaged to another man. From Trent's insinuations, he'd been the one to comfort her after her father died. Had they gotten engaged after her father's death? If so, that meant she was engaged a few months ago. Why did it end?

From Trent's bitterness and the way Emily shrank away from him, he guessed Emily broke the engagement. But why?

A short while later, he helped Emily into his truck. He'd offered to rent a limousine to take her to the cemetery, but she insisted it wasn't necessary. Now, he wondered whether she would let him take her back to the ranch or if she'd insist on going back to her condo.

She propped her right elbow on the door and rested her head in her hand. She looked exhausted, and Jake's heart melted.

"Are you okay?" he asked.

"No."

"What can I do for you?"

"Take me home, please."

"Home...?"

"To my condo," she said with conviction.

A vice squeezed Jake's heart. "Emily, please come back to the ranch and give yourself more time to finish mourning and healing."

She glared at him. "Finish mourning? Is that even possible?" Then in a small voice, she added, "I guess it is, since I have no one left to lose."

Why did Jake get the feeling he was about to lose her? "I don't want you to be alone."

"But I am alone, Jake. I have no one and no family. I need to do this on my own at some point."

He opened his mouth to argue that she had him, but she raised her hand.

"I've let this go on too long. You'll become a casualty of my grief, like Trent."

She may as well have thrown ice-cold water in his face.

"Tell me about Trent, please," he said through a tight throat. "The whole story."

Emily closed her eyes and leaned her head back against the seat. She let out a long sigh. Finally, she opened them but didn't look at him as she spoke. "Trent is... was my brother's best friend. They've been inseparable since the second grade. When my father passed away, he was there for Cameron and me. He came over almost daily. He brought food, made sure I ate, and spent a lot of time with me."

Jake's gut clenched. He wasn't sure he liked where this was heading.

Emily rubbed her forehead with a shaky hand. "About a month after my dad died, he kissed me. I thought I felt a connection with him, so I encouraged it. Trent filled the empty space my father's death created. Strange, I know, but I welcomed the relationship. He proposed two months later, and because I craved the comfort and sense of family a relationship provided, I accepted."

Jake gripped the steering wheel with one hand as his chest tightened. The thought of her becoming another man's wife stole the air from his lungs.

"A couple months later, after I'd dealt with my grief, he pressed me to set a wedding date. I couldn't do it because I realized I wasn't in love with him. I cared about him... but only as a dear friend. I didn't have the strength or courage to break off the engagement, though, because he'd done so much for me."

Jake's thoughts turned to the explosive kisses he and Emily had shared. Were the sparks between them enough for her? Did she feel more for him than she'd felt for Trent? Did she care for Jake as much as he did her?

He wanted to ask her, but he feared the answer. Instead, he said, "What made you finally break it off?"

"A few months ago, he borrowed two thousand dollars, saying he needed the money to help a friend. Then two weeks later, he wanted to borrow more. I confronted him about what the money was really for and found out he..." Her voice dropped to a whisper. "He had some large gambling debts."

And Maxwell Garrison's gambling problem cost Emily her father and brother. She must hate the gambling industry like no other right now.

Emily spoke again. "I was angry that he'd kept something like that from me. It finally gave me the courage to break off the engagement. A few weeks later, he decided he wanted help with his addiction." She gave a sad nod. "But I couldn't help him. I wasn't strong enough. I still struggled with so many of my own problems and couldn't give him the help he needed. So I referred him to someone who could. It hurt Trent that I didn't love him enough... to help him."

"And now he's getting help," Jake said.

"I'm glad, but it doesn't change anything. I have even less to give now than I did before." She looked at him, her eyes full of tears. "That's why you need to take me home, Jake. I appreciate everything you've done for me, but I can't keep taking from you. I have nothing to give right now, and I don't want to hurt you by letting things go too far. I can't do that again. You understand, don't you?"

A chill swept over Jake despite the warm day. He gripped the steering wheel with both hands to hide their trembling.

"I'm not asking anything of you, Em," he said. "And I do understand, but it's too late." When her brow creased, he shifted to face her so he could caress her cheek. "Things have already gone too far. There is no way I can walk away from you and not feel like I'm leaving a piece of me behind. It will hurt like hell, but I'll take you home, and I'll drive away. I'll give you the time and space you need because I love you."

Emily pressed her cheek against his palm. She closed her eyes, causing a tear to fall on her cheek. "That's the problem. You've fallen in love with an emotional, needy woman who has taken advantage of your compassion and generosity. But I'm not normally emotional and needy. And I don't use people, either. Usually, I'm confident, self-reliant, and stubborn, even downright bossy. I need time to deal with everything that's happened, and I need to do it alone."

He wiped the tear from her cheek. "You are never alone, Emily. I know you blame God for taking away everyone you love, but He loves you and will not leave you comfortless. If you won't let me help you, please let Him."

Emily dropped her eyes. "I'll try, Jake, but I don't know if I can."

"Will I ever see you again?" Jake was almost afraid to ask the question.

"I do care for you, but I don't trust my feelings right now. I can't allow myself to fall in love because I'm alone and craving a replacement for my father and brother, or because I want a family. I won't make that mistake again."

Her inability to answer his question left the weight of a half-ton hay bale sitting in his gut.

"There's nothing wrong with wanting those things, Emily. It makes you human, not weak." Dropping his hand from her cheek, he turned in his seat and started the truck.

How do I walk away from the woman who holds my heart in her hands?

A VICE CLOSED around Jake's heart, and his legs felt like lead as he walked away from Emily, leaving her on her doorstep. It was the hardest thing he'd ever done. It hurt worse than losing his father.

After everything they'd been through in the past couple weeks, walking away from her was the one thing that brought tears to his eyes.

He thought of how painful his break-up with Lydia had been. It had taken a long time to get over her rejection of him and the ranch. But this pain... he wasn't sure he would ever get over this.

He'd asked Emily if he could call her to check up on her, but she'd put him off, saying she didn't even have a cell phone right now. And she hadn't promised to call him when she got a new phone. She said she cared for him but leaving her standing there with no promise of future contact felt so final.

Why had he let his mom and Ben convince him it would be okay to fall in love with Emily?

Like I could have stopped it.

As soon as Jake arrived home, he found Joe's number on his phone. Pressing the talk button, he waited for the call to connect.

"Hello?"

"Joe? Jake Winters. I felt you should know..." Jake swallowed hard to clear the lump in his throat. "Emily insisted I take her back to her condo after the funeral today."

Joe let out a heavy sigh. "I had feeling she was going to do that. I had hoped she would take a little longer to recuperate at your ranch. Give herself some time, you know? But I should have known. She can be stubborn."

"She told me about Trent," Jake blurted. He wanted Joe to know he hadn't abandoned Emily. That he understood what she was going through.

"Did she tell you everything?"

"I assume so. She told me how he helped her after her father's death, and about their... engagement." The word felt like barbed wire coming out of his mouth. "She told me about the difficulty she had breaking it off when she realized she didn't love him and for not being able to help him with his gambling problem."

"So you understand why she needs to distance herself from you?"

"Yes," Jake sighed.

"She needs some time. Emily needs to work through everything without getting her feelings for you all mixed up in it."

"She said she cared for me, but..."

"She does. But she's afraid to let herself care too much because she can't separate her feelings for you from her grief. She's not sure her attraction to you is genuine or if she's trying to replace all she's lost."

Jake pictured how small Emily looked standing on her front porch. "I don't want her to be alone."

"She won't be. Beth and I will insist she come stay with us for a while. If she refuses, then Beth will stay at her place with her. Thank you for taking such good care of her."

"I feel better knowing someone is looking after her."

"Your concern tells me you care about her too. Would you like to talk about your feelings, Jake?"

Jake almost laughed out loud. He didn't need to talk through his feelings. He was well aware he was in love with Emily. That's why her decision to shut him out hurt so bad. He didn't need a shrink to tell him how painful this would be.

"No thanks. I do care a great deal about Emily, but I understand why she is doing this. I don't like it, but I'll respect her wishes."

"If you ever feel the need to talk about any of this, call me. Sometimes, talking about things can help put them into perspective."

If Jake wanted to talk, he'd talk to his mom. Although, he didn't think his mom's listening ear or all the hot cocoa in the world could take away the darkness pressing in on him right now. The thought of never seeing Emily again sucked the air from his lungs.

Jake ended the call. He'd work through this on his own. Over the years, he'd learned the best way to work through something was by doing just that. Work.

But with the extra hands they'd hired this summer and Zane's efficiency, everything was running smoothly. He'd appreciated that while Emily was here, but now he longed for something to demand his undivided attention. He glanced at the clock. Daniel would be doing his evening workout soon. Perfect. After that, Jake would go for a long ride.

He'd find something on this ranch to do.

CHAPTER 32

"Do you trust God?"

"What?" Emily looked up at Joe.

Why had he brought up her faith, or lack thereof, again? Emily talked with Joe almost daily, but she was at an impasse. She was coming to grips with her loss, but she couldn't understand why God had taken away her entire family. And she couldn't move forward in her life when she felt so unsettled.

They sat in Joe's office in matching armchairs, facing each other. Joe leaned forward, holding her gaze. "I know we don't often discuss God and religion in these offices, but you've suffered great loss, leaving you with deep spiritual wounds. Unfortunately, those wounds don't heal as easily as broken bones." He tipped his head toward her arm.

Instinctively, Emily bent her elbow and flexed her arm. When she'd gotten her casts off a month ago, walking had felt so foreign.

It had been six weeks since she buried her brother. She'd stayed with Joe and Beth for a week before returning to her condo. After another week, she'd begged Joe to let her return work—for her sanity's sake. Sitting at home and missing not only Cameron, but Jake too, had driven her crazy.

"I know you still believe in God," Joe said, pulling her thoughts away from Jake. "but do you trust Him?" His eyes bore into hers. "Suffering the kind of loss you have, it's understandable that you question God's love for you. But you need to recognize that the events that took your dad's and Cameron's lives were set in motion years ago because of one man's selfish choices. God didn't take your father and brother from you, Maxwell Garrison did."

Balling her fists, Emily tamped down the anger that consumed her every time she heard Max's name. Forgiveness wasn't a possibility. Not for a very long time. The anger and hatred would eat at her if she didn't let it go. But she couldn't. Not yet.

Being alone, she struggled with enough, she didn't need to fight that battle too. It was easier not to think about the person responsible for Dad's and Cameron's deaths. It was the only way she'd been able to cope.

"God, however, was mindful of you," Joe continued. "Being able to escape that trunk when you did was not a coincidence, Em."

Emily had regained her full memory except her escape from the trunk of that car. She remembered the inescapable fear she'd felt when the two men shoved her in there, knowing they planned to kill her. And she remembered Jake trying to calm her as she lay on the floor in the back of the car. But she had no idea how she'd managed to escape from the trunk into the back seat. It remained a blank spot in her memory.

"Emily, He brought you to people who would not only take care of you but also care about you. He didn't leave you alone."

This wasn't the first time Joe had led their talks around to Jake. He knew she missed the compassionate, handsome rancher. She fought the urge to call him daily. Joe kept telling her she didn't need to fight it, but she wasn't sure she could trust herself to make rational emotional decisions.

So many things still felt out of her control, and she hated it.

What if it was only her desire to have a family again that attracted her to Jake? Her heart began to race as she thought of the warmth and security she'd experienced in his arms.

He didn't leave you alone. Joe's words pierced Emily's thoughts and struck something deep inside her.

She *had* felt so alone. And she'd blamed God for that because he hadn't stopped Maxwell Garrison. But Max had been on this path for ten years. How many times had God tried to change Max's course? But Max refused, and her brother and father had paid the price. God had spared her though. He'd led her to people who would care about her.

Peace flooded over her, filling every cell in her body with warmth and love, as she acknowledged this truth. *God loves me, and I am not alone.*

Her thoughts turned to Jake again. She loved him, and she was certain he loved her too. This was so much more powerful than anything she'd felt for Trent. Jake was her rock. She felt safe with him. She felt whole. She didn't need to be alone.

She only needed to trust God and let Jake in. *If he still wants me.*

Hope filled her chest, stealing her breath, and the peace that had settled over her was so intense she began to cry. The tears flowed hot and heavy, but she didn't try to stop them. She didn't care that Joe sat across from her, watching. She simply propped her elbows on her knees and buried her face in her hands.

These weren't tears of sadness for those she'd lost. They were tears of joy because of God's love for her and the things He'd given her.

The tears were cleansing and healing. Somehow, amid her crying, she found peace in being alone, and recognized that she didn't need to be.

It was her choice.

JAKE CURSED UNDER HIS BREATH. "Can you reach that nut?"

Now free of his cast, Daniel dropped to his knees and reached under the tractor. "Chill man, I got it."

Jake took the nut from Daniel's grimy hand with his equally filthy one and fit it onto the bolt. Daniel's reminder to chill grated on his nerves.

Jake had been unbearable the past six weeks. The hole in his heart had made it difficult to eat, sleep, and even breathe at times. Worrying about Emily and whether he would ever see her again kept him on edge. So much so, he'd avoided everyone as much as possible.

Daniel had been as upset as Jake when he returned from the funeral without Emily. But the kid was working hard to stay sober. He'd kept an incredibly positive attitude since his court appearance a month ago that resulted in a mandatory sobriety program, suspension of his license, a five hundred dollar fine, one hundred service hours, and fifteen days in jail—to be served on weekends.

What bothered Jake the most was that Emily had invited Daniel to come in for counseling. He knew it was purely a professional relationship, but it hurt all the same. Emily was doing well enough to return to work, but she hadn't contacted Jake. He'd also heard through the family grapevine that Ben had met with her a couple times too, concerning the sale of her father's company.

She *had* sent a message with Daniel for him though. A message that eased his concern a little but made him miss her even more. *"Tell Jake I'm eating plenty of strawberries along with everything else."*

The memory of Emily licking strawberry juice from her lips sent an electric shock through him. And he was right back to thinking about Emily's lips again. That's what caused him to drop the nut in the first place.

With each day that passed since that message three weeks ago, Jake's hopes of hearing from Emily dimmed.

Maybe she has no desire to come back to the ranch.

Not for the first time, Jake considered turning the ranch over to Zane entirely. He could own the ranch without having to live on it. But every time he entertained such thoughts, something inside him withered and died.

He needed to face the truth: the reason Emily hadn't contacted him probably had more to do with him—and the fact she didn't love him—than it did the ranch.

Jake and Daniel both lifted their heads as a blue Nissan Rogue approached the stables. Not recognizing the car, they both watched to see who the driver was.

A woman with long auburn hair climbed out, and Jake's lungs seized. His heart raced like a runaway stallion. He'd never seen Emily in anything other than sweatpants and loose dresses. So, the form-fitting skinny jeans and red blouse she wore did crazy things to his insides. She looked downright sexy in jeans.

Daniel obviously thought so too. He let out a long, low, wolf whistle.

"You can say that again," Jake said, catching his breath.

Daniel started to whistle again, but Jake smacked him in the stomach with the back of his hand, causing him to cough.

Emily turned their direction. A smile lit her face when she spotted them. Her gaze remained on Jake as she walked their way.

Jake watched her, realizing he'd never actually seen Emily walk. She had the sexiest walk—fluid motion, with a bit of a sway and lilt in her step. There was something different about her face though. It wasn't only the absence of bruises; it was the light that shone in her emerald eyes. A light he'd never seen there before.

The closer she got, the faster his pulse raced. He took a few hesi-tant steps toward her, feeling like an eager puppy. If he had a tail, his whole body would be quivering from its eager wagging. And like a dog, he was eager to smother the woman who owned his heart in kisses.

He tried to tamp down his excitement. Just because Emily was here, didn't mean she would welcome his kisses. For all he knew, she'd come to tell him there could never be anything between them.

Emily walked right up to him, ignoring Daniel and the fact Jake was covered in grease and oil, and wrapped both arms around his neck. She pulled Jake's head down and kissed him with a passion she'd never shown before.

Her boldness caught Jake off guard, even as desire rushed through him. He wanted to crush her to him, but his hands were greasy, and he didn't dare let the front of his filthy shirt touch hers for fear of ruining it. He bent forward drawing his body away from her while keeping contact with her lips.

Her warm, soft mouth against his set every nerve in his body to tingling. A wealth of emotion passed between them. Excitement, anticipation, desire, and dare he hope love?

Daniel let out a dramatic cough, and Emily pulled away, color filling her cheeks. "Sorry."

Jake didn't know if she apologized to him or Daniel, but he wasn't one bit sorry. Actually, he was. Sorry he was filthy and couldn't return the kiss like he wanted to.

She smiled at Jake, her dimples cutting grooves in her cheeks. "Hi."

"Hey." Heat raced up Jake's neck to the tips of his ears. The woman he loved kissed him like there was no tomorrow and all he could say was *"hey?"*

Daniel snickered behind him, and he fought the urge to smack him again.

"Can you take a break so we can talk?" Her voice was soft, but the words spoke volumes.

Did she want to talk about *them* and *their* future? He searched her eyes for the answer and got lost in their emerald depths.

"For you? Absolutely." He turned to Daniel.

"Go on. I can finish this up." Daniel waved his hand toward the tractor they'd been working on. "Better get her far away from here, Jake, because the two of you are likely to make the diesel fumes here in the shed combust."

Scowling, Jake turned and threw a jab at Daniel's shoulder. The younger kid easily dodged the punch and laughed.

Jake's one goal today had been to get his best tractor running again since it was time to cut third crop. But now, with Emily here, he could care less about the tractor and the alfalfa.

Turning back to Emily, he let his gaze linger on her face. "Do you mind if I take a quick shower? Then maybe we can go for a ride."

"On horses? I'd love to ride with you. Take your time. I'll visit with Daniel for a bit."

Jake planted a quick kiss on her lips, before walking away whistling, wondering if this was all a dream.

◇

EMILY PERCHED on a semi-clean piece of farm equipment and talked with Daniel as he reached his hands back into the tractor's engine.

They discussed trivial things for a while, then Emily said, "You look good, Daniel. How are you feeling?"

Daniel scratched the back of his neck with a greasy hand, leaving a black streak there. "Good, I guess. The cravings aren't as strong as they used to be, but I still struggle."

"Are there certain triggers that cause the cravings?"

"I've recognized some. Whenever I get angry, frustrated, or upset about something, I get thirsty."

They continued to talk about his triggers and coping mechanisms and first AA meeting he'd attended until Emily spotted Jake headed her way leading two horses.

Her heart raced as thousands of winged creatures took flight in her chest. She patted Daniel's shoulder. "I'll talk to you later. Right now, I need to have a long talk with that handsome cowboy." She nodded her head in Jake's direction, hardly registering Daniel's chuckle as she walked away.

As she drew near, Jake dropped the horses' reigns and pulled her into his arms. "Now, I can greet you properly." He lowered his lips to hers, sending her pulse skyrocketing.

The touch of his lips was light, but it ignited a spark deep inside Emily, and she wanted more. She pushed up on her toes, pressing her lips more firmly against his. Jake claimed more of her mouth, deepening the kiss.

Pleasure rippled through her as electric warmth spread through Emily. She felt like she'd glimpsed the sun for the first time. It was bright, warm, and powerful. In Jake's arms, with his lips on hers, she found something she hadn't realized she'd been longing for. It was so much more than the desire to belong to someone.

It was home.

The kiss was thorough, but it ended much sooner than Emily wanted it to.

"Wow." The word came out a breathless whisper. Not wanting to leave his arms, she buried her face in his chest.

Jake tightened his embrace, as she hoped he would. The fresh clean scent that always wreaked havoc on her senses hit her full force and she sniffed. "Mmm... you smell nice."

Jake chuckled. "I'll never be able to change my soap and deodorant, will I?"

"Not as long as I'm around."

Jake's arms loosened, and he pulled away enough to look into her eyes. "Dare I ask if that will be often and for an extended period of time?"

Emily pulled back and smiled at him. "Let's ride and talk. Do you think we could go to that place with the little waterfall?"

Jake pointed to the bulging saddlebags. "That's my plan. I had Lottie fix us some lunch."

"Mmm... any strawberries in there?"

"I hope so," he said under his breath. They exchanged a heated look. "Get on your horse already. We should talk before we kiss anymore."

"Good idea." She turned toward the horse, and a shiver of anxiety shot through her. "I haven't ridden for years. I'm a little nervous."

"Honey is the gentlest horse I have. You'll be fine." He stood by and helped her get into the saddle then adjusted the stirrups.

They rode in silence for a while, Emily not yet ready to broach the subject they needed to discuss. She knew Jake was leery of her intentions, but she wasn't sure how to explain to him what she experienced yesterday. There was still a lot she didn't know about this handsome rancher, but she knew she could trust Jake with her heart, and she looked forward to getting to know him better.

Peace and contentment filled her as she settled into Honey's smooth rhythm. Her revelation in Joe's office yesterday had lifted a burden from her shoulders. An incredible sadness filled her every time she thought about Cameron and her father, but she recognized that God had a plan for her. All she needed to do was learn to let Him guide her.

They slipped into easy conversation as they rode, Emily enjoying every minute. When they reached the waterfall, they worked together to lay out the picnic.

"I have to admit," Jake said as they ate, "your greeting surprised me back there. I wasn't sure when or even if I'd ever see you again. So I wasn't expecting to be attacked." He gave her a teasing grin, triggering a flutter in her abdomen.

Heat filled Emily's cheeks at how brazen she'd been. "I had to know if what I'd felt every time we kissed in the past was real or if I was remembering a passion that wasn't really there."

Jake looked at her, eyebrows raised. "And? Was it real?"

She couldn't keep a sigh from escaping. "It was definitely real."

"Good." A grin split his face. "Because that kiss sure felt like... a promise."

He was right. It had felt like a promise to her too. It promised a future. A future with Jake.

"It was."

"Was what? A promise?" Disbelief overshadowed the hope on Jake's face.

"I had a... revelation yesterday." She fiddled with her napkin as she spoke. "I'm kind of a control freak, and losing my dad and brother took things out of my control. But I realized yesterday, even though I'd lost control there was someone who hadn't." Emily's throat grew thick as she remembered the peace she'd experienced in Joe's office. "Joe helped me see that I needed to trust God. And I've come to realize, even though I can handle being alone... I don't want to." She leaned into him. "I don't want to be alone, Jake."

Jake sucked in a sharp breath as he wrapped his arm around her. "Does this mean you won't shut me out again?"

She slid an arm around his neck. "It means I'm choosing to let you into my life. Into my heart. Being apart from you these past six weeks has made me realize how much I love you. It happened so fast and at a difficult time in my life, so I couldn't trust my feelings. I was so afraid of making the same mistake I made with Trent."

He slid his hand into her hair and pulled her face close to his. "I love you too, Em." He lowered his lips to hers for a long, lingering kiss that left her mind muddled. Finally, when they parted, with his hand still cupping her head, he whispered, "How can something that feels so right be a mistake?"

"It's not a mistake. I know that now. I've never felt like this before." She stroked his cheek. "This feels so right. It feels like this is where I belong."

"It's exactly where you belong," Jake rasped as he lowered his lips to hers again.

Emily leaned closer to Jake, encouraging him to deepen the kiss. The warmth permeating her body reacted to a sudden ice-cold dampness against her thigh.

Jake gasped and pulled back at the same moment she did.

They looked down to discover a water bottle with a loose cap had tipped over. Jake's thigh was as wet as hers and the narrow expanse of blanket between them.

"Wow, that's cold." She laughed as she shifted away from Jake and the wet spot.

He shifted away as well. "I think I needed that."

Their eyes met, and Emily caught her breath at the obvious desire in his gaze. He gave her a killer smile. It was obvious neither had wanted the kiss to end, but it was probably a good thing it had.

Jake cleared his throat and looked away. Picking up a grape, he popped it in his mouth before a smile stole across his lips again.

Emily couldn't wait to get to know this amazing man better.

AVOIDING the damp spot on the blanket, Jake laid back and laced his fingers together behind his head. He sucked in a deep breath. The air near the river always smelled so fresh, so crisp. He studied the tree branches above him.

Are the leaves always this green?

The food had been cleared away and Jake was content to relax, with Emily. Ben and his mom were right, it wasn't as hard to make time for a woman as he thought it would be. In fact, at this moment, he couldn't think of a single thing more important than being with Emily.

He wanted to build a future with her, but there were still some hurdles to overcome, for both of them. Emily had said she loved him, but that didn't mean she'd be willing to walk away from her life and move to the ranch, where one could often feel lonely and isolated.

Emily had a life and career in Spokane, one he could never ask her to give up. But if she wasn't willing to accept him and the ranch as a package deal, was he willing to walk away from the Double Diamond? Would she ask that of him?

He loved Emily so much he was willing to do anything for her. He could leave the ranch in Zane's capable hands so he could be with Emily. If he spent weekdays with her in Spokane, maybe she'd be willing to spend weekends here with him.

He'd probably go stir crazy after a few weeks, but a long-distance relationship held no appeal.

Emily laid down beside him, laying her head on his shoulder and her hand on his chest.

Propping one arm farther behind his head, he wrapped the other arm around her. Peace swept over him. They'd find a way to make this work. They had to, because he couldn't bear to lose her.

They lay quietly for some time, and if not for the hardness of the ground beneath him, Jake might have dozed off.

Emily shifted her head to look up at him. "What now?"

He looked down at her. "What do you mean?" They needed to have this conversation, but Jake feared what the outcome might be.

Emily pushed herself to a sitting position, her face serious.

Jake sat up too. "I love you, Emily, and I want to be with you

293

forever. I'm willing to do whatever it takes to make this relationship work. I'll leave the ranch in Zane's hands if I need to."

Emily gasped and tears filled her eyes. "Why would you even consider doing that?" Before Jake could respond, she continued. "I'm touched you would be willing to make that sacrifice for me, but I would never ask you to do that. Ranching made you into the wonderful, compassionate, hard-working man I love. This ranch was my refuge during the darkest time of my life. I'd never ask you to walk away from it."

Jake pulled her close to his side. Her words filled him with hope. He wouldn't have to choose between Emily and the ranch. "It's not fair of me to expect you to leave your life behind and give up everything you've worked so hard for to join me on the ranch."

"I'm not giving up anything. I'll simply be exchanging what I have for something else. Something better. I plan to talk to your uncle and see if he thinks the hospital board would like to take on a psychologist. If I need to, I'm sure I can find a job in the Tri-cities area. It would mean a bit of a commute, but it's closer than Spokane."

Jake's heart swelled. It was all he could do to keep from crushing Emily in his embrace.

"As much as I love you, Jake, I couldn't give up that piece of me either. I need to be a therapist for myself as much as for others."

"I'd never expect you to give that up, but I need to know if you can accept me and the ranch as a package deal. I sleep very little during calving season, which can drag on for months. And when it's hay cutting time, I spend my nights baling and the days hauling. There may be times you feel neglected and lonely."

Emily shifted to sit on his lap.

He wrapped his arms around her waist, reveling in this new bold version of the woman he loved.

Her breath tickled his ear as she whispered, "If I get too lonely, maybe I'll just have to spend the night baling hay with you."

A pleasant shiver rippled through him, sending his pulse racing. Jake tightened his hold around her waist and chuckled. The thought of Emily in the close confines of his tractor with him warmed his blood.

"Hmm... that could be fun, but it could also be disastrous." He pressed his lips to hers in a lingering kiss.

"I'm sure I can manage to keep myself busy. But don't worry, I'll be sure to make time to watch you break the colts. I enjoy watching that."

"I remember," Jake said before claiming her lips again.

CHAPTER 33

ONE MONTH LATER.

ake hit submit on the final phase of the government's paperwork for the solar project and pulled his checkbook from the drawer. Today's paperwork was almost done, and this was the last time Jake would have to do it.

Emily had insisted he hire a part-time secretary after pointing out how ornery he got every time he did the paperwork.

Jake had easily caved, because it freed up more time to spend with Emily. And because he really did hate the paperwork.

Ben had hooked Jake up with his own secretary. Sheila would come to the ranch for one hour every afternoon and for two to three hours on Friday mornings.

Jake's head snapped up at the sound of tires on the lane. Electricity shot through his veins as his heart kicked into overdrive.

Emily was early.

Jake bolted to his feet and met Emily on the front porch. "Hello, Beautiful." He pulled her into his arms and pressed his lips to hers.

It had been a whole week since he'd seen her. Though they talked on the phone nightly, Emily had insisted he couldn't visit this week, because she had too much to do.

She'd been working to get her patients set up with other therapists, packing up her home, and listing her condo. But tomorrow... Jake, Robert, Ben, and Daniel were moving Emily to Providence. She'd be renting the apartment above Knight's repair shop from his Aunt Charity until they got married.

Jake hoped that would be sooner than later, but he wouldn't rush Emily. She was still mourning her brother.

Come Monday morning though, Emily planned to start seeing patients at the hospital. Knowing it would take a while to build up a clientele, she also planned to work part time at the high school as a school psychologist.

"Hmm... I've missed you." Emily buried her face in his chest when the kiss ended.

Jake pulled her to the porch swing where they shared more passionate kisses until Ben drove down the lane. He was bringing the paperwork for the sale of her father's company for Emily to sign.

They greeted Ben and led him into the house. Jake planned on leaving them to their business, but she held his hand and pulled him to the table.

Thinking she needed moral support, he sat beside her.

Ben opened a file folder and one by one spread documents in front of Emily. "This is your brother's life insurance, his investments, and the sum of his accounts."

Jake noted the amounts on the checks Ben placed in front of Emily. If she wanted to, Emily could live comfortably on the money from her brother. But Jake knew money wasn't important to her.

Emily slid the checks to the side without a word. Her face remained impassive while Ben explained about the sale of Andertech Solutions and Denise and Jeffrey Garrison's insistence that all the money Maxwell had embezzled be returned to Emily, along with her portion of the sale of her father's company.

Jake sucked in a sharp breath when he saw the amount of the

check Ben slid across the table. Then he coughed uncontrollably from the saliva he'd inhaled into his lungs.

Ben gave him a wry smile.

Jake was a successful rancher. He both wrote and received checks on a regular basis with four and five zeros, but the check in front of Emily had double the zeros of any check he'd ever seen.

As Jake recovered, his eyes met Ben's again. Ben's brow furrowed, and he tilted his head toward Emily.

She had her head buried in her hands. Her shoulders shook, and a soft sob escaped her.

Jake shot Ben a give-us-a-minute look.

Understanding, Ben left the room.

Jake scooted his chair closer to Emily's and pulled her into his arms.

"Oh, Jake." Emily laid her forehead against his chest.

"What's the matter?" He stroked her hair.

"It's so much money. It should make me happy, but it doesn't. I feel repulsed and burdened by it. I would give it all away and that much more again to have my father and brother back."

"So, do it."

Emily pulled away and looked at Jake's face. "What?"

"Give it away. It won't bring them back, but you can honor your father and brother while giving it away."

"You mean like a scholarship fund or something?"

"That's exactly what I mean. You've got enough money you could put many students through college and give large amounts to your favorite charities."

Emily's eyes lit up. "I could set one up in my mom's name too."

"You can do a lot of good with the money, Emily. And you don't have to decide right away. You can let it sit while you decide what to do with it."

"You're right," she said, wiping her eyes. "Ben!"

When Ben rejoined them, Emily pointed at his legal pad. "Write." Pushing all the checks Ben's direction, she said, "Set up an account, or multiple accounts if necessary, in a bank somewhere other than Providence. I want anonymous donations of one million dollars each given to the city of Providence, the Medical Center, the Sheriff's Office, and... the School District."

Ben's eyes widened, and he wrote quickly, trying to keep up with her.

"I want to establish the Anderson Scholarship Foundation. It will give away multiple scholarships each year to various students throughout the state. We'll discuss the particulars of that later, but the scholarships are the only thing I want my family's name linked to. Everything else must be done anonymously." She paused to take a breath as though contemplating who else she could give money to.

"Finally, someone who can give Widow Wheeler a run for her money," Ben mumbled under his breath as he wrote.

Emily's eyes narrowed. "What did you say?"

Ben's face flushed. "Nothing, I'm sorry, Emily. That was horribly inappropriate of me. I shouldn't have—"

"You're right." A mischievous smile spread across her face as she looked at Jake.

He chuckled. "I'm not sure I like that look. What's going on in that beautiful head of yours?"

"I'm thinking how much fun it will be to give Debbie a run for her money at this year's bachelor auction."

The mention of Debbie and bachelor auction in the same sentence made Jake's skin crawl. "I don't think I like the sound of this."

She clasped his hand. "Don't worry. I've got it all figured out. I'll bid on Robert and drive the price way up before I let Debbie have him. You go last, and I'll make sure I win you."

He leaned toward her, and whispered, "You've already won me." Their lips met in a lingering kiss.

Ben cleared his throat and chuckled. "Hey, you've still got an audience. Emily, give me one more minute of your time then I'll be out of your hair and you two can..." He waved his hand in their direction, allowing the action to finish his sentence. "First, I need your signature on these documents." He pushed several papers her way, explaining what each one was. When she'd finished signing all the papers and checks, Ben tucked everything back in his file folder. "I'm comfortable with the legal dealings for the Scholarship Foundation and the other charitable stuff, but I'm not an accountant. You should hire someone to help manage these funds. I recommend Henry Fenway. His office is two doors down from mine. He's an excellent accountant."

"He's a good man," Jake said. "He does my taxes and helps manage the ranch and my personal accounts."

"That's fine but try to keep my name out of it if possible. I don't want everyone in town knowing I'm independently wealthy. It will affect my credibility as a therapist. If my clients think I'm only practicing because I have nothing better to do, they won't be interested in my help. I want the people I counsel with to view me as an equal, as someone who understands them."

Ben made a few more notes, then Jake and Emily walked him out.

As he climbed into his truck, Emily said, "Make sure you triple your hourly rate, Ben, and withhold your payment when you deposit the checks."

"That's not necessary."

"Yes, it is. You don't understand the peace of mind it has given me to not have to worry about any of this."

"I'm happy to do it, but—"

"Please don't make me look for another lawyer." The tone in Emily's voice held a warning.

Ben's eyes widened in surprise, then his lips turned up. "Looks like you've got your hands full, Jake. Good luck."

Jake and Emily both chuckled as Ben started his truck. Jake returned to the porch after Ben drove away. He let out a sigh as he sat once again on the swing.

"What's wrong?" Emily sat beside him.

He was quiet for a long moment. He wasn't sure how to voice the overwhelming feelings racing through him.

Realizing how much money Emily had made him feel insignificant. Ever since he met Emily, he'd wanted nothing more than to take care of her. There had been a time when he'd felt like she truly needed him. But today, he'd realized she didn't need him at all.

There was nothing he could give her she couldn't provide for herself. Except love. But Emily was a beautiful, amazing woman, she could easily find a dozen men who would easily fall in love with her.

"Jake, please talk to me." She picked up his hand and laced her fingers with his.

"Why did you want me to be here while Ben went over all of that with you?"

"I thought we were planning a future together." A spark glinted in her eyes. "Like it or not, this is me, Jake. It's not who and what I want to be, but this is who I am."

"I guess I'm overwhelmed by how wealthy you are." Jake tightened his grip on her hand.

"You're overwhelmed? I'm so glad I can let Ben worry about it all. I want nothing to do with all that money. I'm afraid I'll always associate it with what it cost me."

Jake pulled her close to his side. "I thought when I fell in love and got married my wife would be as eager for me to take care of her as I am to provide for her and a family. I'm not saying I expect her to stay at home and take care of the kids all day, although I do want kids..." Jake ran his hands through his hair in frustration. The words were coming out all wrong.

Emily leaned into him. "I've always planned to live within my husband's means when I married. My income will simply be a bonus. What I really want is something money can't buy."

"I always thought I had a lot to offer a woman, but you..."

Did Emily need him, like he needed her? She'd become his fresh air. He couldn't breathe without her.

"You have everything to offer." Emily held his face with both hands. "You have something I don't. Something money can't buy. The one thing I want more than anything else in the world."

Understanding dawned on him and his heart soared as he pulled her closer. "Emily, I can't bring your father or brother back, but I can give you a mother and brother. As annoying as he can be at times, Robert's a cool big brother. And I'll even throw in a little sister, although I must warn you, she can be a pest sometimes."

Tears filled Emily's eyes. "That's a good start."

"I'll give you cousins, aunts, and uncles."

"That sounds wonderful, but I want more than your family, Jake."

His brow furrowed in confusion.

She dragged her finger along his jaw and down his neck, igniting a fire in his veins. She rested her palm against his chest. Dropping her voice to a low, seductive whisper, she said, "You have so much to offer, Jake."

Jake's pulse raced, and he sucked in a sharp breath. "I'll give you your own family, Em. I'll give you sons and daughters, as many as you want. So many, you'll wish you could be alone again for a while."

She smiled, her dimples creasing her cheeks. "That's exactly what I want." She gripped his shirt in her hand and pulled, closing the remaining distance between their lips. When the kiss ended, she added, "And as far as I'm concerned, you're the only one who can give it to me."

Anxious to start a life with Emily, Jake released her and slid off the swing. He dropped to one knee in front of her. "I wasn't planning on doing this right now, but..." He scratched his neck. He should have thought this through better. "I don't have a ring or anything, yet, but Emily, will you marry—"

"Get back up here. Of course, I'm going to marry you. You aren't getting rid of me."

Jake wrapped her in an embrace and kissed her again. Finally, when they parted, he picked up her left hand and stroked her ring finger with his thumb. "So, what kind of ring do I buy for an heiress, who doesn't want to put on airs."

"You're not buying me a ring."

"Didn't you just agree to marry me?"

"Yes, but I don't want you to buy me a ring."

"Listen, Em, I'm very comfortable financially. I don't have the kind of money you do, but I can afford a nice ring for you."

"I don't want you to buy me a ring, because I want to wear my mother's wedding ring when I marry."

Jake took in the sheen of tears in her eyes. "I think that's a wonderful idea, but I hope you'll give them to me and let me place them on your finger to make it official."

"Of course I will. What makes you think I wouldn't let you do that?"

Jake smiled. "I don't know, maybe because you're no longer the docile, emotional woman I fell in love with. You're stubborn, smart, and sassy."

Emily's eyes widened in feigned offense.

Jake rushed to add, "And when you see something you want, you go for it."

"Aren't you glad I do?" She wrapped her arms around his neck and pulled his lips back to hers.

"Very glad," he said breathlessly when the kiss ended. "So, when do I get to stake my claim and put your mother's rings on your finger?"

"Not until after the bachelor auction."

"But that's not for two more months."

"Yes, and we've only known each other for three months, and we weren't even together for half of that. Don't worry, I promise we'll have a short engagement."

"A very short engagement, please." When she nodded, he pulled her to her feet. "Come on. I've got a present for you. Since I don't get to buy you a ring, I hope you'll consider this an engagement gift. Unofficial of course, because we won't technically be engaged for another two months." He made his voice sound like he was being tortured.

But he was having the time of his life with this woman.

HAND IN HAND they walked to the stables. A flutter tickled Emily's stomach. Maybe she could talk Jake into taking her for a carriage ride. A romantic one this time.

He led her to the tack room where a large, bulky, tarp-covered object sat.

"Sit here." He led her to a wooden bench and placed a box on her lap. "Open it."

Emily pulled the lid from the box, revealing a pair of lady's cowboy boots in brown leather with a fancy design stitched in turquoise thread. She kicked off her tennis shoes. "I love them. Can I put them on?"

Jake knelt in front of her and helped her put the boots on, then he pulled her to her feet. "I thought since you're becoming a permanent fixture around here you should have your own boots and..." He pulled the cover off the sawhorse. "Saddle."

Emily gasped. "It's beautiful." She ran her fingers over the gleaming leather with high-quality stitching. At the back of the saddle, she traced the initials E.W. stamped and dyed into the leather.

E.W. for Emily Winters. Her heart swelled. This was way better than an engagement ring.

Ben's words echoed in her head. *"Someday, you'll find happiness. It will be different from the happiness you experienced in the past, but you will be happy again."*

He was right.

"Pretty sure of yourself, weren't you?" She teased Jake as she traced the W.

"Are you kidding? After the way you attacked me a few weeks ago?" He pulled her into his arms, and his voice dropped to a seductive whisper. "I admit, it totally turns me on when you come on strong like that."

"You like that, do you?" She wrapped her arms around his neck, pulling his head down until their lips almost touched. "Looks like I'll have to be careful about that for the next few months." Laughing, she pushed him away and stepped out of his arms.

With a chuckle, he pulled her back to his side. "Come on. I have one more gift for you." Entering the stables, he led her to a stall halfway down. "When I was at the auction the other day, I saw a beautiful mare that reminded me of you." He stepped aside. "Emily, I'd like you to meet Jewel."

Emily gasped as a beautiful chestnut horse stuck its head over the stall door. She reached her hand up to stroke the horse's nose. "Jake, she's beautiful."

"Like I said, she reminded me of you."

Emily rolled her eyes, while her heart pitter-pattered at the compliment. "And you named her Jewel. That's so sweet."

"I didn't name her Jewel, the previous owner did. She's registered by that name."

Tears flooded Emily's eyes. She blinked them away and hugged Jake. What were the chances a beautiful mare named Jewel would be auctioned the day Jake attended?

It's providence.

Just like it was providence that God led her here, to this ranch and this wonderful man. The ranch had become her refuge. And Jake would always be her rock.

~

If you enjoyed Refuge, please consider leaving a review on Amazon.

~

Continue reading for a sneak peak of Robert's story.

RECLAIM

CHAPTER 1

"*S*heriff Winters," Robert answered with his official title in case Debbie was still close enough to hear. He leaned back in his chair when his brother's cheerful greeting came through the line. "Hey, Jake. What's up?"

"I have some news to share with you." Jake said, a smile in his voice.

"Do I have to guess, or are you going to tell me?" Robert asked when Jake didn't volunteer more information.

"Emily's pregnant. You're going to be an uncle." Pride and excitement filled Jake's voice and brought a smile to Robert's face.

"Congrats. You guys didn't waste any time, did you? But I hate to break it to you. That's not news to me."

He'd noticed Emily's struggle not to give in to the nausea the other night, just like Amy had been doing the past couple months. When Emily placed her hand on her lower abdomen—like Amy always did—it was a dead giveaway.

"What? Who told you? I haven't even told Mom yet."

"Good thing, unless you want the whole town to know."

Robert loved his mother, but she was about as big of a gossip as they came *and* she was eager to be a grandma. She was the only one out of her sisters who didn't have grandkids yet.

"No one told me, bro. Emily looked as green around the gills as Amy did the other night at dinner. I thought morning sickness was supposed to be in the morning though?"

"Apparently it's different for every woman. Most only have it for the first couple months, but and some have it the whole nine months."

"Well, I hope for Emily's sake hers doesn't last the whole nine months. When is she due?"

"About a month after Amy," Jake said. That meant late January.

"Congratulations, Jake. I'm happy for you both."

"Thanks. Uh...hey, don't tell Mom yet, will you? I don't think we're ready for the entire town to know yet."

"My lips are sealed."

The call ended a short time later, and Robert planted his elbows on his desk. *I'm going to be an uncle.*

He already felt like an uncle to Ben and Amy's daughters. Kallie and Cassey were the cutest three-year-olds. He enjoyed spending time at his cousin's house, playing with the sweet little girls. Ben and Amy were expecting in December, and Robert couldn't be happier for them.

Now, Jake and Emily, who had only been married five months, were expecting a baby this winter as well.

A heaviness filled his chest. This wasn't how things were supposed to turn out. As the oldest, he hadn't expected to become an uncle before he became a father.

If anyone had asked him five years ago where he saw himself at thirty-one, without hesitation, he would have responded, "Married with a couple kids, maybe a third one on the way." Back then, he knew exactly who the mother would be.

But things hadn't turned out like he'd planned. This one-horse town was too small for the woman he'd loved since he was seventeen. Jessie needed more. More than he could give her.

His head shot up at a knock on his office door. He gripped the cell phone he still held. If Debbie had come back, he might do or say something that could hurt his chances for re-election.

The door opened, and Robert sucked in a sharp breath.

"Have you got a minute?" Sylvia Sorenson, the woman he'd thought would be his mother-in-law, stood in the doorway. Her resemblance to Jessie—tall, slender, with dark hair—brought a pain to his chest.

Had his thoughts of Jessie conjured her mother? Too bad they couldn't summon Jessie. That would be an amazing feat since she lived in New York. Not only was she about as far away from Providence as she could get without leaving the country, she was married to another man.

"Mrs. Sorenson, come in." Robert stood and extended his hand. "Have a seat."

"Robert, we left formalities behind a long time ago. Call me Sylvia, please."

Robert dropped back into his seat. "How have you been, Sylvia?"

"I'm doing good, but…" her words died on her lips.

He took in the silver threads in her dark hair and the lines around her eyes. She was still a beautiful woman, but she'd aged over the past five years since he'd hung out at her house regularly.

"Is something wrong?"

She sucked in a deep breath. "I need your help. I know this is asking a lot, but I need you to help me bring Jessie home."

Robert's heart pounded against his ribcage. *Bring Jessie home?*

"I'm sorry, I don't understand." He rubbed his palms against his thighs, attempting to calm his racing heart.

"Jessie has been living in an abusive relationship for the past four years. I've finally convinced her to leave Patrick. But she's scared—" Sylvia's voice caught.

Jessie's husband abuses her? Why would anyone hurt such an amazing, creative, beautiful woman? How had she ended up in an abusive relationship?

Robert cleared his throat. "Why don't you explain to me what's going on."

"I suspected Patrick was abusing Jessie a long time ago, but she wouldn't admit it. A little over a year ago, Jessie and Patrick moved to Seattle. I've visited her occasionally, and my suspicions were correct. I've been trying to get her to leave him, but she's too afraid. Patrick threatened to kill her if she ever left him."

Robert's hands balled into fists. It's a good thing they were in his lap and Sylvia couldn't see them.

"She called me from the hospital an hour ago. Patrick beat her pretty badly before he left for a work retreat."

"The hospital? Is she okay?" This kept getting worse.

"She has a mild concussion, a broken wrist, and two bruised ribs. They're keeping her overnight for observation."

Robert bolted to his feet and walked the few steps to the window, barely able to contain the rage tightening his chest. He took slow, steady breaths as he stared out at the back parking lot. He couldn't understand why any man thought it acceptable to abuse a woman.

"And she says she's ready to leave him?" He spoke through clenched teeth. He couldn't bear to help her if she wasn't ready to leave the jerk.

"She is, but she's afraid he'll come after her. I know this is a lot to ask, considering your history with Jessie, but I need you to help me bring her home and...keep her safe. If I take her to my house, Patrick will find her in no time and force her to go back."

Robert stared at his fleet vehicle, a Chevy Tahoe. *Bring Jessie home and keep her safe?* Could he protect her from a psycho husband without providing round-the-clock detail? Despite hiring two more officers after receiving the anonymous donation last fall, he didn't have those kinds of resources.

He had enough personal leave built up that he could take a full month off. But he couldn't protect her himself. As sheriff, he had responsibilities he couldn't shirk, nor could he spend that kind of time with her. He feared he'd fall for her again, and he couldn't afford to let that happen.

An image of his family's cabin on the lake filled his head. He could take her there. It was remote enough Patrick wouldn't find her. She'd be safe, and he wouldn't have to provide constant protection.

"Will you help me?" The pleading in Sylvia's voice pulled at him, and he turned to look at her. He read the depth of concern in her eyes.

Staring at her, he saw glimpses of the woman he'd fallen in love with. Pain pricked his heart. It had taken him years to rid Jessie from his thoughts. And just like that, she was back in his head.

"I'll help keep her safe, but..." Robert rubbed his jaw. "It might be better if you took one of my deputies to bring her home. I'm not sure Jessie—"

Sylvia scooted to the edge of her chair. "She was so scared on the phone, I promised I would bring you along in case Patrick showed up. It was the only way I could convince her to leave him."

"You're sure she wants *me* to come?"

Sylvia nodded.

"When do we need to leave?"

"She'll be released from the hospital in the morning."

This might be the toughest protection detail of my life.

❧

Read Robert's story,
Reclaim
Finding Providence Book 3,
Free on Kindle Unlimited, or get it from Amazon.

❧

If you enjoyed Refuge, please consider leaving a review on Amazon.

Be sure you join my newsletter, so you don't miss a new release.
www.jillburrell.com/newsletter

ACKNOWLEDGMENTS

As always, thank you to my critique group whose feedback on my stories has been invaluable. Thank you to my beta readers Michelle, Marie, Jessie, Laura, Britney, and Jenessa.

Thank you to Aaron and Megan Walker for proofreading and cleaning up my manuscript. Thank you to Kelli Ann Morgan at Inspire Creative Service for this amazing cover. Thank you Tia for the chapter heading art.

And a special thanks to the man who is my rock. Thank you, honey, for your unfailing support and encouragement. And thank you to my children for patiently helping with the laundry and fixing yourself dinner on occasion.

ABOUT THE AUTHOR

JILL HAS always been an avid reader, and romance has always been her favorite genre. If she's not writing or folding laundry her head is usually in a book.

When her father told her, "I've got a story I want you to write," she didn't think she'd ever actually do it.

But after twenty years of being a stay-at-home mom with seven children, the idea of writing and publishing a book sounded less terrifying than entering the workforce again. Boy, was she wrong!

Keep in touch with Jill Burrell
www.jillburrell.com

amazon.com/author/jillburrell
facebook.com/authorjillburrell
goodreads.com/authorjillburrell
bookbub.com/authors/jill-burrell